THE HELL THAT FOLLOWED

By RJ Law

This is a work of fiction. Any names or characters, businesses or places, events or incidents, are fictitious. Any resemblance to actual persons, living or dead, or actual events is purely coincidental. No part of this eBook may be reproduced or transmitted in any form or by any means, electronic or mechanical, including photocopying, recording or by any information storage and retrieval system, without written permission from the author.

Copyright 2020 RJ Law All rights reserved.

CHAPTER 1

Cesar Ortiz stood among twenty armed men next to a plane on a desert landing strip in west Texas. Each stared into the blinding horizon as it swallowed up the last red sliver of afternoon sun. They cupped their hands to their foreheads, slick with sweat. In the distance, an orderly procession of rippling vehicles approached through the heat blur wafting up from the cooked earth.

One of the men peered through a pair of binoculars at the oncoming train of Army National Guard Humvees. He lowered the binoculars and ran his fingernails against the coarse mustache hairs above his lip. He motioned toward the plane, and his workers set to unloading stacks of wooden crates.

When the Humvees reached the landing strip, the drivers wheeled them around and lined them side-by-side, rears directed toward the plane. Two of the drivers stepped out, while the workers filled the vehicles with crates.

"They said there'd be eight," the man said to one of the drivers. "These won't hold it all."

The two soldiers stretched and grunted, their limp faces offering fatigue.

"We were lucky to get the six," one said.

The man studied the soldier, his face pallid and clouded with too many freckles to count. The other soldier took a few steps to the side and relieved himself in the parched, sucking dirt.

"Just stack it high," he said. "No one's gonna stop us."

The man shook his head and instructed the loaders accordingly. When the vehicles were full, the soldiers climbed back into their seats and waited. The mustached man said something to Cesar and another man, and each nodded and took a place in the backseat of the lead vehicle.

An hour later, the Humvees hauled their cargo across an uneven desert terrain. The carriages jostled as the tires thumped the stony land, the two passengers bracing against each impact, their faces duplicate with pinched eyes and wide gritting teeth. By the time they reached a disheveled dirt road, their muscles ached and burned, and they were much satisfied to see the Interstate swelling in size upon the horizon.

They reached the first police checkpoint after only twenty minutes and fell still behind a long line populated with all different makes of vehicle. The soldier studied the two men in his rear-view mirror, each much sweatier than before, eyeballs darting about as if untethered from within.

"Just relax," he said, and then the lead officer at the front of the checkpoint waved his hand to motion them around the other cars and past the police cruisers. The soldier tipped his cap as he passed and the officer reciprocated. Cesar and the other man looked back over their shoulders as the growing distance reduced the flickering colors to a blur. Then they looked at each other, and the soldier grinned.

They hit five more checkpoints on their way into Houston, and each time, their mossy military colors checked them through. Hours later, they drove into the city and turned south toward the I-45 Causeway into Galveston. When the bridge appeared in the distance, Cesar's partner gaped his mouth. The 4-mile reinforced concrete structure jutted from the dark ocean waters like a monument to the will of man, and he studied it like some traveling witness to foreign spectacle. He tapped his partner with an elbow, but Cesar only rolled his eyes and looked away.

It took six minutes to travel from the mainland to the island, and when they entered the city, Cesar saw the Sorrento Resort Hotel sign flickering ornate above a group of blunt concrete buildings. He pointed to it, and the driver nodded and led the trailing vehicles onto the exit ramp. They drove down a city block and wheeled around the back of the hotel, where a group of five nervous looking men stood at wait. When they saw the parade of green vehicles, the men opened an immense metallic door, revealing a paved concrete service road that declined sharply into a small parking garage four floors beneath the hotel lobby.

The convoy descended beneath the building and set still in an empty concrete parking garage. A group of square-shouldered men began unloading the Humvees not less than a second after the vehicles crept still. The soldiers remained seated as Cesar and his partner stepped out and looked around.

An old man in a tailored suit stood next to a polished steel elevator that gleamed brightly within the muted concrete. He wore a pink tie and a matching kerchief tuft in the pocket of his suit jacket, and one side of his face was ruined with a sunken brown scar. He stood buttressed by two expressionless men who looked to have been carved from large granite stones.

Cesar and his partner approached, and the old man shook each of their hands and grinned. The soldier in the lead Humvee lit a cigarette and watched as the three traded words. Then the old man said something to his men, and they broke open the boxes with an iron wedge. The old man inspected the contents of each and nodded, and then he and Cesar went into a small office and closed the door, while the workers sealed the boxes and towed them off on two-wheeled dollies. Minutes later, Cesar exited carrying two black vinyl satchels. He and his partner climbed back into the lead Humvee, and all six vehicles growled to life and drove out of the garage and back onto the street.

This time, they headed southwest along the moonlit powdered coast of the island across the Blue Water Highway that made a thin bridge over the gulf. By the time they crossed onto the mainland, it was nearing midnight, and the white summer moon basked down on the six rumbling vehicles high in its neutrality of all things good and evil.

They thundered through a marshy wildlife refuge with glassy little ponds that gave back the stars, each one sparkling in the dark ambling waters like bits of crushed jewel. And as they passed, nesting waterfowl fluttered airborne, and then, the disturbance having passed, drifted back downward to vanish in the tall grassy cover.

By the time they exited the reserve, the landscape had turned flat and barren, and there was no other traffic to force them to speed or slow. They drove on for a while, and then the road veered to the right like an arm bent at the elbow, and the freckled driver had to slow his Humvee to make the turn. As he did, an explosion of dancing light ignited in the darkness ahead, and he knew that they were approaching another checkpoint.

He brought the vehicle to a stop and told Cesar and his partner to stay silent and set the satchels on the floor. Two black unmarked cars blocked their way, and when the driver checked his rear-view, he saw that two more had pulled from the dense brush behind the Humvees to bar retreat.

The night glittered with siren light, but the soldier heard nothing except the wind and some quiet little voices coming from behind the barricade. He checked the passengers in his rearview, and he saw in that glass Cesar's partner biting his lip and bleeding sweat. The figure in the mirror eyed the dense six-foot plumes of dried grass along the road, and his hand curled about the door handle, trembling fiercely enough to make it rattle.

"Now, now," the driver said in a low tone. "You don't want to do that. If you do that, it'll all be over."

His voice was steady, but strained, as if he spoke to a man endeavoring to breech the hatch of a submarine and drown all in the process.

"Take it easy. It's all under control."

The driver reached for his military ID, but before he could get it, a booming voice yelled, "FBI," and then the doors of the Humvee jerked open, and men with machine guns ordered them out.

The driver dropped the ID in his lap and raised his arms. Men stood on either side of the vehicle, each with flashlights that flooded the interior with a wash of blinding white. The driver squinted into one of the bright round spots and started to speak, but before he could, Cesar's partner snatched up a satchel and drove his boot heel into one of the agent's knees.

The agent cried out and buckled to the ground. Cesar's partner stepped over his body and bolted toward the shroud of tall sapped grass, his head lowered, boot heels kicking bits of dirt and rock upward into the air.

"He's got loose," one of the agents yelled, but another had already leveled his gun. The agent popped off four shots into the small of the fleeing man's back, and the man toppled forward in an awkward heap.

The driver watched all of this with a face made odd by horror, his jaw slack, ovular eyes leaking brine. He looked at the fallen man, coughing and gagging under a bloody congestion, legs bicycling frantically at search for traction in the air. Then he stopped moving altogether, and each limb thumped flat.

The agents pulled the other two men from their seats. They shackled Cesar's wrists with metal cuffs and put him in the rear of one of the unmarked cars. They bound the driver's hands and ankles in zip-tie handcuffs, and propped him on his knees, his forehead pressed against the side of his Humvee. They repeated this with the other five soldiers. Then they read each prisoner his Miranda rights, and when it was the freckled soldier's turn, he sobbed.

An agent collected the two satchels and nodded to another. Then, one by one, they got into their vehicles and drove away, as if beckoned by some signal only they could hear.

Some of the soldiers had fallen over onto the ground, and they lay next to their Humvees with hybrid expressions of fear and bewildered relief. The freckled soldier stared forward, his face smeared with salt and snot; and his weeping persisted even after the red lights of the cars winked out within the rolling blackness, and they were alone.

Three weeks later, Cesar sipped from a glass of white tequila at a table in a Texas cantina. Two young Mexican girls with long false eyelashes sat across from him, faces tilted forward, doe eyes blinking bashfully. They sipped big fruity drinks from tall glasses, the rims smeared with bright lipstick from their red sucking mouths. They asked him questions about his bulky gold jewelry and the meanings of his tattoos, and he replied to them with teasing little jokes that made them giggle and squirm in their chairs, like schoolgirls afflicted with the warmth of sudden crush.

The bartender eyed Cesar from behind his station as he polished beer mugs with a soiled towel. He was a thickset, bald man with a handlebar mustache, and he knew who Cesar was, and his face was painted with concern.

The two girls talked of themselves, mostly, and Cesar nodded, ingesting little of what he heard. He studied their soft blushing faces as they rambled about school and travel, each flaunting so well the prettiness of youth.

A small checkered dance floor in the center of the cantina sat barren save for one drunken girl who performed a solitary dance of sudden knee jerks and elbow movements. She swept about the floor, leaping at times and bowing in a false swoon at others, and things remained as such for a long while until a shrieking woman staggered through the entryway and commanded the eyes of the bar.

The woman wore a heap of makeup on her cross face and she ground her teeth and scratched at her knotted hair. She stumbled toward Cesar and the little girls, cursing his name all the way. The young ladies stumbled to their feet and hurried to the far side of the cantina, their colored drinks swashing back and forth in the oversized glasses within their delicate painted hands.

Cesar ascended from his seat and met her halfway across the floor, his boots pounding the wood like big rubber hammers. She raised her hands high and brought them downward like slashing claws, but he caught her wrists and clenched them with such force, her fingers turned an immediate blue. She stopped her noise and the courage ran from her face. He nodded to the bartender who dropped his rag and hurried forth to escort her away.

Cesar looked around for the two young girls, but they were gone. He shook his head, and looked at the foul woman: discarded by her lover, restrained and sobbing in a dim corner of the cantina, her wasted form given to her addiction to methamphetamines, little left to maintain what had only been lewd interest in the first place. He lifted the glass of tequila and drank it empty. Then he slammed it on the wooden table, and went outside.

He stepped out into the night and breathed deeply. It was coming on midnight, but the air was still hot and thick. His shirt clung against his skin, and he peeled it free and flapped the cloth in the breeze, but it would not dry. He strode across the gravel parking lot, barely illuminated by a single orange bulb atop a warped telephone pole in the center. He slid a cigarette between his lips and held it with his teeth as he set it afire. He didn't need that bitch anyway. With the money he had coming, the pussy would find him.

He walked across the parking lot toward his car, all quiet except for the wind licking the tree tops and the gravel crunching beneath his boots. When he got to the vehicle, he passed the cigarette from his right hand to his left and worked his fingers into his crowded jean pockets. As he closed his hand around the jagged metal, the gusting wind kicked whipping bits of rock and dirt against his face and into his eyes and mouth. He pressed his lids shut and spat, and when he opened them, he saw two men approaching from the other side of the lot.

He recognized them immediately by their size: one short but formidable with a wide neck laden with colored tattoos; to his side, a massive, brutish man with a large sagging belly and legs like tree trunks. The short man walked with a brief, choppy gate, and his monstrous partner slowed his pace so they moved in near synchronicity.

Cesar removed his empty hand from his pocket and turned his body to greet them. The two approached and stood before him, the blunt man scanning Cesar from head to toe, the huge man staring forward like some soulless creature meant only for function, his hazy eyes devoid of any real expression.

"You're looking pretty good," the squat man said. "Better than you should."

Cesar tried to speak, but the man raised his hand and shook his head.

"Not to me," he said. "Save it for the others. I'm only here to collect you."

Cesar swallowed the words in his mouth and nodded.

The three stood quiet for a moment, and then Cesar felt a searing in his hand as the cigarette burned against his finger flesh. The pain startled him, and he threw the smoldering butt to the ground in a demonstration of false anger.

The squat man shook his head and made ticking noises with his tongue.

"Now, now, such a temper."

He looked at the large man, and then back to Cesar.

"Vamanos."

The large man took Cesar's arm and led him toward a black van fitted with garish chrome rims that twirled in the blowing wind like glinting pinwheels. The big man directed Cesar into the passenger seat and sat down behind him. The short man took the wheel, and the van crawled out of the parking lot and out onto the street.

They traveled a lightless network of backroads that left Cesar disoriented. After an hour of silence, he spoke.

"Will you tell me where we are going?"

A crack in his voice brought a smirk to the driver's face, and the man raised a finger to his lips and shook his head.

The dense trees blotted out the distant city light and a murky shroud of black enveloped everything to the horizon. Cesar looked out the window at the whizzing hints of shadowed scenery. He noticed the hulking creature in the backseat watching him in the rearview mirror, and he locked eyes with him for a terrifying moment and then looked away.

After a long while, the driver turned onto an ill-made road, the van jostling against the uneven aggregate. They rolled up the path, tree branches raking the windshield like angry wardens. In the near distance at the end of the disheveled road, an old shack lifted from the darkness. The brakes cried as the van stilled in a matte of thick flowing grass.

Cesar studied the gray structure, an ominous lull in his heart rendering him weak and nauseated. This did not look like a place where people came to talk no matter how dark their vocations. The wood had worn gray from years of weather and neglect, and the roof sagged in the center under the piled weight of severed tree branches and rotted leaves. The tiny black square windows showed no signs of life, their forms warped into funhouse geometry, jagged shards of broken glass jutting from the frames.

Cesar pursed his lips and looked at his lap.

"So this is where you plan to kill me, is that right?"

The driver looked at the man in the backseat, and then back to Cesar.

"Not for a while."

He nodded to the behemoth, and the hulking form slid the van door open and ducked his towering frame in exit. The van dipped sideways under his weight and then lurched back and forth in a rhythmic sway as it settled back to its default state. When the passenger door swung open, Cesar looked at the driver. The man gave a polite smile and waved his hand in a circular motion, as if to offer the courtesy of first opportunity.

Cesar stepped out amongst the bull frog and cricket calls audible from where, he could not tell. His legs wobbled as his feet gathered footing on the dusty earth. The burly man wrapped a massive hand around Cesar's muscled biceps, enveloping it whole.

The shorter man stepped out and stretched. He bent and flipped the seat forward and removed a collection of instruments from the backseat. There was a lantern, a plastic five-gallon bucket and a very large pair of tree trimmers, and Cesar took inventory of these things, his mind frenetically mapping escape against all reason. The man placed the tree trimmers in the giant's free hand, and then the two men guided Cesar forward into the shack.

Inside, it was cold and simple, one-room and square. The squat man lit the lantern, singeing his finger in the process, and he cursed in Spanish, and sucked at the wound. He pointed to the center of the cracked concrete floor, where a splintered wooden chair sat fastened by silver bolts that looked bright and new. Cesar moved obediently as the man strapped him in place.

The short man withdrew a straight edge razor from inside his denim jacket and wiped it against his leg, as if cleaning some unseen gore from the flawless blade. He trimmed the tips from each of Cesar's wiggling fingers, a casual expression set upon his face, as if he sheared not flesh but bits of carrot for some obscene salad. Each snip brought new questions, and the men considered each answer with furrowed brows, interpreting the broken words from the wails that seeped from Cesar's tight, tremoring lips. When the fingers were gone, the men processed his toes, repeating the same questions and matching the answers to ensure agreement.

When they ran out of fingers and toes, they removed his shirt and dragged the razor in linear patterns against his back like ghoulish artists working a canvas of supple flesh. They asked more questions, but there was nothing more to know, and when the short man was sure of this, he removed a pistol from his belt and quieted the room of screams.

They untied the body, and it fell limp to the ground. The burly man kicked it over so it turned face up. He fired several shots into the cheeks and forehead. Then he raised his over-sized boot and drove it into the skull, again and again until the vacant face was little more than shattered bone and pulp, unrecognizable to all comers and maybe even God, himself.

The thick, blunt man removed a pair of rusted vice grips from his back pocket and slipped them between Cesar's lips. He wrenched the teeth from side to side until each plucked free. He placed the three gold ones in his right pocket and scattered the rest inside the five-gallon bucket. The large man used the hulking metal tree trimmers to pinch Cesar's hands from his wrists. These he plopped into the bucket, as well, each slapping audibly against the plastic bottom like dead fish.

    A brief argument erupted over ownership of Cesar's watch and the six crisp 100 dollar bills found folded in a clip within his left pants pocket. The giant man relented almost at once, cowering away and resetting himself a few feet from the other, a small welt growing upon his massive forehead. The smaller man wiped his hands on a handkerchief, and then he added the bills to the gold incisors that had once helped Cesar chew his food.

CHAPTER 2

Edgar Porter and his family rolled into the sand covered parking area at the Douglas Reservoir, his brand new Cadillac freshly washed and gleaming. He pushed into the last space available, way on the end and impossibly tight. His young daughter opened her door and gracefully slipped from the vehicle, her uninflated vinyl raft in tote. His 17-year-old son followed, bouncing the door off a blue Camaro parked a space over.

"Godammit, Sam," Edgar said, as the two bolted for the glimmering oasis a hundred yards away. He mopped sweat from his forehead with a handkerchief and cursed the weather: 100 degrees and still only June. Madelyn opened her door and exited with great effort, the car rocking and groaning as if from relief. Was she getting fatter? He shook his head and loaded his lip with a sticky brown hunk of chewing tobacco. He watched from the rear view mirror as she opened the backdoor and carefully withdrew a huge platter of over-stuffed deviled eggs.

"Come on, Edgar, we're late."

"Dammit, Maddy, I'm comin," he said, as she waddled toward the others.

He waited until she made the lake, and then he removed a white envelope from beneath his seat. He thumbed it open, six one hundred dollar bills inside. He glanced over his shoulder and then back to the money. He fingered one of the bills for a moment and then snapped it up and jammed it into his left front pocket. He sopped a fresh coat of sweat from his forehead and went to join his family at the barbecue.

A mix of foreign and familiar faces had gathered in the desiccated grass on the edge of the manmade beach that skirted the Douglas Reservoir. Conflicting genres of music boomed from large box radios, each pinned to dissimilar stations, and those who could dance, danced, and those who could not sat in lawn chairs and drank beer. Grills crackled with peppers, onions, and swelled up crispy sausages, and a cloud of meat-borne incense floated stagnant overhead like a heavenly smog, potent enough to satisfy mild appetite by scent alone.

    The barbecue was hours old, and drunken men with boisterous voices laughed and argued, while drunken women dealt gossip and shook their heads in disbelief. Most of the children were already sunburnt, though few realized, and their mothers pursued them with handfuls of dripping skin cream and expressions of real concern. An adventurous clan of mobile toddlers kicked at a bright blue rubber ball, while those less sure watched longingly, their diminutive hands pulling at their mothers' cotton dresses. A group of teenage girls plotted an excursion into the woods to smoke cigarettes, while their younger siblings played in the water, pounding their arms against the lazy wave ripples born of a passing jet ski no longer visible.

    Edgar made the necessary rounds with all the right families before seeking out the other deputies. He asked around, and a woman with red curls told him they were by the volleyball pits playing catch with the football. Edgar looked to where she pointed, but his attention stayed with the lush odor of grilled foods. He stacked three flimsy paper plates together and buried them in a mountain of steaming meats and a slurry of potato salad and salted gravy. Then he hurried over a gentle hill of spiny summer grass toward the other deputies.

    He saw Seth and Levi smoking cigarettes by a girthy oak, no football in sight. Each wore his uniform, and neither looked to be saying much. Levi had his hat propped back, and he studied the ground from behind his glasses, his elderly body looking thin and frail. Seth stood beside him staring off into the smoldering afternoon sun, a stony expression upon his face. When he saw Edgar approaching, he suffocated his cigarette against the bark of the tree and flicked the butt into the air. He started toward him, his chiseled shoulders heaving with each breath, bounding strides closing the distance efficiently. When he was within range, he brought his palm against the bottom of Edgar's sagging paper plate, and an explosion of food particles flared upward. Flecks of potato salad spattered against Edgar's startled face and he slammed the greasy plate to the ground in disgust.

    "What the fuck was that for?"

Seth fired up a new cigarette and looked at him over the curling blue flame.

"You're late."

Edgar wiped his neck with his sleeve and looked down at the succulent meats, now wasted by flecks of dirt and strings of grass. He shook his head and spat.

"Where the hell is Tom and Bud?"

Seth bent forward and spat.

"Tom's home with the bad knee. Bud's not comin."

Edgar picked potato salad from his chin and shook his head.

"Well, that just figures," he said. "I hate these fuckin community things. Bunch of know-it-all douchebags and drunk, fat bitches."

He pulled a wrinkled pouch of chewing tobacco from his pocket and worked it open.

"So what's his damned excuse?"

"He's got business," Seth said.

Edgar jammed a huge wad of wet tobacco into his mouth and sucked on it. He looked over each of his shoulders and then back at Seth's square face.

"What's so important that he'd miss all this?"

Seth smoked and spat.

"They found that Mexican's car abandoned at one of them cantina's up yonder."

Edgar looked at Levi. He stood leaning against the tree, his old thin body cocked rigid, as if it held the big oak up.

"Is that right?"

Levi looked up and blinked a few times, as if he'd just come to noticed Edgar's presence. He nodded and looked back to the ground.

"Well, that's just great," Edgar said as he worked the tobacco around in his lips. "That motherfucker was supposed to stay low."

"Well, he proved unreliable," Seth said. "Imagine that."

Edgar put his hands on his hips and looked up at the top of the lofty oak. A gust of wind howled to life, and the green leaves twinkled in the brilliant sunlight, and no one spoke until it died away.

"Well, maybe it's broke down," Edgar said. "Did they try crankin' it?

Seth nodded.

"Fired right up."

Edgar looked down at the ground.

"Shit."

He cut a half-buried stone from the dirt with the heel of his boot and kicked it a few feet away.

"I knew that fucker weren't listenin'," he said. "The whole time Bud was talkin' to him, I knew he wouldn't pay no mind."

He spat and looked at Seth.

"Them young ones," he said. "They think they know better. Mexican or not, they's all the like."

Seth nodded, and so did Levi, though he hadn't appeared to be listening.

The three stood silent for a while, and then a man in a white tank top stepped over the hill about fifty yards away. He tilted his head, as if to assess the physical stature of the men before him.

"You fellas want to play some football?" He asked.

They shook their heads, and the man shrugged and went away.

They stood silent for a while longer, each studying the ground in place of an alternative. Edgar shook his head and spat a mucousy stream of chewing tobacco onto some ants gathering atop the ruined meat. He propped his hat back with his index finger and looked at Seth.

"You think they got hold of that ole boy?" He asked.

"I reckon we'll find out one way or another."

Edgar reached in his right pants pocket and withdrew the envelope, and Seth snatched it away and gave a heated look. He glanced over his shoulder, but Levi wasn't watching. He peeled it open and counted the contents, and then he put it in his pocket.

"I tell ya what," Edgar said. "If they did get that little fucker, and he talked about us, you can cancel Christmas."

Seth nodded, and Levi did, too. Edgar bent his body to look past Seth's muscled frame toward the worthless old-timer resting against the tree. The baggy deputy's uniform looked comical draped over his bony frame, and Edgar couldn't imagine what had possessed Bud to hire him in the first place. He shook his head and looked at Seth.

"Is that it?"

Seth nodded, and Edgar turned and walked back toward the noise issuing from the other side of the knoll.

When he was gone, Seth asked Levi what he thought. The old man removed his hat and ran his fingers through what little hair remained.

"Same as you fellas, I reckon. It looks bad."

Seth sucked the last of his cigarette and stamped the smoking fragment against the tree trunk.

"You said this was likely to happen. But I just didn't see it." He coughed and spat. "I woulda had no part in it if I had."

Levi pursed his lips and nodded.

"Ain't the first time I didn't take my own advice," the old man said. He shook his head and frowned. "It's easier to be wise for others than for yerself."

Seth hooked his thumbs into his back pockets and tapped his boot against one of the big oak's burly roots that jutted from the ground like the back of a petrified snake.

"Well, let's see what Bud finds out. Whatever it is, he'll know what to do."

Levi didn't say anything, his eyes burning the ground in a thoughtful trance.

Seth drew a new cigarette, and set it afire.

"Don't ya think?"

Levi looked up.

"Oh yeah. If anybody would, it'd be old Bud, I reckon."

Seth nodded and looked out past the yellow summer grass toward the trees waving in the distance afar.

"I guess somebody needs to tell Tom what's happenin."

Levi shook his head.

"If Bud tells you to do it, then you do it. Otherwise, I'd leave it to him."

Levi looked over his glasses at Seth.

"You keep that little boy of yers close, you understand? All you fellas is gonna have to watch over yer families like a hawk, cause that's how these people work. I mean, if it ends up bein what we're thinkin."

Seth drew from his cigarette and tapped the ashes in the wreath of rust-colored dirt that edged around the tree.

"I tell you what," he said. "I'll bring hell upon anyone that messes with my boy."

He said anyone, as if he meant God the like, and he said it in a way that made Levi pity him somewhat.

"This ain't somethin you can throw yer fists at, son. Killin's part of these people's business, and they don't square up in front of you like in a fair fight." He started to say something else, but he just put his hat back on instead.

They stood for a while longer, and then they went back to the barbecue. When they got there, Edgar and his family were gone, and most of the men looked sick from drunken exertion. Seth fished around in one of the coolers and withdrew two cans of beer. He handed one to Levi, and the two sat down in a pair of brightly colored lawn chairs. Seth spotted his son sitting alone on the beach, his little head dipped in a sullen daze. He called him up, and the boy sat down on a towel next to his father, and all three sat quietly watching the children dance and play, until dragonflies gave way to lightning bugs, and everyone went home.

CHAPTER 3

Ellie Moreno's Volkswagen squealed into the cracked drive outside her scrimp stone brick home. It was late afternoon, and she'd just finished a long night shift at the 24 hour restaurant, where she waitressed for few in return for little. She flashed a hopeful glance to the curb at the front of the yard. Tom's gray Buick sat parked in the street, but she knew that was only a thin promise. She pushed open the door and stepped out. If he wasn't there she would make a cup of tea and take a warm bath.

She entered the house and listened. The antique clock in the corner of the living room measured time in little pecks, but beyond that, all was silent. She dropped her purse and hurried down the compressed hallway that ran to the bedroom. The door was open, and when she saw into the room, she rested her head against the wooden jam and gave a soft smile.

Tom lay sleeping on his stomach in the bed, his hair muddled in disarray. She crossed the room on the balls of her feet, and stripped off her skirt and underwear. She lifted the covers and slipped underneath, her soft thighs needled by the coarse hair on his bare legs. The velvet warmth of her skin broke Tom from a forgettable dream, and he turned over and stroked her cheek with his fingertips, as if testing for realness the image his eyes gave. She bent forward and kissed his lower lip, as he traced with his fingers the sheet outline of her rising thigh.

"You're here," she whispered.

He smiled and nodded his head, still blurry from sleep.

Her hand fell across his arm and landed on his shoulder, and he collected it with his and moved it to his chest. She smelled of food and sweat, but he barely noticed for the nature of her gaze. They kissed, and she curled her cool body against his back. He felt her feet against his bare leg, sharp and callused by duress, but beyond that, her body like raw silk.

He flipped over and positioned himself atop her, his head congested with rude thoughts. He worked his body between her thighs and she felt a rush of warmth as she received him. They moved together with a continuity only familiar lovers know, and then they froze still while their bodies throbbed to a climax.

When they finished, she brought fruit from the kitchen, and they ate in bed and talked. He bunched grapes inside his upper and lower lips, molding his face to a mask grotesquely swollen by severe allergy. She giggled and tried to imitate, but her mouth tightened and curled with laughter causing the grapes to spring forth upon the bed.

He frowned and touched her chin.

"Why do you always wear a shirt to bed?"

She withdrew and cast her face downward.

"You know why."

He shook his head slowly.

"You don't have to. I don't care."

She looked up.

"I don't care if you care," she said, her eyes beautiful and wet. "I care."

They sat without speaking, some wrong thing taking on weight between them, his mind busy conjuring words to save the moment. But if there were such things, he'd not the skill to cultivate them, and when the phone broke the silence, he took it as a gift.

Her face grew somber as he crossed the room and took the receiver, she, half knowing the caller's identity.

"Hello?" He said.

"It's Bud."

Ellie watched him, her face painted with dejection and fatigue.

"What can I do for you, Sheriff?"

"Come down to Riley's. We gotta talk."

"Yes sir," he said, and he hung up the phone.

Ellie lifted to her feet and left the room. He followed her to the paltry dining area outside the kitchen. She sat at the little table, her expression like that of a child digesting failed plans. He moved behind her and put his hands on her shoulders, and she reached across her chest and brought one to the side of her face. They stayed that way, rejecting time for as long as prudence would allow, and then he turned and walked away.

He walked the hall and claimed his pistol and badge from the bedroom closet, and when he came back, she stood at the door. He kissed her somber lips and said goodbye, and then he shut the door in her beautiful face against whatever sanity still nested in his mind.

Outside, the air filled with cricket noise, as the sun reddened in its descent. He slogged toward his old Buick and wrenched open the heavy metal door. It gave way with a hollow metallic bong, and he got inside. He fired up the clattering engine and headed toward Riley's.

When Tom arrived at Riley's, only three cars populated the dirt lot, and Bud's was not one of them. He stowed his Buick in the dusty spaces out back and limped around the rusted dumpsters on his way to the front. The entrance to the bar was pitted below street level, and a fire raged in his injured knee as he descended the tall choppy steps.

He pushed open the door and looked around. A heavy-set bartender dusted flecks of peanut shells from a scarred oak bar, while a customer to his left sucked beer froth from an overflowing glass mug. On one side of the room, a middle-aged couple filled the boxes of a newspaper crossword puzzle, their faces lit with broad smiles, their demeanors odd to all but themselves.

On the other side of the bar, in a dim corner, Bud sat hunched over a glass of warm scotch, his face focused downward toward the burnt orange liquid in his hands, eyes reading the alcohol, as if it held the answer to an impossible question.

Tom ordered a beer and went to join him.

"Where's your car?" Tom asked.

Bud looked up and stared for a moment, the lids of his eyes asquint, as if a stranger had manifested to pose a riddle beyond his equipment.

"I had someone drop me off," he said at last.

Tom slipped into the booth and looked the sheriff over. He was not a young man, and he sat in a manner that aged him greatly. The bartender approached, and Tom leaned back to give him a place to set his beer.

"What's going on, Sheriff?"

Bud looked up from his drink and waited for the bartender to leave.

"They towed that Mexican's car away from one of them bars last night." He shook his head. "One of them places where all them types gather. Bartender said it'd been there for three days."

Tom sat back in his seat.

"There weren't nothin in it," Bud said, "but it was definitely the one we give him. Same plates."

Bud raised his glass and drank, and Tom let him swallow before he spoke.

"I thought you told him to hole up a while."

Bud shook his head and aired an exasperated sigh.

"I guess he got tired of waitin," he said.

He put a cigarette between his lips and the bartender flashed him a look from beneath a no smoking sign. Bud stared into his eyes as he set the cigarette ablaze, and the bartender shook his head, stuck a soiled towel into his back pocket and walked to the other side of the bar.

Bud smoked and exhaled. "I tell you something," he said. "Youth and patience are foreign to one another." He took off his Stetson hat and set it on the table.

Tom stared down at the beads of moisture bleeding from the side of the glass in his hands. It was all turning out just as Levi had said. He raised his head to see Bud studying him, head tilted and eyes probing as if to penetrate deep enough to tap his thoughts.

"Maybe he'll turn up." Tom said.

Bud straightened his head and frowned.

"Might as well think positive, anyway," Tom said. "I don't see what other choice we have."

Bud took a pull from his cigarette, and then he looked it over, measuring its length. He had it in his head that he was quitting, and he only smoked them half at a time. He must have thought he was weaning himself back, but Tom noticed he only smoked them twice as fast.

"You know, my mother always tried to tell me that," Bud said. He squinted through the stinging smoke as he crushed his cigarette dead. He put the unsmoked portion inside his shirt pocket like some deranged collector hoarding trash for jewel.

"She always said to think positive. That it was the secret to bein happy."

He stared directly into Tom's chest and fell into a thoughtful daze.

"I never could do it, though." He shook his head and frowned. "It's not that I expected the worst. Just always felt myself preparing against it. Sorta just in case. After a while, it got to be so I was miserable from it."

Tom squirmed in his seat. He'd only known Bud for a year, and in that time, he'd not heard the man speak personally about anything.

"I used to be interested in readin old quotes," Bud said. "And, one time, I read one that said thinkin in a negative fashion is akin to takin a weakening drug. I figured that made sense, so I used to try to make myself think positive thoughts. It didn't work, though."

He smiled to himself, still lost in the daze.

"Of course, it didn't work," he whispered almost inaudibly.

He snapped back into the moment and rubbed the heel of his hand against his eye.

"Anyway, as I got older, I just quit tryin. Now, I kind of figure that bein positive is somethin yer either born with or yer not. Some people cain't make themselves think positive thoughts any more than they can take flight. I come to think it's just another one of them genetic things. Like who's fast, who's tall."

He took out his wallet and thumbed it open.

"Ain't no use in fighting against yer nature," he said. "Yer just burnin energy if you do."

Tom looked across the bar at the couple working on the crossword. They were smiling and laughing, and they touched each other, and they sat on the same side of the booth.

He rubbed the back of his neck, and looked at Bud.

"So you think they got hold of that Mexican and now they probably know about us?"

Bud shook his head side-to-side.

"Yer still breathin ain't you?"

"So what do you think happened to him?"

Bud took out a five dollar bill, placed it on the table and stood up.

"I don't know."

Tom scratched his neck and thought for a moment.

"So what do we do?"

Bud patted him on the shoulder and gave an easy-looking smile.

"Think positive," he said. "If you can manage."

He put his hat back on and waited for Tom to finish his beer.

"I need a ride home if you're up to it."

Tom nodded and followed him out the door.

By the time they pulled into Bud's neighborhood, it was completely dark, and the streets were empty save for the occasional shadow cast by wandering man or loose dog, each drifting amidst the yellow street light, like uncertain figures wandering through uncertain land. They breached the mouth of a cul-de-sac, and Bud made him stop and let him walk the last of the way.

"How's your wife?" He said before he got out.

Tom tapped the steering wheel with his thumbs.

"She's doing ok. Full remission."

Bud nodded and rubbed his whiskered chin.

"That's good. That's real good."

He opened the passenger door and started to get up. Then he stopped and sat back down, grunting under the strain of age.

"You just go on like we talked about," he said. "You got a job to do, same as the others. You're still a deputy of the law. Just do your job like you always would. Me and Seth's got an ear for what's goin on, and if we feel like somethin ain't right, we'll let the rest of you know."

He got out, shut the door and crouched down to say something else.

"What I don't want to see is you doin somethin dumb like leavin town, runnin away or anything like that. That's what'd get us all in trouble. You understand, right?"

Tom nodded.

"You've got nothin to worry about, Sheriff," he said.

Bud popped his hand against the roof of the Buick a couple of times, and then he walked away. He had his hands in his pockets and his hat pulled down low, and he was whistling. Tom watched his silhouette disintegrate outside the Buick's halogen beams like some unworldly apparition, bound not to this world but some other place altogether, strange to those outside that place and perhaps to those within. He rubbed his eyes and then turned the car toward home.

It was after midnight by the time he punched his key into the deadbolt lock of the front door. It stuck like it didn't recognize the carved metal, and then he gave it a calculated jiggle, and it spun free. He opened the door and went inside. The house was dark and the only sign of life was the flashing green neon digits of the microwave which cast the entire kitchen in a dull, alien glow.

He laid his keys on the table, quietly and with care, as if he baited a live mouse trap. The subtle metal clatter made a faint racket, but not enough to wake her. He sat on the couch and removed his boots. They were old and ill-fit, and he wriggled his toes to make the warm blood return.

The floor creaked as he made his way through the narrow hallway adorned with framed photos of family loved ones, some alive, others not. He traced these with his hands for bearings as he negotiated the pitch black. When he got to the bedroom, he squeezed the cold brass knob and twisted the door open. Ellie lay sleeping on her back, a book face down on her chest. The dim reading lamp on the end table was still on and so were her glasses.

He approached her on his toes like a burglar, and when he was close enough, he collected the book and slid the satin purple marker between the page she had finished and the one still full of possibilities. He set it on the nightstand, and then he carefully navigated the weightless eyeglasses over her ears and set them on top of the book.

He looked down at her face, ruddy around the cheeks and twitching under the influence of a private dream. He looked at her chest and saw the awkward slope of her nightgown, flowing upward and over from flesh to void. He considered the scar beneath, though he'd not seen it for over a year; curved and barbed like a great purple caterpillar, it had likely set to a waxy brown. He pulled the covers up over her arms and gave her forehead a silent kiss, and then he extinguished the lamp and left the room.

He went to the kitchen, and opened the refrigerator. He took a beer and drank it empty next to the glow of refrigerator light. He pressed his palm against his forehead and looked down at the torn carpet rug under his socks. His thoughts grew morbid, and when he shooed these, more torturous ones filled their place.

He dropped the empty can in the trash and looked around. Unopened bills littered the dining room table, some hinting threats by way of pink blush. He'd take them and tear them apart if it be to his will. But she would not allow it, and there they sat, not as simple debts writ to paper, but like dark organisms empowered to crumple ambition and hope.

The treatments that had saved Ellie were entirely unaffordable, but rendered nonetheless. They'd crossed paths with death and grappled against it, finally frustrating it to the point of withdrawal. But in its recoiling, it transformed, persisting by way of threat and financial toll. The debts were insurmountable, and there hadn't been anything else to do but what he'd done with Bud and the others.

    He stared through the window at the oak in the backyard, its branches stretching wildly, leaves shimmering in the moonlight like falling coins. There was a way past all this, but it was beyond his mind to cultivate such broad plans. If it was beyond Bud's, too, they'd all be dead by week's end. He stood for a while longer, tapping his foot against the floor; eyes fixed downward, mind sorting. But there was no reckoning with the dark thoughts rooting within his brain, and after a while, he quit them altogether and went to bed.

CHAPTER 4

Swollen drops of rain popped against the parking lot outside the Crystal Café, where Edgar sat eating the same breakfast he'd eaten every day for the last two years. A formidable storm front had shifted in around sunrise. Wind howled and hail ticked, and the simple idiots of the town acted as if it was the end of days.

He speared a flabby chunk of ham with his fork and ran it through the brown gravy leaking from his two soggy biscuits. He pushed it into his mouth and chewed, as he read baseball scores in the sports section of the local newspaper. He marked the winners with a blue pen, and when the ink failed, he drew a black one from his shirt pocket and went through the remaining box scores.

When he had finished, he matched the circled names with the ones he had written on a torn scrap from a yellow legal pad. All but three matched, and he was glad he'd snuck away to call his bookie during the barbecue the day before.

He smiled at the smeared ink print. He'd rendered that bookie dumbstruck when he gave the sums for each bet. The son of bitch had chuckled first, as if it was all some joke. Edgar had set him straight, though. Told him to mark it down and get used to it. And now he'd made a killing. Things were finally going his way and he wasn't about to let up. Let those other chicken-hearted pussies sit on their shares. He was going to parlay this thing into something really special.

He heard a rush of clatter and saw the hail picking up through the window glass. Men and women scurried about the broken blacktop in their work clothes, hoisting briefcases and purses above their head as makeshift shields against the sheets of stinging ice. They scattered in all directions as if unsure which way to go. Edgar watched from behind the glass, an amused smile trickling across his hairy lips. They moved like rats dumped wet upon a linoleum floor, feet ticking against the slick ground in a mad panic for traction. He watched them all with a legitimate hatred pointing forth from his dark eyes. He felt it, hot and pungent and seething from a place inside, dark and unrevealed, a mystery to even himself.

He collected a handful of bacon and smeared the yellow jiggling ends against the gravy-soaked plate. The red-haired waitress watched him from behind the counter as he mashed the whole wad into his mouth.

"Careful, Deputy. There ain't nobody here can fit their arms around you if you go and choke yourself."

He raised his middle finger without looking, and then he lifted his empty coffee cup and shook it like a blind vagrant at the mouth of some gritty urban alleyway. The waitress grabbed a pot of decaf marred with floating bits of coffee grit and toted it around the counter. She bent to fill his cup, but he yanked it back like it was on a string. Murky brown droplets of coffee spattered and sizzled on the cheap orange Formica table like crackling spots of battery acid.

"Goddamit, Edgar."

"Is that decaf?"

"Hell no."

He slid the cup back beneath the carafe and she filled it and walked away.

He scanned the diner. There was a fat guy flipping oversized pancakes behind the counter. His grease-tarnished white t-shirt looked as if slugs had skidded across it, and Edgar wondered if it was any dirtier than when he'd put it on this morning. A truck driver with a red baseball cap sat directly across from him, and Edgar could hear that they were talking about the economy. Enough about the goddamn economy, he thought.

On the far side of the room, that widow, Johnson or Jacobson or something like that, sat across from her retarded son. A pool of slobber collected on the table beneath his mouth, and she mopped at it with a crumpled paper napkin. Edgar shook his head and pushed his meal away.

Behind them, a man in a tailored suit sat alone reading a magazine. When Edgar looked at him, the man raised his head and gave a peculiar smile, a bit too personal like those donned by door-to-door solicitors. Edgar shook his head and returned to his newspaper.

He finished with the previous night's results and began circling the games he liked for the coming evening. He'd totaled six, all certain locks, when he sensed someone standing beside him. He set down his pen and turned his head.

"Pardon me, officer. Do you have a moment?" The man in the suit said.

"Not really. I'm eatin, here."

"I understand. I only need a moment of your time. Do you mind if I sit down."

The man slipped into the torn vinyl booth seat before Edgar could tell him to go fuck off.

Edgar looked the man over. He had a bad greasy haircut and a thin, manicured mustache. A purple length of scar ran across his cheek, and it turned white when he smiled, which seemed to be most of the time. He held a magazine in his hand and he placed it on the table.

"You know, I was just reading this fascinating article in this magazine, and when I saw you sitting over here, I just had to get your opinion on it."

Edgar gave the man a disgusted look, ill-concealed by intent.

"I really ain't interested," he said. "And, like I said, I'm eatin, here."

"Yes, I see," the man said as he thumbed the magazine open. "But please, just humor me for a moment."

Edgar rose back in his seat and placed his right hand on his thigh. The man looked down at the magazine, and when he did, a blade of congealed oily bangs separated from his scalp and swung in front of his face, adhering to his forehead for an awkward amount of time before he finally smeared it back in place.

He flipped the magazine to a page marked with a yellow sticky note. He tapped the page twice with a hairy finger. Edgar looked down and read the title of the article: US Soldiers, Law Officers Snared in Border Drug Sting.

Cold adrenaline ran through Edgar's chest. He took a second look at the man, appraising him anew. He didn't seem like a federal agent. But what kind of agent would he be if he did?

"Have you heard of something called Operation Lively Green?" The man asked.

"No, sir. Can't say as I have."

"Really? You know, that surprises me, someone in your line of work. Well, no matter. I can tell you all about it. You see, it's an ongoing operation by the FBI to clean up police corruption in this area, which I must say, judging by this article, is truly getting out of control."

The man searched the article, running his index finger across several lines, as if he had a sensor in it that could read printed text.

"Yes, here. You see, apparently, the National Guard, who had been assigned to support the local police with border control, drug trafficking, and so on, had actually been helping to smuggle narcotics across the border. Or, at least, a few of them had."

He spun the magazine around and tilted it toward Edgar.

"You see, it says: they used their color of authority to prevent police stops, searches and seizures of narcotics as they drove the shipments on highways that passed through checkpoints."

Edgar shrugged his shoulders.

"Ain't heard nothin about it. But it don't surprise me."

"No?" The man had a quizzical look.

Edgar shrugged his shoulders.

"A lot of money in drugs. A lot of people who like money."

The man made a frown and nodded.

"Well, you are probably right. It says in here that authorities believe this is just the tip of the iceberg. It intimates that there are many other investigations currently underway."

Edgar shrugged.

"Is that all?"

The man grinned, and his scar went pale.

"Not quite. And again, I do want to thank you for your patience."

Edgar swelled behind the table.

"Look, fella, my patience is all but run out with you. Now, you need to leave, so I can finish my breakfast, or I'm gonna give you some trouble."

The man raised his hands in a sign of surrender.

"Absolutely. No, I don't want that. It's just that it occurred to me that all of these covert FBI investigations resulting in these huge busts could present interesting opportunities for a clever someone. Someone who likes money, as you say."

He closed the magazine and stared directly into Edgar's eyes, setting in deep.

"Someone who enjoys a good masquerade."

Edgar lifted his coffee cup and sucked in a long, thin stream. He studied the man from behind the dull glass rim and for the first time, he noticed his eyes. His original impression had written them off as ordinary dead brown. But now they seemed darker. Deep and hollow and strangely vacant, like implants on some stuffed head laughing down from a taxidermist wall.

"Do you think you know somethin?" Edgar said.

"I do know something."

"What do you know?"

"I know everything."

"What, exactly, do you think you know?"

The man leaned forward.

"I know that you and your friends posed as agents in order to steal drug money from the cartels." He leaned back in his seat and smiled. "Is that clear enough for you?"

Edgar swallowed the void in his throat, nearly gagging on the nothing.

"How do you know?"

The man leaned back and frowned gravely.

"I think you probably know how I know. And if you don't. Well, you can probably guess."

The two said nothing for a while, and then Edgar removed a deflated pouch of chewing tobacco from his pocket and used his middle finger to swab it clean. He put the tacky wad in his mouth. It was dark and sweet and it stung his tongue.

"So you work for who? The Feds? The Cartels?"

The man sat silently, his hands folded on the table. He looked Edgar over with squinted eyes.

"You know, you are a fat man."

Edgar's face remained set, but his jaw flexed, and the man noticed this and smiled.

"You know," the man said as he relaxed backward in his seat. "I've always thought that law officers should be sleek, and well-maintained. Not this."

He motioned his hand toward Edgar, as if brushing something away.

"I feel they should be commensurate to whatever challenge they might face. Otherwise, well."

He turned his palms upward and shrugged.

Edgar remained silent.

"That would be best." The man nodded, as if agreeing with himself. He looked at Edgar and rubbed his chin thoughtfully.

"But you know, I've come to notice that power in all its forms tends to stimulate the appetite."

He tipped his hand toward Edgar and smiled.

"But something tells me you've been a fat man all your life, is that right?"

Edgar didn't react, and the man chuckled, before clearing his throat, as if he'd heard a joke.

"Why don't you quit fuckin around, and tell me who you work for?"

The man gave an abrupt nod.

"I work for whomever pays the most."

"So who's that?"

"Well, it could be you. It should be you. And it will be you, or else it will be the ones whom you stole from."

Edgar spat in the coffee cup and stared down at the table. His eyes fired about within their sockets, as if he tried to add two huge numbers together in his mind.

"You know," the man said. "They're looking for you, the Cartel. That's why they hired me. To find you."

Edgar spat in the cup.

"They don't know who you are, and they don't have to know. If you do the right thing."

Edgar cleared his throat, and the man tilted his head in a look of artificial sympathy.

"These men," he said. "They'll never stop looking. Not for that much money. And if they find out. Well, they will do things to you and your family. Horrible things that involve knives and razor blades and, well."

Edgar looked out the window. The hail had stopped and only the rain remained, thin and flittering, like weak splatters from the shag of a wet dog. The big purple thunderheads beat back the morning sun, but a faint golden tinge now outlined the masses. Edgar stared at this for a while without noticing its beauty.

He looked back at the man.

"So what do you want?"

The man shook his head, as if growing weary of the conversation.

"I think you know what I want."

"You want money."

The man smiled and touched the end of his nose.

Edgar tapped his foot on the linoleum floor. He spat in the coffee cup, and then looked over his shoulder like he thought someone might be listening. He leaned forward, and the man did the same.

"Well, first off, I ain't admittin to nothin," Edgar said. "I'm sayin I don't know what the hell yer talkin about, and that's all yer gonna get me to say. But if I did know what you was talkin about, how do I know yer for real. I mean, how do I know you ain't workin with that Cesar fella, tryin to pull a fast one on me?"

The man folded his arms and stroked his chin. He smiled and nodded, as if truly impressed by the man sitting before him.

"Well, there really is no way to know, is there? In that case, I will have to prove it to you."

Edgar leaned back in his seat.

"What the hell does that mean?"

The man's face hardened, congealing into a cool mask that made him look like a serpent. His upper body relaxed and settled back into his seat, and his leathery, sunbaked skin constricted around his false marble eyes. Edgar looked into them: mostly pupil, the color of wet soot.

The man's right hand traveled across his chest, fingers dancing like little feet across his polyester jacket. It slid inside the coat pocket and there is stayed for several seconds.

Edgar had already slipped his pistol from its holster, and now he held it beneath the table against his thigh. His heart throbbed, pumping blood through his bulging neck, causing it to swell against the binding collar of his dress shirt, choking him until he saw a shiny stipple of bright hallucinated light, like random bits of hot glitter.

The man remained frozen for what seemed like a long time, but was probably only a few seconds. Then a runny smile slipped from behind his hard mask, and his hand reappeared, a cheap blue plastic pen within his fingers.

Edgar let the breath slip from his lips.

The man tore a blank corner from one of the pages of the magazine and wrote a phone number across it. Then he got up and put the pen back in his pocket.

"You call me when you feel convinced."

He turned and walked across the diner toward the exit. When he went out, a gray sedan sped to meet him at the door. Edgar looked through the window, but he couldn't see the driver's face. He watched the car exit the parking lot and disappear within the vehicle hoard.

He stared at nothing in particular for a long time before the waitress finally broke the spell.

"You want anything else?"

Edgar shook his head, and she laid a bill for $12.26 on the table and walked away.

He looked at the jagged slip of paper sitting before him, the area code unfamiliar, the handwriting neat like calligraphy. He put it in his pocket and looked across the room. The handicapped boy stared at him, a big gooey grin upon his face. He hooted and clapped and his mother tried to hush him. Edgar laid a ten and three ones on the table, and then he got up and walked out the door.

CHAPTER 5

A brand new Dodge Charger barreled down one of the deserted back roads in South Texas, throwing clouds of red dust high and wide into the air. The carriage jostled and squealed along the bad dirt road, but the young driver only pushed faster.

Inside, Sam Porter had it made: a 40 ounce bottle of cheap beer between his legs and Abby Buhner to his side. God she looked good: long shiny olive legs, tanned to an optimal state; frayed denim shorts, two feet above the knees; her long wavy hair kissed by the summer sun. She had a bottle between her legs, too, but it was still almost full. Damn, he thought, how am I gonna get anywhere if she keeps milking that shit.

"Drink up," he said.

"I'm drinkin. You just mind your drivin."

"You're drinkin like I'm pissin," he said. "Here."

He plucked the bottle from her lap and jammed it in her hand.

"We'll each take three big drinks at the same time."

"I don't want to, it makes me sick."

"You ain't gonna get sick off no three drinks."

"Fine," she said.

He brought the bottle to his lips and guzzled three huge swallows, and when he took it away, the contents were greatly diminished. Abby made a grisly face as she sipped, her expression pinched with concentration. Sam shook his head.

"It looks like yer trying to build a ship in that bottle with yer tongue."

When she put the bottle back in her lap, it didn't look much different.

"It'll take you til next week if you keep takin them Mickey Mouse sips."

"I told you, I don't like it. It makes me sick."

She folded her arms and stared out the window, a pissy little look across her face.

Well, that was that, Sam thought. There's no way I'm gettin anywhere with this shit.

He raised his bottle and slung back the last of the contents.

"You'd better be careful," she said. "There's Sheriffs out here. Some of em don't care who your daddy is."

"There ain't nobody out here," he said. "Look I'll show you."

He jammed the accelerator until it met the floor, and the car fish tailed as it gathered a grip on the powdered surface.

"Don't you scare me, Sam," she said, her polished nails boring handles in the soft vinyl arm rest.

Stupid bitch, he thought. Lucky for her, she was hot, or he'd dump her skinny ass out here in the middle of nowhere, let the coyotes eat her.

The sound of knocks and clicks filled the car, as bits of rock and dirt clods pinged up from underneath. Abby's heart tapped against her chest as the car gained speed.

"I mean it, slow down."

The Charger ate up a huge span of land before he finally let off the gas. He saw a glint of metal on the horizon and tapped the brake. Shit, he thought, that better not be a cop.

"I told you," she said. "There's Sheriffs out her that'll plant you up under the jail for drunk driven."

Sam gave her a sour look, and then turned his head toward the vehicle growing before them.

"Shit," he said. "That ain't no cop."

He hit the gas again and approached the black van coasting over the road before them.

The old road wasn't quite two lanes, and Sam dodged and weaved side to side, trying to make the driver dip over. But the van kept going straight ahead, 45 mph: the posted speed limit.

Sam hit the brakes and let the car ease back a few feet.

"Goddammit, let me by."

Abby studied a crack in one of her fingernails.

"Damn you, Sam Porter, you done made me break a nail."

He ignored her, gunning the Charger right up to the van, inches from the back bumper.

"Don't be tailgating," she said. "You don't know who this person is."

He started on the horn, but the black van pressed on unchanged, seemingly oblivious to the commotion behind it. A flat stretch of shoulder manifested just ahead to the right, and Sam seized his chance. He mashed the gas, and the Charger's Hemi V8 rumbled like a crack of thunder. He dipped the car into the rough grassy shoulder, and easily made it around the van and back onto the road. He smiled at Abby and she shook her head. Then he saw the vans headlights flash in his rearview mirror.

"What the fuck?"

He tapped the brakes until the van closed the distance built.

"Goddammit, Sam. What the hell you think yer doin?"

"These fuckers want to play, let's play."

He pressed the brakes and the car slowed, then he gunned the car forward.

"Dammit, Sam. Quit bein an idiot. You don't know who this person is. They could have a gun."

"I ain't afraid of no man," he said. He snagged the empty 40 ounce bottle from the floorboard between her feet and flipped it in his hand. He hung it out the window with his left arm and looked at Abby, her face painted with a worried confusion, like that of an animal recognizing a weapon without fathoming its function. He smiled at her and then pitched the bottle several feet into the air. It drifted end over end in the air and descended flush on the shiny hood of the trailing vehicle, exploding against it with the percussion of a tiny bomb.

Abby looked back in horror, but the van's speed did not vary. It proceeded as if nothing had happened like a soulless machine programmed only to drive.

"You see?"

"You're an asshole," Abby said.

A wrinkly grin ran across his face as he punched the accelerator and left the van in a rust-colored curtain of dust.

Abby was a pretty face without a mouth for the next hour, and every time Sam looked at her, she turned her head toward the whizzing scenery outside the window. She saw a pair of buzzards pulling strings of leathered flesh from a dead rabbit on the side of the road, and her lips wrinkled up toward her flawless little nose.

"Come on, Abby," Sam said. "I was just foolin about."

She turned her face and tilted her little head.

"You stoppin to get gas at the truck stop when we get on the highway?"

"Probly."

"Will you get me some nachos?"

The inflection of her voice settled on the familiar tone proven most effective in her short, easy life. It was whiny, but made of silk, and Sam was bewitched by her beauty for a moment, her wide sea-green eyes, oval and pressing, and crested with long curling lashes.

They pulled next to a gas pump at TT's Truck Stop just after 5 PM.

"Get me a soda and some donuts, too," she said.

"What kind?"

"Powdered."

Sam jogged across the lot and into the truck stop. He claimed a paper bowl of corn chips from beneath the orange glow of the heat lamp and drowned it with a ladle of melted cheese. He pulled a soda from the refrigerator and took a sleeve of donuts from one of the racks.

"Thirty dollars on pump twelve," he told the fat man behind the register.

He reached into his pocket for some cash but something stopped him. Outside, through the oily plate glass, he saw a black van parked next to the pumps immediately behind the Charger.

"You know we got some cold ones in that there cooler."

Sam looked at the man. He held the soda in his hand.

"That refrigerator's been actin up. This one's kinda warm."

"It's fine," he said as he paid the man with more coins than bills. He gathered his things and walked outside.

"You don't wanna bag?" The fat man said as he exited, but Sam didn't hear him.

Forty yards of pavement spread between the store and the pumps, and Sam eyeballed the van the entire way. It was just an ordinary piece of crap van save for the oddly-fitted chrome wheel rims, spinning in the breeze like the blades of a blender.

Guess there might be trouble after all, he thought.

He wasn't worried. At six-foot, 200 pounds, he was the most formidable member of the varsity wrestling team, and the only man that had ever beaten him in a street fight had been another wrestler.

The van's passenger window was lowered, but he saw only nebulous shadows working within. As he crossed the lot, an arm extended from the interior and rested on the frame. Just the sight of it made the soda bottle slip from Sam's grip and thump against the oil-stained pavement. He gulped back a dry swallow. The arm, colored with a web of disordered tattoos, was easily the largest he'd seen in actual life. He bent to retrieve the soda and hurried to the car with his head pointed down. He crossed the front of the Charger and slipped into the driver's seat, as if he'd just robbed the store.

Abby sat busy working her broken nail with an emery board. He dumped the junk food in her lap and studied the van in the rearview mirror. The sun refracted off the tinted windshield, making it impossible to see inside. A grapefruit-sized dent marred the hood, and a wild pattern of abrasions webbed outward from the great flaw.

"This soda's hot," she said, and as she turned the cap, a spray of carbonated froth ejected onto her t shirt and face.

"Godammit, Sam."

The van's driver's side door cracked open and a short, thick-set man stepped out. Sam saw a pistol in the belt of his pants, obvious to anyone with the audacity to look. He turned the key over in the ignition and punched the accelerator. The car surged forward sloshing more soda on Abby's shirt.

"What about the gas?" She said as she wiped her face with her bare wrists.

Sam looked in the mirror but the van still idled next to the pumps, the inverted figure growing smaller and smaller in the reflective glass, becoming less real by the second.

He drove that way for at least thirty minutes, dodging all comers, a singular look of terror pressed upon the girl's face, as they wove in and out through a mob of vehicles. After a while, he exited the highway and started down one of the beaten back roads that led to Abby's house. She dabbed at the wet soda marks on her shirt with a wadded napkin she'd found in the floorboard, and when she noticed him watching her work the area around her breasts, she turned away toward the window. She caught a glimpse of the instrument panel as she turned, and she looked at him and shook her head,

"We're gonna run outta gas," she said and before he could correct her, the engine started knocking.

Shit, Sam thought. They were still a good thirty miles from Abby's house, and it was another thirty from that to the next service station. He pulled the car to the side of the road just shy of a railroad overpass that hunched awkwardly over a creek. He scanned the area: vast hilled pastures rambled into the horizon on either side of the road, and a herd of cattle grazed near the tall oaks that skirted the length of a dry creek.

"There won't be no cars out here for the most part," Abby said. "We'd better get to walkin. My daddy'll give you a ride to the station and back to yer car."

They exited the vehicle and shut the doors. But before they could raise a knee, the burbling sound of an engine swelled over the hill, up the road behind them.

"Hot dog," Abby said.

But when the black van cleared the horizon about a hundred yards away, each of their faces went white.

"Is that the same van as before, Sam?"

He went to the back of the Car and popped open the trunk.

"Sam. Is that the same van?"

He found the tire iron and curled his hand around the hard metal. He held it in both hands, as if taking its weight, and then he closed his eyes and set it back down. The van pulled off the road and stopped two car lengths behind them. Sam closed the trunk, and they each stood watching as the two men got out.

They wore loose black clothing, their bare forearms, overcast with all sorts of homemade tattoos. The short man approached, but Abby's eyes affixed to the behemoth to his right: his legs, thick as the stump her daddy chopped wood on, arms like other men's legs. He looked like a thing broken loose from a bedtime story, something unreal.

"You having car trouble," the short man said with a grin.

Sam took one step forward and the men stopped.

"Sir, I want to apologize for what happened back there a few miles ago," he said in a shrill voice not his own.

"Shut the fuck up," the man said as he removed a black 9mm pistol from his waistband.

Abby screamed and staggered backward, while Sam raised his hands into the air.

The man looked at his hulking partner and gestured his head toward the girl. The giant nodded, and approached her, mouth agape, his big purple lips wet and slick. She screamed some hellish noise none were accustomed to, and the man leveled the pistol at her tiny head.

"Shut your mouth, or I'll put a bullet in it."

She froze still as the big man wrapped his meaty fingers around her wrist and curled her arm behind her, fast and easy, as if he manipulated a doll made of weightless rags.

The man moved the gun toward Sam and looked him over. He squinted his eyes thoughtfully, as if running over his options.

"Get on your knees," he said.

Sam looked at Abby: whimpering and petite, her body bent and dangling below the slobbering beast-man, her face contorted by despair. The giant watched her from above with a bizarre contemplation, his head tilted acrook, as if he'd snared some exquisite fairy from a storybook tale his own.

Sam looked back to the squat man.

"Why?"

"On your knees."

He crouched to the ground and waited, a swell in his throat that would not go away. The man turned his body and paced back and forth, his eyes small in his bony skull.

"You throw a jar at my car and think it's ok?"

Sam looked to the ground. He almost told the man his father was a Deputy-Sheriff, but ultimately opted against it. That was for other backwoods lawmen and teachers at school.

"Answer me, boy."

"I'm sorry."

The man looked to his partner and gave a grin.

"Yeah, but a lot more in a second."

The man looked at the girl. She wore a skin tight t-shirt with the word 'juicy' printed across the front in large flowing glittered script. He stroked at the faint black hair on his chin and hummed his lips, as if he'd caught the scent of something rich and delicious. He looked at his partner and nodded, and Abby screamed as the large man dragged her toward the sloping gravel that descended into the creek beneath the railroad overpass. She dug the heels of her flat-soled sandals into the dirt, but they only plowed linear grooves as the giant man pulled forward. Sam stared down at the shattered edge of pavement where the shoulder met the road, while Abby filled the air with great choking sobs that pitched for a moment and then muffled as she vanished below the bridge.

The short man chuckled, and then pushed the gun against the top of Sam's head.

"Look at me," he said.

Sam raised his head.

"Open your mouth."

Sam began to cry.

"I'm so sorry."

"Open."

He opened his mouth and the man put the gun inside, teeth clicking against the metal as it forced a path through. The metallic flavor made him gag, and this brought the man a curly smile. Sam closed his eyes and sobbed.

Below the train tracks, the large man manipulated Abby like a doll. With casual ease, he forced her into the creek bed: waterless but damp, her feet skidding against it like skates.

The giant bent Abby forward and pushed her onto all fours. He tugged the denim shorts down past her olive hamstrings and unbuttoned his pants. Abby screamed and tried to wiggle free. But the man swallowed up the back of her head with his palm and pressed it down into a filth of mud and runoff pollutants from the road.

She struggled fruitlessly, the septic smell making her throat lurch and gag. And then, she felt the weight of his huge gelatinous belly resting on the small of her back, as he positioned himself behind her. He used his free hand to open her thighs, but before he could do more, the overpass rumbled above their heads.

The giant man raised his head to the sky and held it there, like some primitive animal exacting scent from a passing breeze.

"Vámonos," the short man called from above.

The large man pulled Abby's face from the mud and studied it through huge vacuous eyes: the delicate features marred with snot and mud, her candy pink lipstick smeared around her lips.

He held her firm by the back of the neck with one hand and brushed the hair from her face with the other. He leaned forward and kissed her on the lips, pressing long and hard, so his great yellow teeth clacked against the flawless ones within her mouth. When he'd finished, he shoved her back into the grotesque mud and ascended the gravel embankment.

She remained there for a while, staring up at the vacant flawless sky, her face devoid of expression, giving neither gratitude nor blame. She tugged her matted hair from the sticky creek bottom, pulled up her shorts and rose to her feet.

When she got back to the road, the black van was gone, and an old Ford pickup sat parked in the shoulder a hundred yards ahead. Sam sat upon the back bumper of the Charger, his hands on his knees, silent tears streaming down his pimpled cheeks. She passed him without looking and staggered toward the truck.

The driver watched the young female figure approach within his rearview mirror, unable to discern more than superficial characteristics. As she grew closer, he saw the mud streaks and torn clothing, and within her eyes, he saw an emptiness where something beautiful might once have dwelled. A thing not lost, but taken, abruptly and without warning, using method so thorough as to alter a soul.

Three hours earlier, Madelyn Porter sipped a full-bodied red Bordeaux at the Cafe Rabelais in Houston. A tall man with dark-rimmed glasses sat across from her, a woman with a face like a saucer to her right. They discussed politics and toothless generic social issues as they nibbled a pasty cheese appetizer the waiter had said was made from the milk of Portuguese goats.

She ordered the Salade de Bleu d'Auvergne and when it came, she sent it back, because it tasted of Walnuts. The waiter brought her a Salade Jardin instead and she ate this without relish. When they were finished, the waiter asked if she wanted a box for the leeks and avocado she'd picked from her salad, and she rewarded his sarcasm with a roll of her eyes.

Outside the restaurant, they browsed the windows of some of the local high-end clothing stores. They entered one called Hemline where she tried on three dresses that were all too small. The round faced woman bought an expensive handbag and some over-sized sunglasses, and the tall man held the door open as they exited back onto the street.

Madelyn thought she saw one of the employees, a thin pale woman with wet pitchy lipstick, roll her eyes as they left the store. She turned to re-enter, and as she did, a young man in a light brown leather jacket approached from the street. He withdrew a pistol from his pocket and shot the tall man in the bridge of the nose, splitting his glasses in two. He then raised a straight edge razor and dragged it down the length of Madelyn's back, carving a vertical groove in the flesh next to her spine, an arch of blood spewing from the wound as he cut. The woman with the oval face turned to run, but the man shot her twice in the back, and she dropped face forward on the gritty cement walk.

People screamed and the sidewalks ran empty. The young assailant walked to the edge of the street and stood casually, as if waiting for the next bus. A few seconds later, a gray sedan squealed up next to the curb, and the young man got inside as it drove away.

Madelyn lay face down on the ground sobbing, her back slick and sanguine. The blood ran from her body in a pulsing seep, and her head began to swim. She looked at her male friend, his eyes murky and crossed outward, his brain matter an inch away from her face. She vomited out the expensive lunch from the restaurant, and then her eyes rolled back in their sockets, and the world fell dark.

CHAPTER 6

Ellie's frantic voice came through like raw clatter on the radio, and Tom pulled his patrol car to the shoulder of the road and strained to listen.

"Calm down," he said. "Tell me what's wrong."

"Madelyn. They cut Madelyn's back."

"What?"

"They cut her back with a razor blade."

"Who cut her back?"

"Someone. They tried to kill her for nothing."

He listened. Great choking sobs. What have we done?

"Where are you," he said.

"At work."

"I'm coming to see you."

When he got to the restaurant, she buried her face in his chest, and he hugged her until her shivering body stilled. They drove to Harris County Hospital in Houston, the sirens on his cruiser splitting the rows of traffic in two. When they arrived, Levi met them at the front entrance, his face tired and sullen in a way that made him look more elderly than old.

"How is she?"

"She's all right, I guess," Levi said. "The main thing is she lost some blood. But they've got that under control now."

Ellie hugged him and went inside. When she had gone, Levi turned to Tom and shook his head.

"Not good, I guess is what you're thinking," Tom said.

"Nope. Not good at all."

"What happened?"

"They were comin out of a store or something, and this guy comes up, shoots this fella she was with in his face, this other woman in the back, takes out a straight edge and pulls it down Maddy's back like he's opening a cardboard box. Then he gets into a car and drives away."

"What kind of car?"

"A gray car."

"That's it?"

"I guess when he fired, everybody took cover. Nobody could remember the make."

"What about the guy?"

"Young, dark hair."

"That's it?"

"That's it."

They went inside the hospital and looked around. Down the hall, they saw Edgar and Ellie embracing in a small pink waiting room positioned off to the side.

"Where are Seth and Bud?" Tom asked.

"Over at Henry Thompson's."

"What are they doing there?"

"He had a tractor stolen."

"That sounds important."

Levi nodded.

Edgar left Ellie in the waiting room and walked the hall toward the other two men, his eyes webbed with bright red veins, two big salty smears soaked into his uniform from where Ellie had been crying. He offered his hand, and Tom shook it.

"How is she?"

"She's got staples down her spine from her neck to her ass," Edgar said. "She looks like fuckin Frankenstein."

He spat into a Styrofoam cup filled with a foul slurry of saliva and spent tobacco

"This ain't all, neither," he said.

"What do you mean?"

"They got after my boy today, too. Put a goddamn gun in his mouth. Scared the bejesus outta this little girl he was with. Made her crawl around in the mud. Probably woulda raped her if someone hadn't come by."

Tom's stomach turned over. A taste of sour vomit. A snap shot of Ellie's face smeared with mud. A gun in her mouth. A man pushing inside her, his gargoyle face grinning down from above.

"So I guess we're feelin like we know who did it?" Levi said.

"Oh, I know who did it," Edgar said. "He come to meet me this mornin, down at the Crystal Cafe. Come up to my table like he knew me."

Edgar told them about the man, the magazine article and the phone number in his pocket. He told them about the man's white scar and how it filled with color under his reptilian grin. And he told them about his eyes, obsidian and null.

"What are you gonna do?"

"It's already been done," Edgar said. "I called him an hour ago. Told him ok. Told him he could have it all, so long as he leaves us be and don't tell nobody nothin."

Levi shook his head.

"You shoulda talked to Bud, first."

Edgar's face turned a blotchy rose.

"That motherfucker's the one that got us into this. Him and that goddamn Mexican who's probably chopped up in a suitcase somewhere. I'm done listenin to Bud and you should be, too. I don't wanna ever see that cocksucker again. I'm quittin. I'm done with it. Gonna give this fella what he wants, and then we're lettin out right after."

"Where you gonna go?" Levi asked.

"Movin up to Tennessee, so Maddy can be close to her Momma. Gettin the hell outta here, and you all should do the same."

"They say she can travel?" Tom asked.

"I don't give a flyin fuck, and I ain't waitin around."

The three men stared at their toes with dull, spacy eyes, the procedural happenings of the hospital burgeoning around them. Tom looked to his side at a very old Mexican woman sitting alone in the lobby waiting room. Her little body rocked back and forth, the thin wrinkled skin around her eyes squinched in a mighty concentration. Her waxy skeletal fingers traced a plastic turquoise necklace of rosary beads, and her lips moved gently as she mumbled silent words. He watched her for a moment without really seeing her, and then a couple came through the doors behind them, and they all moved out of the way against the wall.

"When are you supposed to meet this guy?" Tom asked.

"I don't know yet. I don't know where. He's gonna call me and I'm gonna go."

"Let us come with you," Levi said.

Edgar shook his head.

"He said alone, and I ain't fixin to test him. You can color me convinced."

He spat in the cup and set it on the edge of an over-filled waste basket.

"I'm sure you'll be hearin from him soon enough. Ain't no need to be in a hurry."

"You need to let us come," Tom said. "What if this guy's planning to take the money and shoot you dead just the same?"

Edgar gave an exasperated laugh and shook his head as if pestered by the questions of a young child.

"You just don't get it, do you? What the fuck choice I got? What choice do you got? This shit is miles past fucked up beyond all recognition. You can either do what this fella says, or you can let him cut up your woman. Or, if you can stop that, he goes and tells the cartel and they come and hook battery cables up to your balls and light you on fire."

He looked at Levi.

"You think Bud's got answers for that? Cause he don't. No matter what he tells you."

Levi looked at the ground and sucked his false teeth.

Edgar shook his head, and then looked back at the waiting room where Ellie talked to a nurse.

"I gotta go," he said. "Thanks for comin."

He took a few steps down the sterile tiled hallway, and then he stopped and turned back.

"You best be careful. This guy don't fuck around. Case you hadn't noticed."

The two men watched him walk away, his big, bulky frame looking smaller than they'd ever seen it.

"I'm calling Bud," Levi said, and he left the hospital for the parking lot. Tom watched him leave, and then he turned to see Ellie coming.

"You ok?"

She nodded, eyes still welling over.

"This is just crazy," she said. "They shot Madelyn's friends, and they did that to her, and they didn't even take anything."

"I know," he said.

He held her and they rocked, and he hushed her gentle crying, while blotting out the fear and shame within his head.

He put his arm around her, and they turned to go, and as they walked out the door, he turned to take a last look at the old Mexican woman. A nurse talked to her as she cried, and the rosary beads lay abandoned at her feet on the cheap carpet floor, the plastic within them unabiding, as if it thought itself a simple toy charm instead of something holy.

CHAPTER 7

The sun hung small in the sky, and that meant too much time had already been squandered. The day's work waited, and Henry Thompson's patience was at its end.

"You ain't even listenin to me," he said.

"I'm listenin," Seth said. "I just need to make sure I get everything the way it happened."

The old man hocked a layer of mucous from the back of his throat and deposited it in the plumes of dried grass growing long and free around an old, warped fence post. He put his pipe back in his mouth and frowned.

Seth looked at the pad in his hand. It had "John Deere 346 Square Hay Baler" written on it and something about Mexicans, but that was it.

"Now, why do you think it was Mexicans who stole your tractor?"

"I already told you why, goddamn it. Is he even gonna get out the car?"

Seth looked over his shoulder at the police cruiser. Bud sat in driver's seat talking on the radio, his left arm slung out the open window and his fingertips tapping against the outside of the door as if keeping up with a tune.

"He don't need to come down if you just tell me what happened."

"I already said. I come out here lookin for my tractor, and it was gone."

"So why do you think it was Mexicans who took it?"

The old man stared past him. He clicked his long tarnished fingernails against his pipe.

"Henry," Seth said.

"I ain't deaf."

"Fine. Why do you think it was Mexicans who took your tractor?" He spoke with a big, clear voice despite the old man's assurance.

"It's these goddamn Mexicans is what it is. There ain't never been nothin like this til them Mexicans started in. I growed up in this same house in this here same town and there ain't never been no trouble like this til they started in."

Seth looked back at the cruiser, but Bud wasn't coming.

"What the hell would Mexicans want with your tractor?"

The old man pulled the pipe from his mouth and spat.

"To sell it, you dipshit."

Seth closed his pad and flashed a look that made the old man take a step back. He raised a finger and aimed it at his wrinkled face.

"You best watch how you talk to me, or I'll kick your ass all around your own property, old man or not."

Henry studied the man before him. He had a big frame, and his muscle fibers twitched beneath the fabric of his uniform, like water disturbed by electric current. He was big and mean-looking, alright. But Henry doubted he'd hit an old man. He put the pipe back between his lips and worked it to the corner of his mouth.

"You don't wanna help, then you can go on back to town." He pulled the pipe from his mouth and spat in the same spot as before. "Hell, I don't even know why I'm talkin to ya. All you fuckers is so corrupt. You probably helped em load the damn thing up."

He put the pipe back in his mouth and folded his arms.

Seth looked back over his shoulder at the cruiser, and then he threw the pad on the ground and started toward the old-timer. Henry's mouth went slack, and his homemade pipe fell to the ground and stuck upright in the dirt. He unfolded his arms and put his hands out in front of him, stumbling backward and falling onto his backside. He raised his forearm against the hulking creature bearing down on him, but the police cruiser's horn blared just in time and broke Seth's trance.

The old man stumbled to his feet as fast as he'd ever done it in his younger days. He hurried toward his house looking back over his shoulder like he'd just encountered something he didn't understand.

Seth retrieved his pad and shook the dust from it. He looked back at the old man's house and then down at the ground. He saw the pipe jutting out from the dirt, and he raised his leg and crushed it with his boot. He headed back to the police cruiser, and when he sat down inside it, Bud looked at him and shook his head.

"Goddamn it, Seth."

"I can't help it. These old-timers out here got no respect for anyone under sixty."

Bud lifted his hat and wiped the sweat from his forehead

"You shoulda heard that old fart," Seth said. "The way he's got it figured, the goddamn President's sittin in the White House with his feet propped up on his tractor."

Bud smiled and shook his head.

"I ain't lookin forward toward gettin old," Seth said. "I don't know how you do it."

Bud put his hat back on and put the car in gear.

"Hell, my idea of hell is bein young, again."

When they hit the highway, Bud told Seth everything Levi had said on the radio.

"That goddamn, Edgar," Seth said. "I always knew he was gutless, but I never knew he was this stupid."

Bud didn't answer.

"So what are you gonna do?"

"Nothin." Bud said.

"You're gonna let him do this?"

Bud frowned and shrugged his shoulders.

"Last I checked, it was still America."

Seth shook his head and spat out the open window.

"Godammit, Bud, he's gonna wreck the whole deal."

Bud lit a cigarette and propped his hat back.

"Things is pretty much wrecked as it is, I'd say."

Seth looked out the window, a hot glowing rage in the place where most feel fear. He flexed his jaw, and turned back toward Bud.

"You really think this fella'd tell the cartel about us?"

Bud took a drag from his cigarette and squinted his eyes, as if reading the license plate of an invisible car driving in the vacuous road ahead.

"I reckon not. Seems to me, they'd have to give back what they get from Edgar if they do."

Seth thought for a second.

"Yeah, but the cartel would probably pay em just as good."

Bud nodded.

"But they wouldn't a gone to the trouble and the risk of goin after Edgar's family if that was their plan."

"I don't follow."

"Well, when it comes to shakin somebody down with threats, a meal's as good as a feast."

Seth looked at him liked he expected more.

"What I mean is if you're gonna tell the cartel, then tell the cartel. Don't make no sense to do what they done, unless they done the math and figured it'd be better for em if they had the whole pie, stead a just a slice."

Seth tilted his head down in thought. He rubbed his chin.

"So you figure they'll be comin for our shares, too, then?"

Bud looked at him with startled disappointment.

"All right, fine," Seth said. "What do we do when they come?"

Bud shrugged.

"What can you do? You got a boy. You have to think about that."

Seth squirmed in his seat, a gathering rage polluting his body, making him sick. He looked down to his hands, where supple pink flesh grew in the places rugged jags of callus had once been. That callus he'd earned through years of working construction and riding bulls, a youth of hardness to set him apart from other men whose sole claim to manhood was that they carried the correct dangle of flesh between their legs. But now the bloody bar fights and other glories of youth had been replaced with back-aching drives through long open country to quell drunken domestic disputes. He rang his hands waiting for Bud to speak, but the man just kept driving.

"I could send him away."

"Where would you send him to?"

"I got places I could send him. Places they wouldn't know to look."

Bud shook his head.

"They'd figure out where to look." He looked at Seth with bold serious eyes. "People like this, this is their profession. If they're connected to the cartels, they got money and they got experience, hell, they got expertise, in killin and probly worse."

Seth looked back down at his hands and molded them into big white fists.

"So what are you sayin? I should do like Edgar? Just give it all up. Just like that?"

Bud shrugged.

"I cain't make that decision for you, and I won't. Every man's gotta do what he thinks is right for him and his."

He crushed the partially-smoked cigarette out and put the unspoiled half in his shirt pocket. Seth rolled the window down against the stink.

"Besides, what advice can I give you? Just cause you give it back, don't mean they don't kill you just the same. To keep you from talking, to tie up loose ends, or just for the hell of it for that matter. Ain't possible to gauge somebody you ain't never met."

A cow stood in the road ahead, and Bud slowed the car and blared the horn. But there it stayed: solid cinnamon and motionless, like some extravagant decoy put there for incomprehensible reasons.

"What are you gonna do?" Seth asked.

Bud fished the crooked stub of cigarette from his shirt pocket, and lit it, and the car filled with a burning fetor that made Seth feel a little green.

"I ain't ready to decide. I don't need to decide yet. And there ain't no use tryin to make decisions til you got all the information."

They sat there with the car running, each looking at the cow and he at them.

Seth took off his hat and set it in his lap.

"So I take it we ain't all in this together no more."

Bud raised his chin and scratched the itchy gray whiskers pushing through the sweat on his neck.

"In what? We got what we aimed for. Now somebody wants it from us."

Seth shook his head, and Bud turned to face him.

"What do you want to do, Seth? Band together into some rag tag army?" He rubbed his eyebrow with the thumb from his smoking hand. "Hell, I ain't never even seen Tom or Levi shoot their guns outside the firing range."

He took a puff from his cigarette and the air filled with a curling fog of white smoke that crawled along the top of the car like something infectious and alive.

"You want to stand in a row next to men with wobbly knees? Put yer life in their hands?" He frowned and shook his head gravely. "Cause if that's what yer thinkin. Well, you might want to take a step back, reassess things."

He turned his head toward the cow and leaned back in his seat. Seth watched him for a moment and then he did the same. They sat for a while without talking, and then Bud suffocated the cigarette against a pile of old butts and black cinder in the ash tray. He put both hands on the wheel, and tapped his thumbs a few times.

"Listen, son. I know yer lookin for me to tell you what to do, but I cain't do that." He stared forward as he spoke. "You want my advice? Well, here it is. Don't take no advice and don't give none neither."

Bud lurched the car forward, and the cow flinched and stepped aside. They drove on down the road without speaking, Seth stone-faced, his mouth closed, jaw working, a bitterness growing between him and the man he'd once admired.

That night, Seth arrived home later than usual, and his neighbor wasn't happy about it.

"I said I'd watch him after he gets home from school," she said. "I said I would. But you cain't be leavin him here past supper time, because then I gotta feed him, or else me and my kids gotta set and eat in front of him, and I ain't wired to be like that."

Seth said it couldn't be helped, and he palmed the top of the boy's head and guided him through the woman's door out into the front yard.

The boy studied the ground as they moved, and Seth eyed him with worry.

"What'd you eat?"

"Green bean casserole," the boy said.

"Any good?"

The boy shook his head.

The sun had set, but a faint pastel haze lingered in the mid-summer sky. Seth took its measure, and looked at the boy.

"We got about fifteen minutes fore it gets dark."

The boy looked up.

"Where's that old baseball you found?"

A smile leaked from behind the boy's somber face, and then the thing withered like a little flower growing someplace infirm.

"Go." Seth pointed toward the house, and the boy went.

When he came back, he had a peeling oblong baseball that looked like something wrestled from a dog's mouth. Seth took it from him and turned it over in his hands. He looked at the boy, and the boy looked back, his face possessed with mute excitement.

"Alright," Seth said. "Let's hurry."

They tossed the ball back and forth, their hands bare and stinging, the boy's face noticeably live. After a while, the darkness closed, and when the streetlight didn't come on, Seth held the ball.

"Just a little longer?"

"You can't see nothin."

The boy looked around with desperate little eyes.

"I can see."

"No you can't. You're gonna end up with a busted lip, and the teachers at school are gonna think I slapped you upside the head."

They went inside, and separated immediately, the boy toward the television, and Seth down into the basement to deal with the sagging drywall. A bad pipe had spit water for a long time before he'd noticed it, and now the ceiling was bellied like the abdomen of some bloated dead animal turned upside down.

He had a refrigerator down there dedicated solely to beer, and the shelves were packed so tightly, when he took one, another seemed to fill the void instantaneously. He opened a beer and set it on the old plywood table he used as a makeshift workbench. He turned on an old box radio and finessed the knobs until the crackling settled into what sounded like old-time country music.

He picked up an iron wedge and sunk it into the edge of the rotted ceiling. He whacked at it with a hammer, and it tore through. The rank smell of mildew filled the air, and he coughed and spat as he tore chunks of drywall loose with his gloved hands. He'd gotten about half of it down, when he noticed the boy standing in the stairwell.

"What do you need?"

The boy shrugged.

"You wanna help?"

The boy nodded.

"Well come on, then."

The boy crept in, hands stuck tightly in the pockets of his jeans.

"Put those gloves on, and then take all these pieces of old drywall and start tearing em into smaller pieces, and then put em in those five-gallon buckets."

The boy worked in silence while he listened to his father sing along with the radio. The dust grew thick and after a while, they both put on the thin paper masks he'd bought from the drug store. After they'd hauled the last of the old foul drywall up the stairs and into the trash, the boy sat on the floor and watched as his father used a power drill to pluck out all the old screws from the wood joists.

"Get up and grab that coffee can and start pickin up these screws."

The boy jumped to his feet and moved across the floor like a beach comber intently scavenging the sand for tiny precious shells. His hands grew orange with powdered rust, and these he wiped against the hips of his jeans.

"You know you gotta wear those again tomorrow," his father said.

The boy dusted his hands together and stared at the floor.

"Christ," Seth said. "You're the one's gotta wear em. If it don't bother you, it don't bother me."

When they'd cleared the screws and swept up, Seth took two beers from the refrigerator and propped an old fold-out steel chair in front of his son. He sat and looked at the boy: small upon the floor, his fingers tracing on the faded wood in an invisible delineation uncertain to all but himself.

"You want one?"

The boy shook his head.

"Come on. I don't mind."

The boy took the beer and looked it over. He watched his father open his, and then he pulled the chalky silver tab. The bubbling foam rose upward and threatened to overflow, and he cupped his little hand around the cylinder until it receded.

He looked up.

"Take a drink."

The boy raised the can to his nose and smelled, his lips wrinkling back as if he'd caught the business end of a skunk.

"Just drink it."

He took a sip and froze, the rich bitter liquid quarantined in a pool upon his tongue. He looked at his father with stunned eyes.

"Just swallow it."

He swallowed with an audible gulp, and a sick look advanced over his face. Seth laughed and drank some more. The boy drank more, too, a warmth diffusing across his flesh, gathering and crawling with every sip. They sat drinking for a while, the boy putting up two beers to his father's six.

"You did good tonight. Helpin, I mean. You did real good."

"Really?"

Yeah. You did good."

The boy smiled and looked at his beer.

"When do we put the new stuff up?"

"I don't know. When I have time, I guess."

He watched the boy, his little body lilting in a wobbly teeter.

"Alright, let's get you in bed."

He skipped his bath, but Seth made him brush his teeth, and by the time he got into bed, the easy warmth he'd felt in the basement was made into something sullen.

"Do you miss mom?" He asked the shadowed silhouette sitting on the edge of his bed.

"No."

It was quiet for a moment.

"Do, you?" He asked the boy.

His little head nodded in the dark.

"We're better off," he said, but the boy began to cry.

Seth picked him up in his arms and held him for a while. Then he laid him back down and pulled the covers up to his chin.

"That's enough of that, okay?"

The boy nodded.

"You gotta be tough. That's what men do. You wanna be a man, right? And not just a little boy."

"Yes."

Seth mussed his hair with his engulfing palm and walked out.

He went down into the basement and got another beer. He hadn't been lying. They were better off. The boy didn't know it, but he did. She was little more than a drug addict now: no longer a human feeling creature, but a parasite, who sat around all day conjuring ways to spin misery where none was occurring naturally.

She'd burned up all their money trying to stay high. Sold the same goddamn stereo she'd bought the boy for his birthday, snuck into his room like a stranger and took it off the shelf not two weeks after she'd given it to him.

She'd disappear and then show up again, like some starving diseased animal that you pity but are afraid to touch. The boy would come home from school and search the house every day until she'd finally appear, eyes sunken and yellow, lips tacky and cracked: characteristics unbelonging to something alive.

He'd care for her, bathe her and bring her soup. And the boy, distrusting and reserved at first, always succumbed quickly and fell into her embrace. She'd make promises that they both wanted to believe. And they would make themselves, because it seemed the thing to do. And that was the way things went for a long time until the one final day Seth pulled a bag of crystal meth from the bottom of her purse. He remembered it well, her eyes searching the floor, glassy and shamed, until he flushed it, and then she transformed into her true form, hysterical and sinister, her eyes wild in their dark sunken sockets.

She clawed at his cheeks with the split shards of yellow nail growing from the bleeding beds of her fingertips, and he drew his fist back in a rage and drove it into her stomach like a great battering ram. She fell to the ground, coughing and gasping, the boy huddled over her, frantic and crying. But when she caught her air, she shoved him away, said they could both go to hell, and walked out.

The boy wept for weeks and then got better. He still had fantasies of her return, but Seth knew better. Bud told him that she had been arrested in Arlington for prostitution and drug possession, and that she had skipped out on the bail. She was either dead or someplace far away or both. And it was a good thing, because, there were many nights that Seth fantasized about killing her and dumping her body in the county reservoir.

He sat in the basement drinking as fast as he could. He thought about the woman for as long as he could stand, and then he thought of Edgar and Bud, and then he thought over his options, and when he became too drunk to think about anything at all, he turned up the radio and tottered in his chair until he passed out onto the floor.

He awoke hours later, his mouth parched, a genuine agony within his skull. He shook the boy awake hours before sunrise and had him pack a bag.

"Where are we going?" The boy asked.
"On a trip."
"Am I going to school?"
"Not today."

The boy asked what he should pack and Seth told him to pack everything.

"Everything?"
"All your clothes."
"Should I pack swim trunks?"
"Pack everything."
"Will we go swimming?"
"We'll see."

The boy made a disappointed face.

"Yes," Seth said. "We'll probably go swimming."

They loaded their things into his pick-up and covered them with an old frayed blue tarp. They got into the truck and Seth stuffed a green army backpack under his seat.

"What's in the bag?" The boy asked.
"Bathroom stuff."
"Where are we going?"
"You'll see."
"Is it far?"
"Yes."

They drove out of the driveway and onto the road, venturing forth into the horizon: spacious and empty, hanging before them blackly, and offering little else but the promise of the red morning sun.

CHAPTER 8

The baby spoke in Tom's dreams, its voice similar to that of any other baby's, except it gave perfect speak inappropriate for its age. It asked why it had been made. It wanted to know the point. Tom didn't know the answer, and he didn't ever respond. He just stared at its tiny pallid body, watching it breathe and then die.

When the dream woke him at night, he often went to the kitchen to make a drink. Ellie always slept through his tossing. A skill owed to what, he did not know. He both envied and hated her for it; she, drifting away each night with a suddenty that often left him feeling lonely and bereft.

On this particular evening, torment rose on two fronts, the past and the future, converging like a mass of wild-eyed soldiers with stony faces that would hear no reason. Ellie remained unaware, but he could tell she perceived something. If his poker face gave mystery to the rest of the world, to her, it was thin as a child's lie. He'd have to tell her something soon, else send her out into the world oblivious to the danger set against her. They might be sitting together the very moment, conjuring some terrible procedure, brainstorming about their unsavory craft as musicians compose music within their heads.

He stood drinking again by the sterile refrigerator light, its radiance fluttering in and out: the quiet threat of a coming failure. The clock on the microwave said three in the morning, but that meant little. He didn't want to sleep anymore.

He turned on the burnt yellow bulb above the stove and looked around. A meek little dining room table sat before him: bought at a flea market from an old man who had probably since died. The old man wanted thirty for it, but all they had was twenty; and once satisfied they weren't bargaining, he let them have it. He'd eyed them with pity as they hauled it off, and Tom had seen this and set his mind to hate the little table, though Ellie had always loved it.

A few waxy scratches cut into the table's varnished top, but Tom couldn't see these now because of all the bills. He thumbed through the envelopes as if working through an oversized deck of cards. One particular letter caught his eye, and he plucked it separate and tore it open. The bill didn't say St Gregory's Hospital, but he knew it had originated there because of the amount, the account now taken by a collection agency that didn't stop with paper threats, but relied on unyielding phone calls meant to shame. The first calls angered Tom, and he'd curse and make threats of his own through wild spitting lips. But fighting that broad apparatus was akin to firing wildly into a locust swarm. After a while, they stopped answering their phone altogether, and now it just sat there hasped to the wall, useless as a stage prop.

He studied the bill, a sum amount hanging bluntly over concise rows of words that blustered mutely between his hands. He hated the apparatus and those it employed. But in truth, he feared their articles less than those from the Hospital, which itemized its bills into painful little memories, each one appearing at a month's pace, each packed with little bulleted reminders of illness and agony in case you'd allowed yourself to forget or forced yourself to try.

But this particular bill didn't have a thing to do with Ellie's illness, and so it remained in his hands. He held it closely to his eyes, as if trying to exact visions, like a psychic reading the dusty possessions of one long dead. The mind flows toward painful recollections as water creeps along a slant. And he knew this, and he thought it to be natural. And so he allowed himself to remember once more.

Ellie was healthy back then, and they each looked at the cruel nature of the world as most anyone with little experience of it would. It was real and it all around them, but they walked above it or through it untouched. It teased them from behind television glass and whispered to them through impersonal text on the local newspaper. It existed, and they knew it, but it seemed safely foreign, and they wouldn't worry about things beyond their control. What fools are those who spend their time constructing a mental defense against those things there are no defenses for; and this was their philosophy at the time.

Though young, they believed themselves the owners of a grace and wisdom beyond their years. But in truth, it was but an arrogance born of youth: a faith that they were special in some way, that their destiny should be different from those beaten down by hardships they did not deserve. They weren't big dreamers, but they were dreamers, nonetheless. And why not? Their life was a canvas and their love, a golden base coat to light the edges of the many moments they would paint across it.

They loved deeply in those early years, as it is common for young lovers to do. They fantasized of their love as divine planning and viewed her pregnancy much the same. To say it was all falling according to plan wasn't accurate. But things were coming together as well as one could hope from such a world as real as the one they thought they knew.

They papered the walls in their spare bedroom with images of small cartoonish animals and other childish things. He bought a crib, and she watched him assemble it, a fevered rose glow flushing her cheeks. In one corner, they placed a rocker for her to rest during late night feedings, and each evening, she would sit alone in it holding an invisible baby in her arms for practice.

Parenting books appeared on Tom's nightstand, and he dutifully read them each night while he chewed the lid of a bright green highlighter. The books forbade the ingestion of certain foods, and she lived by this code, like a monk on some holy quest. They knew it would be a boy, and she was happy about this and he was, too.

They took regular walks around a serene little duck pond at a nearby park, under the deep cooked orange of the setting weekend sun. They stretched out over the mossy arching stone bridge and tossed hunks of bread to the bright-eyed yellow ducklings that buzzed across the spring waters, like tiny motorized winding toys. All the while, children raced about them filling the air with sweet little cackles, chasing insects and each other.

They sat on benches near the swings and watched the children pump their tiny young legs, his arm hooked over her shoulders, and hers cradling her swelling belly. And when the darkness shooed them all away, they'd sit at the table eating dinner, talking of future responsibilities and the undeniable miracle of conception, and life.

A suitcase appeared toward the end. It sat next to the closet stuffed with everything the books said they would need when the time came. And when it did, they collected it and drove to the hospital: all very much as they'd planned in their heads.

The hospital admitted her, and she quickly lost focus from the pain. But Tom guided her back with a seduction of loyalty and understanding; the future whispering through his lips, begging her to come along through the blinding haze of pain.

And, she felt better for a while. But then the baby's heart monitor beeped suddenly, and the nurses moved about in an unsettling manner. A doctor burst into the room and spoke with a controlled voice free from emotional inflections. He jammed his hand inside her, and his eyes rose in concentration, as if he strained to recall the combination to some dark corporeal safe.

He watched the heart monitor and frowned. Tom looked at Ellie's face, but she didn't seem completely aware of what was going on. The doctor said that both baby and mother were in jeopardy, and within minutes, other people came into the room and wheeled Ellie into the hall.

Tom watched as she vanished behind a pair of flapping metal doors. They told him not to follow, but his body trailed behind them like some thoughtless zombie corpse. The nurses stopped him and led him to a waiting room where they tried to calm him with words that seemed practiced, routine as a fire drill.

In what seemed like no time at all, another doctor approached and told him that Ellie would be fine. But when Tom asked about the baby, the doctor said that there would be no baby because the baby had died.

He sat next to her bed all night, and she awoke often, though still heavily sedated. She'd ask about the baby, and he'd tell her, an agonized little cry slipping from her lips as she drifted back into a medicated slumber. Then she would awaken some hours later, unremembering, and the entire thing would repeat like some hostile recurrent dream.

One day, he snuck out into the bright glinty morning while she lay asleep. He drove with the radio playing, the disk jockeys behaving as if nothing had happened. After a while, he turned the knob silent and listened only to the shrill wind, as it leaked past the gap in the rear window that refused to ascend the way entire.

When he arrived home, he went straight to the nursery and stood leaning against the jamb of the door. He flipped on the light switch, and then turned it back off. He saw transparent images moving about the room: a ghostly Ellie changing a diaper, and he in the chair embracing their son. He kissed his fat little cheeks and the baby laughed, and then the sunlight shifted behind the curtains and everyone disappeared.

He tore at the wallpaper with his fingernails, and then he got his tools and disassembled the crib and the rocker, screw by screw. He took everything to the basement and packed it into the corner, and when he was finished, the empty room looked different, and he felt better.

But when Ellie got home and saw what he had done, she collapsed in the middle of the floor and lay there sobbing into the carpet, her body limp and aching. He held her and said he was sorry, but it didn't seem like she was really there. They sat there for a while on the floor amidst the emptiness, and then he carried her out of the room and shut the door.

CHAPTER 9

They'd packed everything by the time Edgar made the phone call. Madelyn and Sam gave no argument, but the girl was tight to some boy. She screamed about injustice and swore she would never love again: none of it unexpected.

They loaded everything as if they're lives depended on haste, and the house they left in a ragged state. Madelyn remained loopy from the pain medication, so Edgar handed Sam a wad of cash and told him to drive straight through. He said to keep moving, and he tried to make this point clear as best he could without revealing too much. He said he'd be along after he finished up some business with Bud, and then he told them to go, and they did what he said.

When they'd gone, he called his bookie, who took a long time coming to the phone.

"Hello, deputy," the bookie said. "What you got for me tonight?"

"Nothin. I'm comin to see you."

The other end kept quiet.

"You hearin me, Daryl?" Edgar said.

"Yeah, Edgar, I hear you. It's just, I ain't sure I'm gonna be here for much longer is all."

"Well, I'm comin. And you best be present when I get there."

Daryl was quiet, again.

"You understand me, boy? If I get there and you ain't, I'm gonna shut down everything you got."

"No, it's no problem. It's just--"

"It's just what?"

"It's just. I don't have your winnings right now. Well, I mean, not all of it."

"Now why don't that surprise me?"

"I'm awful sorry. I just don't tend to set anything aside for the ones that like to let it ride."

Edgar swallowed and looked out the window.

"Well, I'm gonna be there in ten minutes, so you best give me what you got."

When he arrived, Daryl met him at the door.

"Listen, Edgar, you can't just take everything. I mean, you're gonna put me in a real bind."

Edgar walked past him into the bar.

"You put yourself in a bind."

One of the scraggly looking waitresses smiled at him, but he didn't respond.

"Let's go," he said. "I got places to be."

Daryl led him to his office and opened the safe. He brushed aside a stack of papers from a metal desk and dumped all the cash in its place. Edgar sifted through the pile and raised his eyes. The thin man cowered and put his hands forward.

"Look, man, it ain't like you're thinkin."

"Oh, it ain't?"

Edgar shook his head and slammed a wad of cash against the desk.

"Cause what I'm thinkin is you smoked up all my winnings."

Darryl shook his head.

"No, man. It ain't like that."

Edgar drove his forearm into Darryl's bony chest and pinned him against a tall aluminum file cabinet.

"You get everthing out of them drawers out there, and you bring it to me, or I'll drive you to the city lockup myself."

When he returned to his truck, Edgar added Daryl's cash to the rest and looked it over. It still looked light, but a lot better than before. He cranked the pickup and peeled out into the road.

The voice on the phone had said eleven, but Edgar set out at about a quarter to nine. He wanted to have a look at the area beforehand, though he didn't know what good it would do him. They held all the cards, and that was that.

He met the highway and drove straight toward the blaring red sun. He lowered the visor without effect, the radio offering something gentle, fit for an easy Sunday drive.

He stopped at the gas station and purchased chewing tobacco and a cup of coffee. When he reentered the truck, he took his pistol from the glove box and put it under his seat. They'd said unarmed, but they could go to hell just the same. He wasn't going anywhere without his gun, least of all, to meet soulless killers. In the truck, the weapon would stay, available only if he could somehow get to it. It wasn't great, but it was something.

He hit an early exit and journeyed the backroads a ways. He'd steal a glance at his rearview mirror from time to time, but all he saw was a picture of the horizon: serene as any replicate painted from mind. The radio became an irritant, so he shut it off and listened as the wind licked the open windows. The air grew fragrant with the smell of cut grass, and the chirping insects gave the early evening a pulse. It would be a perfect night for anything but this.

The light petered out by the time he made it to the chunky red dirt road, and he couldn't see much outside the aura of his headlights. He thought there were fields stocked with cows on either side of him, but he couldn't be sure. He knew there weren't any houses, because he didn't see the reassuring glow of porch light. It was all pretty barren and lifeless except for the animals and the bugs. He felt like he'd been on this particular road at some point, but he couldn't remember why or when. He thought he might have seen an old house on it then, but he must have been mistaken because he didn't see any driveways sprouting from the left or the right. Maybe that was a different road, he thought.

Ahead, a stretch of the road arched low between two hills, and when he descended into it, he noticed the bridge. He pulled up to it and stopped: just a little one-laner that looked in awful shape, the wood warped and rotted, the hardware ancient and misshapen.

He tipped back his hat and leaned forward. No way was this thing going to hold 10,000 pounds of modern metal. He spat in the coffee cup and let the tires creep forward. The wood groaned as if pried from the dead. He almost stopped, but something in his head said not to; and so he pushed the pickup over the straining, wobbling relic as fast as his courage would allow. When he reached the other side, he looked back at the bridge: rocking some, but still there.

He pulled off the road into a big swath of red dirt that sat at the foot of an imposing tree line, the trunks running in order alongside the creek that ran beneath the bridge. He parked the truck and killed the lights. The fingernail moon offered little light, so he gathered a flashlight from behind the seat. He sprayed light behind him onto a large red bag pack he'd jammed behind the passenger seat.

He pulled it upward and took its weight. Not that heavy. A goddamn lifetime of unending possibilities for anyone who held it, and it wasn't even that heavy. He thought it strangely odd that there should ever be such a fuss for a thing of this weight, but then he remembered that people killed for things so small as ideas. He shook his head and spat into the empty coffee cup.

He threw it over his shoulder and got out. The seat had swallowed the pistol some, and he had to fish around for it, his fingers negotiating through fragments of stale food and chewing tobacco wrappers as they went. When he found the pistol, he raised his sagging belly and shoved it into his belt. He draped his shirt over the butt of the gun like a curtain and closed the truck's door without making much sound.

He ascended the road a ways and cut off into a hay field. He made a wide half-circle around the bridge, flicking the light all around him as he went. The cut hay offered few places for anyone to hide, so he moved into the tree line and surfed the shifting rocks down into the creek. The bed lay sandy and dry, and the tree branches from either side lengthened toward their reciprocates like giant black claws. Their dry tentacles smothered the light, leaving the creek like an open cave. He pointed the flashlight to his right where the creek ran away from the bridge. It went about 100 feet and then veered out of sight.

He turned back to his left and lit the side of the bridge with the flash light. He couldn't see beneath it, so he moved in for a closer look. He took out his pistol and held it in his right hand as he approached. He went cautiously, the pistol leveled toward points of anxiety.

"I can see your ass, so you better come on out fore I light you up."

He listened, but his heart throbbed loudly in his ears, washing out all other sound. He bent and filled the bottom of the bridge with light: nothing but glittering sand and leaves. He took a closer look at the bridge. The supports looked so dilapidated, he thought he'd drive a hundred miles out of the way to keep from having to cross it, again. He ran his fingers against the wood and some of it disintegrated into black dirt. He shoved one of the vertical beams, and it gave a little.

The large, flat rocks on the other embankment looked like ominous places where snakes might hide, so he ascended the steep incline carefully on the toes of his boots. When he got up out of the creek, he searched around some more, and when he was satisfied that he was alone, he went back to the truck and put the gun back under the seat. He closed the door and walked to the back of the truck. He lowered the tailgate and sat upon it, legs swinging slightly, the toes of his boots cutting vertical patterns in the dry, dusty earth. He worked his finger under his gums and flung the old used chewing tobacco out onto the ground. A flood of anxiety passed over him, but he beat this back with his mind. He waited there for what seemed like a long time, but was probably only twenty minutes. And then he saw the air above the hill line illuminate, and two glaring star bursts crested at the end of the road. The car sailed down the hill and crossed over the bridge without hesitation. It glided up to Edgar's pickup and idled beside it.

  He hopped off the tailgate and approached the driver's window. It lowered to reveal a young man's face.

  "Get in," he said.

  Edgar scratched the back of his neck and looked over the little sedan.

  "Why do we have to go somewhere? Why can't we just do it here?"

  The driver eyed the red backpack and licked his lips.

  "Just get in."

  Edgar bent lower and peered into the backseat to be sure it was empty. He crossed the hood, opened the passenger door and got in. The interior of the car smelled new, and the driver looked ill-fit behind its wheel.

  "Where are we goin?"

  The young man put the car in reverse and glanced over his shoulder. Edgar looked at the pickup as they backed out. He thought about the gun under the seat and felt a little foolish for ever thinking he might have had a chance to use it.

  The young man turned away from the bridge and gunned the motor. Bits of dirt and rock sprayed from the tires as they gathered traction, and Edgar had to hold the door and the seat between his legs to keep steady as they jostled up the steep incline.

"Yer gonna drive this thing into a ditch, you don't slow down."

Debris spat up against the fender, and the driver reined it in some, his feet tabbing the brake enough to make the vehicle lunge. The air grew live amidst the headlights, bug fragments freckling the windshield with splashes of coagulate. Each explosion smeared the glass with green and purple swaths, ornate in their morbid patterns, like some repugnant artistry laid out by a demented mind. The young man lit a cigarette, and Edgar lowered his window and tipped his head out into the gushing wind.

They came upon an oak tree, its vast arching branches leafless in these late summer months: a twisted corpse still upright in the ground, firm and brooding, as if ignorant of its death or defiant to the world that gave it. The driver pulled off the road and flashed his lights. Ahead in the thick night, a pair of headlights clicked on and flooded the road. Through the darkness, a large black dually pickup crept forward and stopped before them.

"Get out," the young driver said.

Edgar stepped from the car and the driver did the same. He took a pistol from his belt and used it to direct Edgar to the front of the sedan. He told him to face the windshield and put his hands on the hood. Edgar did so, and the young man frisked him with brambly fingers that felt like instruments of wire. Once finished, the man turned his head toward the big dually and nodded. Edgar turned to see the man from the cafe step down from the passenger seat. He looked much the same, except his hair looked neater, and instead of the tailored suit, he wore a light windbreaker jacket and a pair of gray slacks.

The man approached and smiled, his solid, dark eyes demonic in the white aura of artificial light.

"Good to see you, again, Mr. Porter. I'm glad you came to see things my way."

Edgar took the bag pack from his shoulder and held it out.

"Here, you can take it. I just want this all over with."

The man made a serious face and nodded.

"Yes. Indeed. It is best for everyone that this all be over and done with."

He nodded to the young man who took the bag from Edgar and unzipped it. He dipped it toward one of the sedan's headlights and rifled through it, then he handed it to the other man, who did the same. He studied the money, tilting the bag and shifting the contents from side to side. Then he shook his head and made ticking noises with his tongue.

"No. I'm afraid this will not do," he said.

Edgar spat on the ground and stuck his hands in his coat pockets.

"Hey, that's all that's left. I spent some and I can't get it back. So that's all I got to give you."

The man gave the bag to the younger man who took it to the truck and handed it to someone inside. Then the man reached into a holster underneath his jacket and removed a pistol. Edgar backed against the front of the sedan.

"Hey, now. I gave you what you wanted. Now you need to let me go."

The man took hold of Edgar's shirt collar and cracked the pistol against the side of his face, the impact sounding very much of metal against bone.

"Goddamit," Edgar said. His body lurched backward, but the man yanked him so they were face to face.

"Do you think I'm playing around with you? Is that it?"

He spoke through gritted teeth, and his breath smelled a warm sour. He cocked the pistol and worked it into Edgar's mouth. He leaned in closer and whispered in his ear.

"I am not playing with you."

Edgar gagged as the barrel invaded his throat's delicate rear. The younger man returned, the corners of his mouth turned upward, his pointy face eager and excited, as if he longed to feel the pistol in his grip.

The man drew the gun from Edgar's mouth, and a glutinous filament of translucent mucous stretched between his lips and the barrel. It bowed downward and then severed, one end sweeping against Edgar's chin and neck, the other upon the man's fingers and arm. Edgar vomited something orange into the dirt, his hands braced against his wobbly knees.

"You can't lie to me," the man said as he wiped the gun down with a handkerchief. "I tell you that not because I know all the missing dollar amounts, which I do, but because I would know it if you did."

Edgar heaved dryly, his eyes wide and strained and facing the ground. The man tickled his fingertips against Edgar's slobbery chin and directed it upward.

"Look at me while I talk to you."

Edgar looked up, his torso heaving, his face an unhealthy red.

"You see, I have a special little gift, and it has always been of great service to me in my field. I guess you could say that I always know when someone is lying. But that's not it exactly."

The man dried his fingers with the handkerchief and then handed it to the younger man who put it in his pocket.

"It's not that I can tell when someone is lying."

He shook his head and looked down at Edgar. His face grew concerned, as if he lectured a young, reckless child.

"No, that's not it at all."

He pressed the barrel of the pistol against the center of Edgar's veiny forehead,

"It's that I can always tell when someone is telling the truth."

Edgar's eyes darted between the two men, his mouth gaped open and panting, his broad back damp with sweat. He gave a great trembling heave, as he sucked in enough wind to speak.

"Look, I'm tellin you, it's all I got."

The man looked over at the other man and then back to Edgar. He pushed the barrel further, and it sunk into Edgar's flesh until it felt like a bruise against his skull.

"And, we didn't split everything even, neither," Edgar said. "Bud's got most of it, including that Mexican's share."

The man's lizard eyes twitched rapidly, as if downloading information from Edgar's brain. The three stood frozen for a long time, and then the man flashed a manic grin that choked the blood from his purple scar.

"I believe you," he said, and he retracted the pistol from Edgar's forehead leaving a purple spot the size of a dime. He said something in Spanish to the other man, and then turned and walked back to the truck without speaking further. Edgar looked at the young man. He had his gun out, and he motioned Edgar back into the car.

Edgar got in as instructed and waited for the other man to join him, but he did not. Instead, a voice shouted from the truck, and he jogged over to listen. Edgar studied the man through the windshield. He stood short, perching on his toes to see into the passenger window of the stilted truck, like a young boy bargaining for ice cream on a neighborhood street. His head nodded, and he looked to pay perfect attention to whatever things he heard, and something about the way it all looked made Edgar more nervous than he had already been.

Edgar glanced at the sedan's ignition, but saw no keys. He ran his fingertips across the tender indention in his head and frowned. They'd free him to better their chances with the others, he thought. Yet, something in the base of his brain pestered him with dark thoughts. They could have killed him already, he thought. But there was no figuring the strategies of routine assassins. They might just be moving him to the place where they wanted to dump him, because they didn't feel like carrying such a weighty corpse. He tried to diffuse these thoughts by humming a tune aloud, and by the time the young man returned, he felt an acceptable excuse for calm.

The man wasted no time drowning Edgar's voice with the radio, and within a few seconds, the sedan plowed down the road back toward the bridge. He kept his eyes on the driver's rat face: serious, but calm as before. Edgar rode mutely, secure of his eventual freedom, contemplating his life elsewhere, void of money at least until he sold the cars. But then he noticed the driver did not smoke as he had before, and the thing in his brain spewed forth a fresh dose of paranoia.

The halves of his mind warred over the possibility of getting himself killed by reacting upon a bad feeling. If these guys weren't planning to kill you, ain't no reason to give 'em one, he thought. But then he felt headlights bathe the rear of the sedan, and the thing in his brain finally choked out all other reasoning and took control.

The sedan had been so loud on the bad road, he hadn't noticed the truck's growling engine behind them, but once he caught sight of it in the rearview mirror, the noise seemed deafening. The driver continued along as if all was ordinary, while Edgar chewed his bottom lip raw. When they reached the crest of the hill, he saw a hint of the tree line that ran along either side of the bridge. They sailed down the hill, and Edgar expected the driver to breeze across the aging structure just as he had before. But the man must have caught a better look at it this time, because he brought the sedan to a stop and leaned up on the steering wheel with squinted eyes.

Edgar scanned his brain for second thoughts, but none arose. He looked past the driver, to his truck parked in the dirt across the road. He could maybe make it, but only if things went perfectly. His eyes drifted back to the driver's face. The young man assessed the bridge, his fingernails clicking against the steering wheel, tongue poking his cheek.

Edgar sucked in a full, warm breath, and swung his brawny forearm against the driver's face, crushing the bridge of his pointy nose, which gave with an audible snap. The man cried out, and Edgar felt a warm sensation, as blood spurted into the fabric of his sleeve.

"What the fuck?" The man said.

Edgar hammered his face again, and this time, he felt the man's front teeth cave. The driver cried out once more, and Edgar swung the door open and lurched toward the road. The car rolled, and when Edgar's feet touched the ground, he tottered forward like a drunk man: his upper body out in front of his legs, anchoring his face toward the earth. When he hit the ground he was at a tumble, and his big frame rolled awkwardly down the steep embankment and smashed face down into the creek bed.

He climbed to his hands and knees and wobbled, his face dusted with dirt fine as cinnamon, his mind stranded in an incoherent fog. He watched the parched earth drink in the blood drips from his broken face, and then he heard the big dually truck blare its horn; and this made him fully aware. He ran through the dark hall of trees, his boots slipping against the grainy, giving sand.

Behind him, the sedan sped across the bridge and the growling dually pickup pulled onto it. The driver of the sedan stepped from the car and leapt upon the hood of the truck, his pistol in hand and ready to fire. He hurdled the cab and landed in the bed, firing wildly down on the fleeing man.

Edgar pumped his legs, his eyes fixed forward at the bend where the creek veered out of sight. His lungs burned under the fury of his gulping breaths, while the sound of popping pistol shots echoed into the air and racketed against the thick oak trees encompassing the creek. The passenger window of the truck lowered and someone from inside joined in the firing. Edgar felt a bullet stab his left arm, and then a shearing metallic pop sliced through the night, and a great wobbling sound filled the creek as the bridge buckled and gave way.

The rear of the truck dipped, and the man in the bed fired into the air as he fell backward. One of the support beams remained erect and kept the front of the bridge stable, causing the truck to roll backward and slam against the embankment.

Edgar rounded the bend and staggered several yards into the darkness. He plodded through the creek bed sightless, his arms stretched out waving against the whip-like thicket lashing his face. He pressed forward into that black nothing, his feet clumsy upon the loose land giving beneath them. He ran on, until a coldness swept his body and a taste of iron filled his mouth. He stopped and ran his fingers along the front of his belly: two exit wounds gushing fluid. He poked his trembling fingers into them and massaged the slickness in his hands. His mind fell into a panic, and he ran faster than before; but soon he sat upon the ground, and voices and dancing flashlights appeared in the distance.

He fell onto his back, and gazed up at the tree branches, their willowy silhouettes wavering above in the warm summer wind. Blood pooled in his mouth, and he pushed at it with his tongue until it trickled down his pallid cheeks. His head swam, and soon, he saw three dark men standing above him. But beyond them, he saw the stars.

They hung above like pin pricks in a dark oblivion, glittering frenetically in a way he'd not noticed before. His malfunctioning mind exacted messages from the throbbing pulses that said to come forward and join them forever in the eternal sky. He smiled at them, and they twinkled back as if just for him. But then he remembered that they did this for everyone, and a profound sadness overtook him until his mind finally winked out, and the three men raised his lifeless body and carried it away.

CHAPTER 10

Bud sat in his cruiser facing the sheriff's station, a Styrofoam cup of coffee in his left hand, the morning newspaper in his right. He raised the cup to his lips and sensed its temperature, cooling the contents with a thin stream of breath as he read. He skimmed the text through horn-rimmed reading glasses, but too many thoughts already glutted his mind; so he folded it over, and placed it flat in the empty seat beside him. He sipped the dark liquid as he glanced around the parking lot. He'd arrived first, as always, but something told him the reasons weren't the same this time.

A small winged insect had landed upon the cruiser at some point during the drive in. It had somehow managed to survive the battering winds the way entire. He'd watched it with casual curiosity, its legs stretched awkwardly in the violent wind, wings whipped into odd angles. Now, the world having slowed, it pressed itself against the glass, and for a moment, he thought it too crippled to move. But then it took flight, passing from one wiper only to land against the other: stayed affixed to its situation without thoughts of escape, its brain, a basal mechanism of minor functions.

Bud rubbed his whiskered chin and fidgeted in his seat. The early sun looked a sickly yellow, but the interior of the car had already grown sticky and hot. He watched Tom's Buick pull into the lot and park in its usual space. Tom stepped out and looked around. He tipped his body sideways to see into the cruiser through the open passenger window.

"Morning, Sheriff," he said, a half smile upon his face. "You gonna sit out here all day?"

Bud leaned across the passenger seat and peered over his glasses.

"I gotta make my way up to the Fredrick's place."
"Oh, yeah?"
"Yep."
"What's the problem?"
"Ah, probly nothin. We got some complaints from a neighbor, some other people who been out there."

Tom nodded and looked at the front of the station.

"I'm thinkin I'll have you come with me," Bud said.

"What about Seth?"

"I ain't expectin him in today, or tomorrow for that matter."

Tom spat and looked back at Bud.

"I take it you're not going to say it's because he's sick."

Bud removed his eyeglasses and slid them inside his shirt pocket.

"You take it right." He leaned forward and pushed the car door open from the inside.

Tom sat down in the passenger seat and ran his hand over the back of his neck.

"So what's the problem out at the Fredrick's place?"

"Oh, well, it's got somethin to do with his boy, I reckon." Bud said.

He wheeled the cruiser backward and put it in drive.

"Are we going to talk about what's going on?" Tom asked.

Bud tipped his coffee cup up and finished it dry.

"Let's wait til after we handle this. There'll be plenty of time."

He turned the radio up and hummed along, his window open, his left arm resting upon the frame. His right hand worked the steering wheel, and Tom looked it over from the corner of his eye. The skin wore wrinkles from its years weathering in the pitiless Texas sun; but beneath that, the muscle looked strong as wire.

Bud eyed the insect as he drove. Only two of its six legs hooked to the wiper, and the others stretched in the wind as if pulled by invisible tweezers. He worked a wrinkled half of a cigarette from his shirt pocket. It had a stubby used tip that turned his fingertips black, and he wiped them clean on a paper napkin he pulled from the cruiser's console.

"I don't think you ever been up to the Fredrick's place, am I right?"

"Not that I remember."

Bud tipped his hat back and wiped the sweat from his head with the back of his hand.

"Well, this fella's a bit of a hot head, I guess you might say. I know that won't be nothin new to you. I just don't want you to be surprised, is all."

"What's his problem?"

Bud shrugged.

"I don't know. Maybe feels like he's got somethin to prove."

"Is he a big guy?"

Bud thought for a second.

"Depends on who he's standing in front of."

"What if he's standing in front of one of us?"

"Then we'd be lookin up, I reckon."

Tom looked through his window at an old tractor moving upon the rugged ground, marring the serene blue sky with a smog of billowing earth.

"I guess you're wishing you had Seth with you, then?"

Bud smoked and blew through his nose.

"Actually, the opposite's true. He's got a sizable temper on him, too, and that complicates things worse from time to time."

He took another drag from the cigarette stump and shook his head.

"That boy's always been rash. Since the day he first come to work for me. I've had to push like hell to reel him in. Gets that look in his eye like a crazy fella. I'm sure you seen it."

"Oh, yeah. I've seen it."

Bud nodded.

"I know you have. You and the rest of em. You think it's bad, now, you shoulda seen him in his twenties. I'd of had to fire him if anyone knew about the beatins I seen him give. Probably woulda had to throw him in jail just the same."

He smoked the cigarette until he tasted filter, and then he smothered it in the car's ash tray and added the butt to a pile of at least twenty.

"I knowed him for a good ten years, and he ain't never changed, no matter how many times I told him. Temper's a young man's flaw, usually. Most of em outgrow it."

He looked at Tom.

"Youth reacts, age responds," he said. "Or usually, anyway. He still acts like he's twenty even though he's pushin forty. I always had him pegged as one of these fellas who needed to be put on his ass at least once in his life for his own damn good. Just ain't never seen nobody who could do it."

He exited the highway and turned onto an old gravel road that looked as neat as the day it was laid.

"Don't get me wrong," he said. "I'm fond of him. I think everyone knows that. I just woulda liked to see him settle down some. Sort things out a little better with his mind."

He coughed productively and spat something vile out the window.

"Anyway," he said. "He's still a relatively young man, I guess. Cain't say I never made mistakes when I was his age."

They broke from the gravel after only a mile, turning onto a one-lane dirt road with tall blades of parched grass growing between the tire paths. The path cut into a wooded area that grew more dense the further they drove, the low ground overgrown with a curling thicket of barbed thorns. Above that, tall bent trees blocked the sun, shrouding the land in a veil of sepia that seemed fit for a dark fairy book setting where bad things happened to good people.

Things looked similar for a while, and then the vegetation thinned to sparse grass and ringlets of dwarf pines. The road swelled into a hill, and when they crossed over it, they saw a small house and a large barn surrounded by many acres of unkempt farmland.

Bud drove the cruiser through an open wire gate, and traveled the uneven dirt drive that led up to the home. Large antiquated steel farm equipment, colored maroon with baked rust, littered the yard like brittle relics from a long-ago era; and an old refrigerator set upon the grass waiting patiently as a perfect trap to suffocate curious children.

Tom looked over each of his shoulders taking in the lay of things, and then he looked at Bud who pursed his lips and nodded.

"Well," Tom said. "I don't know what trouble this Fredrick fellow has with his boy, but I've seen enough out here already that social services could use to pluck him free."

Bud nodded.

"Yeah, but half the time you take em outta someplace like this, they end up somewhere worse. So let's just wait and see."

They'd barely breeched the front drive, when a pair of broad shouldered pit bulls bolted from the barn and swarmed the car like frenzied bees.

Tom gripped the vinyl armrest as the animals circled the car. Their fur looked scant and mangy, but their rippling bodies seemed to be well-fed. A commotion of slobbering snarls fell from their huge snapping mouths, and Tom felt weak chills infiltrate the bones of his legs.

Bud slowed the cruiser to keep from hitting one, and when he did, the other lunged at Tom's half-raised window, its teeth clacking against the glass, sagging streams of saliva thick as adhesive left against the window. Tom flinched and raised the window.

"Goddamit," he said. "I hate those fucking things."

Bud wheeled the car in front of the barn. He put it in park and leaned back in his seat. Tom looked at the house to see eyes peering from between a pair of stained curtains. He pointed toward the window and Bud nodded. They sat in the car for a few minutes longer watching the dogs orbit like satellites, their teeth polished and glowing amidst the motion blurs.

"I don't think he's planning to come out," Tom said.

The dogs ran in opposite circles around the vehicle, pausing only to clash with each other for brief moments with each pass. They hurled their muscled bodies against the doors, and Tom ducked his head with each dull metal pong.

"What do you want to do?" He asked, but Bud already had his pistol out.

He lowered his window a few inches and stuck it through the space. One of the dogs saw this, and stopped abruptly, its feet skidding the dirt against its momentum. It steadied itself, and surged forward, veined hind legs overlapping the front ones as it charged. When it was within a few feet, Bud pulled the trigger and Tom's left ear went deaf. The bullet sailed impotently into the hanging air, but the thunder sent both animals scampering toward the barn.

Tom stuck his index finger into his ringing ear and rubbed around.

"How the hell did you know that would work?"

"I didn't."

Tom raised his hat and ran his palm up over his hair. He looked at the window, but the curtains hung closed. They stepped out of the car and stretched their legs. Tom looked into the barn, his eyes squinched trying to interpret the shapes within the shadows. Bud moved toward the house, but a shirtless man in a pair of overalls stormed through the front door and met him in the yard. Oily strands of black hair stretched from one side of his bald head to the other, and his natural facial expression seemed frozen in such a way that it seemed he smelled something that others did not.

"Mornin, Bob," Bud said.

"What can I do for you fellas?"

Bud dusted his pants and scanned the ground as if looking for something.

"We heard some complaints, so we're gonna need to have a look around."

Bob stuck his thumbs underneath the straps of his overalls. He had patchy black facial hair, and his sunburned shoulders were caked with waxy scales of healing skin.

"Well, I don't know what you heard, or who you heard it from, but there ain't nuthin fer you to look at."

Bud looked at the man and gave a half-friendly smile.

"Well, there won't be nuthin for you to worry about then. But we do need to have a look around."

Bob sucked his teeth. He looked at Tom and took his measure from head to toe.

"Well, like I told you," he said. "Ain't nuthin for you to look at."

Bud bent to look over Fredrick's shoulder, but the man took a step over to block his view.

"Now you fellas can get on outta here, cause I got work to do."

Bud worked a brand new pack of cigarettes from his pocket and peeled the plastic open by the dainty gold ribbon. He tore open the silver paper that sealed the cigarettes, and pulled one out. He placed it between his lips and cupped it with his hand as he lit it with a match.

"Now, Bob," he said from the corner of his mouth, smoke rolling up from his palm. "I'm gonna have me a look around."

He puffed the cigarette to life and waved his hand to kill the match.

"You can either walk next to me while I do, or you can watch from the back of the cruiser with cuffs on yer hands. It'll be up to you."

Bob bent over and spat in the space between the two.

"You do what you got to, Sheriff." And he turned and walked toward the barn.

Bud puffed his cigarette. He looked at Tom and held his hand out.

"After you," he said, and the two men followed Bob into the barn.

A smell met their faces as they entered: a combination of bitter mildew and wet dog hair. Broken bales of hay lay scattered about, much of it looking moldy and wasted. Rusted tools hung from nails on the walls, and others lay scattered carelessly on the bare dirt floor. As they moved further inside, the foul smell of spoiled meat filled their nostrils. Tom's stomach turned and he slowed to let the others go ahead.

A big twelve-by-twelve support beam blocked their view of a portion of the barn, and when they cleared it, they met the source of the odor. Tom turned his head in disgust. A six-foot length of chain hung from one of the horizontal beams running across the roof. Attached to the end, a deer carcass hung by its head, the chain curled around the beast's neck and cinched together with a pad lock. Tom looked it over: its face a black leather, its eye sockets picked clean by green flies, its big herbivorous teeth locked in an eager-looking, satanic grin.

Bud picked a hoe from the ground and poked the carcass. It spun three times and stopped. He shook his head.

"You lettin this place go to hell for any particular reason?" He asked.

Bob spat.

"If I was, it'd be my business."

Bud looked at Tom who frowned.

"Alright," Bud said. "Let's have a look at the house."

Bob folded his arms and looked at the ground.

"I done showed you all I intend to."

He looked up at Bud and raised his eyebrows.

"And if you think I'm messin about, you're fixin to find out different."

Bud looked over at Tom. He had his right hand resting on the butt of his pistol again. Bud frowned and looked up at the man before him: large and breathing fast, hands clinched into great fleshy hammers. Bud looked down and tapped the hoe against the toe of his boot.

"Well, then. Let's head on back to the front of the house, I reckon."

He turned and left the two men behind, using the hoe as a walking stick in a way that made him look old. Bob looked at Tom and wrinkled his lips in disgust. He turned and followed Bud out into the open air. Tom took a final look around the barn and then followed suit.

In the yard, they stood much as before. Bud leaned against the hoe and looked around. A single nomadic cloud drifted across the endless blue sky and landed in front of the grueling sun, placing a welcome if temporary shadow onto the tiny specific area of the world that held the three men that very moment. They stood within the quiet until it passed over, and then the sun struck back with all its fury, and Bud spoke.

"Alright, Bob. I guess I can see where this is goin. If you don't want to let me in yer house, well, I guess I can understand that. And I have to respect it, cause I don't believe I have any reasonable cause to do it."

Bob studied the man with lowered brows, as if parsing the words of a salesman.

"But there's another side to that pancake, and I'm gonna tell you what it is," Bud said. "I'm gonna ask you to show me yer boy, and yer gonna do it, too. And if you don't, well, I suspect that's gonna give me reasonable enough cause to go ahead and take a look around in yer house. And then at's what I'll do."

Bob's face filled with color, the bands of his comb-over peeling slightly from his greasy, bulbous skull. He squinted his eyes and took a step forward, but Bud didn't move. Bob's eyes shifted toward Tom, and then they settled back on Bud.

"Alright, Sheriff. You know what I'm gonna do? I'm gonna go get my shotgun, and if yer here when I come back out, I'm gonna spray both yer faces with bird shot."

He turned toward the house in a cold fury, but before he got further than a couple of steps, Bud whipped the hoe forward and curled the metal end around his ankles. The man's balance went top-heavy, and he sailed to the ground, palms slapping loudly against the hardened earth. He tried to turn over, but Bud had already set upon him. Tom had his pistol out, but he only watched as Bud gathered the man's greasy hair in a vice of fingers. Bob cried out, as Bud yanked his head back and curled an arm around his neck. He locked down and pulled until he heard gurgled choking noises.

"Why don't you come around here, and lay them cuffs on him."

Tom did as he said, and a few minutes later, Bob sat in the backseat of the cruiser, his wrists bound with cuffs.

They stepped onto the front porch and withdrew their pistols. A ragged screen door blocked their way, and when Bud pulled it open, the hinges gave a thin cry. The smell slapped their faces as soon as they stepped inside. It lingered heavily in the humid air, a marriage of sharp chemical deodorizer and some ungodly heaping spoilage. Tom looked to his right into the living room: trash everywhere. He stepped inside, kicking through spent beer cans and empty containers of potted meat. They saw empty bologna casings, and bags of chips; and each thing disturbed released its own brand of vile smell. In the few areas devoid of garbage, the brown carpet floor lay matted with grease, the fibers sculpted and smeared, as if licked by a great mucilaginous tongue.

Tom looked at Bud and nodded toward the hallway that led toward the bedrooms. Bud went ahead, and Tom stood back, his gun drawn and aimed over the sheriff's shoulder. The bedroom doors stood closed, so Bud turned his attention to the open bathroom coming up on his right. He raised his gun, and made a sharp turn, a dense fecal stink violating his nostrils. He reached his hand around the corner and flipped the light switch. Tom watched him, his pistol focused on the closed bedroom doors. Bud lowered his gun and looked at Tom. He tipped his hat back and rubbed his eye with the heel of his hand.

He brought Tom forward with his index finger, and they both looked inside the tiny room. The sinks looked surprisingly neat considering the plight of the home. But in the bathtub, a cat litter box sat abundant with crusted feces. In the tub beside it, the author of the waste rested, its eyes dried and sunken deep within the recesses of the skull sockets, the white fluffy belly bloated with undulating larvae that moved about like tiny wriggling fingers stretching out against a latex shell.

Bud flipped off the light and stepped back into the hall. He looked at Tom and motioned his head toward the bedrooms. When they reached the end of the hall, Tom leveled his gun at one of the bedroom doors, while Bud turned the knob on the other. He swung it open and looked inside the empty room. A whirring ceiling fan dangled from above, caked with dust and cob webs and wobbling difunctionally with each revolution. It turned awkwardly, bending the thin white light from the window to form amorphous shadows along the walls and floors. Piles of unwashed clothing littered the carpet floor, each article soiled and twisted and radiating a musty scent that smelled like mildew borne of sweat. A single stained mattress lay upon the floor; and on it, lay stacks of erotic magazines along with more empty food wrappers and beer cans.

 Bud stepped out of the room, and closed the door. He turned his attention to the other bedroom: the last place to look. If they didn't find the boy inside, they'd have to bring out dogs to search the property. He looked over his shoulder at Tom, who gripped the handle of his revolver and nodded his readiness.

 Bud turned toward the door and wrapped his palm around the knob. The metal felt slick with something wholly vile, and he jerked his hand back as if scalded by surprise. He turned his hand to see a chunky unfamiliar residue. Jellied and pale brown, it glistened grotesquely on his skin, and he turned his hand from side to side watching the sheen shift in the available light. He wiped it on a handkerchief from his pocket, and then used the handkerchief to turn the knob. He pushed against the door, and Tom moved in from behind, his gun cocked and trained at the growing slit. Bud backed against the wall and let Tom pass in front, and then he followed him into the small unlit chamber.

 The room offered barely enough space for a single man to stretch out in. The hall gave enough light to prove the room empty, and that was a good thing, because when Bud reached for the switch, his fingers sunk into a vacant square hole.

 The two men lowered their pistols and looked around. An ungodly odor flushed forward; and it seemed that if a smell could actually kill a man, this would be the one to do it.

 A black sheet hung tacked up over the window, and Tom tore it down to let the smell out; but nailed boards blocked the window from the outside, so they pulled their shirts up over their noses, instead.

 Streaming sunlight sprayed through the slits between the boards, exposing in one of the corners a ratted blanket marked by dog urine and diseased hair. In another corner, a hoard of flies clustered atop one another along the edges of a plastic 5-gallon bucket half filled with a slurry of urine and excrement. The rest of the room consisted of nothing but soiled carpeting, slick and matted with a putrid glaze. At the center of one wall, a closet door stood closed, a sliding barrel bolt lock fastened on the outside.

    Bud approached the door and pulled the bolt back. The door creaked open, unleashing yet a fouler smell trapped within. The tricks of shifting light ran the shadows away, revealing a wasted figure curled against the corner: emaciated and covered in fragments of ill-fitted tattered clothing. Bud stepped back, and the little boy scuttled against the closet wall, his bare feet kicking the worn carpet floor of his cell.

    Bud squatted with his palms down, as if to warm them above a fire. The boy pressed the side of his face against the wall like a cornered animal awaiting consumption.

    "It's alright, son. We're gonna help you."

    The boy studied the ground like someone who had done something wrong, while Bud made shushing noises so gentle, they nearly vanished in the tainted air. He sent Tom to collect a blanket from the cruiser's trunk, and as he passed the car, the man in the backseat locked eyes with him for a moment and then looked away at once, as if he might be seared to cinder by the deputy's gaze.

    By the time Tom returned, Bud had coaxed the boy out into the room. Tom wrapped the blanket around him, and then he went into the abominate kitchen to collect a cup of water. Roaches infested the countertops and floors, and not a dish looked serviceably clean; so he claimed a large glass jar of rice from one of the cupboards, and shook the contents onto the ground. He rinsed it under the tap and filled it for what it was worth, and when he brought it, the boy drank in a desperate rush, as if it was the first time he'd tasted such a thing, or the last time he thought he would.

    They led the boy out into the living room and sat him upon the linoleum entryway. Bud left to use the police radio, the boy emptying two more full jars in the space of his return. When he reappeared, Bud said social services was on its way, and instructed Tom to wait with the boy, while he delivered Bob to the state police. Then he turned and left, his boots punching against the wood porch on his way out.

Tom looked down at the frailty engulfed within the folds of the coarse blanket, and then he took a couple steps out the door.

"Sheriff."

It was a forceful whisper, and Bud turned and moved toward him.

"What is it?"

Tom looked back at the boy, traumatized and empty-looking: just a shell. He turned toward Bud, eyes wet in the orange burn of the late afternoon sun.

"Look, Bud, I know this isn't the time, but I have concerns. I need to know what we're going to do about our problem." He swallowed. "I want to know what we are going to do."

Bud leaned to the side and looked at the boy, and then he looked back at Tom.

"You was right the first time. This ain't the time." He looked over his shoulder at Bob and scratched the back of his head under his hat. "But I'm gonna tell you the same thing I told Seth. Ain't nuthin we can do til we see this fella for ourselves."

Tom looked down and shook his head.

"And what about Seth, Sheriff?" He looked up at Bud. "Why aren't you expecting to see him? Where's he at? Where's Edgar? Why won't anyone tell me what's going on?"

Bud shook his head and spat.

"I don't know where neither of em is, and that's the truth."

He looked up at Tom, and put his hand on his shoulder.

"Everbody's doin what they think is right and I don't judge none of em for it. What you got here is a worst case scenario, son. It's beyond yer control, and there ain't nuthin you can do to change it. Now what I'm gonna do is wait and see. I ain't gonna worry, and I sure as hell ain't gonna run. When this fella met Edgar comes to me, I'm gonna hear what he has to say, and then make up my mind. You can do the same if it suits you."

He turned and walked down the porch steps toward the cruiser.

Tom stepped forward, his fists clenched white.

"What about Ellie, Sheriff? What about my wife?"

Bud threw his head back and turned around.

"What about her?" He shook his head and spat. "She's yer wife. These ain't hard questions to answer, son. Look after her as best you can. What more can you do?"

He turned and walked to the cruiser, and when he reached it, he put his hand on the door handle and stopped. He looked through the glass at the sulking figure in the backseat. He had cracked the window for air when he'd first put him in there, and now he couldn't think of a single thing from his life he regretted more.

He looked down at the hood, and saw the little insect much as it was before. He watched it for a moment, its legs clenched down waiting for the world to speed up again. He looked across the yard at Tom, and then he opened the door and sat inside.

They drove a long while before anyone spoke, the wind lapping the edges of the open window, whistling when conditions were so. Bud watched the prisoner in the rearview mirror, something stoic about the man's carriage: some misplaced pride founded perhaps in the knowledge that no man and no law had dominion over his choices; and whether this posture was authentic or a trick of Bud's mind, it was tolerable no longer.

"Hey, Bob, do you remember that time I come out to yer place back when yer wife was still alive?"

The man raised his head and squinted his eyes.

"Yeah, you was a tough one to handle back in those days." He removed the pack of cigarettes from his shirt pocket and pulled one out. "Not like now." He shook his head. "Nope, you was somethin back then. Big and mean. I guess they call that yer prime."

They traveled the back roads to the state police station: thirty minutes longer by mileage, but sixty less in real time what with traffic. Bud lit a cigarette, and as he breathed life into it, he spoke between puffs.

"You beat the hell outta that women more than once as I recall."

Bob rubbed his cuffed hands together behind his back.

"Yeah, yer a real hero, Sheriff. You got everbody fooled includin yerself."

Bud took a long drag from his cigarette, and then he withdrew it from his mouth and looked it over.

"Yeah, you was a hard one." He looked at Bob in the mirror. "Til I cracked it outta ya."

Bob shook his head, and Bud smiled.

"You ain't gotta worry, Bob. I ain't like that no more."

A grassy road shot off to the right, and Bud turned onto it, Bob glancing out both windows at the desolate spread. They drove a half a mile, and then Bud pulled into the shoulder of the road and stopped the cruiser. He parked the car and killed the engine, his eyes affixed to the insect, clinging against the windshield wiper like some obscure ornament. It would never let go, he thought, lest somebody extracted it, and then it'd probably spend the rest of its life trying to find its way back.

"You know, Bob, there was a time I woulda shot you between the eyes for what you done to that boy."

He studied the cigarette in his hand, half gone but still burning. He looked out the open window at a hay field swaying beneath the sun like a flowing ocean of polished gold. A single tree stood amidst it, an island of cool shade lurking beneath. He smoked into the forbidden half of the cigarette, and tapped the ash outside.

"You know," he said. "I used to smoke these things like it was the end of the world, I reckon. But now I just smoke em a half at a time." He held the cigarette up and looked through the gray ash at the hot orange kernel glowing inside. "I guess there ain't no real point to it, but that's what I do."

Bob leaned back in his seat.

"Shit or get off the pot, Sheriff."

Bud looked out the window and nodded.

"Yep, I reckon so."

He opened the door and got out of the car.

When they pulled into the state police station two hours later, Bud flagged down an officer and told him who he was and that he had a prisoner to drop off. The officer went inside, and minutes later, Myron came out.

"Afternoon, Bud. What do ya got for us today?" The fat man had a toothpick in his mouth, and his lips worked it around as if they wished it a cigarette.

Bud put his hand out, and Myron shook it.

"Well, Sergeant. This ole boy here's been beaten on his son. Social services is out at his place gatherin the boy, investigatin and whatnot. You can probly find out all you need to know from them."

Myron leaned back and looked at the figure in the backseat: his face grotesquely swollen on one side, a gouge of skin missing from his forehead. The sergeant looked at Bud.

"He give ya some trouble did he?"

"Nuthin I cain't handle, I reckon. I'd put him up if I could, but I just assume be done with him, less I'm called to testify anyhow."

Myron took another look at the man.

"Not a problem, Bud. We'll take it from here."

The sergeant flagged down a pair of officers who gathered the prisoner and helped him inside the station. Bud went inside to fill out forms, and then Myron walked him back outside to his car. They stood alongside the cruiser for an awkward moment.

"How you been, Bud?"

Bud took his hat off and scratched the top of his head.

"Aw, you know. Bout the same."

He put his hat back on and spat, while Myron leaned over and looked at the empty backseat. Puddles, a quarter's size, stood red on the upholstery, alongside a crinkled glop of pulp that looked like the missing piece of the prisoner's head. He looked at Bud and took the toothpick from his mouth.

"Looks like you got some cleanin to do." He flicked the toothpick away and put his hand out.

"Good to see ya, Bud."

Bud shook his hand.

"You be good."

He took the freeway back, the traffic sparse in that early evening for reasons he could not conceive. He drove with the window open, the air slipping through the fibers of his shirt and cooling his sweating skin. The wind smelled of summer, and the sun set behind the levels of highway architecture: red light cascading over the sterile concrete, bathing everything in a considerate glow.

He looked at the insect clinging still to its spot on the windshield wiper. He lit a cigarette and shook his head. The highway speed engineered a pitiless wind, and he watched one leg uncouple, and then another, and then without knowing why, he slowed the cruiser slightly, and the insect recovered, though it appeared greatly diminished by its struggle.

The sun had set by the time he pulled into the station, the surviving light casting oddly the manicured grass in a fluorescent glow: lucid and beautiful and easy on tired eyes. Tom's Buick sat in the lot, which meant he hadn't returned from the Fredrick's place yet. Beside it, a plain gray sedan idled, thin whiffs of exhaust putting out the backside. Bud parked the cruiser and stepped out, and when he did, a man got out of the sedan and approached.

"Hello, Sheriff," he said. He had a scar on his face, and his eyes were like pellets of coal.

Bud held up his finger, and the man stopped walking. Bud turned his back and looked down at the insect still bonded to the cruiser. He pinched his thumb and forefinger around one of its legs and lifted it into his other cupped hand. He took a few steps toward the grass and swept his hands upward, as if releasing an unseen dove. The insect flew forth and dipped toward the ground. It nosed earthward for a moment, and then its wings puttered to life. It ascended into the growing purple shadows in an arc that sent it over Bud's head and back toward the cruiser in a great circular loop. It hovered over the vehicle for a few seconds, and then on the windshield wiper it landed, drawn by misguided love or loyalty or perhaps by nothing at all.

The man viewed all of this as a witness to something incomprehensible and autistic. His smile had disintegrated, but after he cleared his throat, it returned.

"Hello, Sheriff. I think you and I should talk."

Bud stared at the bug for a moment, and then he looked at the man with an expression of surprise, as if he'd just noticed his presence. He rubbed his chin and spat.

"Well, if you say we do, then I guess I won't argue with you."

He reached his hand toward the windshield wiper and picked the insect, its miniature body writhing between the warm fleshy tongs. He studied it for a moment and then smashed it between his fingers, its exoskeleton crunching aloud like the hollow shell of a seed.

He flicked the organic fragments to the ground and went inside the station, the door splayed open behind him. The man looked at the cruiser, an expression of dumbfounded bemusement upon his face. He looked at the sedan and then at the sky, and then he turned and followed the sheriff into the station.

CHAPTER 11

They'd driven all day, the other vehicles falling behind their progress, the nameless people within dismayed by their speed. Seth sucked coffee from a soda cup, his mind failing, his body fueled poorly by the thin drunken sleep from the night before. The taillights before him appeared as star bursts in the closing darkness, and the boy's body seemed taut with worry. Seth rubbed his eyes and set the coffee in his lap.

"We're gonna stop at a hotel, fore I drive this thing into a ditch."

The boy rubbed his ear.

"Are we gonna get somethin to eat, first?"

Seth wheeled the pickup toward an exit ramp.

"We can stop at that drugstore yonder, and you can get what you want."

They entered the lot and parked a good distance from the entrance. Seth handed the child a fifty-dollar bill and told him to get all he wanted. The boy took the bill in his hand and eyed it with no ordinary wonder, his eyes blazing, as if they studied an object plummeted from outer space. His face turned cautious as he looked at his father.

"It's alright. Take it and do as I say."

The boy opened the door and hopped out of the pickup. Seth watched him cross the cement lot, his little sneakers tapping the smooth pavement as he went. An old man with a curved wooden cane exited the store, and when he saw the boy coming, he stepped aside and held the door. The boy sailed through, and the old man lingered in the wake, as if some of the trailing youth might somehow soak into his withered frame. He smiled faintly as he watched the boy rumble about the store, and then he walked away with his head down, his body wholly reliant on the cane.

Seth rubbed his eyes and bowed his head. They'd eaten up some decent ground, and with every passing mile, he felt an advancing relief, whether based on something reasonable or fraudulent, he tried not to care.

He had a map, but it stayed pressed neatly in the glove box at yield to his recollections, which had proved correct enough thus far the journey. He teetered upon his seat, willing himself back from brief suspensions of consciousness, his face dark with growing hair, his stomach sick from too much coffee.

When the boy came back, he had a soda and a bag of licorice and nearly forty-seven dollars in change. Seth ordered him back into the store and he returned with a large paper bag, his face lit like a contest winner.

They pulled out of the cement lot and drove back toward the highway. Seth had seen a hotel on the way into town and they backtracked toward it, the boy eating sparingly, and then after a while, not at all.

"What's wrong with you?"

The boy stared down into his bag of synthesized sugar.

"Are we ever going back?"

Seth turned into the hotel parking lot and parked across from the front lobby. He killed the engine and looked at the boy.

"Do you want to go back?"

The boy shrugged his shoulders without looking up.

"Well, then the answer's, no. I suppose we ain't."

The boy didn't say anything.

"That alright with you?"

The boy nodded.

The child followed him into the hotel and waited in the front lobby. He found a shiny leather chair big enough for three, and he sat upon it, his eyes gazing into the mute television, his feet dangling inches above the bad carpet. Seth approached the front counter and popped the dull tin desk bell. A young man with jaw pimples appeared from a door behind the counter and asked how he could help. Seth asked for one night near the pool, and the desk clerk advised that the pool had closed at eight. Seth looked over his shoulder toward the boy.

"We'll have one next to the pool anyways."

He paid the clerk in cash and asked for the key card.

"We need a credit card to insure against damages."

Seth slid four hundred dollars across the desk and flashed his badge. The clerk took the money and nodded, saying nothing when he saw that the signature on the paperwork conflicted with the one printed on the badge id.

They left the office for the pickup, and Seth drove it around to the backside of the hotel. They unloaded their suitcases, and Seth put his pistol in his pants and slung the green army backpack over his shoulder, his face like that of a weary traveler put upon a senseless quest.

They used the key card to enter the building and walked a hallway lit by florescent light. One of the bulbs threatened to die, and it flickered forth in random bursts that set the hall in strobe lighting. The hotel room doors flashed a freshly painted red, and they counted numbers until they came to room 112. Seth used the key card to open it, and they took their things inside and shut the door.

Twin beds sat parallel atop the floor, a single veneer nightstand bolted between them. Upon it stood a single lamp and an alarm clock you'd only trust if you were made to. The room smelled of harsh disinfectant and the bedspreads looked cheap and itchy. Seth slung his baggage onto the nappy floor and sat on the bed. The boy set his things next to his bed and awakened the air conditioner unit just below the window. Then he headed for the door.

"Hold up," Seth said. "Where you goin?"

"To get some chips from the vending machine."

"You ain't got no chips in that bag a shit from the store?"

The boy shook his head.

"Fifty damned dollars' worth a sugar, and you ain't think to buy no salt?"

"I got some peanuts," the boy said.

"You bought peanuts?"

"Chocolate covered peanuts."

Seth shook his head and yawned.

"Alright, but hold up, and I'll go with ya."

He stood and went into the bathroom to look for an ice bucket, and when he didn't find one, he took the empty plastic trash can and rinsed it in the bathtub. When they reached the machine, the boy studied the selections with care, as if he feared some of the bags empty. Seth filled the trash can from the ice machine, and then he leaned against the wall and waited for the boy to decide. The child's index finger floated toward the glowing digits on the machine, hesitating an inch from impact. He looked back at his yawning father nearly bent over from fatigue.

"Godammit," Seth said as he reached into his pocket. "Here."

The boy looked at his father's hand and then his face.

"Take it, goddamit."

He took the ten and held it.

"Get all you want, and put an end to this shit, so we can get back to the room."

The bill felt crisp, and when the boy slipped it into the machine's horizontal slit mouth, it went in like it belonged. The child punched in a letter and a number, and a metal coil came to life and rotated until a bag of corn chips pushed forward and plummeted downward into the metal reservoir. The boy tabbed numbers until he had a dozen bags total, and then, on the final selection, the bag stuck. Seth nudged the boy aside and pressed one of his large hands against the top of the vending machine. He pushed it back so its front legs levitated off the busy carpet floor. The machine came down hard on the ground, but the bag held; and after several more attempts, he gave up, and they left the bag there: teasing and teetering on the very brink.

They went back to the room, and the boy spilled his loot across his bed. Seth opened his suitcase and removed a pint of scotch. He went into the bathroom and took one of the two plastic cups he'd seen earlier. He gathered four cubes of ice with his fingers and dropped them inside, and then he filled the dainty container with liquor. He set the cup on the nightstand and pulled off each of his boots. Then he lay back on the bed and wiggled his toes to let the coolness filter through. The scotch had grown warm inside the suitcase, and it ate through the ice until a clear level of water gathered atop the surface. Seth lifted the cup and drank it empty in three swallows. He set it back on the nightstand and lay against the bed, while the alcohol ran a soothing course through his veins.

The boy had the television going, and he flipped through channels trying to decode the foreign number associations between the stations there and the ones back home. After a while, he gave up and went back to his feast. Seth watched the boy shuffle through the packages of candy, the faint joy on his little face bringing forth a great sucking grief, as if he watched a desperate animal scavenge the sparse resources of a barren world.

He got up from the bed and refilled his cup. He stood before a broad mirror hung above the veneer dresser and drank with a poor, older representation of a man he once knew. He watched it watch him, and he hated what he saw, and then he shook his feelings away and looked toward the boy.

"You got yer bathing suit?"

The boy looked up, his cheeks engorged.

"The man at the desk said it was closed."

"I asked if you had yer suit."

The boy nodded.

"Well, get it on."

The pool had a skin of leaves, and the water looked a murky green. Seth eyed it with distrust, as the boy scanned him for signs of retreat. He approached one of the tables and sat down. The boy watched as he spun the lid off the bottle of scotch.

"You waitin on an invitation?" He said as he filled his cup.

The boy neared the choppy steps descending into the unkempt bath. He tip-toed into the cool water; goose flesh spreading over his skin like a visible infection.

"At ain't the way you do it," Seth said. "You gotta go all at once."

The boy looked at him and pressed forward a bit, and then he sat down on the last stair step and splashed water onto his shoulders. He looked over at his father and saw his foot tapping the ground. He pinched his nose with his fingers and plunged forward, the pool sludge enveloping him like a hungry bog. His head popped up over the surface and his arms flapped frantically. And then he settled and swam as best he knew, his father watching him and the uncertain space around them, his fingers tracing the butt of the revolver jutting visibly from his belt.

When it was over, the boy stank like a sewer, and once they were within the room, Seth sent him to the shower. When he got out, his father was asleep on the bed, his hat tipped over his eyes. The light from the muted television was all there was, and the boy tilted his suitcase toward it in search of a shirt and a pair of shorts.

Several coins lay scattered across the dresser, and once dressed, the boy scooped them into his hands without making any noise. He collected the other key card and crept across the room on the balls of his bare feet. He opened the door and slipped out, the catching latch snapping softly as he rounded the corner through the flickering hall toward the little room that housed the vending machines.

The bag of chips still dangled from the chrome coil as if it waited for only him, and he punched in the letter and the number that were its name, and a clone came forth and pushed it over the edge. He collected each from the reservoir, his small face bright and proud. He added a soda to his bounty and entered the hallway with everything bunched tightly against his chest.

He'd nearly made it around the corner when he heard the tapping against the glass door at the end of the hall. He turned and looked down the long flickering corridor. A man stood outside within the luminescence of exterior lighting, his hands cupped around his eyes to see within the darker interior. He wore black denim, and when he realized the boy had seen him, he rapped sharply his bare knuckles against the glass.

The boy looked around the corner down the other hall toward his room, and then he looked back at the stranger. The man called to him, his voice made muffled and incoherent by the thick clear pane. The boy looked at the room again, and then he turned and made a few steps toward the dark figure. The man called out, and the boy leaned forward as if to better hear. The man motioned him closer with his fingers, and the boy took several more steps until he was within twenty yards of the door.

"Hey, little man," the figure said. "I left my room key inside. Can you help me out?"

The boy held the chips and soda against his chest. He looked behind him, but no one came. He turned back toward the man.

"Yer stayin here at the hotel?"

The man bent his head and spat on the ground.

"Yeah, man. I need some help."

The boy turned again, and when he looked back the man's face took worry.

"C'mon, kid. You can't leave me out here all night. Where am I supposed to sleep?"

The boy studied the figure behind the glass, his eyes asquint, as if he contemplated a suspicious creature within an aquarium.

"I'm sorry, mister. But I don't know for sure that yer stayin here."

The man smiled without opening his mouth.

"Good boy. That's the way to be. I have a son, and I tell him that he should be careful with strangers. But then I also tell him that fear makes strangers of people who would be friends."

The boy looked back over his shoulder, and then he turned and sunk his chin into the two bags of chips.

"Just let me in. Otherwise, you will be hurting a good, honest person. You don't have to come outside, just push the handle there, and then you can go back to your room, and I can go to my room, and everyone will be happy."

The boy stood for a moment longer, and then he walked to the door and put his palm against the handle and pushed it until he heard the latch release. The man wrapped his hand around the exterior handle and yanked the door open in a sudden motion, the cool conditioned air sucking past the boy's hair outward into the humidity. The child staggered backward, and a bag of chips dropped to his feet. The man watched him with an amused little grin, his face changed in a way the boy hadn't known possible.

"Good boy. You can go back to your room now."

The boy turned and hurried toward the bend in the hall.

"Momento," said the man behind him. "You forgot your food."

The boy looked at the bag, and there his eyes stayed.

"You can have it," he said, and he held its twin in the air. "I've got this one."

The man cocked his head sideways and squinted.

"Gracias, niño," he said. "Now, you go."

The boy stood, his little body paralyzed by the seeping brown stare.

"Vamanos," the man said, and he made a forward movement that sent the child scurrying down the hall and around the corner.

When Seth awoke, it was still very dark, and the boy lay sleeping, entirely hidden within a pile of covers in the other bed. He rose to the edge of his mattress and rubbed his eyes with the heels of his hands. He found his boots and put them on, and then he went into the bathroom and sucked from the faucet until his belly was full.

He went back into the room, his head a racket of ringing pain. He put his hat on and ran his fingers across the brim. He collected the bottle of scotch and looked at the sleeping boy bundled fetal within the cheap hotel quilt. He walked past his bed and turned off the air conditioner: old and dusty and humming warnings of its forthcoming end. The boy stretched and mumbled as the white noise went, and in the quiet disturbance, he crossed into a shallow, twitching sleep. Seth moved across the room with a grace unsuited to a man his size, and when he got to the door, he opened and closed it like the hinges were freshly oiled.

Outside, his hangover screamed under the blinking light, and the busy carpeting stirred a nausea that nearly coaxed everything forth. He steadied himself against the door jam and spat a sour taste onto the floor as deliberately as someone who'd inhaled a fog of gnats. He wiped his mouth with his shirt sleeve and walked the hall toward the pool.

When he opened the door, everything looked much as before except the fresh moon now soaked the area with a pale haze of soft light. He walked over and sat down in the same chair he'd chosen hours earlier. He worked the plastic lid off his scotch and held the breathing bottle, his face fixed as someone set to perform a great feat. He slung his head back and siphoned a pair of thin sips through his puckered lips. Then he lowered the bottle and pushed back his impulse to heave. After a few seconds, his headache softened and his body relaxed.

He leaned back in the flimsy plastic chair and crossed his extended legs. The air was thick and soaked with the smell of pool filth, and he noticed it now as he hadn't before. He leaned back and admired the stars, pale and spread thin in conflict with the city light. He tipped his hat over his eyes and entered a seamless doze: scant in duration but rich with dream. He dwelled in this state for several minutes before the pitchy squeal of the door jolted him loose. He rose in his chair and swung around to see a short Mexican man dressed in black denim.

The man paused for a moment and looked back over his shoulder. Then he proceeded forward and sat down at a table across from Seth. He took out a thin, sweet cigar, and lit it under the bill of his baseball cap. Seth watched him for a moment without demonstrating interest, and then he turned his head away.

The man sucked the cigar and leaned back with relief. He watched the large white man with lazy eyes.

"Hey, man," he said.

Seth swiveled his head toward the man and raised his eyebrows.

"You here alone?" The man asked.

Seth looked away without speaking.

"Ah, I get it. You don't want to talk, is that it?"

Seth bent forward and spat.

"You seem like you can probably do enough talkin for the both of us."

The man laughed.

"That's funny."

They sat in silence for a while, the man seeding the sour air with a perfume of sweet smoke, Seth sitting as if he was alone. The man finished the entire cigar and flicked it into the pool, where it danced across a bridge of soggy leaves and sunk into the living muck. He removed a compressed bag of chips from his deep denim pockets and pulled it open. He stuck his hand inside and scooped a handful of crumbled fragments. He stopped short of his mouth and pushed his hand forward.

"Quieres?" He said with a curved smile.

Seth looked at him and down to the slick, greasy hand. He raised his head and smirked.

"At's alright. I'm good."

The man shrugged.

"Suit yourself."

He ate the bag empty and then sucked at his fingertips in a way that seemed almost sexual. He dusted his wet fingers against his black denim clothing.

"Hey, man," he said. "You got any money."

Seth's jaw undulated. He looked at the man, and the man looked back from beneath the bill of his cap; eyes brazen and reckless.

"Yeah, I got money," Seth said. "But not for you." He turned his chair and stood up, an imposing shadow stretching from his muscled form. "Now, you've bout run through all the patience I got for yer type, and I think it's best you be gettin on."

The man sucked his fingers, his eyes affixed to the danger before him. Finally, he raised his hands and looked down.

"Ok, take it easy, I no want trouble," he said in an exaggerated accent.

He stood up from his chair before the figure nearly twice his size. He nodded graciously and turned toward the door, and as he walked, Seth watched him, his body taught with adrenaline and power and rage.

The man reached for the door handle and pulled it open, but he did not pass through. Instead, he stopped and turned toward the white man.

"Is that your little boy I saw earlier?"

Seth lowered his head, his eyes feral from beneath the brim of his hat, his body seething and athirst for conflict.

"He's a good looking little boy. How much would it take to get an hour alone with him?"

The man smiled, and turned toward the door, but before he could move through the passage, Seth was upon him.

The short Mexican proved formidable, and Seth had to work to get him to the ground. But once he did, the man had no answer for the sea of fists that befell him; and in no time at all, the thick purple flesh surrounding his mouth pulverized into a mealy, processed smear.

The man cried out something specific, and when he did, a presence filled the space behind the two of them, and Seth felt an arm loop under his jaw and swell against the bones in his throat. He tightened his neck on instinct and pulled opposite the squeezing vice, but the arm seemed anchored in stone, and though he worked against it using all his strength and his vast experience of such things, its control was certain.

Seth's face flushed a blotchy rose, and flecks of white glitter swept across the plane of his vision. He kicked his legs back and felt his heel tap against a toe. He raised his own boot high and brought it down on a very large foot. The arm's owner moaned, and he yanked Seth backward and up into the air. Seth's legs split apart, and his booted feet skidded against the walls of the hallway. He let his legs go high into the air until his toes tapped the ceiling, and then he hunched forward and brought himself back to the ground with all his weight, the two standing flat footed in that hall, secure in a muscled impasse. The man pulled hard from behind, but Seth's strength balanced them together in an unproductive strain, and that's how they remained for several seconds: like pulsing waxed figures posed in a museum of oddities.

Seth's face grew purple, and he knew he owned only moments of consciousness. In a panic, he let go of the massive, flexing arm and let the thing constrict absolute.

The flitters of white light coagulated into full on blindness, and he knew he would be gone in a few more seconds; so he turned his body and slipped his left leg behind the other man's right leg. Then he swung his left arm against the man's immense chest and used the leverage from his positional advantage to trip the confused giant backward. His practiced technique sent the big man tumbling, and he released Seth's neck and sunk into the wallpapered drywall, rendering a concave flaw the size of a large child.

Seth stumbled several feet back and straightened, the corridor around him softly blinking behind his silhouetted body, sweaty and heaving, electric and eager. Ready.

The big man worked to his feet with impressive speed, and when he rose, his head nearly scraped the ceiling. Seth watched him engorge into his true size, an immense mass of bones and meat, two beads of thoughtless eyes staring out from within a bulbous, inhuman skull.

Seth staggered back, a genuine doubt rooting in his mind. The freakish man sensed this, but it brought him neither pride nor satisfaction, his mind operating only in a consequenceless domain of deliberate execution. He moved forward like a falling building, and Seth reached into his belt and removed his pistol. He leveled the gun at the approaching and pulled the trigger; but the bullet did not slow the man nay a simple flinch; and when the monstrosity laid his hands upon Seth's frame, the finality was as sudden as it was absolute.

The short man had ascended to his knees and was snorting and spitting above an apple red pool of blood and drool. He spat and looked at his partner and then down to the sprawled man upon the floor: motionless by death, jagged bones protruding from within his neck skin like sticks within a plastic bag.

The short man rose to his feet and spat a tooth into the puddle. He kicked Seth over and withdrew the keycard from his pants pocket.

"Vámonos," he said, and the behemoth followed him down the hall, the white man's body there in the hallway behind them: as much a stranger to them as he had been to himself.

CHAPTER 12

Social services arrived much sooner than Tom expected, and that was a welcome relief. The boy had refused to speak no matter what he'd tried. In the end, he wasn't like a boy at all, but more a feral animal: slinking and reticent, taking kindness for allurement. Whatever had happened to him in that house had taken its unholy toll, and whatever he had been before it had started, or whatever he might have been if it hadn't, wasn't worth talking about anymore.

When they dropped him off at the station, it was late, and no cars populated the lot save his. He stood outside the driver's door and made small talk with the social worker, but she was as tired as he, and they each showed mercy enough to act according to the truth, which was that they would almost certainly never see each other again.

He took one last look at the boy before they drove off to wherever it was they were going. Huddled in blankets, pressed against the door, he didn't look like he wanted to be touched; and the man that sat beside him didn't look like he had much interest in touching him. And that was how they left: tired and missing their own homes, couriers of the abused and forgotten. As he watched them drive away, he thought about his baby that never was, now a distant wish; and he considered that a large sect of life's cruelty lay in the rewarding of those undeserving. And then his mind changed the subject, and he hurried across the parking lot to his car.

He called Elli and gave her a brief account of his day. He made her promise that the doors were all locked, and he reminded her of the pistol in the nightstand, how to cock it and release the safety. She humored him with an earnest voice, and then they said goodbye, and he headed that way.

He made a second call, this time to Levi, and when the old man answered the phone, Tom knew something was off.

"I gotta tell you somethin," Levi said.

"Okay."

"It's gotta be face to face."

"Can't it wait until tomorrow?"

"It won't take long. Just swing by the house. I'll have ya in and out."

Tom rubbed his eyes and thought for a moment.

"Alright. I'll be there shortly."

The road before him grew into a barren concrete snake, and a wavering mist in the air forced him to start and stop the windshield wipers. The moisture loosened the settled car exhaust of the earlier day, and the road grew slick and dubious. He kept his speed as low as he could tolerate, and by the time he made it to Levi's home, the night had established itself completely.

He parked along the curb out front and stepped into the warm summer air. He left the door unlocked and trotted the brick pavered walk and up onto the four wooden steps that ascended the deck porch. He tried the plastic handle on the screen door, but it was locked; so he wrapped his knuckles against the aluminum frame hard enough to force a racket the old man could hear. When Levi opened the door, Tom could tell he'd been drinking.

"Are you just sitting here alone?"

Levi scratched the back of his neck.

"The tv's on."

His feet stood bare, some of the toenail beds yellow, those that weren't, a dead black.

"Gimme a second," he said, and he went back inside and turned off the television.

Tom sat in one of the steel chairs on the porch and looked around. Ceramic flowerpots clogged the large deck, trowels, pruners and cultivators propped against them. Each container sat barren, devoid of flowers, and the season had grown far too late to think that any would be coming.

Levi returned dressed in boots and an old Stetson hat. He sat in the other steel chair across from Tom, his body and mouth whining with strain. A small wooden folding table stood between them. It held a clear glass ashtray and a half-empty pack of cigarettes, a sheet of matches stowed inside the cellophane wrapper. The old man lifted the pack and thumbed out a hard, stale-looking cigarette. He lit it and sucked until it had a life of its own, and then he set it in the ashtray. He put his hands together in his lap and leaned forward.

"So what's happened?"

Tom rocked back in his chair so the front legs lifted.

"That's what I'd like to know from you."

Levi nodded and rubbed his hand over his mouth. He raised the cigarette and sampled a taste. Then he fit it back into its nook on the glass tray with a delicate placing, as if it was the last of its kind.

"Well, I met that fella't met Edgar."

Tom lowered his chair and leaned forward.

"When?"

"This mornin."

"Where?"

"Right here."

Tom shifted in his seat.

"Here?"

"You darn right. Pulled right up here in my drive and knocked on my door, like he come to preach the word of God. Sat right there where yer setting."

Tom shook his head.

"What did he say?"

Levi rubbed his hands together and rocked back and forth like he'd had too much coffee, or too many cigarettes, or both.

"Said what you'd expect, I reckon. That he aimed to kill me less I give him the money. At least in so many words, he said that."

He took the cigarette up and smoked it, and this time he didn't put it back.

"What did you say?"

"I told him he could have it, and I got up to get it. Only he stopped me and said he didn't want it right now. Said he'd tell me when and where to bring it to him."

He took another puff and coughed.

"Well, I told him that weren't alright, and I did get up, and I went and got it from behind my water heater, and I brought it back out here and set it in front of him and told him he could have it now, or he could wait forever."

Tom waited for more, but Levi said nothing.

"What did he do?"

"He took it. Picked it up and nodded to me. Then he turned around and walked off. Didn't say nuthin. Just walked off and got into his car with some fella had a bandage on his nose."

Tom leaned back and stared at the ceiling, where a rusted aluminum light bathed the porch through the tangles of insects butting blindly in the glowing air beneath it.

"Let me tell ya," Levi said. "That fella's a cold one. If you was to say that I'd been settin across from devil himself, it wouldn'ta surprised me."

Tom looked at Levi's driveway and wiped his mouth with his palm. He looked back at the old man like he'd had a thought.

"Did he say what his name was?"

Levi nodded.

"He said his name was Soto."

"Soto? He said that?"

"I asked him, and he seemed happy to tell me. Like it was nothin at all."

They sat for a while without speaking. Tom rocked back in his chair, his face painted with thought. Levy smoked his cigarette and watched him patiently, as if he waited for the dust to settle inside the young man's brain.

"There's somethin else, too," he said. "I got a call from Madelyn today, askin where Edgar was. Said they took out yesterday mornin, and he was sposed to catch up."

He smoked the last of his cigarette and snubbed it out in the ashtray.

"Only he didn't."

Tom didn't say anything.

"I told her that I hadn't heard nuthin from him, and that she oughtta call Bud, and she said she would, but I don't know what he's got to tell her."

Tom shook his head and his eyes made a slow arc from one side of his face to the other. He spat over the porch rail into a dying shrub. Levi leaned forward and rested his chin on his fist, his elbow propped against his knee as if he posed for a sculptor.

"You got somethin on yer mind?" He asked.

Tom leaned forward and clasped his hands.

"Let me ask you a question."

Levi pushed out his lower lip and nodded once.

"You go right ahead."

"What's Bud said to you about all this."

"What do you mean?"

"I mean, has he given you any advice on what to do?"

"I ain't had much chance to talk to him. Sure as hell ain't fixin to pick up the telephone and discuss what we done."

Tom shook his head and looked off into the darkness that curled around the dimly lit porch. Levi leaned back and slapped his palms on his knees.

"Anyway, what's he supposed to say? He's in the same spot we're in."

Tom looked at Levi and let his eyebrows drop.

"What's he supposed to say?"

Levi nodded.

"Yessir."

"He's supposed to say something." He crossed his arms. "For God's sake, Levi. Say something. Say anything. Christ, he wants to act like everything's hunky dory, while there's guys slicing up his deputies' families and then making them disappear." He looked at the old man. "He ought to say something, shouldn't he?"

Levi pursed his lips and shook his head.

"Son, you made a choice you got to live with. Same as the rest of us. Same as Bud. Ain't nobody can help ya now but yerself."

Tom tucked his chin into his chest and nodded.

"Well, I'll tell you what I think if you'll hear it."

Levi nodded.

"Let me have it."

"I don't trust Bud. There's no more to it than that. I don't have specific reasons. But something doesn't make sense about all of this. There's just something that doesn't make sense."

Levi rubbed his chin and crossed his legs.

"You're worryin that Bud might be behind all this. Is that right?"

Tom shook his head.

"I wouldn't say worried. It did cross my mind, though. I guess it did yours, too."

Levi spat on the deck and smeared it into the dust with the toe of his boot.

"I guess it did, but it left about as soon as it came."

He looked at Tom.

"Are you thinkin he's connected with this Soto fella? Like Bud might be pullin the strings on this to gather up all our shares? Is that what you think?"

"I don't know what to think," Tom said. "All I know is that Edgar and Seth are gone, and no one seems to know where they went, and he doesn't seem to want to talk about it, or do much of anything except walk around like nothing's happening."

He looked at Levi with his palms turned up and shrugged his shoulders as an invitation for a contrasting assessment. Levi shook his head and looked at his boots.

"You don't know Bud like I know him."

"And how's that?"

Levi looked at Tom and then back down to the deck.

"I've known him for fifteen years. He got me this job when ain't nobody woulda hired me on account of my age. Me and my wife, God rest her soul, we was struggling. We was in some real bad trouble."

He leaned back in his chair and straightened one leg out, his weathered face easing a bit.

"This was a long time ago mind you, but I was still an old man."

He looked at Tom.

"You'll come to find that a large percentage of yer life's spent bein old."

He dusted his lap.

"Anyways, Bud hadn't been here very long at the time, and I'd only talked to him once or twice in passing. He'd only been the sheriff here for a few months, and I think everone was still tryin to feel him out. He kind of had a reputation for bein hard on some people when he was a lawman up in Tyler, but I ain't never talked to nobody who seen evidence of it here. At least not in that first year."

He pushed his lower lip out and scratched his whiskered neck, as if struggling to remember his thoughts.

"Anyways, I talked to him only a couple times. Told him a little about my situation. How I'd had to give up the farm on account of the drought and the bank loans, and he listened, and then I didn't think nothin of it after that. And then one day, he just come up to the house, and told me that he wanted me to work for him. I asked him what use I'd be, but he just said to let him worry about that, and that was it. Told me to show up to the sheriff's station the next day, and he wouldn't hear no arguin about it. I just shook his hand and thanked him, and he said there weren't no thanks required. Said he needed somebody who knew the people and the area better'n him."

He looked at Tom and lifted his bushy gray eyebrows.

"I tell you what. He didn't know it, but he saved our lives. Or, maybe he did know it. I don't know. Whatever the case, I ain't ashamed to tell you that me and my wife hugged and cried the moment he left. We was that close to endin up on the streets or somethin worse."

He looked at Tom's boots, his eyes squinted, his mind trying to remember. He shook his head and wiped his right eye.

"Anyways, the next day, I went to the station like a nervous child on the first day of school. He put me to work, showed me how to go about things. Was real patient. I used to tell him that the only reason he hired me was so he wouldn't look so old standing next to his deputies, but he'd hear nothin of it. He always made me feel like I was a big help. And he always has."

He looked directly into Tom's eyes.

"I realize that I don't know Bud all the way through. He's got different versions of himself, same as anyone else. But I can tell you that he ain't the type to turn his back on a friend. And I'd be offended if you couldn't take my word on that."

Tom looked off into the dark sky above his Buick. The other houses on the block looked cold and sleepy, the people inside having already committed to the following day.

"I don't know what to think about him. I wasn't ever sure I liked him. Something about him has always made me uneasy. I don't think it's just me, either. I know Edgar doesn't like him."

Levi spat on the porch.

"Hell, Edgar don't like nobody."

Tom leaned forward and rubbed his eyes.

"No, it's something else. There's something about him. Something that's no good. I don't know what I was thinking trusting in him in the first place."

"Yeah you do."

Tom looked at Levi.

"You was tryin to make things better for you and yer wife. To make up for all you been through and all yer dealin with. And there ain't nuthin wrong with it. Nuthin at all."

Tom looked down.

Levi reached over and collected the pack of cigarettes. He took one and slipped it between his lips. Then he raised his eyebrows and offered the pack to Tom.

"No thanks."

Levi smiled and nodded.

"Just thought I'd see."

He lowered his head and set fire to the cigarette, smoke lifting from under the lowered brim of his hat, like ghosts racing toward the sky. Tom leaned forward and tilted his head sideways to see the withered face below.

"So why'd you do it, Levi?"

Levi raised his head and Tom could see directly into his eyes. Crystal blue within a shroud of wrinkled flesh, they could have been the eyes of a twenty-year-old, except they flashed a wisdom: unmistakable yet overlooked, invisible yet visible withal.

The old man pursed his lips and thought.

"I don't know."

Tom looked down and shook his head.

"You told me something like this might happen."

Levi leaned back in his chair and gave a soft smile.

"Desire precedes stupidity," he leaned forward again and opened his right hand toward Tom in presentation. "Desperation, too."

They sat for a while listening to the insects thumping against the aluminum like kamikaze entities, spellbound by a something only they understood. After a while, Tom spoke.

"Do you think Seth and Edgar ran off?"

Levi shook his head.

"Seth, maybe. I mean, that makes some sense. But Edgar? It seems awful odd for him to send his family on and then cut out like that, don't it?"

Tom rocked his chair onto its rear legs, again.

"The Edgar I know? I wouldn't put it past him."

Levi nodded and looked out into the night.

"Yeah, but it's just as likely he give them fellas a reason to shoot him by sayin somethin stupid."

"Maybe they didn't need a reason," Tom said.

Levi sucked his false teeth.

"You insuatin them fellas might come back to put me to rest?"

Tom didn't say anything.

Levi looked down at the ground and smiled.

"Well, they can have at it, cause I done had my fill."

Levi bent down, stubbed out his cigarette on the porch, and stood up.

"I'm gettin a drink."

He went inside the house and returned holding a bottle of whiskey and two glasses. He handed one to Tom without asking and filled it half-way.

Tom drank, a satisfying warmth rushing over his body. Levi filled his glass to its limit but sipped from it as if the fluid might burn his lips. He set the glass next to his cigarettes and collected the pack.

"Maybe you oughtta know something else about Bud."

Tom looked at him.

"It's supposed to change the way I feel, I suppose."

Levi shook his head.

"Nope, just somethin. That's all."

He worked a cigarette from the pack and lit it. He puffed on it while he stared at the ground, his eyes darting gently, as if his mind played out the webbed repercussions of what he might say.

"First off," he said. "I wouldn't tell you this if I had ever been told not to tell no one. And that's a fact. It's been said that those at gossip to you will gossip about you, and I believe that's true, but this here ain't gossip. Though, I admit that I didn't come into it firsthand."

He puffed his cigarette and looked up, his eyes squinting as he picked the details from his fading memory.

"I come to hear about this through my wife, God rest her soul. She come to hear about it through Bud's wife, or ex-wife now, I reckon."

Tom looked at him, and Levi gave a flat smile.

"You didn't know Bud had a wife before now?"

Tom shook his head.

"Well, that don't surprise me none, cause Bud don't talk much about hisself, and ain't many people like to talk about Bud on account of they fear the man."

He puffed his cigarette.

"And, you can count me in that group, but I'll tell you this just the same, cause I think it might help you understand the man yer dealin with."

He tipped his hat back and scratched his head.

"Well, like I said, I come to hear this through my wife, and she come to hear it through Bud's. They moved down here bout fifteen years ago from Tyler where he'd been workin before. They moved into that very same house he's living in now. When Bud came to town, he brought a reputation for bustin people up, sometimes for good reasons, sometimes fer reasons at weren't so good. He had a helluva temper on him in those days is what I hear. Though, I ain't seen but a flash of it here and there since he come. Age tends to put the hose on that sorta thing is what you'll find."

He spat and nodded to no one in particular if only to agree with himself.

"Anyways, I think somethin happened up in Tyler at put him over the edge, and he did somethin at was real bad, and there weren't no way he could stay there no more. But he had some pretty important friends at liked him a lot, and I think they fixed it soes he could come here. Anyways, that's the way I got it figured, but ain't nobody knows fer sure cause he don't say much about it, and ain't no one likes to talk too much about Bud."

He watched the swirls of white smoke rise from the cigarette and twist in the light, his eyes pinched, as if they read messages from within its evolving schematics. He shook his head clear.

"So as I was sayin, he come down here with a wife at first, but she done left town not more than two months after they got here, and that was that. Ain't nobody asked where she went, or if she was ok. Everbody just went right on like she ain't never been here in the first place, cause they figured at was the way Bud wanted it, and at was alright with everbody round here cause most of em believe in keepin only to the business at's yers."

He added to his shrinking glass of whiskey.

"But my wife, God bless her, she come to meet Bud's wife in one way or another. I only seen her once, and she was a pretty little thing. Kinda mousy lookin. Walked around real quiet, sorta sad little look on her face, but it didn't do nuthin to take away from how pretty she was. Anyways, she was a librarian over in Tyler, and that's what she came to do here, too. She started working at the old library in town, and at's where my wife met her. They got to talkin a little, mostly casual, polite stuff. Anyways, one day, she up and told my wife all these things. I don't know why and neither did my wife. I guess sometimes people just gotta say somethin to someone, and maybe my wife looked as suitable a person as any. I don't know."

He smoked and exhaled thoughtfully.

"Anyways, they went off into the corner of the library behind some of the less popular books, and the poor girl got to cryin and talkin about all the troubles they seen up in Tyler. Said she come to meet Bud when he was investigatin a case she was witness to. Said she didn't like him at first, and her mamma was all over her with warnings. Told her at the only thing a man like Bud could give her was a reputation. But she said he won her over eventually on account of his looks and charm, and what her mama said didn't hold up in the end. Anyways, they got married and had them a little girl, and I guess that put a change into ole Bud, or that's what she told my wife, anyways. She said he sorta calmed down and acted happier than what he had been."

He sipped his alcohol with the steady face of a trained drinker, and when he lowered the glass, it looked near empty.

"Well, everthing was fine fer a while is what she said. But then she told my wife that one night, they was leavin from a movie. One of them with the cartoon characters. She said they went to it cause the little girl was fixed on it, and she said that precious little thing giggled the whole way through. And when she told my wife at part, her voice dried up on her, and she stopped talkin altogether for a few minutes."

Levi bent forward and spat.

"Well, when she started talkin, again, she told my wife what had happened, and that was that they got in a car wreck with a fella'd been drinkin, and the little girl died on the spot, right there in the road. She said Bud held her in his arms, and she was all bloody and hacked up to the point to where it didn't even look like a little girl no more."

He stopped for a moment and lowered his head as if in prayer, and Tom waited in silence until he began again.

"She told my wife it was the only time she'd ever seen Bud cry, but that it wasn't a normal cry, but somethin at seemed to come out of a raging panic. Somethin crazed. Well, she musta been right, cause apparently, he set that poor girl down, and he got up and walked right past his wife who was in pretty bad shape herself, and he set to work on that fella't hit em, only there weren't no point to it, cause he was already dead. But she said that didn't stop ole Bud, and by the time the ambulance and police got there, he'd turned at fella's head into not much more'n goop, and she said he was still stompin on it when they pulled him off."

He made a sour face and spat, as if his mind had painted a better picture of the story than he wanted.

`Well, she said that they buried the girl out in the cemetery, and they gave the fella at the mortuary a little white dress to bury her in, cause it was her favorite, but they had to take his word that he done it, cause the casket was closed on account of what she looked like. Anyways, after that, she said that Bud just went to nuthin. Said he got to drinkin, and didn't talk much, and after a while, he just quit talkin altogether. And then she told my wife that after a couple months, she made herself go into the girl's bedroom and she sat in the middle of the floor and cried. Hugged the little girl's clothes and whatnot. But after that, she picked herself up and started to take the room apart."

He looked at the ground and shook his head slowly.

"Well, Bud come home and caught her doin it, and she said he just went crazy. Balled his fists up and nearly beat her. And then he started puttin everthing back the way it was and said that she wasn't ever to change a thing, or else he'd kill her dead, and she said that she believed him, and my wife said that she believed that she believed it, and that she had a look in her eye that made my wife believe it, too."

He raised the glass to his lips and drank. He lowered the glass and a hissing noise slipped from his lips, as the raw liquor scorched his throat.

"Well, they went on like this for two years is what she said. And then Bud did whatever he did that got him sent down here. Well, when the time came to move, there weren't no choice no more with the girl's room. And so he went into the room hisself and closed the door, and when he came out, she said he had everthing put away into cardboard boxes and the walls were white and bare, and she said it made her sad as can be, but it also made her feel a little bit better, too. She said when they moved, things were bad between the two of em, but she said she felt like maybe they'd get a fresh start down here, and that's why she agreed to come in the first place.

"Well, they was here not more than a couple weeks, when she said she went up to the library for work. She was gone for a few hours, and by the time she got back, Bud had put that little girl's room up in the spare bedroom of their new place, piece-for-piece like he'd used pictures as a guide. She said she just couldn't believe it. Said it was like seein a ghost or somethin, and when she told him she wouldn't stand for it, he just looked at her and walked away. Didn't say nuthin."

He took another cigarette and turned it over in his hands.

"Anyways, my wife listened and tried to comfort her, but it weren't a couple more weeks fore she packed up all her stuff and drove off for good. I don't know what the thing was that finally put her off, but I reckon it coulda been him not bein able to let go, or maybe she tried to take that room down, again, and he off and hit her. I don't know, and don't nobody else neither, cause he don't never talk about it, and ain't no one likes to talk too much about Bud."

He struck a match and cared for it with his cupped palm. He held it to the cigarette and then shook it out.

"I think that's a sad thing, you know. I mean, I cain't say I'd hold hard feelins against his wife. At ain't no way to live locked up in the past like that. But it sounds like to me, when that girl come, old Bud made a place for her in his heart. And just cause she's gone, don't mean that place ain't still there. I figure he's tryin to keep her alive somehow with that room."

They sat for a while without talking, the humming insects looping above in sweeping oblong orbits. Tom leaned back and watched them gather around the deceitful light, each beguiled by a compelling genetic obligation to worship the cold nutritionless radiance, each thoughtless and disposable to all but itself.

Levi added to his glass and tipped the bottle toward Tom who held his hand up, no. The old man gave a friendly smile, and he sat the whiskey on the table.

"How did Bud know that Mexican, Ortiz?"

Levi shrugged behind a cloud of freshly exhaled smoke.

"I think he met him in Tyler."

A haze of cigarette smoke clouded the porch, and Tom leaned forward and looked at the old man through the stinging scud.

"Do you mind if I ask you a question?"

"Go right ahead."

"You ever take a bribe, Levi?"

Levi leaned forward and looked at him from beneath his bushy gray eyebrows.

"You mean from the cartel runners?"

Tom nodded.

"No."

"Have Edgar and Seth?"

"Yes."

"What about Bud?"

Levy leaned back and shook his head.

"Son, you just don't understand how things work around here nowadays. They don't ask you to take a bribe. These fellas don't like to be told no. It ain't in their business model. If they's to ask you to take money to look the other way, then what they's really sayin is take the money or else."

He pointed at Tom with his cigarette.

"This area's a dangerous place for an honest lawman. Ain't no place for one atall, to be downright truthful with you. And you'll find that out if you allow yerself to stay around long enough."

Tom rubbed his chin and searched the deck with his eyes.

"Why haven't you gotten involved?"

Levi chuckled to himself.

"Well, I reckon they probably think I'd be a poor long-term investment on account of my age."

Tom gazed into the empty glass upon his lap, as if the truth of things lay not quite visible within.

"I've made such a mistake." He shook his head slowly. "I have no idea what I'm going to do."

Levi leaned forward and set his palm on Tom's shoulder.

"Yes you do. You're gonna do the right thing. You're gonna go home and tell yer wife what you done. Then you're gonna give this Soto fella what he wants, and then you're gonna move on. Get outta this line of work and outta this town, and you ain't never gonna come back, cause this ain't where you belong, son. I could tell that the first day I met you."

Tom ran his fingers through his hair.

"She won't forgive me. Wouldn't believe I'd ever do something like this."

"I don't think that's true," Levi said. "After everthing you kids have been through, she ain't the type to cut and run."

He patted Tom's shoulder twice and leaned back in his chair.

"But you gotta tell her cause that's the right thing to do. That's what a man does. Even when he's scared or don't want to, he does it cause he's a man."

Tom checked his watch and stood. He held his hat in both hands.

"I thank you for everything, Levi."

The old man stood and put his hand out.

"Everthing's gonna be ok, son. You just do like I said."

Tom shook his hand, and turned. He descended the porch steps and walked to his car. Levi walked the porch and set his old wrinkled hands on the railing. He raised one hand in the air as the car pulled away, and Tom rolled his window down to do the same.

The old man turned and went inside the house, and then the porch light went off, and the insects dispersed, and the hollow flower pots disappeared. Tom watched as Levi's silhouette vanished within the interior lighting, and then he drove away, and the two men never saw each other again.

CHAPTER 13

In the small living room, a large candle soaked one far corner of the plain white drywall with a honeyed glow, the shadows born from it lunging and retreating and undulating, like spirits confine; their prison a paltry one, lowly and unpretending.

Ellie sat processing, her legs crossed, a bare foot bobbing, her expression concealed within an impregnable silhouette. Tom sat across from her with his forearms on his thighs and his hat on the couch cushion beside him. He almost spoke, wanted to, but there wasn't anything more say, save for questions to answer.

Ellie's black shape ran its hand over its head.

"So what happens now, Tom?"

The voice she used sounded foreign to him.

"I'm still waiting for him to get in touch with me. When he does, I'll give him what he wants, and then it will be over. We can leave or we can stay. It will be whatever you say."

She said nothing for a while.

"I'm so sorry, Ellie."

"Don't," she said. "Why?" He watched her head shake slowly. "What good does it do now?"

He lowered his head.

She looked into the kitchen and saw that it was two in the morning.

"Christ," she said. "I have to be at work in a couple of hours."

His head sunk lower.

"I don't understand this, Tom. Not any of it. But of all things, you waited this entire time without telling me, and then you decide to jolt me from sleep and spring it on me just hours before I have to go to work? What in God's name were you thinking?"

He looked at her, his eyes wet.

"I don't know. I couldn't hold it in any longer. I was worried."

She shook her head, again, and looked away.

"Madelyn," she whispered. "You unbelievable bastards, all of you."

He didn't speak.

She ran her fingers over her lips as she thought.

"So what's to keep them from doing that to me, Tom? Are you going to follow me around all day?"

He shook his head.

"That was Edgar's fault, Ellie."

He leaned forward and put his hands together.

"That's not going to happen to you. I promise."

She looked away.

"Don't," she said. "Just don't."

He examined mutely the cheap brown carpet.

She rocked in her chair and studied him: as despicable as any man irresilient to the shallow temptations of this life, and yet, he also, a lovely creature, selfless as any she had ever known. And she knew the man she saw was the same who'd coaxed her back to life when but one will existed between the two of them, his eyes and his voice, a comforting fixation throughout the uprising within her body. And amidst the cold irrefutable logic, when they'd carved her breast from her being, he had not allowed her to recede into self-loathing, but instead, lifted her from the sour comfort of despair through unyielding and intimate dedication. And this had bound her to him, and if there existed occurrences potent enough to dissolve such a bond, she knew that this thing did not wear the markings.

Her foot stopped its manic waggle, and she spoke, her tone more delicate than before.

"I understand you, Tom. I understand what you were trying to do. But I didn't ask for this. I did not ask you to do this."

He looked at her, his eyes red and teared.

"You have to accept that this is our path in life, "she said as she raised her hands toward their surroundings. "You can't change things by wishing for miracles and taking risks."

He swallowed hard and shook his head.

"Why, Ellie? Why is this our path?" He looked away and chewed his teeth. "I don't think there is a path. I think it's just fucking chaos. You tell yourself that everything will be alright. But it won't. And if it is, it won't be because someone designed things that way. You think that there's some plan directing all of this? It's not fucking true. It's just the haves and the have-nots and not anything more. It's being born in the right place, under the right circumstances. It's the ones who get struck by lightning and the ones who don't. The ones who get fucking cancer and the ones that don't. There's nobody looking out for us, Ellie. There is no plan."

She raised her finger.

"Don't," she said. "I don't care what you believe. But I need to believe, and I have found a way to do that. And I won't let you destroy that for me."

She smoothed the wrinkles in the lap of her nightgown.

"I've been to the edge of this life, Tom. To the edge of sanity." She shook her head slowly, her tearless eyes stable and sharp. "I won't let you, or this thing, or anything else take me to that place, again."

She put her palms on her thighs, and he watched but said nothing.

"Now, I've heard what you have to say, and the only thing I can do now is tell you to go ahead with whatever you have to do. I want you to be careful. I truly do. But I don't want you to ever speak about this to me, again. Not until it's over."

She looked down and nodded as if agreeing retroactively with her own words.

"Now, I have to get ready for work. We can't afford to let this take over. We can't afford even one lost day."

Tom wiped his palms across his face, and then he collected his hat and put it on so the brim left a shadow over his eyes. Ellie stopped rocking and leaned forward.

"This thing, Tom. This thing that you're experiencing, that you think of as so partial and unjust. It's called survival. It's not supposed to be better than what it is. It's not supposed to be anything, because it isn't anything at all. It's a state."

She shook her head slowly, her eyes wide and direct.

"You can't look at the whole thing at once, or you won't be able to take it. You have to take every day, every moment as it comes. You have to siphon life. If you can't do it, then you have to strive to do it. And if you fail, you have to try again."

She leaned back in her chair and put her arms on the rests.

"These worries, this hopelessness. They're based on assumptions. That bad things are going to happen, because they have before. Tom, there are infinite possibilities ahead of us. You can't see it, because your view is obstructed based on where you stand right now."

He tapped his foot a few times, and then let it still.

"I don't know how to see things any other way then what they are."

She propped her elbow against the armrest of the chair and rubbed the back of her neck.

"I am sorry for you, Tom. I'm sorry you can't find a way to get past it all and move forward."

He pursed his lips and looked toward the ceiling.

"There is no forward, Ellie. Not like this. We are circling the drain. We can't afford to live as is, and those people, those collectors. They are not going away. They will put out whatever fire we've got left. It's their craft."

She leaned forward.

"You can't keep that money. Not any of it. We will have to find another way. On our own. There is always some other way."

He nodded and stood like some weary negotiator met by an intractable impasse.

"I am very sorry for this. I will do everything I can to make it go away. You have my word."

She rose to her feet, and they stood before each other awkwardly, as if their forking views might prove irreconcilable. But then she reached for him and righted everything with a touch of her hand.

He leaned forward, and she leaned into him, but he would not kiss her.

"Everything will be alright," he said. "But I need to take you to work, and you need to let me, because I just need to."

They arrived at the 24-hour diner at a quarter to four, and she sat beside him in the Buick, her uniform still clingy and warm from its time in the dryer. She touched his whiskered face with the back of her hand, and the tenderness of it made his stomach fall. Her touch and her scent weakened him in a way he did not like, so he collected her hand in his and looked into her eyes and told her he had to go.

She looked at him, her hair pulled back, stray bangs drifting over her drowsy, soulful eyes. She leaned in and kissed him, her lips, fleshy and pink. She took him in for a long while, and he, her, as if they engaged in something holy and potentially final. And if it wasn't that which moved them, then it was their bond through recovery and loss, and the fear of further loss, and of all the infertile unknown.

He held her a moment longer amidst that sacred space within that car upon that asphalt parking lot, sunbaked and expelling fumes even at that hour. And then he released her, and the door opened, and she was gone.

He drove to the station, but the building stood empty. He unlocked the front door and collected the keys to the police cruiser, and then he went back outside. He entered the vehicle and cranked it to life. He started toward Bud's house, his head congested with ill visions of what he might find.

When he arrived at the sheriff's house, he found the man in a lawn chair upon the front porch, his body awkward and angular, as if it'd been tossed there. Tom studied him from the yard. A .45 pistol sat in the sheriff's lap, choked within coiled white fingers like some article of lustful possession.

Tom looked over each shoulder and made his way toward the porch. The steps creaked as he scaled them, and the dead wood brought Bud to life. His body jerked as if he himself was the intruder on another's property, and he spun and raised the pistol and leveled it at the visitor's midsection. Tom stopped and put his hands in the air.

"Calm down, Bud, it's just me."

He held the pistol steady and looked around through a set of wired eyes. He seemed to have not heard the words, but then he swallowed and relaxed and draped the gun across his leg.

"What are you doin here? What time is it?"

"It's almost five."

Tom looked around. The screen door stood skewed from its post, and the jamb of the damaged entryway showed raw wood. He looked at Bud: busy gathering himself within his seat.

"What happened, here?"

He looked at Tom and then to the ramshackled entryway.

"What does it look like?" He coughed and spat a volume of mucus onto the porch. "I mean to your trained police mind?"

Tom rested against the rail of the porch.

"Looks like someone kicked your door in."

Bud dangled his left hand over the chair and gathered a half-empty bottle of scotch.

"I knew there was a reason I hired ya."

He loosened the cap with one hand and raised the bottle as if in a toast. Then he drank, his face passive as if he tasted a substance benign as apple juice. He lowered the bottle and nestled it against his sternum.

"That there's our friend's handiwork."

Tom approached the door and ran his fingers against the gnawed looking splits of wood.

"Where were you?"

Bud wiped the drying slobber from his chin.

"Busy bein kept occupied at the station by the very man hisself."

He leaned to the side and spat.

"They done sent somebody over to rifle through the place while the fella was talkin to me."

He looked up and gave a closed-lip smile.

"Christ," Tom said.

Bud nodded, and set the bottle of liquor down on the porch beside him.

"Well," Tom said. "Did they get what they were after?"

Bud searched his empty shirt pocket for cigarettes.

"Oh, yeah. They was more thorough than I am smart."

He gave up searching and slapped his thighs. On the porch rail next to him, an ash tray sat choked with spent cigarette butts from another time. He leaned over and dangled his fingers above the heap, searching for the least vile of the bunch. He snapped one up and put it to his lips. Tom watched as he worked a match free from the booklet in his lap. He folded his leg and struck the red tip against the sole of his boot, but it raked off and fell to the deck floor. He shook his head and tried twice more before he got fire. And then he lined the flame with the tiny stale butt, like a far-sighted man trying to thread a needle.

"Christ," Tom said. "Hold on."

He bent and collected the half-full pack of cigarettes that had fallen beneath Bud's legs.

"Here."

Bud spat the wasted butt over the porch rail and took the pack. He thumbed one loose and lit it. Then he leaned back and tipped his hat up.

"Yep, they took it all. They took everthing. Everthing and more."

He leaned and tried to spit, but the mucous flung like molasses and swooped against his sleeve.

"Goddamn, Bud. How drunk are you?"

Bud looked up, his eyes flashing hell.

"What the fuck business is it of yours, Tom?"

He sat up in his chair.

"What the hell are you doin here, anyway?"

Tom raised a hand and tipped his head down.

"Take it easy, Bud. I'm on your side."

Bud kept his eyes fixed on Tom's a moment longer, and then he sat back in his chair and looked off at the little leaves flickering under the moonlight.

"I'm sorry, son. You're right."

He smoked and exhaled.

"I ain't never been sorry to see ya, Tom. And that includes now."

Tom looked around the porch and wondered how much snarl and tangle the ransackers had authored, and how much existed before they'd arrived. He rubbed the whiskers on his jaw and squatted.

"I suppose they're saving me for last. Why would that be?"

Bud shrugged.

"Maybe they figure you'll be easy once you've seen how they go about things."

He shrugged, again.

"Well, if that's what they're thinking, they figured right," Tom said. "I'm set to give them what I have if they'll let me."

Bud leaned over and spat.

"Oh, I'm sure they'll let you. But then what?"

Tom looked down and nodded.

"That's what's occupying my mind, lately."

He waited for Bud to say something, but he didn't.

"I'll tell you this much. If we get out of this, me and Ellie are going someplace where this drug shit isn't running crazy."

Bud shook his head.

"Ain't no such place."

Tom walked back to the rail and propped against it.

"This shit's like a leviathan," Bud said. "It cain't be stopped. There's too much money, and where there's money there's men that'll do anythin to protect it. It'll go anywhere there's people at. You'll find these same cartels' fingerprints in Bumfuck, Idaho or Maine, or Saskatchewan. Ain't a damn thing anyone can do to stop it. It's like pissin on a forest fire."

He picked his hands up and pushed the air away.

"Hell, ain't no one really wants to try and stop it anyways. Everthing at's done is only to provide the appearance that those at's in charge is tryin to do somthin about it. They all know there ain't no point to it. "Everthing's a lie. Even the things you know is true. Them's lies, too. All of it, lies."

He rubbed his forehead.

"Anyways," he said. "At least with this drug business, things make sense."

Tom tipped his hat back.

"How do you figure?"

Bud looked at him like he'd forgotten what they were talking about.

"What do you mean?"

Tom raised his eyebrows.

"What do you mean?"

"I mean all the killin that goes with it."

"I don't think I follow your point, Bud."

Bud took his hat off and sat it in his lap. He sucked the cigarette and thought for a moment.

"Well, how can I explain it to you? Let's see." He made a stiff frown and rubbed the pointy corners of it with his thumb and forefinger. "Alright, if you'll allow this, I'll point out that killin happens all the time, everday. It's all fer different reasons. Most people say there ain't no good reason to kill. And the hard ones argue about eye for an eye, and say at anyone who would kill somebody ought to be killed theyself."

He smoked and thought for a moment longer.

"Less there's a war. And then most people line up with their country like they're rootin for a football team. It don't make no difference if somebody dies in a war. That makes sense to em. They think, well, hell, that person, they put theyself in harm's way. For good or not, they knew what might happen when they signed up. They took the risk for whatever reason. For whatever it was worth. People accept it. Celebrate it, even. Less there's a draft. But in them cases, people are more worried than concerned."

He scratched under his right ear and turned his left palm over in the air.

"Anyways, dyin in a war makes sense to a lot of people no matter the circumstances, cause them that die was put there to do somethin with cause. And whether it was a good cause or bad cause. Well, at's for people who ain't in the war to argue. But whatever they argue, most people agree that those who die in a war at least had some control of their fate, and even though it makes em sad, most people can digest that kind of dyin a little bit better.

"Where killin don't make no sense to people is when it happens to somebody who ain't made no choice. Them they call victims. The ones who are just livin their life when killin comes upon em."

Tom rubbed his forehead hard as if Bud's words made it ache.

"You're saying that those dying from drugs are in a war?" Tom asked. "That they chose to put themselves in harm's way?"

Bud raised his cigarette.

"Not all of em. Now, that cain't be argued for. Yeah, there's those who get gunned down cause they was in the crossfire, and there's the ones who get hooked on drugs and wither away to nothin. That's always sad. But when you take the numbers, the ones who die within the world of drug traffickin and drug use, most of em had control. Even if they didn't realize it, most of em did. Not all, but most. And though it ain't ideal, it does make sense. Of all the things I've seen since I been in law enforcement, drugs have made the most sense to me."

Tom raised his arm to check his watch.

"I don't see your point, Bud. I really don't."

The sheriff pursed his lips.

"Let me tell you a story, then." He looked up at Tom. "If you'll allow it."

Tom turned his palms over.

"This thing happened in Tyler where I was workin at the time. Long time ago. Back when you was probly still in middle school."

He looked off for a moment and rubbed his chin. Tom watched him, the toe of his boot tapping the deck. The old man might have been analyzing the repercussions of what he had just said, weighing age and meaning and relationships. Or he might only have been willing down a throat full of vomit. Whatever it was, it finally abated, and he went on with what he was saying.

"Anyways, it seems there was this young fella, thought it'd be a good idea to kill somebody. Weren't no one he had a problem with. No vendetta. Nothin like that. Fact is he didn't even know who it was he was goin to kill. It was just somethin he'd been kickin around in his head for a while. That he wanted to kill somebody. Take a life. Somethin like curiosity. Somethin wrong in his brain."

He raised one palm up and shrugged.

"Anyways, what this fella done is come up with a clever little way of gettin what he wanted. It was all plain as hell once we started lookin back at it. But at the time, it had the people involved scattered to shit. Those directly, anyways."

He leaned over and spat.

"So, this fella knew he had an ambition to kill, only he didn't do it like most in his position do. Didn't foller some lady home from her work. Didn't pluck some kid up off the playground. Nothin like that. See, cause that'd be too easy. Anybody could do it, and this fella understood that. No, this particular fella I'm talkin bout had a flare for the dramatic. He didn't just wanna smother somebody out. Didn't just wanna watch the light die out in somebody's eyes, while he strangled em in some dark concrete basement. Nope. This ole fella wanted to test hisself. Or at least at's what I come to think of the whole thing."

He sipped the scotch and his lips curled and hissed mutely.

"You see, this fella I'm talkin about wanted to know if he could kill somebody in a populated area. Sorta like killin in plain sight. Wanted to see if it was possible, I guess."

He sucked smoke from his cigarette and then pointed it at Tom.

"See crazy ain't rare like most people think. There's lotsa people out there who's crazy. Just most of em are too lazy or too scared to unleash it on the world. Your problems come when you get somebody who's crazy and motivated. At's when you get these flare-ups. The ones at show up on yer night-time news broadcasts. The ones at tap at yer very bones. Make you start to question things. Check yer locks twice even when you know you done locked em."

He smiled and nodded, as if he read agreement in Tom's face. Then he sat up and put his hands together.

"What this fella come up with was pretty damn smart. You know, in its own sick way, it was. He knew if he was to kill somebody in front of other people, then them other people was gonna be disturbed by it, and they'd either jump on him all at once, or they'd call the police, and he'd be all but done. So, what he did was go someplace where blood weren't no issue."

He leaned back and rubbed his chin. Then he gathered himself up again and sat with his forearms on his knees.

"See, they got these haunted houses all around these parts in October. Big elaborate things out in the country. They put a lot into em. Advertise em on the radio. It's a big deal for the teenagers. They get to drinkin and the fellas take the girls out there to get their adrenaline pumpin. Then they go off and do more drinkin and all them other things at follow.

"Well, what this fella did was get a high-carbon stainless steel knife from his kitchen drawer and head on out to one of these haunted houses set up in one of the hay fields in Tyler. It was late by the time he got there, but there was still lotsa folks lined up to go inside. Mostly high school kids."

He rubbed his chin.

"Weren't supposed to be nobody under fourteen, on account of all the carnage and the overall realism of the thing. But I know a few of em snuck in, cause they was there when we showed up."

He stopped and looked for the bottle of scotch. When he found it, he drank until his eyes watered. He swallowed and lifted the bottle like he might take another, but instead he set it back on the porch.

"So, like I was sayin, this fella went down to this ole haunted house with a knife hidden in this black trench coat he was wearin. He drove up, got out the car, bought hisself a ticket and took a spot at the end of the line. He waited for a long time. Just standin there with the rest of em. Hands in his pocket. Plain lookin guy. No expression on his face is what the witnesses said.

"Anyways, he just stood there in line and when the time came, he went on inside with everbody else. Past all the cob webs, the moaning corpses with their guts hangin out, the guy with the leather mask and the chainsaw, and whatever else there was."

He lifted the pack of cigarettes and tapped it on his knee as he spoke.

"Well this ole setup had curved passages in it, and things would lunge out of the darkness at all the people as they went past. And everthing was all random like, so nobody would know what to expect. And the people who worked in there would pop outta dark corners and reach and grab people and scare the living hell out of em."

He looked at Tom.

"I don't know if you ever been in one of these things, but this one in particular was really pushin the limits. I mean, some of these people could have filed assault charges if they wanted to.

"Anyways, this fella went through the thing once and when he came out, he had a pretty good idea of what things looked like, what to expect. And he knew there was some empty areas where there weren't nobody hidin. So what he did was go and buy another ticket and get back in line. And he followed everone back in like before. But this time when he got toward the end, he stepped outta line and ducked into one of them empty areas.

"Well, he stood there waitin a long time. Just watchin all the people shuffle through the darkness. Watchin their faces freeze like pictures between the black frames of the strobe lights. And then after a while, he took that knife out and held it. And when he saw what he was lookin for, he made his move."

Bud raised the pack of cigarettes to his mouth and pulled one out with his teeth.

"Anyways, this fella reached into the line and plucked out this little sixteen-year-old girl. Grabbed her by the hair and pulled her to him. Then he flipped her around and locked his arm around her neck from behind. And he reached around and dug that knife into the soft part of her stomach right near her belly button, and he worked that thing all the way up until it got underneath her rib cage."

He struck a match against his boot and held it against the cigarette until the tobacco glowed orange.

"She screamed right away, but nobody could tell what was happenin from the rest of everthing else they was seein. Nobody knew it was real. Except the other two girls she was with. They damn sure knew it was real. And when they saw that dark circle of blood all soppy against her sweater, well, they started screamin and beggin the people around em fer help. But hardly nobody could hear em, and those at could just thought they was screamin fer the same reason as everone else. And the ones behind em pushed everbody forward, and they left that girl behind just bleedin and cryin while that fella butchered her right in the face of all comers."

He took the cigarette from his mouth and tapped the ash against his boot.

"Well, at some point, that fella left her settin there and got back in line, and it looked like he was gonna get outta there just like he was hopin. But them two girls happened to find a fella outside at had some sense. And he'd gathered a few other people and closed off the parking area. Well, when the fella saw that, he took out toward the woods. Didn't take us no time at all to find him with the dogs and when we did find him, we let him have it pretty good cause we all been in the business long enough to know that whatever we gave him that night was probly gonna be the worst of what he got from then on.

"Anyways, when they found that little girl, she'd been cored out from her belly button to her tits. I saw her and I looked at her eyes. They was just all glazed and soulless like somethin made of gelatin. There weren't nothin in em. She didn't even look like a real girl no more. Her whole body just looked empty. Not human at all. More like a carcass. Like the meat you get at a grocery store."

He tried to smoke, but the smolder had burned the cigarette to its filter; so he set the butt in the ashtray without pressing it dead. He continued, while a pale string of smoke extended flawlessly from the ashtray, high into the air as if pulled tight by fingers from above.

"She didn't have no look at all on her face. It just held blank. I know that point is true. I remember that particular point. She wore no expression."

He raided the pack of cigarettes for another. He slipped it through his lips, and it dangled unlit.

"But for some reason, when I remember her face, it ain't like that. In my mind, she has this tortured, confused look on her face. Like the kind a puppy or a very young child gets when they been hurt and they don't know the reason. When they first get that taste of what the world has in store for em. That first unveiling. That kinda look. The kind at makes you feel an ache in your soul. Like you have a responsibility in everthing sick and wrong that men do in the world just cause you belong to the same race."

He snapped a match against his boot and raised it against the cigarette. It flamed to life, and he worked it to the side of his mouth with his teeth.

"Anyways," he said, the cigarette dangling from his lips as he spoke. "It didn't make no sense to me at the time, and I don't expect it ever will."

He leaned back and wiped his hands against his jeans.

"You ask me why all this is better, and I say it's cause it makes sense. That little girl didn't die for drugs or for money. She died cause some sick fuck was born with crossed wires. I say, again, if yer gonna be in law enforcement, drugs is the least of the evils. Less you wanna audit parkin meters."

He stopped for a moment and thought, his drunken body bobbing like a corked bottle drifting without will in some vast and disturbed patch of ocean. Tom watched him, half hoping the man might fall unconscious. But instead of passing out, he seemed restored by a new thought.

"Let me ask you a question," he said as he squinted his eyes against the stinging cloud of white smoke. "You ever have a feelin about how you might die?"

Tom pushed his hat back, and rubbed his palm against his eye.

"I don't know, Bud. What's this got to do with anything?"

Bud drew another match, and snapped it against his boot. Fire spewed from the tip, and he held it in his fingers. He observed the tailing flare, his eyes blaring forward like those of an arsonist worshiper of flame.

"Just answer the question."

Tom exhaled and scratched the back of his neck.

"I guess. I mean, you know, just little feelings in passing. Probably the same as everyone else."

Bud let the flame taste his flesh, and then he snapped it cold.

"Yeah, that happens to everone probly," he said. "But what about strong feelins? You ever have them?"

"I don't know, Bud. I guess you're saying that you have? Is that it?"

Bud nodded and spat on the porch.

"From time to time. Yeah, I sure have."

"Like what are you talking about?"

Bud hunched over and pressed his forearms against his thighs.

"Well, for a while, I had this feelin that I was goin to die chokin on somethin."

He peered up at Tom, his eyes shadowed beneath his hat.

"Certain things, I wouldn't even eat for a while. Nuts and popcorn, stuff like that. Wouldn't touch em. Least not when I was alone to where I couldn't get no help if I needed it."

He scratched his chin, and stared off into the vacant black night.

"Some things were ok. Grapes and ice. I don't know why. Just some things made me uneasy for some reason. Others didn't."

Tom tried to speak, but Bud cut him off.

"Hard candy weren't no good."

He looked at Tom.

"You know like the little peppermints they give you at restaurants when yer done eatin?"

He pressed his lips together and shook his head.

"I'd take em and give em away to kids."

Tom raised his eyebrows and pressed his lips together.

"Well, that ain't that weird, I guess."

Bud adjusted his hat.

"Yeah, I guess not. I just don't know why it ever started."

"Maybe you choked on something when you were a boy. What difference does it make?"

Bud shook his head.

"No. Wasn't nothin like that. It was more like, one day, I didn't ever worry about it, and then the next day, I did. It just come up on me all of a sudden is what I remember. Don't know why. Maybe it was somethin I dreamed, but I don't know, cause I don't remember my dreams."

A distant train blared and chugged toward someplace else, and neither spoke, again, until it passed too far to hear.

"Well, you haven't choked yet."

Bud nodded.

"I reckon."

His shot-red eyes towed low down toward the porch, where specks of ants combed the boards for nourishment. He leaned forward and spat on one. It struggled against the sudden lake of goop for several seconds until it broke free, and then it went on searching unquestioningly, exactly as it was programmed to do.

Tom checked his watch, again.

"You don't gotta be here," Bud said.

"Maybe you should get some sleep," Tom said.

Bud put the scotch to his lips and drank.

Tom stood and dusted his legs.

"Alright then," he said. "I'll leave you to yourself."

He turned to go.

"Let me ask you somethin, Tom."

Tom stopped.

"What is it?"

"You ever think about havin another kid?"

Tom leaned back against the porch railing.

"No."

Bud tilted his head.

"That simple? Just, a flat no?"

"That's right."

Bud put his hands behind his head.

"I guess I could see why you'd be a little gun shy."

He stretched his legs out and crossed them at the ankles.

Tom lowered his hat and turned to go, but as he reached the steps, he stopped and turned back around.

"What about you, Bud? Where was your second try?"

Bud looked at him crossly, and Tom's eyes narrowed as he assessed the gun in the drunk man's lap.

"It weren't my choice."

They watched each other's faces for a while, and then Tom looked down.

"Anyway," Tom said. "I'm not gun shy."

Bud uncrossed his legs and sat up, his drunken body wavering.

"I take it yer one of these, the world's too dark a place to bring a child into folks, now. Is that it?"

"That's pretty close."

Bud shook his head.

"That's bullshit. No matter how many times I hear somebody say it, it never sounds no truer. The real reason is you don't wanna get hurt. Yer tryin to keep yourself safe from the world. But you cain't do it. Ain't no one can."

Tom's eyes trickled upward.

"It's normal," Bud said. "Believe me cause I know what I'm talkin about."

He propped his elbow on the chair's armrest and leaned over, but his elbow slipped over the edge, and the chair capsized over the top of him. Tom walked over slowly. He lifted the chair and set it to the side. He reached down and took Bud's arm.

"You need to stop this," he said.

Bud grabbed his shoulder and tried to raise himself, but his legs gave out, and he fell backward, his head cracking against the wood deck. Tom looked down at the mess before him. Bud had bitten his lip on collision, and the blood, made thin from the alcohol, dribbled like red water from each corner of his mouth. Tom bent down and collected the pistol, and then he gathered the limp, awkward heap of a man and guided him inside.

By the time Tom got him into the house and onto his bed, Bud's awareness seemed much reduced. He propped the man upon the end of the bed and let him fall, hands flailing back over his shoulders.

The room sat barren, save for the bed and a cheap veneer nightstand that seemed only a platform for a lamp and a small plastic alarm clock. Tom walked over and collected the tiny thing. He set it for noon and placed it back down. He turned to leave, and as he did, the slumbering inebriate burst to life as if struck in the chest with an adrenaline plunger. He reached for Tom's arm like a panicked man lost in the dark, and when he found it, he held it firm.

"Listen, son," he said, as if there'd been no delay in their last conversation. "I know you're scared. But it's all gonna be alright. However things turn out, it'll be alright."

Tom ripped his arm away.

"I'm not scared, Bud. I know what needs to be done. Go to sleep."

Bud turned over on his side, eyes watering, his face a sickly green.

"I don't mean that." He shook his head. "I ain't talking about that. I mean your boy. The one you lost."

Tom shook his head.

"I don't need to hear this from you, Bud. I don't even really know you."

Bud shook his head and spat on the carpet.

"It don't matter. Just listen. This idea you got. About keeping safe from pain. Not tryin no more. I understand it. I've lived it. But you need to know. It don't matter what you do. What you don't do." He tapped his fist on the mattress. "It don't work. If life wants to hurt you, it'll damn well do it. You cain't make yerself exempt from it. No matter what you try. Yer alive, and as long as yer alive, yer gonna be hurt. Over and over. It's best to just foller your heart. Do it blindly. Do it like you ain't got nothin to lose. You cain't insulate yourself against life by keeping the stakes low. I know it, if I don't know nothin else."

Tom looked down at the carpet and kicked at a melted cigarette burn with the toe of his boot.

"Go to sleep, Bud."

He left the room and closed the door behind him, Bud's face flooded by the thinning thread of light from the hall, and then gone, like a specter, conjured by sufferers of ill-thought and unable to exist without them.

He waited there, his hand on the door knob while he thought. His eyes panned the closed door to his right. A piece of rectangular wood dangled from a centered nail, the word "Anna" scrawled across it in glittered script.

The door stood closed, the locking mechanism incapacitated by a booted foot, its impression stenciled into the white finish just below the knob like a beveling stamp: a brutality, invasive on something sweet and serene.

He approached the door and grasped the knob. He could see his hazy image reflecting darkly within the painted sheen, like some antecedent from another world bent on escaping the very place his other headed.

He knew what the room was and what he'd find before he entered. But he couldn't calculate the weight of its punch. And as the door swung free, he covered his mouth at what he saw.

All things lay shattered beyond provocation, beyond reason or need. With proper context, things identified. Without it: litter and scrap. A doll house, splintered by a hammer or possibly a crowbar. A miniature vanity, hacked apart by a clumsy axe. Dainty dresses with their frilled sleeves and necklines, torn and piled in the center of the room like fuel for a makeshift bon fire.

He saw the innards of companion dolls, still wafting in the draft, like cottonwood seeds in a spring wind. And fragments of porcelain figurines, smashed and scattered across the carpet, like crushed sea shells bleached white upon an open beach. And within the debris, he saw photographs of Bud and his wife, the stunning child set upon their shoulders, her face lit by the gift of the single day: pictures of a once-was family and of dreams unrealized.

He shut off the light switch, stepped back into the hall and closed the door.

He turned to Bud's bedroom door and studied his darker reflecting twin. He paused there for a while, as if he expected reassurance from the fleshless double or at worst a shrug.

After a while, he turned and walked out of the house. When he got into the cruiser, he started it and sat quietly, inhaling the scent of fresh exhaust and staring forward into the new horizon: brightening before him, blue like a robin's egg amidst the relinquishing night. A few moments later, he was gone and Bud was alone.

The man that stepped from the restaurant seemed stricken by the brightening dawn. He moved one foot onto the exterior walk before snapping his fingers at the larger subordinate who held the door. This man retrieved a pair of expensive looking sunglasses from his jacket pocket and passed them over with polished haste. The first man slid the frames over his ears and onto his nose, and then he raised his eyebrows, as if the glasses had not just subjugated the glare, but transformed his view of the world into something serene and correct.

There was another younger man behind the first two, and though small was his body, large was his intensity, and forceful and forged in doings of violence and ill-deeds, and none that met him dared to comment on his height, and few had come to notice it anyway.

They emptied through the exit and spilled out into the honest world very much a crew of threatening men, tidying their suits and straightening their hair, as if something from inside the restaurant had disturbed their refined veneers.

They moved across the parking lot quickly but in no discernible hurry, and Tom knew who they were as soon as he saw them, and if he was unsure, the sight of Ellie sobbing in the arms of a coworker through the restaurant's window glass, removed all doubt.

The men seemed curiously unready for what happened next, and as Tom swerved his car before them, only the small man reached for his pistol. He leveled at the unknown driver, his associates still busy parsing the circumstances for meaning. Tom exited the car in full uniform, and the man with the sunglasses instructed the bearer of the gun to lower his weapon. He smiled and approached the deputy, but before he could speak, Tom removed his pistol and slammed it across his ear. The younger man raised his gun, again, and this time it seemed he would shoot, but the first man called for restraint, and so he obeyed.

Tom held his pistol steady on the smaller man, his eyes wild and perspiring.

"What is the meaning of this?" The sunglassed man said.

Tom looked at him.

"That's my wife in there." He pressed the gun against the man's chest. "I think you knew that already." He looked at the other men, each with a pistol at his side. "Drop them."

Neither responded, each breathing slowly, as if they faced a gun of plastic. Tom moved the pistol toward them.

"Do you know who I am?" Said the sunglassed man.

"Your name's Soto?"

The man nodded.

"That's right."

Tom kept his pistol leveled at the other two men.
"Then I guess I do."
He took a step forward.
"Drop them. Do it right now."
The larger man dropped his pistol and lofted his hands into the air, but the shorter man did not follow suit. Instead, he raised his gun at Tom's head and took several steps forward until the two diametric pistols hovered only a few feet apart.

Tom tried to measure the resolve in the young man's eyes, but he couldn't see past the bulky white bandage across his nose. But by his actions, the small man told the story enough, that the man he saw before him appeared suspect and unsure.

"You wish to die here in this parking lot?" Soto said.

The oranging sun ratcheted its intensity on the men, as a small group of people gathered near the front of the restaurant. Ellie burst from the doors, and a large male coworker grabbed her firm in his arms. She screamed something across the lot, but her words were swept up by the wind.

Tom strangled the pistol grip.
"If I have to."
The gathering people pointed and whispered to one another. Soto looked at them and then to Tom.
"This is not the way out for you," he said. "This is a fool's play."
Tom kept the pistol on its mark, his shoulder now burning at the base of his extended arm.
"I don't care."
Soto sighed and evaluated the crowd once more. He rubbed his forehead and then turned to the young man. He said something to him in Spanish, but the young man remained fixed in his position. He spoke the same words louder, and finally the man released his hold on the pistol and let it fall clattering against the asphalt.

Tom inhaled as if he'd risen from underwater. He gathered the three men into a bunch with a wave of his pistol.
"What now?" Soto said, his arms spread to his side.
Tom walked to the cruiser and opened the back door.
"Get in."
Soto smirked, and for the first time, Tom felt the sucking gravity of his glare.

"You are planning to arrest us?" He shook his head. "You are more a fool than you look."

Tom shook the pistol toward the cavity.

"Let's go."

The two men looked at Soto, who was busy eyeing the curious mob of servers and patrons outside the restaurant. He leaned forward and looked into the backseat.

"How are we all to fit?"

Tom shook the gun again.

"Awkwardly, would be my guess."

Soto looked to the restaurant once more.

"Very well," he said, and he ushered the two men inside, each's eyes aflame as he dipped into the interior, each's skin a membranous restraint against a seether core. Each, but not for Soto, for he pressed into the backseat and dusted his knees not like a prisoner, but a guest, his hands crossed at the wrist, head casually set forward, as if he'd envisioned the outcome of this set of circumstances favorably, and more sets beyond.

CHAPTER 14

The phone's burbled pulses beat on for a long while, and then the line flooded with hoarse coughing.

"Yeah," Bud said, his voice abraded and grinding. Tom told him everything, but none of it seemed to resonate.

"What's this now?"

Tom told him again and waited through a long pause followed by more strained coughing.

"Christ," Bud said. "You got em all there now?"

"Yes."

"Christ."

He cleared his throat and spat.

"I hope you know what you done, son."

"I know it."

"Well."

There was a pause.

"I'll be on my way shortly. I'm gonna swing by and get Levi, first. You keep em there and don't talk to em."

"Alright."

"I'm serious now. Don't you talk to em til I get there."

"I said alright."

He hung up the phone and turned toward the men in the cell. Soto sat on the cot, his underlings propped against the wall on either side of him, as if they were not prisoners at all, but guards at the shoulders of a throne.

"Was that your friend, the good sheriff?" Soto said.

Tom sat at the desk. He raised a newspaper from days before and read over words he'd already consumed.

"You don't want to talk? I understand."

Tom lowered the paper and looked at the men, stolid and wooden like solemn figures within an old black and white photograph. Soto raised his hand and pointed to the corner of the desk where a steel bowl sat congested with the contents from each man's pockets.

"Would you be so kind as to allow me a cigarette?"

Tom placed the newspaper flat on the desk and stood. He walked around the desk and looked inside the bowl. A pack of cigarettes sat within the clutter, its packaging marked with writing he couldn't read. He collected it and approached the cell, but after a few steps, Soto raised his hand.

"Eh, eh," he pointed toward the bowl. "My lighter, too, please."

Tom turned and walked back to the desk. He dug through the bowl and found it: stainless steel and inlayed with spiraling strings of gold. He gathered it in his palm and held it for a moment. Then he set it back inside the bowl and took one of Bud's matchbooks from the desk. He turned and walked to the cell.

Soto smiled as if he approved.

"Very good."

When the taller man sprung forward to gather the items, Tom stopped and motioned him back. He pointed at Soto who smiled and nodded.

"Yes. Very well."

He rose to his feet and dusted his slacks. Tom tore two matches from the booklet and slipped them into the cellophane cover around the cigarettes. He held the pack a few inches from the bars. Soto approached, his eyes never wavering from Tom's face. He moved quickly, and for a moment, his pace seemed to indicate that he thought he might pass through the bars, as if they were conjured images: cell-less particles of light to all save those who believed them real.

Tom looked into Soto's sucking black eyes, passively searching for something familiar, perhaps a hint of humanity or a glint of weakness. But all he saw was void: dead marbles, organic as onyx glass. Soto stopped, his face an inch from the bars, ugly and scarred and marred with a darkening shadow of facial hair. He stood with his hands to his sides.

Tom raised the pack of cigarettes and shook it, and a smile leaked from one side of Soto's thin lips. He raised his hands and slipped them through the bars with the palms cupped upward. His eyes stayed fixed to Tom's even as the deputy dropped the cigarettes into his hands. He withdrew and walked back to the cot and sat as before, girded by his subordinates, as if he was the principle piece on a chess board.

Tom remained there as Soto cleared his throat and withdrew a cigarette. He struck a match to life with the rim of his thumbnail in a way that seemed practiced or remembered from an earlier time. He puffed the cigarette to life. He inhaled and blew and groaned in exaggerated relief.

"Thank you so much deputy. That was very kind of you."

He propped his head back against the cement and stared forward at the other wall.

"What is it you plan to do?"

Tom cleared his throat.

"That's not for me to decide."

"Ah, yes," Soto said, his eyes fixed forward at nothing in particular. "The good sheriff. He will have all the answers in due time."

He smoked and exhaled. He bobbed his knee.

"Is that what you think?"

He rolled his head against the wall and focused at Tom, who shook his head and shrugged.

"It doesn't matter."

Soto smoked.

"But after what you did to him," Tom said. "I wouldn't want to be in your position."

Soto chuckled, and the two men broke from their stony faces long enough to join him.

"I'm sorry," Soto said, as he molded his demeanor into something that looked very serious. "You care for this man. Is that it?"

"Sure I do."

Soto nodded and smoked thoughtfully.

"Well, I must say that it was not me personally who executed this thing you speak of. Though, I am now aware of it."

Tom said nothing.

"It is not to my particular taste. But I try never to micro manage."

He looked over his shoulder at his men, each leaking subtle smiles. He looked at Tom and shrugged his shoulders. He turned his body toward the deputy and crossed his legs.

"You believe he deserved better? Is that it?"

"Yes, I do. You don't think he did?"

Soto flipped his hand in dismissal.

"I don't believe in deserve." He raised his cigarette to his lips and then paused. "I don't believe in any principles dreamt by men. I believe only in survival."

He drew from the cigarette, his eyes black and depthless and engaged firmly with Tom's.

"You don't believe in right or wrong either, I take it."

Soto smiled and a thin ribbon of smoke escaped from the corner of his mouth.

"That is just another principle conjured by men."

He leaned forward and put his hands together.

"Something a man defines as wrong within the social order constructed for widespread survival is only but a means to preserve the social structure, itself. It is only survival."

Tom shook his head.

"You just think that because you're a sociopath."

Soto leaned back in his chair and smoothed his thin mustache with his index finger and thumb.

"Ah, but you are wrong. I feel. I feel very much. But feelings have no place when it comes to survival. Feelings are genetic frailties that put the carer at risk for the benefit of the one they care for. These feelings are coded within men's genetics to entice protection toward those who need it for their own survival. They do nothing for the one who allows himself to care, except coax him into irrational decision making that puts his own survival at risk."

He smoked for a long time, his eyes flaring slightly with each drag. He blew a thick white smog into the air and scratched the growing whiskers on his neck.

"It is more of the same. Constructs meant to preserve the species, but not the man, himself. All social animals operate this way, because that is what they are programmed to do. None have a choice in the matter. Except for man, who has developed awareness and with it, choice. He mustn't waste this blessing, but use it. He must cast off these genetic constraints if he wishes to be more than a faceless cog in the continuation of a species. What value is there in that? A life wasted and mired in troubles until death. Only to be consumed by the insect mites and vegetation, his body dissolved into elemental nutrients for lesser beings?"

He tapped the cigarette with his index finger and the ash dropped and splashed against the epoxy floor. Tom pulled his hat down low and clasped his hand around one of the bars.

"I'm glad I don't see the world like you do."

"You see what they want you to see."

"Who are they?"

"Those bent on controlling people like you."

"Who are they?"

"People similar to me. Those who aren't burdened with the anxiety of empathy. Those who manipulate. Only, the people I speak of do it legally in plain sight. They sit upon boastful leather chairs in high buildings, smoking expensive cigars, busy always, constructing television commercials and false ideas, tweaking interest rates and positioning their influence within the fertile nooks of your government. All of it meant to keep you and those like you pacing rhythmically to their song. Year after year. Until you die and your children take your place."

He sat back on the bed and folded his legs, as if he'd crossed out the world with his words.

Tom dusted his pants, but they were already clean.

"I don't have any children."

"Yes," Soto smoked his cigarette. "I know."

Tom looked into those cavernous eyes.

"You know everything about me?"

Soto nodded slowly.

"It is my job to know everything."

Tom scratched the back of his neck.

"You know about Bud, too, then I guess."

"Yes."

"But that didn't give you pause."

Soto leaned forward and crushed his cigarette out on the floor.

"Why would it?"

"Because of what he's been through."

"What difference does it make?"

"It should."

Soto fished another cigarette from the pack.

"Why do you think?"

"Because he's suffered."

Soto lifted the cigarette to his mouth and bit the filter with his teeth. He snapped a flame from the other match and raised it to the tip. He monitored the fire with his eyes until the end of the cigarette glowed orange, then his eyes trickled up and bored forth.

"That is the way of the world." The words leaked from the corner of his mouth like blood from a wound. He snapped the lighter shut. "What else should one expect?"

He exhaled and relaxed, his legs crossed, his hands the same upon them, the cigarette steaming from between his fingers. Like this, he sat, seeming less a prisoner, but more a teacher, eager to find an audience receptive.

"What else can one petition from the world than what is the world's nature to provide? The life that populates the world operates the same as the world, itself. Whether it skits across the floor of the earth or stands upright. It all does what it is set to do. Man and animal, alike. And plant. All programmed to survive and thrive as best it can. At the expense of others who would do the same. And such is the world, itself. It spins and flourishes and recedes without passion or prejudice. It does so not because it has reason, but because it is programmed to act in this way. It does not stray. They say that things are the way they are for reason, but there is no reason. Reason is a man's device. His necessity. The world has no need for reason and so there is no reason. There is only what is."

He raised the cigarette to his mouth and drew from it, and when his lungs grew full, he leaned his head back and blew a billowing mass of smoke into the air. He leaned over and tapped the ash against the sole of his shoe.

"The locust will feed until there is no more to eat. And then it will die, because there is no more for it to feed on. It does so, because it is automated to function in this way. It does not alter its course based on prudence, because it cannot. And men are the same, though they believe that they are not. But they are. And their destiny is the same as the underlings they judge and despise. They operate from code. These relationships they seek and hoard, they dissolve with equal vigor. They seek their destruction, robotically, through all obstacles, to clear room for more of their kind that will only do the same. Such is the nature of the world. Its function is the same as that of those who dwells upon it. To build and to thrive and then to clear itself and start again."

He shook his head and raised his hand. He traced his cigarette in a horizontal triangle.

"Order is a man's illusion. There is no order. There is only the slow drip of life or death as you see it. Whatever any of it means to you. It occupies your mind. But considering your potential role in the world is as useless as contemplating your role on the moon. You have no meaning in either place."

He smoked and exhaled a looping white cord of smoke.

"But men have long deluded themselves into thinking they are relevant. Men think that, because their minds operate above the crawling underlings, this somehow makes them different. But each is the same at its core. Men waste their time pondering philosophical ideas that have no place in the actual world. No place within the dirt and the water and the wind and the living and the dying. The decay and the renewal."

He raised his finger at Tom.

"You speak of compassion and morality. These are common considerations for the ordinary man. Unjust life and death occupy his mind. But it is only because he is bred to consider these things. He thinks that by considering such things, he may come to affect their outcome. But that is but a child's wish. And he knows it. Somewhere within his core, he does. But men are new to the world, which is ancient in its patterns and its will. Men scathe the world without compunction. They do not grieve when plants nor insects are compelled to extinction by drought or circumstances attributable to men, themselves. Man cares only for how the world serves his interests, though he is prone to testify at great volumes that it is not the case. But it is, and anyone with a clear, impartial eye can see it. Man strives to enslave fish and insect and animal and other men, all to serve his purpose, malignant or benign. And each man is particular in his view. Man bears loyalties only to things like himself. Things that function as he does. Things with hearts that beat. And some men care not even for this. Man is destructive and he destroys even against his own interests. But it is no sin. It is only the natural state of his existence. All beings strive toward their demise, and sometimes these angles coalesce into a balance that allows coexistence between species for a period of time. But never for too long. Because, the world seeks neither balance nor imbalance. It cares not if all things wither and die. It can exist as it does now or as a barren orb of soil. What difference does it make to the world which has neither desire nor ambition?

"But even if man knows this truth, he can do nothing to alter his path. He is required to think and act as he does because of what is writ in the spaces within the very cells of his body. Of these, he is a prisoner to. These writings. They are the deciders. Choice is false. He can only sway and flinch from danger, actual or perceived. He can do nothing to alter his course toward destruction. As an individual or as a whole. No more than the locust which cares not for its brethren feeding beside it. It exists within a frenzy. As do men, which exist within a frenzy too slow to detect. But a frenzy just the same. And the world sees man and locust the same, because it cares not for either. And though man pounds upon it with demands that he be treated differently, he dies at stray or in piles, same as the locust, each mattering equally, none having effect of any measure."

Tom scratched his chin and kicked at the floor with his boot.

"That's a fine speech, but pieces of it don't make much sense to me."

Soto smoked.

"Which pieces?"

"Well, you say men have choice and that they shouldn't care, because it goes against their individual interests."

"Yes."

"Alright. But then you say that men don't have a choice, because of their genetics."

Soto smiled and brought his hands together in a noiseless clap.

"Good. Yes, it is true. But a man is not a man. Though, they may look alike, they may as well be separate species within their own. Some propagate ancient genes, while others demonstrate the cellular mutations within their brains that make them better equipped for the modern world. You've seen it, I'm sure, in your vocation. The hunters and gatherers, fumbling at survival. And the others, equipped with an intelligence that allows them to escalate above the others into puppeteers. Infants on the playground, all resembling one another, but within their heads, maturing brains that will fracture them toward diverging destinies. Separate species within their own, though they will always appear of the same breed."

Tom looked off and shook his head slightly.

"So you're saying that you are the next level of evolution." Soto smirked and shook his head.

"I would not expect you to understand anything I've said."

He sucked the cigarette and hissed smoke through gritted teeth.

"You are a hunter and gatherer." He flicked his wrist. "This is why you live as you do."

The front door of the station opened, and Bud entered. Tom gave Soto a last look, and then he walked to the front door where Bud stood waiting. Tom looked the sheriff over as he approached. He looked wrecked from the night before, his unwashed uniform sagging loosely upon his aging flesh, giving him the appearance of someone grown thin from illness. He stood in the entryway and scanned the room. He pointed to Tom with his index finger and summoned him closer.

"I told you not to talk to those sons a bitches," he whispered.

"I haven't done much talking."

Bud put his hands on his hips and eyed the cell.

"Go outside."

Tom turned to look at Soto and Bud gripped his arm.

"Go outside. I'll take it from here."

Tom ripped loose.

"I'm staying."

Bud pulled his hat low and stepped forward.

"Boy, don't forget who you're talkin to."

The three men passed smiles within their cell.

Bud looked into Tom's eyes and drew his pistol.

"What are you doing, Bud."

"I told you to go outside."

He held the pistol against his hip and stared into Tom's eyes.

"Put your pistol away, Bud."

Bud's eyes watered. He tapped the gun against his hip.

"Bud, you're tired. You need to calm down and put your pistol away."

Bud raised the gun across his face and wiped his mouth with his sleeve.

"Go sit at the desk."

Tom raised his hands and took a few steps backward. Bud motioned him to the desk with the pistol.

"Go on."

He crossed the room and sat.

Bud approached, the pistol dangling at his thigh. An empty chair sat on the far side of the desk, and he took it in his unarmed hand. He looked at Tom with weary, given eyes, an apology somewhere within.

He turned to face Soto, busy sucking the last of his cigarette and impatiently bobbing his knee. Bud carried the chair and dropped it in front of the cell. He sat, the pistol draped across his inner thigh. Soto smoked.

"Do you see what's comin?" Bud asked.

Soto said nothing.

"Well, do you?"

Soto withdrew the cigarette from his mouth and exhaled.

"What is it you plan to do?" He smiled and his purple scar flushed white. "You know that you must release us. We own enough lawyers to put you in here if we desire. You have nothing to bargain with. You should be happy with what you still have."

Bud leaned over and spat on the floor.

"What do I have?"

"Your life, of course. You still have that don't you?"

Bud leaned forward and pressed his forearms against his thighs.

"Yeah. I still have that."

He leaned back in the chair and casually propped the butt of the gun on his lap, so the barrel aligned with Soto's gut. Soto's men swelled at the careless demonstration of disrespect toward their captain. They'd barely the discipline to see into his eyes for a single moment; yet this man dared to tease him like an impotent beast in a public zoo.

Bud tipped the pistol up slowly until the sight lined with the dimple in Soto's whiskered chin. Soto smiled and shook his head.

"I think I like you. You have a sense of humor."

Bud shook his head.

"You just don't get it, do you?"

Soto chuckled. He looked over his shoulders at each of his men and they flared open grins, as if threatened by a small boy with a corked toy rifle.

"What is it?" Soto asked. "What is it that I do not git." He pronounced the last word as an imbecile.

Bud stood from the chair slowly, his face as calm as unbroken water. He raised the pistol and leveled it at the bridge of Soto's nose.

Soto smiled and bent over. He crushed the cigarette against the floor. He looked up from his bent position, his pupil eyes, glossy as wet ink. He rose up again and squared his shoulders in offering.

Bud let the barrel of the gun dance for a moment, and then he lowered the pistol to his thigh. Tom relaxed in his chair, while Soto's mouth contorted into an amused curl.

Bud turned to face Tom. Their eyes locked for a moment, and then Bud looked down at the ground for what seemed like a long time. When he finally raised his head again, his teeth set clenched, and the muscles within his jaw undulated beneath the skin. His eyes drifted upward and then slipped back down. He turned to face Soto once more. He raised the pistol and approached the cell.

Soto sat, his legs crossed, his expression a fusion of amusement and contempt. He flicked his hand in dismissal.

"Don't be foolish and stupid."

Bud cocked the lever.

"Foolish and stupid was the ad I answered to get this job."

Wrinkles shot between Soto's eyes as he considered the meaning of the expression. But before he came to terms with it, Bud pulled the trigger, and the man's head bounced against the cement wall, its contents spilling backwards in a red pop of mist.

Tom stood without realizing it. He looked at Bud, still standing with his back turned. The sheriff stood oddly erect, his breathing calm, the pistol still addressing Soto's slack body, now laying limp and heavy against the taller man's leg.

The man bent and cradled his master like a bereaved mother. He lifted the head and looked at the face. Pallid and uninhabited, it seemed less a face and more a waxen falsity of silicone or latex. He looked at his partner, and the two men searched each other's faces for instruction; but it seemed the brains of the operation now filtered down the webbed patterns of texture within the painted cinder block wall.

Not knowing what else to do, the younger man vaulted forward and grasped the bars. He belched out a rage of curses and beat against the metal with his fists. Bud raised the pistol and emptied a round into his forehead, and the small, hard-looking body tightened and collapsed onto the hard epoxy.

The taller man dropped Soto's hollow head onto the cot and raised his hands.

"Please, no," he said, backing away.

Bud leveled the pistol.

"Stop, Bud," Tom yelled, his feet stowed in shock.

Bud pulled the trigger, and the bullet sailed through the man's gaped mouth and blew out the back of his skull. His knees buckled and his face crashed against the floor, red gelatinous fragments spattering in all directions, like a pie dropped upside down.

Tom stood facing the splay of leaking flesh. Bud faced the bloody men; his pistol hung loosely at his side.

"Put the gun away, Bud."

The sheriff turned suddenly, as if he'd forgotten he wasn't alone.

"For God's sake, Bud."

Bud swallowed, his face appearing ghoulish and strung out. Tom put his hands out to his side. Bud turned and looked back into the cell, and then he holstered the gun and approached the front of the desk. He moved toward the drawers, and Tom stepped aside to give him space.

"What in the hell have you done, Bud?"

Bud opened the top drawer and collected a ring of keys.

"It's what needed to be done."

Tom walked over to the cell and looked inside. Soto lay hunched on his side, his legs dangling over the edge of the cot. The scar on his face flushed white, but it wasn't because he was smiling.

Tom put his hands on top of his head.

"What in the hell have you done, Bud? I can't believe what you've done."

Bud took the keys and went down the hall. He flipped through the collection until he found the one to the storage closet. He inserted it and opened the door. He walked past the toilet paper and the linens and gathered boxes of trash bags in his arms. He walked out into the room and dumped them in the middle of the floor.

"Lock the front door and pull all the shades," he said.

Tom looked to the door and then back at Bud.

"What the hell are we going to do now, Bud?"

Bud stopped and pointed to the door.

"Lock the fuckin door and pull the goddamn shades."

Tom looked into the cell once more. Then he turned and walked to the door. He glanced out the window, the parking lot as empty as he'd ever seen it. He turned over the locks and pulled the shade, and then he went around the rest of the building doing the same. Once finished, he went back to the office and saw Bud in the cell with the bodies.

"What the hell are you doing, Bud?"

Bud hunched over the smaller man's body, a hacksaw in his hand. He pointed to the ground at Tom's feet.

"Put them gloves on and get in here."

Tom stepped back.

"I'm not having any part of this, Bud. This is insane. You've gone insane."

Bud shook his head and spat on the floor near one of the bodies.

"You just don't get it, do you? These motherfuckers was gonna kill you and me both. Gonna kill Ellie, probly."

Tom watched him.

"How do you know that, Bud?"

Bud turned and faced him.

"Where the fuck do you think everone is, Tom?" He walked out of the cell, the hacksaw firm within his right hand. "For Christ's sake. They're all dead, Tom. All of em. Ever last one of em, cept you and me. Edgar, Seth, Levi. All of em. Dead as hell."

Tom swallowed.

"How do you know?"

Bud turned his palms over at his sides, as if in amazement.

"How do you not?"

Tom raised his hat and wiped his forehead.

"What did you find at Levi's, Bud?"

Bud turned his head for a moment and swallowed.

"Blood. Okay, Tom? At's what I found. Lots a blood." He pushed his fingers against the right side of his head and his chin tightened. "Blood everwhere. Furniture turned over. Shit broken up. All to make it look like a robbery, I suppose." He turned to Tom. "What do you believe? At somebody broke into Levi's home to steal things he didn't even have? At Edgar and Seth are lyin on lawn chairs in Mexico sharin a margarita?"

Tom didn't say anything.

"Look, Tom. I know this ain't where you want to be, right now. But you need to put them gloves on and get in here." He spoke softly. "Help me put this thing to bed once and for all."

Bud seemed practiced at efficient mutilation. He used the hacksaw to break tendons only, his pocket knife for the rest. He dragged the blade at precise angles along the most tender portions of meat, severing around the shoulders and groin as if field dressing a deer. After a while, he noticed the sour look on Tom's face.

"I used to butcher livestock when I was younger."

Tom turned and walked out of the cell.

Each victim had evacuated his bowels, and the smell of warming guts and excrement steamed within the office. He stripped off the latex gloves and tossed them back into the cell. Bud looked over his shoulder and then sunk back into the ghoulish enterprise.

Tom walked to the front door and raised the shades. The parking lot showed no visitors. He opened the door and went outside. He walked out into the graveled parking area and kicked at the loose rocks. The careless afternoon sun bore against his skin and the earth, and all life was silent against it, save for the locusts who lay upon the tree bark, creaking. The wind stirred a puff of coiling dust that went rolling across the lot and pecked against the police cruisers.

Tom pushed his hand into his pocket and felt his keys. He looked over his shoulder at the entrance to the station and then to his Buick. He walked to the car and unlocked the door. He looked back at the entrance, and then he opened the door and got in. He shut the door and slid the key into the ignition. He turned it over and the engine fluttered and quit. He turned the key, again, but the car would not start. He pushed his hat back and mopped the sweat from his forehead with a bloody sleeve. He looked up and closed his eyes, but when he opened them, the world looked the same.

He pulled the key and leaned back in his seat. He rubbed the back of his neck and wept. After a while, he pinched the bridge of his nose with his thumb and forefinger until he saw stars. He slammed his fist against the steering wheel until the skin gave way to blood, and then he stepped out of the car and closed the door. He studied his face in the reflecting glass, the skin red, eyes swollen. He rubbed them with his sleeve and breathed deeply. He blew his nose into his shirt and spat on the ground, and then he turned to the station and walked toward the door.

Inside, things had really come together. In one corner, he saw six handless arms lined at the elbows, each sloppy with blood smear. The legs sat nearby, every one folded at the knees and wrapped in layers of duct tape, calves pressed tightly against the hamstrings, the hair matted with dried fluid. Bud stood against one of the cell walls, finishing a cigarette. His posture seemed that of someone who'd worked an ordinary task, and he seemed to regard the flesh piles like nothing more than bundles of wood.

Tom lifted his hat and bent over.

"Christ."

Bud took a final drag and then flicked the cigarette to the middle of the floor.

"We're almost done. But I gotta have yer help with somethin and it's important."

He pointed to the limbless torsos, still donning heads.

"We gotta get them teeth."

Tom put his hat on and ran the heels of his hands hard across his temples. Bud bent over and raised a 5-gallon bucket.

"Fill this halfway with water."

Tom took the bucket and stood.

"Let's go," Bud said. "The sooner the quicker."

Tom turned and walked down the hallway to the utility closet. He stepped into the small room and looked around: a sink jutted from the wall, a hose affixed to the tap. He dropped the nozzle into the bucket and turned the handle. When he returned, Bud already had his vice grips tightened around one of Soto's molars. He looked over his shoulder.

"Come on."

Tom went inside the cell and set the bucket next to Bud.

"Sit down on the floor and hold his forehead."

Entranced by prudence, he followed Bud's instructions and squatted down. He straddled Soto's torso, folded his fingers around the head and pulled until the neck was taut. Soto's head fell back into his lap and the greasy hair slapped against his pants. He looked down at the inverted face, eyebrows bowed and tongue lolling. A milky glaze had crawled over his eyeballs: once coring and black as bottomless cavities, now soulless and rubbery like overcooked hardboiled egg. He looked into them, searching for the unfathomable presence from before. But whatever used to live beneath had long escaped or dispersed, leaving only bones, organs and meat. Elemental nutrients for lesser beings.

"Hold him good, now."

His fingertips pinched and pulled to counter Bud's jerking. His fingernails stretched against the latex gloves and sunk into the temples. Bud rocked each tooth loose and dropped them all into the bucket. When the vice grips grew slick, he dipped them into the murky water and wiped them against his shirt.

When they'd finished with the lot, Bud gathered up all the hands and put them into the bucket with the teeth. Then he set a lid on top and stomped it tight with his boot. They put the limbs in trash bags and hoisted the torsos into bags of their own. They spread plastic coverings over the floor outside the cell and set the bags on top. Then they hosed the fluids down the cell drain and scrubbed stubborn bits of flesh with a coarse brush. When they'd finished, the only stains that remained were those from past inmates. The water pooled around the drain as it slowly sucked juices through strings of hair and clotted flesh.

"I'll snake the drain later," Bud said.

They each stripped nude and placed their clothing in another plastic bag. Then they used the shower in the back and put on new uniforms. Bud chose an identical copy from a closet, but Tom had to settle for one of Seth's.

By the time they'd loaded every bag into the cruiser, the sun burned red in its descent. They drove a short distance from the station and took a dirt road that led to an old isolated farmhouse away from passersby. Bud stopped the cruiser behind the crumbling structure. He put the car in park and leaned back. He lit a cigarette and pointed to the glove box.

"Open that up."

Tom thumbed the latch. A full pint of scotch sat inside, and he removed it and passed it over. Bud worked the cap free and drank. He offered it to Tom who took it and did the same. The scotch gave back the broiling heat from the day, stinging his throat like a sour hot tea. They sat without speaking, each staring at the separate landscapes outside his open window. Finally, Bud spoke.

"I'm sorry for this, Tom. Sorry for all of it." He smoked and exhaled out the window, the smoke looping into ringlets and then claimed by the wind. "I wish to God we ain't never done what we done. Wish I'd never come to you fellas with the notion. Wish ole Cesar hadn't ever come to me."

Tom opened the door and stepped out and Bud followed suit.

"It's not your fault, Bud." He leaned over and put his forearms on the hood. "I shouldn't have gotten involved. I don't have a soul to blame but myself. I would have walked away from it if me and Ellie hadn't been in the bind we're in. But that's no excuse, and I know it."

Bud nodded and put his thumbs in his pockets.

"Well, let's get on with it fore it gets too late."

They left the bucket and the soiled uniforms in the trunk and tossed the rest in some tall grass behind the farmhouse standing just inside the thickening woods. The bags lay stretched over a fallen tree branch, and one of the tines had bored through the plastic enough to reveal a blood-caked shoulder.

Each man stood within the swelling cricket noise gazing at the black bags, the sun slipping away, the tree bark refracting orange. Bud turned and walked back to the cruiser, but Tom stayed a moment longer. The coyotes would be along soon enough. They'd tear through the plastic and take the remains down to bone. Someone would find something at some point, but there wouldn't be any way to identify the bodies. A line in the paper is all it would be.

He looked up into tree tops at the leaves flipping in the wind. Life gathered at the fringes of the coming darkness, and he could hear a thin orchestra of bird calls and animal chatter. A hint of autumn danced in the air. It was going to be a beautiful night.

Full on darkness closed upon them as they returned to the station. Some cleaning remained, and a bullet had sifted through one of the victims and bitten into the wall.

"You go on home, now," Bud said. "I'll take care of everthing else."

"What are you going to do?"

"I'm gonna spackle that hole and touch it up with the paint from the utility closet." He was smoking, again.

"What about the stuff in the trunk?"

"Don't worry about it. This ain't my first rodeo. Now, you go on home. I'll run the nightshift til we get somebody else hired on. I need to get me some new deputies."

He walked to the door and stopped. He looked over his shoulder at Bud, sat propped against the desk.

"What about the money?"

Bud sucked his teeth and spat directly onto the floor.

"What about it?"

"Well--"

"At's yer money. I don't want none of it."

Tom tapped the door knob with his fingertips.

"Thing is, I'm not sure I do either."

Bud nodded.

"Well, I ain't sure we've heard the end of all this, so yer problem might get solved on its own. You go on, now."

He walked outside and stopped. He closed his eyes and pinched the bridge of his nose. When he walked back in, Bud was as before.

"I'm going to need to take the other cruiser."

Bud leaned backward a ways and gathered the keys. He pitched them to Tom.

"Be in real early tomorrow," he said. "I'll need some sleep at some point."

Tom walked out into the dark lot and stepped across the gravel toward the cruiser. He opened the door and sat inside and plugged the key into the ignition. He took the highway home, the black road sailing toward him like an inevitable truth. He tried the radio, but nothing seemed to fit. He hadn't eaten in hours, but his stomach sent no messages to prove it. He took a moment to acknowledge Soto's death, but if there was a reason for relief, he didn't feel it in his heart.

He took off his hat and set it in the seat beside him. He lowered the window and let the cool evening wind sift through his sweaty hair, the air smelling of wild flowers and cut grass. He closed his eyes briefly and saw Soto's mask of a face. He considered the words the man had said before vengeance swept so quickly and directly upon them all. He thought there had been a coarse accuracy in those words, however insane the speaker. He really was just a hunter and a gatherer of sorts, simple in his ways and bereft of whatever it was that made the great, great and the fortunate, fortunate. He'd known it for a long while, and it didn't surprise him that others saw this lack.

    In the end, there was Ellie. And if he had her, nothing else mattered. He'd surrendered to the world long ago, voiding his desires and his ambitions as expense to her illness. If he could touch her flesh and taste her lips, then the world could spin freely, or according to man's whims or some other being's, or could stop altogether and leave all else to hell. If he had her, he would be subdued and leave the world to the ones who wanted it, gone freely to his destiny, inconsequential to all save her. He breeched a hill and saw the moon ascend and flare white. Then he exited the highway and made his way home.

CHAPTER 15

Lino stopped the van in the wide, barren parking lot and shut the engine down. He grasped the door handle and pulled, but before he could exit, the behemoth took his arm. He looked at Reneau, slumped forward within his seat to accommodate his enormous head, his hands signing hunger across his chest, a pathetic look upon his childlike face. Lino jerked free, and a warm rush of blood returned to his fingertips. He shook his head, stepped out of the van and made his way toward the service station.

Inside, the cashier sat on a stool behind the register focused entirely on the newspaper in his hands, oblivious to the world's realities save for that scribed in print. He said hello without looking up, and Lino made his way to the cooler and took an armful of chilled ham and cheese sandwiches. He shut the door and moved down the aisle. He took two gallons of milk from another cooler and carried everything to the front. When he set the items on the counter, the cashier folded down the top corner of his newspaper and looked over his reading glasses. When he saw what he saw, he swallowed and stood.

"There be anythin else?"

Lino reached inside his pocket and fished around. The old man cleared his throat and looked outside at the van. He scanned the desolation: it sprawled outward against every horizon, a vastness of dry powdered earth and rock that rambled on, like some in-between place - a buffer between fertile worlds.

Lino passed a ten dollar bill over and asked for quarters. The cashier nodded. He drew the milk and sandwiches closer and scanned the labels with a pricing gun. When the total came up, Lino reached inside his pocket and produced a hundred dollar bill. He placed it flat against the counter. The cashier took it, bowing slightly like a beggar in receipt of some charitable pittance. He broke open the register and made change. Then he removed a roll of quarters and set it upright.

Lino ran his fingers in a circular motion above the sandwiches and asked for a bag. The cashier nodded and bent down.

When he stood up, the Mexican remained as before. The cashier scooped everything into a plastic sack and handed it over. Lino took the bag and the quarters and went outside.

He walked across the parking lot and opened the driver's door and pitched the bag into Reneau's lap. He set the two gallons of milk in the open seat and stood watching as Reneau tore open a sandwich and consumed it in two easy bites. The giant took a gallon of milk and flipped open the lid without breaking the seal. He lifted it to his dark fleshy lips and drank, his immense throat lifting and buckling with each vulgar swallow. He pulled the jug away, its contents diminished by half, the remaining milk sloshing about, no longer plain white but polluted with bits of bread and cheese.

Lino looked at the ground and shook his head. When he looked up, he saw Reneau staring at him quizzically, his head half-cocked very much like a flummoxed dog. A solid white string of mayonnaise and drool slung low from one corner of his mouth. Lino motioned at it with his finger, and Reneau drew up his arm to smear it away. Lino leaned over and spat. He took the other gallon of milk from the seat and shut the door. He set it on the ground and pushed it beneath the van out of the sun. He turned back toward the station, but the closed sign dangled freshly inside the window glass. He bent to see through the sun glare refracting against the glass, but the old cashier wasn't visible.

He turned toward the van and looked inside at Reneau, busy feeding upon a second sandwich. He turned back toward the station and approached the pay phone on the side of the building. Once there, he tore open the roll of quarters and loaded the slot. He dug out a strip of paper from inside his black denim jacket and entered the numbers. The pay phone accepted the information and offered a connection, but the line pulsed without end just as it had throughout the previous weeks. He hung up the receiver and put the paper and quarter roll back inside his pocket. He walked back to the van and opened the door. He bent for the milk and set it in the backseat. He sat inside and stared forward, his thumbs tapping the steering wheel in rhythmic knocks, thoughts at war within his head.

Reneau gathered the fabric atop Lino's shoulder and shook him for attention. Lino ripped free, his perfect teeth flashing even, dark eyebrows low. The great simpleton signed frantically with indecipherable gestures, and Lino scanned the floorboard and took the empty plastic gallon. The giant man raised his filthy palms into the air and scrunched backward against the door. Lino rose up in his seat and beat the jug against the imbecile's shaved head until the cap popped off and the plastic caved in. He threw the jug down and sat back in his seat.

    Reneau dabbed the fresh cut on his upper lip with a waxy sandwich wrapper, and the blood gathered and dripped onto his lap. Lino stared forward for a long time, his fingers drumming on the steering wheel as before. He looked over to the service station and caught a glimpse of the old cashier peering out from within. He leaned out the window and spat onto the gravel. Then he started the van and pulled out onto the highway.

    Inside, the cashier sat crouched behind a cooler with a shotgun on his lap. He followed the van across each window of the service station until it drifted over the horizon and vanished entirely. He swallowed hard and went back to the counter. He set the gun across the glass and took a pack of cigarettes from the shelf. He tore it open and fished one out. He held it in his hand and stared at it for several minutes before finally tossing it in the trash along with the spoiled package. He put his shaking palms on the counter and bowed his head. Outside, the wind wheezed and cried, as it slurred against the sharp angles of the structure. The old man gazed through the window watching the fine sand lift and turn in tight whirling cyclonic funnels, and it was a long while before he reopened the store.

CHAPTER 16

By the time Bud found his new deputies, the leaves hung bold red and the winds blew cold enough to warrant sleeves. He and Tom had served the county to the point of exhaustion, each alternating in shifts and neither seeing much sleep. The two newcomers were young and inexperienced, but they were bodies equipped with talking heads; and with most of the calls that came into the sheriff's station, this was qualification enough. When the new deputies grew adept enough to man the telephone and patrol, Bud gave Tom a week off, and then the following week, he did the same.

He spent the majority of his vacation drinking scotch and sleeping very little, and by the time it ended, he was much reduced. When he had slept, he dreamt as he always did of Anna at the park, her soft golden hair flipping slowly at close angles within his mind, the spring sun, radiant and flickering between each strand. Her smile, an awful gift. Her eyes, alive and coring. Her diminutive laugh, indisputable proof of God or something similar: something eternal and kind.

He dreamt up makeshift summer evenings comprised of composites, serene and uncertain, crushing and kind. The dreaming coaxed long dead regions of his heart to life, drawing a joy, raw and bold, leaving him exposed when day broke and his eyes opened to see the light from the pale dawn stretch its awful fingers across the walls of his bedroom, assuring the falsity of the dream, putting out the little life he'd resuscitated within his slumbering mind.

On the last evening, he sat on the carpet at the foot of his bed and put the barrel of his pistol inside his mouth. He curled his fingers around the trigger, but the metal tripped his urge to vomit, and he passed out in a pool of emission, dropping the gun and plummeting into a dreamless sleep.

The next morning, he awoke very early and very hung-over. He crawled onto the bed and fell back asleep, but the alarm wailed moments later, and he opened his eyes for good. He flipped his legs over the edge of the bed and sat with his hands over his face, a raw ache clawing the back of his eyeballs like a desperate something that wanted out. He sat there for a long time listening to the crickets call to one another outside the window in that stark chilly morning that waited patiently outside. He rubbed his eyelids and stood. He stayed to his feet for a few moments, and then he sat again and bowed his head. Tears slipped down his nose and dropped onto the carpet, where they disappeared into the dark fibers, like sustenance to a barren soil. He cried in the darkness over the events of his life: the grievous and the sour, the theft of joy, the taking. And yet he knew the world remained unmoved, its essence: spiritless, invested in nothing and partial to none.

After a while, he got up and went to the bathroom. He vomited into the toilet, until his stomach felt it would rupture. And then he crawled into the shower and lie in the tub while the warm water drizzled over his skin like a cleansing rain. After a while he stood and washed, and when he was finished, he felt well enough to shave and dress, and then he was in the cruiser driving a familiar route toward a life devalued from goodish to sufferable to no kind of life at all.

He stopped at a service station and went inside. He tipped his hat to the pimple-faced boy at the register, and then he filled a Styrofoam cup with black coffee. He set the lid on top and rubbed his thumb around the seal. Then he took it to the front and set it on the counter.

"Ole Fred around?"

The boy had a pierced nose, and his fingernails were painted black. He pinched his eyebrows together and looked up, his slick, wet mouth agape.

"Who?"

Bud laid a five-dollar bill on the counter.

"Never mind."

The boy made change, and Bud walked outside toward the cruiser.

When he rolled into the station parking lot, Emmitt's car was absent. He opened the door and went inside.

"Where the hell's Emmitt?"

Kyle sat slouched over the desk, a cup of coffee in one hand, a live cigarette in the other.

"That's what the hell I'd like to know. He's supposed to have been here over an hour ago, and I'm runnin on nuthin but smokes and hate."

Bud approached and set his keys on the desk.

"That dumb sumbitch is fired, he ain't here in the next ten minutes."

He went into the back to use the bathroom. He stood before the only urinal and looked down into filthy reservoir as he did his business. It was plain to see that neither of the new deputies had been schooled in proper work. He finished up and washed his hands. He flicked the water from his fingers and looked at the man in the mirror, fast becoming a more authentic representation of the one beneath the skin.

Just as he came back out, the young deputy walked through the door.

"Where the fuck have you been?"

Emmitt pressed his palms forward against the air.

"I know it. I know it. I'm sorry as all hell. It will not happen, again."

Bud looked over his shoulder at Kyle.

"You get on outta here and go get some goddamn sleep."

Kyle looked at Emmitt, and then he got up and walked out of the room with his head down. Bud sat on the corner of the desk and addressed the other young deputy.

"Listen up boy. You got but one more chance with me. You understand?"

Emmitt nodded.

"Now go on over and finish up yer paperwork or whatever else you been procrastinatin on. I gotta go check on some matters of my own."

He stood up and tipped his head and straightened his hat. Emmitt sat at the desk and looked up, his face like a child.

"If Tom calls, you tell him to make his rounds and then meet me here this evenin, less somethin else comes up."

Emmitt nodded, and Bud walked out the door.

By the time Bud got out to Beaux Shipley's place, his mind was impaired by fatigue not by the events of the day, but by the lack thereof. He'd passed several acres of Beaux's land on the way in, and throughout one of the pastures, he'd seen a dog racing free through the flailing hairs of grass. He slowed the cruiser and pulled over to watch it run. Its front legs hung shorter than its rear ones, and it scooted awkwardly between the threads of pale yellow grass, like some miscreation fruited in a lab. The dog's coat showed traces of mange, and its tongue lolled wildly as it darted within the cattle, until they were disunited, each skipping frantically from the intrusion.

He tapped his steering wheel and watched. He thought that years ago, he might have taken his gun and picked the stray off on his own, presented it to Beaux at his door. But he didn't feel the inclination now, and as he drove on, he judged his younger self for ever seeking such mediocre glories.

He saw the lone mailbox on the side of the road at the top of the hill, and he steered the cruiser off the street and down the manicured gravel path snaking its way toward Beaux's three-story home. He parked behind one of Beaux's pickups and looked over the property. The manicured lawn was shaved low as a golf course fairway, and the wooden boxes beneath the windows were congested with red geraniums. He lost himself for a moment watching their lobed petals flip in the wind like tiny velvet flags, and then he snapped back into reality and rubbed his eyes.

He killed the engine and stepped out of the car. He walked the fieldstone path up to the whitewashed porch and scaled the steps and rapped at the front door. He waited with his thumbs in his back pocket until Helen greeted him.

"How do, Sheriff?"

"I'm doin just fine, Helen. How bout you?"

"Oh, we're gettin on fine, cept for the creaks in our bones."

"I hear you on that one. Beaux around?"

"He's in the day room watchin the television. Do you want somethin to drink? I can get you some lemonade from the kitchen."

"I'd be much obliged if you do."

"You go on in, and I'll bring it to you."

He walked the maple floor down the running hallway that sprouted into variant rooms of bed and leisure and into the generous entertainment area, where Beaux sat reclined in a leather chair watching investment chatter on cable television.

When Bud entered the room, the old man dug his heels into the foot incline and started to stand.

"At's alright." Bud raised his hand. "I don't wanna disturb you."

"I was wonderin when you was gonna find yer way out here, again."

Beaux leaned forward, and they shook hands.

"Things have been a little hectic lately."

Beaux sat back and raised the remote control.

"That right?" He killed the television volume. "How so?"

Bud pushed the thought away with his palms.

"Ain't nuthin of interest, I assure you."

Beaux shrugged and sat back.

"You want somethin to drink? Helen's got some lemonade in there."

Bud sat on the couch.

"Already offered and accepted."

They sat for a moment watching the mute faces prattle within the television glass.

"I seen a dog in yer pastures on the way in."

Beaux nodded silently.

"Mangy lookin motherfucker. I thought about takin a shot at him, but I figured I'd stay out of it. Let you handle it in yer own way. Whatever that be."

Helen entered the room with a silver tray of juice glasses and a pitcher of lemonade. Bud rose half-way as she entered.

"I thank ya, ma'am."

"Well, you're certainly welcome."

She set the tray on the coffee table and stood up. She dusted her sides and looked at the two men.

"Well, unless you fellas need anything else, I'm headed out back to do some cleanin."

Beaux nodded, and she turned to go.

They sat for a while longer, and then Bud got up and filled the glasses. He handed one to Beaux and sat back down.

"Yeah, them fuckin dogs," Beaux said as he sipped his glass. "I seen him, too. Ain't but one of em. But if there's one, there's more."

"Maybe it's just one stray."

Beaux shook his head.

"I seen it before. One shows up and then there's more. They get to runnin the cows and fore you know it, they got all their legs broke."

Bud raised his glass and took a sip. The lemonade was grainy with sugar and ungodly sweet. He withdrew the glass and bit his lip.

"Well, just so long as you don't use no poison."

Beaux raised his hand and pushed the thought away.

"I mean it, Beaux. I don't wanna be hearin at there's poison been found anywhere near here."

"Well, I can't make no such promise. But I can tell you if you do, it won't be none of my doin."

He took a big swallow from his glass and set it down next to the coaster.

"I'll just plug em with my rifle. Each and everone of em til they's gone. At's the way you gotta do it."

Bud took a cigarette from the pack in his shirt pocket.

"I don't wanna hear no more about it. You just do what you gotta do and don't tell me nuthin more."

Beaux looked over his shoulder into the kitchen.

"We better go on out to the yard if yer gonna light that thing. Helen'll flip her lid, she smells that burnin in the house."

Outside, the sun gave the last of what it had, and they lowered their sleeves against the cooling air. Beaux led the way across the yard, and they made a path over an agreeable slope of yellow grass, the wind hissing as it sifted through the dry blades. When they got to the pastures, they stopped at the fence and threw their arms over. They rested forward on their forearms and watched the cattle graze, while the failing sun burned bold in its descent. Bud tipped his hat back and spat.

"I tell you something, Beaux, if you'll allow it."

"Let me hear it."

"I think I'm bout done in this business."

Beaux nodded as if he wasn't surprised.

"Any particular reason, or is it just the entirety of it all?"

"Well, the entirety of it all has got a whole helluva lot to do with it, don't get me wrong. But at ain't the sellin point."

Beaux leaned over to see the back end of a member of the herd.

"Well then, what is the thing?"

Bud looked off to his right.

"Oh, I'd have to say it's the drugs, I guess. All the drugs and the business surroundin it. All the things it makes you do and all the things it makes you not do. Speakin for this line of work, that is."

Beaux nodded.

"I think I understand what yer sayin."

Bud raised his chin. He spat over the fence and pulled his hat down low.

"I ain't got no apologies in me, Beaux. I always done what I had to do to make my way through. What I knew was best. You can enforce the law as best you can. You can try to do what's right. But this place ain't Hollywood, and I ain't no John Wayne. I knew when I come down here I'd have to make allowances for the cartels. Knew I'd have to turn the other way from time to time. I knew I'd have to do it, or they'd make it their position to put a slug in me and replace me with somebody at would."

Beaux waited for more, but nothing came.

"Well, you ain't gotta explain nuthin to nobody but yerself and the Lord."

Bud nodded.

"Most people wouldn't understand. These people got more money than the Lord, hisself, and more firepower than some countries. They got everone in their back pocket. You stand up to em, you'll damn sure get cut down. And they do it in a way at tells the world they better stay down or else."

Beaux scratched his chin.

"Why you tellin me this, Bud?"

"I don't know. I honestly don't." He looked at Beaux and smiled. "Maybe it's an ill-conceived confession." He pulled from his cigarette and blew the smoke into the fresh autumn air. "I'll tell ya the truth. The further on I get, the more I start to agree with them old-timers at say Mexicans bring nuthin but ruin to this country."

Beaux looked back at the house and then made a quick gesture toward the cigarette in Bud's hand. Bud handed it over, and

Beaux took it. He passed another glance toward the house and then took a long drag. He cocked his chin up and let the smoke seep from his lungs. Then he gave it back.

"Lemme tell you a story, if you'll have it."

Bud nodded and laid his left hand out.

"Years ago, fore you come around, I use to have me a hand out here. A real goodun. Back in them days, I used have a lotta hands. Back when things was better, and when I had the energy to push toward better. Fore I got old and fore Helen got to questionin the rewards versus the expense."

He put his right hand on his hip and glanced over his shoulder at the house.

"Women ain't no better at their own lives than men are," he said. "but they gotta helluva knack for auditin others. And she was right on with me. I sat about and thought on what she said. Thought about my age and about my reasons. And then I got up one mornin and decided to sell most the stock and just cut all the help loose." He slid his hand flat across the air. "Just made up my mind to quit fightin and move on with bein old. Just accept it. We had the money, so I done let it all go."

He took hold of a fence post and pushed against it. It wobbled a little in the ground and he cussed it. Then he let it go and they walked the fence line.

"Anyways, back then, when things was bigger, I had me some hands and they was easy to find, but it was hard to find any at knew what the hell they was doin. I'd run off ten to find one. Got to the point where I'd put em through little tests fore I'd hire em on, cause most of em would lie bout what they knew just outta straight desperation for work. I'd run em through tests and look for the tells, and if I didn't like what I saw, I'd send em on.

"Anyways, I had me a hand back then I'd put up against anybody from anywhere. He was a young Mexican feller, come over the border for work, and I knew he was an illegal, but I hired him on anyways. I didn't expect too much from him, but he proved hisself right away. At ole boy'd do bout anythin you'd tell em, and he'd do it bettern anyone else could. He had that desperation in his soul, I think used to be common in this country back in the old days, but ain't no more. Fear is a great motivator, and I think it was his fear what pushed him to be what he was, and I ain't ashamed to say he was a helluva young man. Helen knew it, too. She could tell it, and she used to invite him up for supper sometimes, and I was dead set against it, but after a while, he sorta won me over, and he woulda won you or anybody else over, too, if you had ever had the privilege to meet him."

He stopped and looked to the heavens, his eyes asquint, like he'd forgotten something important. Bud took a puff of his cigarette and waited.

"Anyways, I guess what I'm sayin is I thought highly of the boy, and me and Helen got to sorta thinkin of him like the son we never had. We bought him some new clothes and a new saddle for his own. He wouldn't hardly take none of it. I had to kindly force it on him. I finally throwed it all down on the floor of the barn and walked out. In my day, when somebody give you somethin, you'd say no a couple times, outta respect. But after that, you keep sayin no, it gets disrespectful. But that weren't his way. He was just a good ole boy. At's all there was to it.

"I talked to some people I knew about gettin him some papers, but before I could get the ball rollin, he come up and quit. Just straight quit. I knew there was somethin wrong, cause he wouldn't hardly look me in the eye when he said it. Had his hat in his hand and was just studyin the dust on the floor. I asked him if he was in trouble, but he said no, and at's the only thing I asked him, cause I figure a man's gotta right to do what he wants even if ain't nobody else understands it.

"So, this boy went off to someplace of his own choosin, and we didn't hear nuthin from him for a few weeks. Then we started getting letters from him, tellin us about how well he was doin, how much he appreciated everthing we done for him. Then money started showin up in the envelopes along with the letters. He paid ever last dollar back for everthing we bought him. Helen's still got all them dollar notes in an envelope somewheres inside the house. She planned to give it back to him the day we seen him again, which she was sure would come. Only it didn't. Instead, we got a stranger at the door one Sunday, another Mexican feller with his hat in his hand. He told us at he worked with Miguel, at was his name, in an old abandoned chicken house, other side of the border. They was cookin up methamphetamines fer one of the cartels. They'd come and recruit all the cowboys and laborers. All the illegals. Pay em more in a day than they'd make in three months workin in the honest world, and I mean them figures to be literal."

He called for Bud's cigarette again, and when he tried to give it back, Bud gestured for him to keep it.

"Anyways, I guess ole Miguel had been hearin the siren call from all his Mexican friends for a while. Bout how they was makin good money to send back to their families and whatnot. He kept to his intentions for a long time fore he finally give in. I give the boy credit for it."

He smoked from his cigarette and ashed against the top of the fence post.

"I ain't sayin I'd ever approve of him gettin involved in that poison at's sweepin down on everbody. But when you do the math, you cain't but understand his reasons. It didn't just make for a better life, it made for one atall."

A hair hung in the barbed wire, where a deer had ducked underneath, and he pulled at it as he spoke.

"Anyways, this ole boy at came to our door on that day told us Miguel was workin one afternoon cookin that shit up, when somebody dropped a glass container and let all them chemicals mix up and poison the air. Most of the other workers got out fore things got too bad, but Miguel caught too much of it, and he run outside and fell down, coughin blood into the dirt. The ole boy said they done what they could for him, but there weren't much to be done. Said Miguel told him once if anythin happened to call on us. I stood there and asked him what in the world for? Said he wasn't nuthin but a worker for me, and I had twenty more lined up behind him." He looked down at the ground. "At's what I said. I don't have no idea why I said that. I truly don't. But at's the damned truth of what I said, and it cain't be wished away."

He cleaned the last stiff bristles of hair from the fence, and then they walked on.

"Anyways, this ole boy kinda looked at me like I was a piece a shit, which I expect he was correct in his assessment at the time. He sorta shook his head real subtly, and then he give me an envelope and told me at Miguel said to give it to me and Helen if anythin ever happened to him. Well, I took it from his hand, and then I closed the door in that young man's face like he was trash. And I carried at letter to the kitchen sink and took out my lighter and burnt it up. I don't know why. I was angry with at boy for what he done. Not cause it was wrong, which I think it musta been. Not cause of that, but cause what he done kilt him. Hell, I was angry at myself for allowin myself to care bout him, which I did very much. We ain't never been able to have no children, and at boy was as close as we ever got.

The muscles in his jaw undulated, and his chin trembled so briefly, Bud wasn't sure if he'd actually seen it.

"Anyways, I stood there and watched that envelope burn, and then I felt some kinda overwhelmin panic, and I took my bare hand and started beatin the flame out. But by the time I got it snuffed, it was too late. I opened the envelope and took out what was in it. There was a good amount of money, but it was ruint. There was a letter, too, but it was too burnt up to read. To this day, I don't know what that young boy wanted to say to us. I dream about it, still. Cept in my dreams, the letter's all fixed."

Bud waited for more, but Beaux just stood silently, gazing off at the sunset, watching the colors drain from the horizon. They stood for a while longer, and then they walked the fence line back to the house. Bud went inside and said goodbye to Helen, and then he joined Beaux next to the cruiser.

"No offense, Beaux, but I been runnin that story you told me around in my head, and I still don't know why you shared it with me."

Beaux looked down at the ground and kicked the dirt.

"Oh, I reckon it just bothers me some when people get to pinnin blame when it comes to what's happen around here with the drugs and the crime."

Bud frowned and nodded his head. Beaux raised his hand and tilted his head.

"Don't get me wrong. I feel the impulse, same as everone else. But it just seems to me at if people want to swim in shit, there's always gonna be somebody ready to fill the pool. Don't make no sense to blame the suppliers when the demand is the thing. Maybe at's just my business sense talkin, I don't know. But you talk about gettin older, and I'll tell you what it's done to me. It's made me tired. And hatin takes a lot a energy outta ya. And I got to hold onto what little I got left."

Bud pursed his lips.

"Well, at's why I come out here. You got a way of settin things straight."

He opened the door to the cruiser and got inside. He reached his hand out the open window, and Beaux took it.

"You take care of yerself, Sheriff."

Bud nodded.

"You mind if I ask you one last question?"

Beaux nodded.

"You go right ahead."

"In yer dreams, what does the letter say?"

Beaux leaned over and spat.

"Well, I reckon it's different every time." He pressed his lips together and looked down. "But it ain't never the things I want."

Bud nodded and started the engine.

"It's funny, ain't it?" Bud said. "This life, it beats up on you and those you care about the whole way through, and if you let yerself want more than it's got to offer, yer shit outta luck. But in yer dreams, you could have it all. If you'd only let yerself. Only you cain't, or you won't for some reason." He offered a subtle smile. "Or if you can, you oughtta let me know the secret."

Beaux slapped his hand against the top of the cruiser.

"I ain't got none of the secrets, son. Ain't nobody else does neither."

They shook hands once more, and then Bud drove on.

CHAPTER 17

Tom sat across from Ellie at the 24-hour restaurant where she worked. The place had been dead for a while, but things were picking up. The fat, balding manager roosted behind the bar, eyeballing her from his post. He wore a sour look, but Tom knew he wouldn't say anything as long as she was sat with him.

"I need to get back," she said.

He reached out and put his hand over hers.

"Finish eating. They'll wait."

She stirred her salad and set her fork down.

"I'm really not that hungry."

He leaned back in the booth and took his hat off. He set it on the table and smoothed his black hair with the flat of his palm.

"I just want to sit across from you a little longer."

She looked up and ceded a smile. They sat a moment longer, while the cacophony of tinging dishes and silverware swelled around them.

"I have to get back to work, Tom."

He lowered his head and nodded.

"I know. Me too."

As they rose from the booth and headed toward the door, she turned back to the manager and raised her index finger. He shook his head and watched through the window glass as they crossed the dimly-lit asphalt parking lot toward Tom's cruiser.

Outside, they stood next to the car, his hands locked behind the small of her slight back, the side of her face pressed against his chest.

"I'll be quitting soon. It's only for a while longer, and then we'll go. I promise."

"Where are we going to go?" She asked.

He lifted away from her and looked into her eyes, set like beautiful jewels inside their sockets, soft but live.

"I don't know. Anywhere you want. We can do that now. We can go anywhere."

"Where do you want to go?" She asked.

He drew her chin upward with his fingertips.

"I want to go wherever you are."

She passed a glance over her shoulder at a mass of customers funneling into the front of the restaurant, like a sucking clot around a drain.

"I have to go." She drew back and lifted his hands to her mouth. She pressed her lips against the backs of each, and then she brought one to her cheek. "Please be careful. Be careful for me."

He pulled her delicate body closer and kissed her tender, fleshy lips, and then she turned and jogged across the pavement back toward the restaurant.

On the other side of the lot, a black van idled softly between a pair of foreign cars. Lino sat in the driver's seat, his arm draped outside the open window, a live cigar dangling from his thick fingertips. Reneau studied the girl from the passenger seat, his eyes bulging, lips wet with slobber and nasal mucous. Lino looked at the behemoth and easily noticed that he'd grown aroused.

"You like that one?"

Reneau nodded with earnest enthusiasm, as if the tiny woman were a treat he might be able to earn. Lino cocked his head and watched her as she scampered across the asphalt.

"Yes, I can see the appeal."

Reneau slammed the side of his fist against the vinyl dash, and it caved under the force.

Lino's face flashed hell. He raised his palm high into the air, and the simple brute crumpled into a flinching cower.

"Relax, you stupid idiot. I don't want that skinny whore."

Reneau rose and settled back into his custom built seat.

"You will have her when the time comes."

The behemoth's purple mouth enlarged into a wet, soppy grin, and his massive body rocked forward with excitement, forcing the entire van to teeter on its platform of squealing shocks.

CHAPTER 18

By the time Bud exited the highway, the harvest moon sat full bore in the starless sky. It floated above the Earth like something alien, large and peculiar, its solemn, pitted face gleaming orange. The night grew animate under the false luminescence, the birds chirping, the deer afoot in the pastures and glens. Bud leaned back in his seat and stretched his arm out into the cool wind. He let his hand swim in the washing air, and the spillover lapped his face, and the smell of autumn tipped his mind toward the long ago.

He didn't see another cruiser when he pulled into the parking lot, and he was glad for the chance to rid the station of Emmitt before Tom arrived.

When he entered the building, the boy's head slung upward from his folded arms. Bud shut the door and put his hands on his hips.

"Goddamit, son."

Emmitt wiped the slobber from his face and sat upright, his eyes spidered red, a paperclip embedded flat against the flesh of his forehead.

"I tell you what." Bud shook his head. "Goddamit."

"I'm sorry, Bud. I swear, I just musta dozed off. I been workin all night. Them phones ain't made a single peep."

Bud raised his hand.

"I don't wanna hear none of it." He shook his head." Boy, you mighta met plenty folks in this world at'd be more than happy to drink yer bath water, but I ain't one of em."

He walked across the room and set his keys on the desk. He raised his hand high, and Emmitt tucked back like he expected a blow, but Bud only extracted the paperclip from his skin and slapped it against the desk.

"You get the hell on outta here, and you don't come back til I call you if'n I ever do, which I may not."

Emmitt rose out of his chair and walked to the door. He took his hat from the coat rack and topped it over his long curly hair.

"I'm awful sorry, Bud."

"Just go on, son."

He pulled the hat down firm and walked out the door.

Bud sat at the desk and waited until Emmitt's car sprayed light on the window blinds. He waited for the engine growl and tapped his fingers until it grew faint. Then he took his hat off and set in on the desk. He opened the bottom drawer and removed a bottle of scotch. He poured some in a coffee cup and drank, and then he refilled it and drank some more. The sour taste rooted in his tongue, but after all the years of drinking, he hadn't really noticed. He leaned back in the chair and closed his eyes, while the sensation crawled over his body like a hundred warm fingertips.

He checked his watch and rubbed his chin, and then he rose from his chair and approached the empty cell. He put his hands on the bars and leaned his forehead against the cold metal. He closed his eyes and thought for a moment, and then he turned and went back to the desk and put his hat back on. He raised the coffee mug and took another sip, and then he set it back on the desk and raised the bottle to replace what he'd drank.

He stood watching the window, waiting for Tom's cruiser to pull in. But it never did, and after a while he walked to the front door and stepped outside. He stood on the concrete porch, sipping from the coffee mug, thinking. He thought about the past and the coming, of decisions, significant and less so, times he robbed Peter to pay Paul, and of Anna, always of Anna.

He finished the mug of scotch and let his eyelids drop. He stared into the fleshy black, his memories coloring in the void like projections on a video screen. And then all of it dispelled in an instant, like some substantial dream interrupted by a sudden rush of coarse reality.

He felt the cold circumference of the gun barrel press against his right temple hard like a bruise. He let the mug drop below his waist. At the same time, his other hand traced its way up his thigh, toward his holstered weapon. A low, slurry voice bid him still, and another hand unbuttoned his holster and extracted the revolver.

He opened his eyes and focused on the speaker, a short, stout Mexican, dressed in black denim, his lips ruined with scars. Beside him stood nothing less than a legitimate giant, the largest man Bud had ever seen, an abnormality.

They summoned him forward, down the concrete steps, his boots crushing the shifting gravel beneath. The giant passed Bud's pistol to the other, who stepped forward and flipped Bud's hat upward with the barrel.

"Put your hands behind your back," he said in clean English.

Bud did so, and the large man crossed his wrists and cuffed them with a plastic zip tie.

They led him across the parking lot and forced him inside the back of a dark van. They fastened a fabric ring around his eyes, and then the giant slid beside him, his great thigh pushing in, forging space.

They drove for a long time until they reached an old washed-out road. Bud felt the van slow and turn and jerk violently, as it negotiated the unbalanced terrain. He sat quietly as the vehicle squealed to a stop, and then he heard the door open and felt a set of massive fingers curl around his biceps.

The giant pulled him out into the cool evening and set him upright, and then the blindfold lifted, and Bud could see. He looked around and took an inventory. He saw dense woods and a crumbling gray shack perched atop a subtle hill. The swollen moon set the structure aglow as if through a pale blue lens, and it sat there, alone and dilapidated, pushed awkwardly aslant, its black windows giving it the appearance of a howling face.

The gargantuan maintained his grip on Bud's arm, starving it white with bloodlust. The smaller man stood before him with his arms crossed, a subtle grin trickling forth from within the furrow of his dark facial whiskers.

"Yer waistin yer time," Bud said. "Yer friend's already collected everthing I got."

Lino's grin broadened. He removed a small cigar from his black denim jacket and ran it under his nose.

"We shall see. We will know everything in time."

Bud raised his chin and gathered the scent from the cooling autumn air.

"It's a helluva night. I love this time of year."

Reneau looked upward and snorted. Lino shook his head and clucked his tongue against the roof of his mouth.

"You are a cool one. I will give you that. But you would not be so unbothered if you knew what lay before you."

He lifted the cigar to his lips and lit it, his eyes flaring incandescent beneath the bill of his black baseball cap.

Bud smiled.

"Son, I ain't unafraid." He pursed his lips and shook his head. "I'm just so fuckin tired."

Lino pinched his brows together, and then he looked over Bud's head at Reneau. He nodded once, and they led Bud inside the shack, where the sour boards stunk like rot, and the spiders curled into their nests and flinched at the noise, as the men tore the sheriff's flesh and cored into his body, until his blood spatters sopped the floor. And it was a long while coming before the soul within claimed its freedom.

The wind whipped sharply, twisting the leaves and sending them downward awaft in the rushing air like sinking vessels amidst a colorless ocean, and the ground grew dense with the dried leavings, and they crackled and disintegrated into articles of soil beneath the weight of Lino's heavy black boots.

He made his way to the van and sat on the rear bumper. He cupped his chin with his hand and tapped his wide stub of an index finger against his lips. Reneau emerged from the shack, his arms and hands a slick sanguine. He crossed the grass with great loping steps, his fingers signing frantically before he'd even entered Lino's view.

Lino removed a small cigar and lit it. He rested his back against the rear of the van, his head cocked upwards toward the glinting starlight, a seed of thought rooting within his mind. Reneau approached and stood before him, his vast chest heaving with a rage that looked somewhat ominous, somewhat reckless. His great hands delivered a clump of convoluted messages, but Lino's mind spun busily considering the sheriff's words.

Reneau stomped a hole into the earth and slapped his hands together, commanding Lino's attention. He begged questions with his fingers, his eyes bulging white. Lino casually raised his hand.

"Enough. I understand. What we must do now is finish with the remains." He pointed toward the shed. "Go. I'll follow shortly."

Reneau turned and sulked back toward the shack. He bent low and turned aslant as he entered the narrow passage way, his unreal form giving the battered structure the illusion of a child's backyard playhouse. Lino watched him disappear within, and then he finished his cigar.

Inside the shack, Reneau splashed the flashlight against the cement floor, searching for the sheriff's teeth and fingertips, collecting each in his giant palms and flinging all into a plastic 5-gallon bucket. He'd rounded up most when he captured a silhouette in the moonlit entryway. He rose upward, but before he'd ascended completely, an explosion nulled his hearing, and he felt acid in his nose.

He turned to see Lino in the doorway, his pistol drawn, a faint whip of smoke dancing upward from the barrel, like a formless demonic fairy. Reneau staggered forward, his face infested with confusion.

The bullet had caught the front of his profile, sheering his nose free. He plugged the dribbling hole with the palm of his hand, but the dark blood swelled in the seams between his fingers and seeped down his arm in wild, veiny patterns.

He gathered himself steady and swelled before Lino, his bulbous eyes poking forth, large as hardboiled eggs. He lowered his hand and spurts of mucous-thickened blood shot forth from the hollow in the middle of his face.

The giant stepped forward, and Lino fired again, this time into the thick of his gelatinous belly. The bullet scorched its way into the flesh and a circle of red manifested on his shirt and instantly swelled to the size of a dinner plate. Reneau surged forward, as if nothing had happened, but before he'd gotten within a few feet, a third round exploded, and this one cleaved his skull in two.

Lino lowered the pistol and watched as Reneau's great body slumped forward to its knees. It wavered for a moment in that position, its eyes cloudy and askew, and then the great torso dipped forward and smashed against the concrete floor, its head splitting into two equal-sized portions.

Lino turned and slipped out the door. He put the pistol in his belt and walked to the van. Once inside, he lit another cigar and sat for a while thinking cold thoughts. When he'd finished it to a nub, he flung it out the window and watched the ember die off in the numb soil. He started the ignition and drove the earthy path back toward the highway.

CHAPTER 19

The morning redness bled through the window shades like a seeping truth, and when Tom saw it, he knew Bud was dead. He'd spent the night waiting behind the desk at the station, rising occasionally to pace the floor and spy through the window glass at the barren gravel outside. He'd pressed his mind for an instance where Bud failed an appointment, but it was a futile endeavor. The man was gone, and any other explanation wouldn't do.

Kyle walked in at seven, and when he did, Tom told him to sit at the desk and wait.

"Don't leave here without calling me," he said. "Don't be where I can't get a hold of you."

He took the cruiser home, the sirens blaring, paving the way through the morning commute. He pushed up and through the tether of vehicles, driving them apart like a wheeled god amongst a mass of toys. He'd beat Ellie home by at least an hour if he kept his pace, and though the traffic before him swelled in the distance like a mechanized storm, he'd the will to pass through it slickly and unfettered and, what was more, the power to make it so. When things congested, he invaded the shoulder of the road and plowed over the jags of littered window glass that flickered against the pavement like fractured gems, and when things opened up, he swerved before the slog of shrinking vehicles and punched the gas so hard the tires skipped before finding their bite on the road.

He killed the sirens long before he pierced the neighborhood ingress, and once inside, he bee-lined toward his rented home. When he reached the front lawn, he slowed the cruiser and idled along the curbside, his eyes glassing the property for inaccuracies, anything and everything, neighboring houses withal. When he felt satisfied, he wormed the cruiser through the neighborhood streets, probing for foreign vehicles, things that didn't look quite right. But he didn't really recognize much of what he saw, and after a while, he judged the effort vain.

He settled the cruiser out front along the curb and stepped out. He walked up the driveway, dodging the oil blots left by the

Buick, each spat separately, but all bleeding together to form a whole of splatters, refracting the morning sun in a rainbow of gold, purple and orange, all bound together, like a giant Rorschach blob. He slipped his key into the deadbolt lock and unhooked it with a twist, and once inside, he set everything back.

At once, he noticed the smell of stale cigar tobacco in the air, and then he saw the Mexican propped upon a chair, strategically placed in the center of the living room floor. The man held a pistol in his hand, and he used it to advise Tom away from the door.

"This place is more a shit hole than I expected," Lino said. "I'm taking it you haven't spent much of your earnings." He said the last word as if it tasted like ash.

Tom faced the man, his hand hovering above the gun in his holster.

"Put your palms on your chest," Lino said. "Very good, now slide them down your stomach and unfasten your belt and pull the end with the buckle until your pistol falls."

Tom did so, and the holstered weapon dropped against the floor. Lino pointed the pistol at the living room sofa.

"Take a seat."

Tom remained where he was.

"Where's Bud?"

"The sheriff man?" Lino turned his head to the side and sucked his teeth. "I'm certain he will show up at some point."

Tom stepped forward.

"Did you kill him?"

Lino thought for a moment.

"No. Not me personally. I think it was the bleeding. So much of it."

Tom removed his hat and wiped his hand across his forehead. "Why?"

Lino filled his lungs with breath and exhaled slowly.

"What is it with you people?" He waved the gun in circular motions. "It's like you're ignorant or something. Like you live in the fairy tale land. Or what is it? I don't know. Why don't you explain it to me. What did you think would happen when you involved yourself in this? Eh? Please tell me? Did you think you were so smart? So cunning?" He rolled his eyes. "Please. Come now. You know why he is dead."

Tom put his hat back on and cupped his mouth with his hand. He glanced at Lino's pistol and then to the door.

"What are you doing?" Lino ticked his tongue against the roof of his mouth. "Do you think that is your way? Please. Come, now. Sit with me. It is time to talk. That is all. To talk." He pointed the pistol at the couch. "Sit with me, now. That's it. Just to talk. That is all."

Tom crossed the dining room floor and approached the couch. Lino held the gun loosely atop his thigh, the barrel aimed at nothing in particular. Tom eyed it for a moment, almost lunged for it, but instead he sat down on the couch, his knees towering comically as his buttocks sank deep into the cheap material.

"I bet you planned to buy a new sofa at some point," Lino said. "With all of the money, that is."

Tom's jaw flexed.

"And, what do you plan to do with it?"

"Me?" Lino looked toward the ceiling. "That is a good question. I suppose I had not thought about it very much. But I'll figure something out. Of that, I assure you."

Tom tapped his boot. Lino noticed and smiled.

"Are you so nervous? You, a law enforcement man? So nervous in such a situation. All of your training and experience results in this? Not something to be proud of, eh?"

Tom pushed his lower lip out and shook his head.

"To tell you the truth, I don't think I'm much cut out for it."

Lino nodded. He frowned deeply until the hair above his lip meshed with that below it into a single patch of black. "Unfortunately, you recognize it too late, I'm afraid."

The clock on the wall filled the silence with ticks that seemed to hasten and slow according to Tom's heartbeat. He flipped his hands over, each slick with sweat.

"What's the delay?"

Lino bit the bottom of his lip and bobbed his head in agreement.

"Yes, I am taking my time, that is for certain. But I want to know a few things before. And this is because of personal reasons you would not understand. But you do not need to, so let us begin." He leaned forward and spun the pistol on his finger like an actor in a western movie. "Tell me about Abejundio."

Tom shook his head.

"I don't even understand what you just said."

Lino's face grew sour. He turned and spat on the carpet.

"Soto."

Tom shrugged.

"I don't know anything about him."

Lino closed his eyes and breathed inward as if summoning the patience for an imbecile.

"Tell me of his death. I must know more of it."

Tom looked to the door and Lino bumped the pistol against his chest.

"Pay attention to me. I am your concern now. What I want."

Tom looked at the carpet and shrugged.

"What do you want to know?"

"I want to know what he said, what he looked like, everything. So you will tell me, now." He moved the gun barrel in circles. "Right now. Fast. Let's go."

Tom pursed his lips.

"Well, I guess Bud shot him in the head and he died. Not much more to it than that."

Lino looked up and wiped the gun across his forehead.

"Yes, not much more than that, I suppose."

He cocked his head up and scratched his chin.

"Did he beg?"

Tom shook his head.

"Bud really didn't give him time to beg. I think he was just more surprised than anything else. Like he didn't think it could actually happen or something."

Lino smirked and nodded.

"Now, I know we are talking about the same Abejundio." He chuckled to himself and then cleared his throat. "Your friend, the sheriff man. He begged. He begged very much."

"I find that hard to believe."

Lino pushed the words away with his empty hand.

"It is not a reflection of his character or anyone else's. They all beg in those circumstances. Each and every one. When they know it is come to an end, and there is nothing that can be done about it. They beg and they pray." He turned his palm upward and raised his eyebrows. "What else is left at that point? Why not try, I suppose."

"But it never works, I guess," Tom said.

Lino rubbed his chin and thought a moment.

"Maybe it does with the ones that kill for pleasure or because of sickness. But not when it is a part of business." He waived his finger side to side. "Then it is just about business. Words have no importance, because there can be no other way."

"You don't take pleasure in killing?"

Lino opened his jacket with his free hand. He set the pistol on his lap and reached into the interior pocket. Tom's eyes flicked between Lino's face and the gun. The Mexican grinned, and then in a sudden jerk, he extracted a cigar and pointed it at Tom.

"Bang." He slid it into the corner of his mouth and grinned. "You see there. This is what I find interesting. You saw me place the gun in my lap, and you thought that maybe you could take it if you moved quickly enough. You considered this possibility for a moment. You thought that you either could get it, or you might should at least try, because it might be your best chance. But you did nothing, because you think that maybe you can convince me to let you go. So you know that if you had tried and were not successful, you may end up squandering that chance."

He removed a silver lighter and set the cigar ablaze. He puffed until the end turned a crystal orange, and then he snapped the lighter shut and slid it back inside his pocket.

"Or perhaps you thought I was playing a game, and that I had another pistol inside my coat." He ashed the cigar on the carpet. "Though, I doubt it. No. I think it was like earlier, when you looked at the door before you came to sit with me. You thought for a moment that you might run. You thought that you might make it before I could shoot you. Or you thought that maybe I might miss, or that if I did hit you, it might be a superficial wound, and then perhaps, I would not chase you for fear that others might see me wielding my pistol in your front yard."

He leaned forward and crossed his wrists over the weapon, still lying flat across his lap.

"And now you probably think that perhaps you made the right choice not to act. Perhaps it's your best chance to wait and see. Perhaps your best chances lie ahead. Perhaps you don't have any chance at all. But had you acted, at least you would have taken your opportunity. By your decision. Acted to save your life. Whatever happened, it would have been your choice and not mine."

He pursed his lips and shook his head ominously.

"But you did not act in either case, and now, as every moment passes, your opportunities dwindle, whatever the percentages of each, they become scarcer."

He smoked and thought for a moment.

"I find it curious. It is what people do. Not because they actually think that they have a better chance by waiting. No. It is never really that. It is the human nature. Not fear exactly. Though, that must be part of it. But, no. Not just that. It is more like, they procrastinate against something they do not want to do."

Tom eyed the pistol and bit his bottom lip. Lino grinned, the cigar jutting from the corner of his mouth like a well-placed prop.

"What about you?"

"Me?" Lino asked.

"Have you ever been on this side of it?"

Lino nodded.

"Yes."

"What did you do?"

Lino took the pistol from his lap and leaned back.

"I'm afraid, I wasn't offered enough time to ponder such thoughts."

He gathered the bottom of his shirt with his free hand and raised it, exposing three round, waxy scars fixed upon his abdomen, each set apart like corners of an invisible triangle. He circled them with the barrel of the gun.

"You see, this was my result," he said, the cigar bobbing in his mouth as he spoke, a length of ash bending downward at the tip. "My enemy was immediate, because he believed that a prudent philosophy."

The curl of ash broke and sailed to the floor, and he smeared it into the carpet fibers with the toe of his boot and sucked a mouthful of smoke from the cigar without touching it.

"This man believed that immediacy was an important rule. A strategy that prevented thought. Prevented dealings. Prevented feelings. All the things that keep hard men from doing what is their job to do."

He took the cigar and pointed it at Tom.

"And, he was correct, though it did not serve him well on this particular occasion. But the principle, that is sound. The longer it takes to fulfill the duty, the less likely it will be fulfilled." He put the cigar in his mouth. "So you yourself might be prone to think that your chances are improving with every passing second. And you could be right. But that is only when dealing with those who kill for business." He inhaled and looked upward. "Now, with the sick ones, those who kill for pleasure and curiosity, there is no telling. With those there can be no lessens, though there are many in my business who try to teach it, try to instill it. All of the strategies. But it is a foolish enterprise. With them, there is no taking, because they enjoy the task too much. They like to tempt the sufferer with illusions of escape. They provide hope with false words, only to snatch it back by way of manner. All to satisfy their appetites."

He removed the cigar from his mouth and dropped it onto the floor. He gazed into the orange of the failing coal as it melted the cheap polypropylene fibers, his face tense as if he audited his statements for future revision. Tom shifted in his seat.

"So which one are you?"

Lino's eyes flicked upward.

"Which am I?"

"Yes."

He raised the rear of the pistol to his head and scratched his temple with the hammer.

"So what if I answer? What difference would it make? If I am a man of business, contemplating mercy, then I will say so. But if I am one who enjoys playing, then I would claim to be something else, all to prolong the dance." He shrugged. "Either way, you could not be sure, so what is the point to answer?"

They sat in silence while the clock kept time, the longhand's casual advances drawing Ellie to her home, exhausted and unknowing, an innocent. Lino tapped his fingers against the pistol's ejection port. He breathed deeply and clicked his tongue as if pained by boredom. Tom's palms hemorrhaged sweat as his mind raced for content. He raised his index finger and pointed to Lino's face.

"Who did that to you?"

Lino rubbed the scars on his lip.

"This?"

Tom nodded.

"Your friend. The large one."

"Seth?"

Lino nodded gravely.

"You killed him?"

"Not me personally."

"But he's dead?"

"Yes."

"What about his boy."

Lino shook his head slowly.

Tom's jaw clenched and his eyes glinted wet.

"You killed him? You killed that little boy?"

Lino raised his index finger.

"No. His father did. His father, and the sheriff, and the others and you." He shook his head and pushed the air with his palm. "Not me. Never me."

Tom pinched his eyes shut and tears leaked from the corners.

"Just kill me. Kill me right now."

Lino cocked his head.

"Is that what you want?"

"Yes. God, yes. Just do it and leave."

Lino leaned back in his chair, and a long sigh slipped between his teeth.

"Is it because of your wife?"

Tom opened his eyes.

"I know her," Lino said. "And I know she is coming here." He gave a disappointed frown. "I know everything of her and of you, because it is my business to know." He reached inside his jacket pocket and took a fresh cigar. "I know about her illness, your finances." He lit the cigar and drew a large sampling. "I know about your baby, the one that never was."

Tom leaned forward and wept and Lino rolled his eyes in disgust.

"What is it with you people? A Mexican does none of this. He knows that life is pain and yet, he is grateful for each breath." He leaned forward and raised his index finger in the air, as if imparting knowledge. "He knows that his pain is not novel, that this being lives in everyone's soul. He plods through each day with his eyes on no prize in particular. Just each foot placed before the other every moment of the day on every day, regardless of the outcomes of each, only for one reason, and that is to crawl home and sit at his little table with his family surrounding him, their eyes affixed to him, because they know he has tried." He leaned back in his chair, his eyes vivid and wide. "And this is his heaven, his breath of life. And for this he lives, and for this he is satisfied."

He talked like a pulpit speaker, bits of spit ejaculating from his mouth.

"But you," he shook his head slowly and his lips crept over his gums. "All of you. You think that everything should be just so. And if it is not, then you pump your fists at the heavens, demanding and begging for happiness to be handed to you, and if it is not, then you are content to sprawl in the gutters or lie down to die."

He dismissed the man before him with a flick of his hand.

Tom pressed his thumb and index finger flush against each eyelid.

"I'm not trying to lie down." He bit his lip and looked up. "I'm just trying to give you what you want, so you can go and leave my wife alone."

Lino tilted his head and smiled as if the words amused him.

"You cannot control what I do or do not do to your wife. You could have at one point, but you made a choice that gave that control away. You made a choice that made me pivot toward your direction, and now I am here."

He glanced at the clock and pushed his lip forward. He motioned with the pistol.

"Let's go."

They walked the hallway past the cluster of family photos adorning the wall, each enclosed within its cheap plastic frame, some of the faces bearing great, wide smiles, others flat and stolid, as if they'd been captured by the camera's lens against their will.

The bedroom was free from disorder except for a pink bath towel strewn about the made bed, its torn covers sculpted trim as if molded by someone who cared too strongly for such things. Lino moved the towel aside with the barrel of the pistol and sat in its place.

"Where is it?"

Tom's hand drifted toward the sliding closet door, half-open and glutted with old shoes and luggage. Lino propped his left hand on his knee and aimed the pistol with his right.

"Kick everything out with your feet."

Tom did so until a pile of clutter grew before Lino's boots. The closet floor sat empty, and Lino's eyes burned forth.

"Where?"

Tom rubbed the back of his neck.

"The carpet."

Lino scanned the closet floor and nodded.

"Go ahead. Slowly. So very slowly."

Tom bent to his knees and crawled into the closet. He drove his fingertips into the carpet and raked it back from the baseboard. Then he collected the free end and peeled a good-sized section away. Only plywood lay beneath, but a pair of seams ran within it, each jagged and meandering, as if carved with great effort by a small keyhole saw. Lino leaned forward and stretched upward to see over Tom's shoulders. Tom looked backward and the Mexican nodded once.

"I need something to pry with."

The fingers on Lino's off hand danced across his chest and into his jacket pocket. He withdrew a bone-handled pocket knife not much larger than a pair of fingernail clippers. He pitched it to Tom who snatched it from the air with a definite strike. He fingered it open and looked at the blade, slender and deviating upward and encrusted with plum-colored gore. He looked back at the Mexican, but if he expected a response, he got none.

"This may break."

Lino shrugged.

Tom turned and went to work on the plywood. He sunk the curved end of the knife into the corner where the running seams met and wiggled it until the blade bore through. He pried upward and the wood gave. He put the tip of his index finger against the exposed edge of the wood and cut his nail into the fibers. He pulled upward, but his fingernail threatened to give, so he slipped the knife along the rest of the seam an inch at a time, wedging upward until he'd excavated enough wood to wriggle his fingertips underneath.

He pulled the cover up and wrenched it free from the baseboard. A large paper bag sat beneath, folded, pressed and clean as the day it was put there.

He looked back at the Mexican, awaiting permission.

"Go ahead."

Tom cupped the side of the bag and slipped his fingers beneath. He felt the cool barrel of the pistol, undisclosed beneath the brown paper, buried beneath the money and floor, waiting like an unturned card promising favor in a one-sided poker game. He traced backward until his palm felt the grip, and then he curled his fingers around it and drew the hammer back.

He paused for a moment and solidified his handle against the sweat from his draining palms. His heart slammed against his chest so loudly, he half expected the Mexican to hear it. But if he did, he didn't react. Instead, he sat upon the bedding as before, arching upward and maneuvering side-to-side like a man set unfortunately behind his vertical superior at a movie theatre.

Tom palmed the paper bag with his free hand, the blood rushing to and from his head, as if he spun weightlessly on some howling rotary amusement park ride. His breaths grew short and flecks of white danced across his eyes accordingly, and for a moment, he thought he might pass out.

"Let's go," the Mexican said, his words like cold water, cruel but clarifying.

He sucked a filling breath through his nose, and his vision returned to right. He took a thin swallow and raised the sack of money, his off hand obvious, the pistol unseen on the other side. He lifted the bag several inches and then turned it sideways. He'd pitch the bag to the Mexican and level the pistol and fire before it landed, but while such thoughts crossed and tangled within his brain, the man spoke.

"What are you doing?" Lino asked. He leaned forward, the pistol dangling from his fingers, his demeanor cavalier and condescending. "You intend to kill me like this?" He strengthened his grip on the gun and stood. "You think you can kill me at all? Do you know that I have killed more formidable men than you while they drew blueprints of escape in their mind?"

Tom laid everything down and sat back on his knees, his face defeated and tarnished with shame. He swallowed and lifted his eyes upward.

"I don't care. I don't care about anything you say. I just want you to leave. Take all of this money and just leave. Leave now."

Lino drove his boot into the side of Tom's ribs, and he crumpled forward.

"Get up. Right now, get up." His voice was low but coarse.

Tom rose to his feet, his side stinging as if a great splinter dug at his ribs.

"Lie on the bed. On your stomach."

Tom crossed the floor with his head down, and the Mexican slammed the pistol on the back of his neck, knocking his hat to the floor.

"Hurry up."

He crawled onto the bed spread and collapsed onto his stomach. He pressed his face into the fabric and held his breath. He lay there waiting to die, petitioning his mind for images of serenity, scraping the depths of retention for something beautiful and neat and clean. But he could only conjure a picture of Ellie's face, sapped white and wiped of life.

He turned his body and sat. The Mexican held the open bag.

"What are you doing?" He asked.

"I'm not going to let you kill my wife."

Lino smirked. He looked into the bag and then crumpled it shut.

"Get up."

He forced Tom through the hallway and into the living room.

"Put your nose against the wall."

Tom looked down and shook his head.

"If you shoot me now, you'll have to leave. The neighbors will hear the gunshot, and you will have to leave."

Lino pursed his lips and shook his head slowly.

"I can come back. I can come back to kill her." He turned the pistol in a circular motion. "Now, turn and face the wall."

Tom's draining eyes drifted upward, as if an unseen salvation lie within the water stained ceiling.

"Please," he whispered. "Please."

The Mexican leveled the pistol.

"Face the wall."

He turned slowly, his nose bending sideways against the finished drywall, his closed eyes pinching out the light. He could not collect himself. There was no way of doing so nor reason to try.

"You're right," he whispered through curled, receding lips. "Those things you said before. I made a mess of things. I brought you here, and I know it." He gagged for a moment on his own desiccant throat. "If you've got any heart, let it all die with me. Please kill me and leave. That's all I ask. Just please leave when it's done."

He said nothing more, his mind readying itself for instant oblivion. It spun away from his physical state and made a desperate scramble toward bright thoughts, dredging the recesses within for some suitable image, an appropriate last. But that one thing remained as before, hidden or lost or stubbornly withheld. Instead, he saw only himself, pinned like an impotent against a wall in his own home, a nothing that would die as he lived.

He opened his eyes and searched instead for courage or, at minimum, a raw rage to serve in its stead. He swallowed hard and whipped his body around. He plunged forward, hands contorted into rigid, fleshy claws, his mind conjuring a frenetic madness to will him forward, eyes half-closed but half-open just the same.

But the Mexican had moved from the spot where he'd once stood, and the force of Tom's efforts compromised his balance, and he tumbled downward and landed in an awkward heap, his face smacking loudly against the tile in front of the open door.

He turned over and looked around, but the Mexican had left. He stumbled upright, his nose broken and leaking blood. He ran the hallway toward the bedroom and plucked the pistol from the floor. He jogged back into the living room and out the door, the gun raised forward, the hammer back. But when he'd made it out the door and onto the driveway, he saw only his neighbor standing frozen, eyes wide as saucers, his hand caught within his mailbox.

Tom sat down on the cold concrete and stared forward with hollow eyes. He tried to wipe the blood from his face with his sleeve, but it only smeared across his skin, crossing his face like a red brushstroke. The neighbor watched the uniformed deputy a moment longer, a pile of envelopes scattered on the ground next to his feet. He thought to offer assistance, but the look on the bleeding man's face instructed otherwise. And so, he jogged back up his own driveway, entered his own home and shut himself inside, sealing his worries away with a spin of the deadbolt lock.

CHAPTER 20

Walter Thompson lowered his tailgate, and his three beagles leapt toward the cold hard dirt, each landing awkwardly upon the one that came before it. They gathered around him, their voices low and whining, intermittent breaths of fog puffing out from their mouths. He scratched behind each's ear and then cut them all loose into the cold blackness that lingered stubbornly before the dawn. He climbed into his pickup and sat patiently, sipping black coffee directly from an aluminum thermos. He thumbed the radio and settled on a gospel station, the old hymns soothing his mind, nearly setting him adrift into slumber. But on this morning the hounds took a scent almost at once, their hollow bawling rattling the trees like an obscene violation against the calm.

He jerked astute and opened the door. He withdrew his rifle from its casing and set off toward the noise, his big boots crunching the dried leaves down into the wet soil. He'd gauge the sounds and set up ahead of them, waiting for the fleet-footed animal to trot out in front ahead of the pack. He might see it in an hour or at the end of the day or not at all, but after decades of practice, he liked his chances.

The bellowing moved fluidly ahead in a winding pattern that traced from the right to the left and then back again. It abated for a while, as if the hounds had forced the deer away in the opposite direction, and then everything changed, and their voices grew louder. Walter positioned himself atop a ridge overlooking a dense mass of pine saplings, and there he waited, straining to hear as the tree limbs clattered about in the cold wind.

Roaming cattle had mauled a dirt path through the branches, and he focused his attention on this area, a bold instinct screaming instructions within his head. He waited quietly while the stinging cold worked its way through his boots and singed his toes. An hour passed and then another. He listened until the bawling finally settled in particular area. He rose to his feet and spat. He recognized the sound. They'd slipped loose from the scent onto something other, an opossum or raccoon, no doubt. They'd likely treed the thing and now were circling the ground. He slung the rifle over his shoulder and headed that way, cursing softly to himself over the morning waste.

He crossed through a dense and spiny thicket, ripping his clothing loose from the curling thorns that reached forth to collect the fabric in clumps. He pushed through the mess of clawing tines for a long while before finally popping free of it and stumbling forward into a sea of arching, windswept yellow grass. The dogs called from beyond an orderly line of pine trees on the far side of the meadow, their dull bawling evolved into panicked yelps. Walter picked up his pace, jogging as fast as his age would allow, the wind pushing against his advance, like some unworldly force nudging him away from what lay beyond. By the time he breached the wall of pines, he'd begun to hear spots of growling and snorts. He saw one of the dogs in the near distance, its tongue lolling, eyes seemingly wild.

"Grady," he called. The animal's head jerked toward him, and it trotted forward. When it was within reach, he curled his hand around its neck and set the leash. The dog licked at his hand as he worked, and with each lap, it left a smudge of blood. "Godammit," Walter said aloud.

He let the dog lead as they overtook a formidable hill, the animal lunging and jerking against the leash until its breath turned into hoarse wheezing. When they reached the summit, the animal drove forward, snapping the leash loose and dragging it toward the other dogs. Walter stood watching as they circled the heap of flesh. He reached inside his pocket and removed a metal flask. He tipped it to his lips and took in its contents, then he put it back and went to collect his dogs.

When Tom arrived, he saw the old man set upon the tailgate of his pickup, a rifle set crossways upon his lap. He wheeled the cruiser next to the truck and got out.

"Where are they?" He asked.

"I'll take ya to em."

They both got inside the cruiser, and Tom drove them to the spot. They took the highway down to the old dirt road. When they entered the clearing, Tom could see the giant man, half dragged from inside the warped shack, his body bloated with insect larvae. They pulled forward and parked.

"You stay here." Tom said.

"To hell with at."

Tom took a flashlight from the cruiser and withdrew his pistol.

"Suit yourself."

They each stepped out and approached the corpse.

"You ever seen a thing like at?"

Tom shook his head.

"That fella's eight foot tall if he's a foot."

Tom looked around.

"You didn't go inside?"

Walter spat.

"What in the hell for?"

Tom held his pistol with both hands and positioned himself along the side of the shack.

"Stand behind me, Walter."

The old man pinched his eyes together as if he'd been told to run.

"Ain't nobody in there, Deputy."

Tom looked at him and then back toward the empty doorway.

"This is the police," he yelled. "Come on out."

They waited for several seconds, but nothing happened. Walter shook his head.

"For Christ's sake, ain't nobody in there. Look at this." He pointed to the flow of maggots spilling from the giant's neck hole. "This fella's been settin here for more than a day."

Tom looked at the body and then stepped into the doorway. He flashed the light inside.

"God damn," he said. "God damn."

The old man crept in behind him.

"Who's at? Is he one of yers?"

Tom crouched down.

"Who is at, Deputy?"

The wind erupted outside, pressing the walls of the structure inward, whistling through the gapes between the boards and bending the wood until it moaned. Tears broke from Tom's eyes and he rose to his feet. He put his gun in his holster and walked out into the howl. He stumbled to the cruiser and put his hands on the hood. The old man followed after him, a puzzled expression entrenched within his leathered face.

"Who the hell is at, Deputy?"

Tom stood and palmed his hand over his badge like a dying man clutching a failing heart. He ripped it loose from his shirt and skipped it into the grass, and then he got in the cruiser and drove away.

CHAPTER 21

Natives of the county called it snow, but anyone who'd seen actual snow knew that this was really sleet, and they cursed it for the worthless nuisance it was. But it piled white on the ground, nonetheless, and the children bolted from their homes and dipped their hands into it and slung it wildly high into the air like those long thirsting for rain, and they endeavored to treat the coarse sludge as the real thing in spite of the sound assurances from their parents and other fools.

Tom sat inside watching it all through the window, no particular expression on his face. He wore a bandage across his nose, his nostrils stuffed tight with gauze packing. His eyes fixed upon the children busy rolling ice into misshapen snowmen like jolly laboring elves, but he saw none of it, his mind wondering instead through a mist of blank thought.

He didn't know the phone had rung until Ellie tapped his shoulder.

"It's Kyle," she said.

He held his hand out and she gave it to him, and then she went back down the hallway and into the bedroom.

"Hello, Kyle," he said, his voice made odd by the packing in his nose.

"I don't mean to bother you, Tom. But I need your help with something."

Tom rubbed his jaw.

"Talk to Mr. Hardy, he's running things now."

"I know it, but he cain't help me with this."

"What is it?"

"It's about Bud and his effects."

Tom traced his fingers against his fractured nose.

"What of them?"

"Well, we cain't get in touch with nobody to come claim em."

"What about his ex-wife?"

It was quiet for a moment.

"Well, Tom, we tried to look for her. But the things is, she done kilt herself."

Tom didn't say anything.

"You there, Deputy?"

"Don't call me that, Kyle. I'm not a deputy anymore."

"Yessir, I'm sorry. Well, the things is, when Mr. Hardy found out, he said to just put everthing up for auction, and that's what I intended to do, but there weren't much of anythin that would qualify, I reckon."

Tom pressed his eyes closed and scratched his head.

"Alright, Kyle, go ahead and tell me what you need."

"Well, once I told Mr. Hardy what was there, he said to take everthing and just throw it away, but I just didn't feel right about it cause of what else I found."

"What did you find?"

"Well, I'd just rather you come down and go through it with me, and if you say it's alright to throw it all away, then that's what I'll do. But I just don't feel right doin it myself."

Tom didn't say anything.

"I'd sure appreciate it, Tom. I really would."

"Alright, Kyle. I'll meet you over there in an hour if that's good for you."

"I'll be there waitin."

He walked the hallway and looked through the crease in the open door. Ellie lay in bed reading, her little body warm beneath the covers, thumb and index finger gently twisting her lower lip as her mind tangled with details unknown. He watched her from the shadows, his heart loving toward her only, lungs breathing due only to that fact. She turned pages slowly, drawing long breaths inward at the completion of each. After a while, he felt wrong to watch her and worse to break her thoughts, and so he left without telling and posted a note to the front door instead.

He warmed the old Buick for as long as his patience would allow, and then he backed carefully into the street. He passed through the slew of children frisking through the browning sludge in a mindless revel that left their parents tracing their lips over a faint Déjà vu of experiences easy to remember, but tenuous to recollect.

He drove the highway with caution, moving moderately among those ignorant to the effects of ice on paved road. By the time he reached Bud's old place, he was thirty minutes later than what he'd predicted, and Kyle stood propped against his cruiser, looking as impatient as was proper. He parked along the curb and got out, the Buick's door crying as it opened and shut.

"How ya doin, Tom?"

He reached out a gloved hand, and Tom took it.

"Alright. Sorry I'm late. The ice is pretty thick in some spots."

Kyle nodded.

"I know it. Them roads is thoroughly untended." He put his thumbs in his coat pockets and squinted his eyes against the blowing sleet. "How's your wife?"

Tom nodded.

"She's fine. How are things going with Mr. Hardy?"

Kyle spat.

"Well, I don't reckon I've got much reference point, but it's alright I guess. I kinda take it he wants to make a career of this. From what I understand, he's a real hand in his own county."

Tom nodded.

"That's how I heard it, too."

They stood quiet for a moment, the sleet threatening to let and then recommitting.

"I hope you don't take this the wrong way, but you sure enough left us in a bind."

Tom nodded.

"I know it." He looked at the vacant house. "What is it you need from me, Kyle?"

Kyle looked to the house and then back to Tom.

"Well, just come and have a look."

He looked down and slid his boot across the sidewalk, smearing a swath of pavement through the white, as if exposing something beautiful for a coarse truth.

"I hope I ain't wasting yer time. But I been thinkin on this for the last couple days, and somethin just keeps tuggin at me. You have a look, and then you can tell me if I'm crazy or if I'm just overthinkin. I aim to do exactly what you say, and then forget the whole thing, one way or the other."

They walked the driveway and scaled the steps onto the porch. The door stood locked, but Kyle had a key, and as he pushed it into the slot, Tom considered the toll it must have exacted from the one who'd taken that piece of metal from the bloated corpse that once cared for it.

They went inside, and the sour reek of old vomit flushed forward. Tom glanced at Kyle who returned a look and then cast his face away, as if protecting the legacy of an admired yet fallible great.

"It's back this way."

He led Tom through the hall, past Bud's bedroom toward the closed door marked by the sign. It read: Anna, and it still hung with its glittered script dancing in the dull hall light for all or no one to see. Tom swallowed hard as he approached. Kyle stopped short of the door and glanced over his shoulder, an uncertain look upon his face.

"What's in there, Kyle? Just tell me."

Kyle squinted his eyes and scratched underneath his hat.

"I'd rather just show you."

He took the knob and twisted the door open and worked the wall with his hand until he found the light. He flipped it upward, and they each stepped into the little room dedicated to a child who'd never the chance to know it. Tom put his hand over his mouth.

The bludgeoned vanity now stood erect, composited together with epoxy resin and glue. Hundreds of wood strands bound together with impossible accuracy, meticulous as a ship builder working within a glass bottle. Upon the vanity's flat, sanded face lay tiny dresses, once torn to threads by the mangling hands of wicked men, presently woven together and bound by satin ribbon like bundles of fine cloth. The dollhouse had been made right, too, though its frame meandered embarrassingly in places that could not be helped. Within each tiny room lay small piles of crushed porcelain figurines, stacks of fragments and powder, the color and sheen of each matched to a fine degree, irreparable but portioned from one another like piles of coveted mineral dust. The lacerated dolls sat mended, as well, their cotton entrails pushed back within, the fabric skins stretched and brought together by clumsy rows of stitching, set by a father given appropriate will but fixed with ill-equipped hands.

He'd made things as right as could be, put back together those things felt by her hands, those things made holy by the contact, each preserved to a remarkable degree, as to make the unknowing marvel and all others despair.

Tom stepped forward and took a stack of pictures from the vanity. There were seven, all taken on one particular day at a fair. He thumbed through some and stopped at one that felt weighty in his hands. It was the only to hold all three, the parent's faces brightly smiling, but muted by the child's. For hers flared with an intensity that might floor the world if given the chance. An indescribable something that could not be tempered nor put down. A thing to be stolen and never destroyed.

Tom looked at the picture in his hand, and then he set it back on the shelf. He looked over his shoulder at Kyle through red weary eyes, as the late afternoon shadows crawled across the walls.

"Do like Mr. Hardy says and throw it all away."

Kyle frowned and looked about the room once more.

"You sure? Somethin about it just don't seem right."

Tom stood up and rubbed his throbbing nose.

"No, Kyle, you're right. It probably isn't right, but it's the only answer I've got."

They left the little room and shut the light off behind them, the disjointed figures left at the mercy of strange, indifferent hands.

"What is all that stuff?" Kyle asked, he, looking younger than ever in that uniform.

"Nothing," Tom said. "It's not anything anymore."

And as he closed the door, it occurred to him that love may persist beyond need and reason, and that some things need someone to be anything at all.

That evening, he and Ellie sat upon the bed, a candle warming the corner of the room, the smell of vanilla in the air. She knew of his day and his ultimate decision, and she took in each with ease, as if she'd known these outcomes and digested them long afore.

He sat before her stripped clean, a man devoid of bluster and pretend, surrendering whole his heart without fear of judgment nor promises otherwise. They sat there not as friends nor lovers nor fools commit to unreckonable worry and want, but of each and all together at the same time.

They looked at each other and embraced.

"I don't know what to do with this life," he said.

She kissed his forehead.

"You don't have to decide tonight."

She traced the back of his neck with her fingertips, and his skin tightened and crawled. He looked up, and she offered a soft feminine smile, stunning and mute, fit to soothe or destroy.

"Why do you love me?" he asked.

She shushed him and pulled his head against the barren side of her chest.

"Everything will be ok," she said. "It may not be ok in the way you want it to be, but it will be ok nonetheless."

He found her hand with his and took it like it was the only thing left of the world. And she held him for a long time until he fell asleep into a world of his own making, where their fears had no teeth and love prevailed over all.

THE END

Also by RJ Law

The five-book Girl in a Rabbit Hole thriller series

Available NOW at AMAZON!
https://www.amazon.com/dp/B094DY44FQ/

Girl in a Rabbit Hole — *Read on to preview the first 10 chapters*

Chapter 1

"Have you noticed any insects behaving strangely?" the man asked, his pen tapping the table in consistent rhythmic beats. "Avoiding you, perhaps?"

"No," Claire answered.

"Good," the man said. "That's different from the other subjects."

He scribbled something onto his clipboard.

"What about sleep? Have you slept yet?"

"No."

"Interesting," he muttered. "That's 72 hours."

He scribbled again and set the clipboard aside. He removed his glasses and placed them flat on the table.

"And how do you feel?"

Claire glanced down at her hands. The leather straps had cut flawless red circles into her milky white wrists.

"I have a headache."

"Well, that's to be expected with the dehydration."

She looked at the two guards standing by the door, their bodies impossibly large and still, as if they'd been cut all at once from two granite hunks. The man rubbed his eyes and sighed.

"Let's hurry this along. I don't want to be here any longer than you do."

"I doubt that," Claire whispered to no one in particular.

"Fine then. Let's proceed." He put his glasses back on and collected his clipboard. "Any itching of the skin?"

"No."

"What about sudden blindness, visual impairments?"

"Nothing."

He pursed his lips and nodded approvingly.

"Are your fingernails growing?"

She looked at her hands.

"I have no idea."

"Fine," he said.

She cocked her head to the side and assessed the man before her. He was bald and his Adam's apple jutted forth like a misplaced elbow, its sharp point bobbing with every spoken word. She lowered her head and sucked the saliva in her mouth.

"Water."

The man looked up and frowned.

"I'm afraid it will be a few hours more at least."

"Why?"

He frowned.

"Let's continue."

The questions came quicker now.

"Any lesions? Is your stool strangely colored? Abnormal hair loss or growth? Have your feet begun to curl?"

"No."

He released the clipboard and took the pen by each end, his elbows propped up on the table, a look of embarrassment taking root within his pale gray eyes.

"Have you passed any fluids since the injection? Urine, sweat, anything?"

Claire shook her head from side to side.

"None?"

She shook her head again.

"Are you sure?"

"Yes."

He looked at one of the guards.

"98.6," the shadowed figure said. "We check hourly."

The man nodded and wrote furiously on his clipboard for several minutes, only stopping to brush away a fly that had somehow entered the facility.

"Well then," he said as he stood. "I'll return tomorrow."

He turned and took a couple of steps toward the door.

"Wait," Claire said. "I need water."

The man stopped without turning around. He looked at the guards and shook his head from side to side. Then he passed through the doorway, leaving her alone with the two hulking men, their stony faces unmoved and uncaring, scars throughout.

Both stood stoically until the door closed and then each one relaxed. The larger one removed a pack of cigarettes and worked two free. He handed one to his partner and set fire to them both. He looked at the other man and gave him an elbow, a smile unfurling beneath his broad mustache.

"I can get you water," he said, as big spindles of white smoke curled from his fingers: the thickest Claire had ever seen.

Claire stared at the floor, her long hair draped around her sulking head.

"I'm serious," he continued. "I can bring you a big cup of cold water. It would take me five seconds."

He glanced at his partner and they exchanged smiles.

"You be nice to me and I'll be nice to you."

He approached her from the front and looked down at the back of her neck. The fly circled his head as if it smelled something familiar. He swatted at it and cleared his throat.

"And, of course, you'll have to be nice to my friend here, too."

Claire raised her head and looked up at his face, her mahogany eyes boring forth, jaw undulating beneath the skin. The guard smiled boldly and drew from his cigarette. He started to say something else, but before he could, the door swung open and Demetri entered.

Both guards looked at their cigarettes and nearly swallowed the smoke in their mouths.

Demetri waved his hand against the stinking fog and coughed.

"Outside," he said without looking at either.

The two men rushed past him, heads pointed down, a telling fear within their watering eyes.

Demetri shut the door behind them and approached. He had a small plastic cup of water in his hand, and he held it so it could not be missed.

"I'm honestly surprised to find you here," he said, as he took a seat across the table. "I thought you would have left by now."

Claire pinched her eyebrows together and raised her wrists against the leather straps.

"Please," Demetri said, as if truly insulted, his black eyes like little holes behind the glasses he wore.

He leaned back in his chair and sighed, his expression casual, as if he sat across an old friend on the most ordinary of days.

"So, why are you still in this room?"

"Where would I go?" she asked. "How would I even know?"

Demetri frowned, his dark Latin features bold and handsome despite his age.

"Let me tell you a story," he said.

He brought his chair flat and placed the water on the table. He removed his glasses for a moment to massage his nose and then replaced them with care.

"I come from a place unlike your home," he said. "It is a choiceless place controlled by cruel men. There, children are made to work like adults. Sometimes with men standing behind them, pistols strapped to their waists."

He cleared his throat and put his hands together, his forearms resting on the table, a stern look in his cold, hard eyes.

"I was born into this place a fatherless child. My mother looked over me and my brothers and sisters as best she could, which was to say inadequately. I spent much of my time taking things that were not mine, a common thing in this place. Even at a very young age, children must learn to steal if they hope to survive for very long. Those who do, do. Those who don't."

He shrugged and turned his palms upward.

"One day, I took something from a soldier. A gold pocket watch that looked very important. Very valuable. Having a practiced hand, I easily lifted it from his jacket and casually made my way through the crowds. Simple as always. One of a thousand times."

He leaned forward in his chair.

"Except this time, another man had seen me. This man, a colonel of the army. As I cleared through all the humanity, there he was to snatch my wrist with his gloved hand. I looked up and saw his face, entirely marred by scars, a thick black beard snarling in all directions. Then I saw the butt of his rifle as it came into my face, and then darkness."

Claire looked down and shook her head slowly.

"I don't care about any of this, Demetri," she said.

He gave a patient smile and continued.

"When I awoke, I found myself shackled to a stone wall in some sort of dungeon cell. On this damp wall, a very colorful algae grew to make a stench that nearly choked the oxygen from the room. This I remember the most, even more than the beatings, which were substantial and severe. For five years, I lived in this place, without any way out. Without any sort of hope."

He frowned and looked thoughtful.

"And each day, I became more trained, and with time, my obedience became ordinary. A thing that was taken for granted. And with this apathy came opportunity. More than enough, in fact. And yet, despite these possibilities, I remained a prisoner, because of fear."

He pointed a finger at her.

"Men of power know this one true fact: that more than knives and guns and bombs and steel walls a hundred feet thick, fear is the one true controller. And so it was with me. Until one day, when I finally took my opportunity and freed myself."

He folded his hands and bit his lower lip.

"I had to kill three people to do it, one an old woman who happened across my path at the wrong time. I had never dreamed myself capable of such things. And yet, there I was with a blood-soaked shirt and gore and death in my wake. And do you know what caused me to risk my life and my soul on that one particular day and not the others leading up?"

He waited for a moment as if he thought she might answer, and then he removed his glasses once more and studied her with his naked eyes.

"Because one of the guards I trusted very much told me I would be subject to heinous things if I did not. You see, the bearded colonel who took me by the wrist so many years before had made regular visits throughout my stay. And, each time, he brought some new misery with him. Miseries which left me broken and scarred for weeks following. And this guard told me with earnest words that this bearded colonel meant to visit again in one day's time to make a toy of me in such a way that would have surely left me dead."

He shook his head once.

"And that was when I acted."

Claire looked up and his eyes sunk deep within hers.

"You see, for five years I remained paralyzed with fear. And had my hand not been forced, perhaps I would have died. Or, perhaps I would remain in that place, still alive, even today."

He smiled and put his glasses back on.

"Thankfully, we will never know."

He stood up and dusted his slacks.

"For one hour, you'll find yourself undisturbed," he said, his eyes serious and bold even behind his glasses. "Then the guards will return to do as they please. I will not stop them. The cameras will be off."

He collected the cup of water and looked it over. He took a small sip and set it on the table.

"Of course, that will all depend on whether or not you still occupy this room."

He turned and took two steps toward the door.

"Wait," Claire said. "Please don't do this."

Demetri smiled and put a finger to his lips.

"Sometimes, you cannot win," he said. "But you can still decide how you will lose."

With that, he exited, leaving the door open and unprotected, the hallway outside bright and white and smelling of disinfectant.

Claire bit her lip and wrestled against the straps, their edges biting down on her flesh, blood trickling from her veins and splattering brightly atop the tile floor. From the corner of her eye, she saw the fly land on the table and rush forward, an invisible trail of filth in its wake. It stopped immediately before her and pawed at itself before taking flight once more.

Down the hall, voices murmured, the guards chuckling to themselves, foul plans rooting within their twisted minds. She glanced at the clock, its pace the same for everything in any circumstance: the guilty, the innocent, animal, insect and man. She took several short breaths and reengaged the restraints. But even after 15 minutes of fury, they remained as they had been: firmly fashioned around her bloody wrists, the leather thick and without seams.

She dropped her head to sob, and when she did, the fly landed on the nape of her neck. Without thinking, she jerked her head back and whipped her hair around. The insect took flight and orbited her head a number of times, its buzzing made loud by the hollowness of the room. In a rage, she shrieked and jerked at the leather straps, the chair squealing against the bolts that held it to the floor.

All the noise brought laughter from down the hall, and now the guards whistled and made crude comments, one shouting the time every five minutes.

She settled in her chair and cried dryly, her body aching for water the way the drowning ache for air. But even as she cried, the clock kept ticking, its gentle racket like a train whistle inside her head.

She thought she might take her own life if given the power, but this was a wasted thought. And more came with it: her childhood, her father's face, a boy she once loved. And time held its pace through it all, unmoved by the problems of men, the clock on the wall tracking its progress with gentle, rhythmic clicks.

At last, she resigned to her fate, her body resting weakly, eyes fixed upon the cup of water. They'd enter the room shortly, she thought. And there was nothing within her to stop them. And no one would be coming to her aid.

She rested her head against her shoulder, and when she did, the fly set down on her cheek and scuttled over her nose.

As if poked by something electric, her weakened body jerked to life. She writhed about, but the insect stayed affixed to her skin, its vile extremities tickling their way across this new terrain of supple flesh. At last, something within her broke and she screamed until her lungs ran empty and her mind went black.

Seconds later, her clarity returned, the fly within her right hand, the leather confinements broken atop the floor. She looked at her free hand as if it had just grown from her wrist, the wounds gone, faint bruises where there had been open sores not minutes before.

She glanced at the clock, but the time was gone. In a panic, she gathered the other strap into her free hand and pulled. With little effort, the thing came apart like something made of paper. She held the fragments and studied them, her face pallid and awestruck.

Suddenly, footsteps gathered outside. She stumbled from the chair, her body wavering atop infant-like legs. But before she could take even one step, the two monstrous guards appeared in the entryway, their jaws made unhinged by her inexplicable freedom.

For what seemed like several minutes, she stared at them and they at her. And then all three looked at the cup of water.

In a panic, both men raced toward it, their hands reaching out, eyes wide as dinner plates. But before they could close the distance, Claire threw herself forward and bent over the table. She gathered up the cup and brought it to her lips, even as one of the guards took her right arm and twisted it backward.

By the time it reached her mouth, the cup had nearly emptied, but for a few drops which splashed onto her face and slipped between her open lips. Soon she was on the ground, the two men restraining her, one clubbing her face with what seemed like a two-ton fist.

But even as he whaled away, she felt a growing heat within her body. And soon, she was on her feet, one of the great, giant men cowering against a wall, the other clutching a useless arm that now bent in all the wrong places.

"Please," the other guard said, as he pressed his body flat against the wall. "I'm sorry. Just go, please."

She approached him and bent low, taking his bristly jaw in her small, delicate hand. And then his screams invaded the halls and traveled deep and far throughout the facility, where Demetri sat at his desk, sipping coffee and smiling.

Chapter 2

(9 months earlier)

Claire Foley slept under warm blankets in a cold room. Below her, floor vents whispered. Outside, the sky grew purple and soft. On her nightstand, an alarm clock threatened to sound in 30 minutes, but this didn't matter much. The birds would cut through everything soon, puncturing the serenity with their thin little cries.

When the first one came on, she turned over her body and worked the covers between her naked feet. She watched the clock keep time as her mind made the murky path toward full-on consciousness. She reached out into the coldness and flipped off the alarm just seconds before it brought more unwanted clatter. She withdrew back into the warmth and listened to the ballad of tweets and calls, the birds growing ever louder as if they believed it necessary to coax the sun from its wherever place. At last, she spilled out from the covers and rushed toward the bathroom, the cold tile floor stinging her little feet with every pattering step.

In the bathroom, she dressed, spread makeup onto her skin and studied in the mirror a young but serious face. She ate little before leaving for work, her car parked along the curb outside, abrasive morning radio voices filling the interior with a twist of the ignition key. She zipped onto the freeway and off the curled exit. She slowed to pay the homeless familiar and the ones that looked new. She cleared security without any eye contact. She slotted her vehicle in the parking space that said staff only without really meaning it. All this she did without thought, as if she'd practiced the sequence hundreds of times before.

And so it was, because she had.

For nearly half a decade, Claire had worked at Clairmont University, assisting a brilliant man, while he continued the research of another brilliant man who'd lived many years before. Like most brilliant men, Paul Devaney knew he was brilliant, but he didn't seem to notice that Claire was, too. Or if he did, he intentionally kept it to himself, out of pride or thoughtlessness, who could say?

Over the course of those five years, Claire worked alongside this disgusting man, while his big fleshy nose squealed like a teakettle with every breath. While she worked, he'd pace behind her, years of abrasion patterns marking the cut of his lazy, scuffling path.

"No, no," he'd say. "Do it again."

And she always did, while his tiny black eyes burned holes in the back of her head.

Nearly everyone at the university had contemplated murder fantasies for Paul Devaney; however, most seemed content enough when they learned he'd accepted a job at Viox Genomics, one of the most prominent genetic labs in the country. That was a big day. People passed cute little smiles as they crossed in the hallways: secrets between subjects, better times ahead.

In the summer, Claire had dreamed up a darker fantasy, but she must have wished too hard, because instead of showing to collect his things and claim his long-awaited glory, Paul Devaney just stopped coming to work all together and ultimately disappeared.

The people at Viox Genomics were concerned, the university heads, too. But no one dragged the world's reservoirs looking for Paul Devaney. Instead, they moved forward, the university slotting apt candidates into relevant vacancies, one to fill his void, one to fill the void made by the filling.

This brought opportunity for Claire, but not the opportunity she deserved. It turned out Paul Devaney had hoarded so much credit, she couldn't assemble a portfolio to prove her contributions. And so she took what came: a suitable offering that allowed her to continue the research which had become her life. And for the next several months, she spent each and every day ruining her eyes on microscopic particles and endless strings of numbers unintelligible to all but her.

She spent endless nights in that place, life getting away, neither dates, nor parties, nor invitations to decline. But then everything seemed to change, when a very important person from Viox Genomics called to offer her the job once promised to Paul Devaney. Without hesitation, she claimed the hand-me-down opportunity as her own, a broad smile cutting across her face, mahogany eyes beaming and wet. That night, she drank margaritas from a yawning, salt-rimmed glass, a rush of warmth flooding her core, newfound confidence at root somewhere within.

Over the following weeks, the past closed out with a wink. Free from Paul Devaney, the facility's social atmosphere bloomed. Attitudes improved and so did just about everything else. How-are-yous became commonplace. Smiles occurred out in the open. People transformed into themselves. Did the air smell better?

On this day, bright thoughts accompanied Claire into the building, an overwhelmingly tall man holding the door as she entered. She stepped inside and surveyed the footwork before her. People came and went across the linoleum floor on practiced feet made experienced by days prior. She sucked in a big breath and pushed her way within their ordinary every day.

For half a decade, she'd worked here, subordinate to geniuses, subordinate to fools. But those days were over, and she wore this truth on her bright, beaming face.

Stacey, the young receptionist with the nose ring, saw it at once.

"Hi you," she said through a broadening, slick little grin. "Getting excited?"

Claire nodded, Stacey up on her feet, face drawing soppy and wet.

"I'm going to miss you so fucking much. I just can't believe this is happening."

The young girl fled the desk and offered a hug. Claire forced a smile and bent so only their shoulders met.

"Oh, it's alright," she said. "It'll be alright."

"No," said Stacey, a stern look setting in. "It's fucking not going to be alright."

She looked over each shoulder as if she made a habit of qualifying her remarks by the presence of others.

"It's not alright." She began to cry. "I hate all these fucking people. Each and every goddamned one." She rubbed the back of her hand across her nose and it shined like polished brass. "I hate their faces."

Claire pulled free and patted the top of her head.

"O.k. Alright." She nudged the young girl backward. "We still have another week, don't we?"

Stacey's face went flat.

"Oh, right." She dusted her chest. "Another week. Sure."

She returned to her desk and started working her cellphone.

"That guy's got an appointment," she said, without looking up.

Claire looked over to the man sitting poised upon the lobby couch.

"Oh, hello," she said, taking a few steps to meet him. "I'm sorry. I didn't see you there."

"Hello, ma'am," the man said. He bowed a little and tipped forward his hat, a fedora that suited him well.

"I wasn't aware I had any appointments." She turned toward Stacey, but she was only there in body.

"That's perfectly my fault," the man said. "It was a last-second thing."

"Ok," she said. "Ok. Well, let me just have a chance to settle a few things, and I'll be right with you."

He put his hand up and regained his seat.

"You take your time, absolutely."

She nodded, her expression showing traces of confusion. Normally, she had few meetings if any, and as she entered her office and closed the door, a temptation to straighten overtook. She looked around for signs of loose organization, but there was already too much order, so she took some files from the cabinet and fanned them out on her desk. She opened one of the drawers, removed a handful of pens, set them on the files and looked around. Someone had given her a coffee mug that read, 'cancel my subscription; I'm tired of your issues,' and this she put in the wastebasket.

She checked the messages on her voicemail and then waited an appropriate amount of minutes to show that unexpected appointments must wait if for no other reason than to prove the value of her time. Then she buzzed Stacey, who let the man in.

He entered and gave a little bow, and Claire lifted from her seat slightly, because it seemed like the thing to do.

"Hello," she said as the man approached. He held a black folder in his right hand and a pen in the other.

"Hello to you. Do you mind?"

He pointed to a stiff little chair propped against the wall, and she lifted from her seat once more.

"Please," she said, as she looked over her appointment book. "Mr. Harris, is it?"

"Yes, ma'am," he said. He lifted the chair with one hand and spun it to face her desk. He sat down and organized himself as comfortably as the thing would allow.

"I'm sorry for the chair," she said. "Truth be told, I don't really get that many appointments."

He pushed away her apology with a flip of the hand.

"It's good for my posture."

Mr. Harris wore a bland gray sport coat that seemed too tight and slacks that seemed too short. Burgundy suspenders arched over his belly and stretched thin against its forthcoming weight. He was handsome in the face, but his age and small stature stole greatly from it. Indeed, it took effort to notice his kind, square features over the plainness of the rest. But something about his manner suggested he might not care either way.

"How can I help you," she asked, her hands folded neatly on the empty wood desk.

"Do you mind?" he asked, hesitating to set the folder upon his side of the varnished barrier.

She turned her hand over, and he placed it flat.

"Now, Ms. Foley, I'm here today to offer you a proposal, and I hope you'll listen to me the whole way through even if at times, you don't feel like you need to, or want to, or whatever."

He had some sort of rural accent, but he didn't seem rural at all. She leaned back in her chair and it cried a little.

"I've got enough copy toner if that's what you have on your mind."

"No, no," he shook his head. "This is way better than toner, I assure you."

"Alright," she said. "Well, I think I should warn you that I won't be here much longer, so you might be better off taking your offers upstairs."

He shook his head and pursed his lips.

"No, ma'am. I'm here today to see you and you alone."

She put an index finger to her chin and lowered her eyebrows.

"Okay."

He smiled and wrinkles shot out from his eyes.

"Now, it may not look like it, but I represent some very powerful people. People who have the power to make dreams come true." He put both hands flat against the desk. "People who have the power to give people like you everything they need to reach their goals."

She frowned.

"Ok," she said. "That's an aggressive statement."

"Absolutely," he said.

She picked up one of the pens and set it back down.

"What makes you think I'd be interested?"

Mr. Harris leaned forward and scratched the back of his head.

"Well, because we know a lot about you."

She smirked without realizing.

"Really?" she asked. "What do you know about me?"

He tightened his lips and raised his eyebrows.

"We know plenty. You'd better believe it."

Claire chuckled and shook her head.

"Mr. Harris, is it?"

He nodded.

"Well, I'm not sure what you are selling, but you'll have to do better than this." She leaned forward and folded her hands. "If you really know plenty about me, you'll know I'm uncomfortable with ambiguous language. I deal in certainties, and I'd expect the same from anyone who hopes to do business with me."

He bowed his head and raised his left hand.

"I'm sorry. I'll be as forthcoming as I can."

"Why can't you be 100 percent forthcoming?"

"Because the people I represent don't feel it's in their best interest."

"Forgive me, but these people sound somewhat shady."

He placed his hand flat upon the folder in front of him.

"I assure you, they're as shady as your average corporate or political man, which is to say, somewhat."

He pushed the folder forward and sat back in his chair. He crossed one leg over the other with some obvious discomfort.

"Please have a look, and take your time."

She lifted the folder and flipped it open. A single loose page sat upon a stack of pictures, followed by more pages and still more pictures. She thumbed through the top three, eyes darting around, widening. She closed the folder and looked up.

"Who are you exactly?"

Mr. Harris put his hands together as if truly frustrated.

"Ma'am, it really isn't important who I am, I assure you. What's more important is who you are."

"Who do you think I am?"

He shook his head a little and pushed his hat back to reveal a balding scalp.

"Doesn't matter. It's what they think."

"Your employer?"

"That's correct."

She looked down at the folder.

"And who do they think I am?"

"I know few details."

She looked up.

"What do you know?"

He leaned forward and propped his forearms against his knees, face casual, eyes set.

"Just that you're headed for a position at Viox Genomics after working for five years under Paul Devaney, his death the main reason for it."

She set the folder flat.

"He's dead?"

Mr. Harris nodded without losing eye contact.

"From what I understand."

She bit her lip and closed the folder.

"How do you know?"

He shrugged.

"I don't know, but my employer does, and I have no reason to doubt it."

She put both hands on her desk, the sweat on her palms making suction for a moment.

"I think I'm going to pass on your offer, Mr. Harris. But thank you anyway."

He stood.

"This isn't unexpected." He pulled the fedora back in place. "Please give a look at the rest of the folder. You'll receive a call from me within the next couple months in case you change your mind."

He put his hand to the front of his hat and turned toward the door. She traced the folder's face with the edges of a finger.

"Wait," she said. "Why don't you give me your number?"

He turned and looked at her. She wore an uncertain expression as if her words still hung in the air waiting to be taken back.

"Because my employers don't feel it's in their best interest." He opened the door a crack and then shut it firm without leaving. "I will tell you this. The people I represent, they aren't the type to quit asking."

With that, he put his fingers to the front of his hat once more. Then he opened the door, acknowledged the receptionist and made his way to the elevator.

Claire eyed the folder and considered its contents. During her brief glance, she'd seen an oddly-worded cover letter, a few headshots and not much else. The remaining contents were a mystery and would stay that way for at least a little longer. The clock demanded action and she'd never been late in her life. She lifted the thing and looked it over once more. It was nearly an inch thick and heavy as a book. She opened a drawer and slipped it inside. She left her office and locked the door.

For the rest of the day, she went about the usual routine. But within her mind, Mr. Harris had found a place in which to live. She thought of his words while she ate. She thought of them during phone conversations. She thought of them while she worked in the lab. And she thought of them during her drive home, the file sitting alone in the passenger seat, a few subtle glances here and there.

When she finally arrived home, she gathered the hefty thing up and made her way inside. Without deterrence, she unlocked her front door and hurried to her bedroom, where she opened the folder and spread the contents across her bed. As she thumbed through it all, her heart picked up, its quickened beats audibly thumping within her ears.

No single piece was shocking in itself, but as a whole, the contents were terrifying. They had everything on her: credit scores, middle school grades, bank statements, orthodontic records. There were receipts and phone records. Letters she'd written long ago to people she no longer knew. Car leases, rental agreements, and somewhere in the middle, she found a picture she'd never seen before. It was her as a child, maybe six, maybe nine, brittle-edged and sepia, freckles on her cheeks.

What she didn't find was an offer, a job outline, a copy of her resume or letter of recommendation. The contents were deeply personal, not professional, and it became clear that what Harris had given her was no pitch at all, but a veiled, methodical warning that she should take their offer, whatever it was, whenever it came again. It was their power revealed and nothing more, and as she closed the folder, she felt the threat working within her as designed, and she did not sleep well or much, and by the time morning broke, she was greatly diminished.

The next day, Claire received a call from Gunther Billingsly, the man who'd begged her to accept the position at Viox Genomics in place of the prestigious Paul Devaney. Then his voice had been pleasant, soft and pleading. This time, it was terse, his words as if from a script.

"I'm sorry to say that Viox has withdrawn its offer and will be seeking other candidates," it said without any obvious inflections. And no questions were answered, and no reasons given, and if she'd been a pleader, Claire might have argued on her behalf, but she'd have done so to a fallow receiver, the opposite party removed the moment his words crossed the wires.

In a daze, she left her office and stumbled outside. She looked about as waves of hurrying people split around her without regard. The air was cold against her skin, and as the pale sunlight disappeared behind a passing cloud, it grew even colder.

She walked along the street, alone and afraid, her mind so frayed and so long without sleep. She passed a cafe and stopped to enter, but the tables were all occupied, so she pulled her coat collar up and took a seat alone outside.

The waiter brought coffee to ease her predicament, and she sipped it gratefully, while the human rush moved before her eyes in a blinding mesh of wool coats and brightly-colored scarves. After a while, her disappointment gave way to terror, as she put the author to its effect.

This Mr. Harris worked for powerful people, indeed. Viox was a multi-billion dollar company with its own version of the CIA. There was no lie this behemoth corporation couldn't dismantle, and no person able to stand firm in the way of its goals. But somehow, this entity had gotten to them, made them do its will. And if Viox's defenses were but a day's worth of aggravation, what were hers?

The waiter appeared from inside, his demeanor strained against the weather's cruelty. He placed a bill on the table, the wind nearly seizing it before she could slap it down with her hand. She withdrew a credit card and handed it over. The tall young man took it and hurried to take refuge within the cafe's interior.

She sipped her coffee and thought, the caffeine rush lifting her spirits and sharpening her mind. She considered Mr. Harris and his people. What was her value to them? Where would they stop to get what they wanted?

Without Viox, she would have to withdraw her resignation from the university, but things could be worse. Whatever the case, she would not be won by coercion, and she nodded to herself to solidify the stance.

She looked up to see the waiter approaching, his soft, youthful face apologetic and somewhat sad.

"I'm sorry, ma'am, but this card has been declined."

She looked up, her cheeks growing red without permission.

"That's impossible," she said. "Are you sure?"

He squinted into the wind as it stung his face.

"Yes. I ran it twice."

She lifted her purse and withdrew another.

"I'm sorry. I don't know how that can be. Can you try this one?"

He took it and hurried away, only to return with the same results. After a third try, she paid with stray coins from the bottom of her purse, and when she took her place among the flowing mob upon the city sidewalk, she was truly afraid.

She walked to the bank, where she spoke to a bald man who resembled the Mr. Clean character from television.

"Let me look into this for you," he said, his voice dry as stale bread.

When he returned moments later, he explained that a hold had been placed on her account through legal means that were appropriate and neat. She would have to consult a lawyer for more information. He was obliged by bank policy. She asked for more information, for help of any kind, but bank policy was his god, so she gave up and left the building.

Outside, the winter wind licked her face, each cheek a healthy rose from the gathering daily same. She wept openly for all to see, few taking notice as they hurried on their way. She dawdled within the crowd for a while. Then she caught a cab and aimed it someplace safe.

Chapter 3

Claire wept as she hadn't in years, her mother trying to understand the muddled, furious words pouring from her mouth. The old woman stared at the dining room floor, sipping her tea, eyebrows pinched together, head nodding, judgments. When her daughter had finished, she stood and walked to the kitchen. Seconds later, she returned with two small plates of muffins that looked as if they'd been freshly made for the occasion.

"You need a lawyer," she said, as she centered a plate beneath Claire's chin.

Claire shook her head and leaned back.

"It won't do any good. These people, whoever they are, whatever they are, they seem too capable."

A garbage truck strained and gurgled out front, and they waited for the calamity of crunching glass and plastic to quiet.

Her mother frowned.

"This is why you should always put some cash aside."

Claire shook her head and looked down the hall.

"Where's dad?"

Her mother's mouth firmed, the corners descending.

"Just resting."

Claire turned and studied her mother's face, so weary and weathered by life.

"How is it?"

The old woman looked down the hall.

"Sometimes it's o.k.," she said, and that was all.

Claire tapped her fingernails against the table.

"Should I see him?"

For a moment, her mother's eyes grew pale as his, and Claire found her answer within them. Through the years, a cloud had grown over her father's mind, an unforgiving dementia at root within. At first, its subtleties inspired endearing little teases. He'd forget things, coin odd remarks, like who made ketchup so red? And how do you look at the stars long enough to count them? After a while, though, it became how is a shoe buttoned; why didn't the dog vote; and when will we eat anymore?

At first, her mother sought to best the doctors and all their certain words. But soon more and more memories went like bits of pepper in the wind, and her resolve ultimately fell away from the fight and settled on the caring instead.

"Maybe wait for a better day," she said, as she cleared the table.

Outside, on the stoop, her mother fiddled with her pocketbook under the shamed gaze of her genius daughter.

"This is all I have on me, but there'll be more. I just have to cash my social security check."

Claire took the money with a swift motion, abbreviating the moment.

"I won't need more." She held both her mother's hands, the skin like tissue paper. "I will return this with more upon more."

Her mother smiled.

"What will you do?"

Claire let go of her hands and straightened herself.

"Practical things."

The old woman put her palms on her daughter's shoulders.

"Long ago, I gave up telling you the ways of the world, my dear, but it wasn't because I didn't think they applied."

She leaned in and kissed the girl's forehead.

"Be careful. Life doesn't care about your abilities, will use them against you if it can."

Claire's eyes shot forth.

"Don't worry. The decision is made for me. I can see no way to resist."

They embraced as awkward friends, the bare treetops clattering above them in all the rushing wind. After a quick goodbye, she left in a taxi, the old woman outside, waving even after there was no one left to receive the gesture.

Claire sat back and watched the city flash outside the backseat glass. The driver tried to make conversation without success, so he pinned the radio to something foreign and off-putting. When they finally arrived at her apartment, she paid the man with money unearned, a miserly hand at the end of her wrist. He grunted and forced the gas pedal down, the tires spinning without much noise, despite his best efforts toward the otherwise.

She climbed the steps with a heavy heart and even heavier legs. She opened the door and let her keys splash against the kitchen Formica. She filled her lungs with the familiar scent of home, and for a moment, she was overcome by peace. But within seconds, the telephone broke the spell and brought the outside within.

She lifted the receiver and said hello.

"Ms. Foley?"

She breathed deeply, her stomach lurching at the sound of his voice.

"Hello, Mr. Harris," she said. "How are you?"

"Just fine, ma'am. Do you have a second?"

"Yes."

"Good."

She heard the rustling of papers.

"I'm going to read a statement to you given to me by my employer regarding the opportunity I spoke of the other day. Is that clear?"

"Of course," she said.

"Alright, begin quote:" He cleared his throat. "We'd like to offer you a lucrative position. We value your expertise and believe you can prosper with our organization."

She waited.

"End quote," he said.

"That's it?"

"I'm afraid so."

She dropped the phone to her waist and rubbed her left eye.

"Are you still there, Ms. Foley?"

She put the phone to her ear.

"Yes. I'm still here."

"I'm sorry I don't have more to offer, but that was the only thing given to me."

She said nothing.

"Are you interested, ma'am?"

Her mind worked over all opposing eventualities: risks, rewards and the forever lack thereof.

"I suppose so."

"Good," Mr. Harris said. "Very good."

That night, she laid in her bed with her eyes closed, mind frenetically turning stones at search for sleep. But it would not be found in its usual places.

And each time she drew close, it skipped away, her eyes rolling upwards and then snapping back, body flinching, palms bleeding sweat.

After a while, the light from the windows grew soft and purple; so she quit the enterprise entirely and moved to the kitchen, where she drank black coffee and drew sound, practical plans.

Chapter 4

    Mr. Harris had said noon with an impactful tone, so she left at nine for anxiety's sake. The park wasn't within walking distance, but she didn't care. The journey provided room for thought and chances to reconsider. Cornered and sleep-deprived, she moved over the pavement, each step forced, yet terrifyingly productive. Something waited at the end, but its mystery was absolute. They wanted her; she did not want them, the former everything, the latter, a wrinkle under an iron.
    She navigated the sidewalks, people rushing past, scarves whipping airborne, a mob of expressionless faces paled by the dim autumn light. Each made way toward his or her next thing, heads pointed straight with intent, as if its measure trumped all others, and as theirs, rightly so.
    She bought a cup of coffee at the place with the smallest line, the cashier palming her mother's social security money like any other, no judgment opposite her shame. Outside, she drank as quickly as possible, wisps of steam curling up and wetting the tip of her nose. The caffeine ran its route, and she used it for its worth. But halfway to the park, the muscles in her legs caught fire, so she flagged a cab and rode too quickly the rest of the way.
    At the park, on a bench, Mr. Harris sat against all reason, two hours too early, with the posture of someone anticipating an immediate arrival. She stood behind a big tree, watching him as if he mattered more than he did. But his decisions couldn't save her from this imposed destiny, and after a while, she stepped from her hiding and approached him from behind.
    As she neared, he did not turn to face her, and for some reason, this brought relief. Despite his all-knowing, he could not predict the moment of her coming, and as she entered his field of vision from the side, he seemed to flinch.
    He stood and outstretched his hand, and when she refused it, he did not seem offended. They sat quietly with good space between them, an

obvious awkwardness at root. The weather so, few used the park for its designed purpose. But it made an ideal timesaver for the working lunch-goers, and mobs of white-collared people passed before them in regular flashes with middling breaks between.

Mr. Harris started to speak but shut his mouth at the break of her voice.

"Why the hell are you doing this?" she asked.

He pursed his lips and shook his head.

"I understand your frustration, but I am not doing anything."

She slapped her palms against her knees.

"Bullshit. You are ruining my life."

He shook his head again.

"I understand why it seems that way, but your life is not ruined, and I am not responsible for any of this either way."

A fat, whiskered man sold hotdogs from a wheeled stand nearby, the smell of flavored roasting meats traveling all the cold, surrounding air.

Claire pulled a tissue from her purse and wiped her nose.

"Do you have any idea how freaked out I am?"

Mr. Harris nodded.

"I can imagine."

She waited for something more, but he only sat, his face made no less handsome by its unsympathetic mold. She looked off somewhere and then back to his ardent stare.

"Well, what now?"

"Now, I give you the information you need, and you use it however you like."

She leaned back and rubbed her forehead.

"However I like?"

He nodded.

"Yes, ma'am."

"What I'd like is to have things as they were."

He frowned.

"The job you would've had?"

She opened her hands to the air.

"At least that, yes."

He squared his shoulders to face her.

"Ask yourself what you would have been there." He slid about an inch closer to her on the bench. "Just a background figure cooking up stuff for others to take credit for. That's all. And these places like Viox, they're corrupt.

They bribe politicians to get drugs rushed through trials. Next thing you know, you've got thousands sick or dead and you're responsible for it."

She shook her head and sighed.

"None of it matters, anyway," he said. "What choice have you got?"

She passed a glance at a blue-eyed girl wandering over the dead grass. The mother sat immediately across them on the opposite bench, her interest tied to some publication documenting the activities of the famous and those balanced along the fringe.

"At times, you seem like a nice man, Mr. Harris."

He nodded his head slightly.

"I thank you for the compliment."

She squared her shoulders to face him.

"Are you doing a nice thing now?"

He shook his head.

"I honestly have no way of knowing."

She rubbed her eyes and sat back on the bench.

"Tell me this," she said. "Why do you work for these people?"

He sighed.

"I would have thought you'd know that by now."

She looked off toward nothing in particular.

"Because you don't have any choice," she whispered.

He put his hand on her shoulder.

"If you want to continue what you've started in this life, want to be anything at all, you will have to do this." He took his hand away and moved it flat across the air in front of them. "You will have no consideration, elsewhere. They'll have you cut out until you're like a woodpecker in a petrified forest. No doors will open; nobody's going to want to touch you."

He frowned and scratched with his fingers the corners of his mouth.

"It is what it is."

From the opposing bench across the path, the mother attracted her child and gave her blueberries from a Ziploc bag. The girl winced from the sourness and then smiled with delight.

"Why did this have to happen?" Claire asked the wind.

Harris said nothing.

"Can't you tell me anything about these people?"

He shook his head.

"I'm sorry. All I can do is tell you where to be and when to be there."

He handed her a very small yellow envelope the size of a business card.

"Inside that, you'll find an address and a time." He firmed his position upon the bench. "Now, I need to give you some important information, and I want you to listen to me very closely. Are you listening?"

She nodded.

"Good. Now, I've warned you of the passive fallout that will occur if you refuse this offer, correct?"

She nodded.

"Okay, now I'm going to give you some important instructions, and you need to follow them, or desert this whole thing before you get started."

He waited a moment and then went on.

"If you decide to come to the specified location inside that envelope, you need to be on time, and you need to go alone. Don't bring someone else, or they will be in danger. Don't call the authorities, or you will be in danger. Do you understand?"

She took a breath and nodded.

"Do not disregard my warning, okay?"

"I understand."

He shook his head.

"No, I mean it. Violence to these people is like you or me having orange juice in the morning."

The two from across got up to leave, and Claire watched them go forward, the child at a stumble, mother at a considerate pace until they were smalled by the distance and lost in the flowing human mass.

"What's your first name, Mr. Harris?"

"I'm not allowed to say."

"Say it anyway."

He scratched hard the skin above his eyes.

"Henry."

She tipped her head back and closed her eyes.

"Henry Harris," she whispered.

The wind kicked up and desiccated leaves rushed between the benches, some whirling, some atomized under boots and heels.

She wiped her eyes, but they were dry.

"What's all this for?"

He slapped his hands against his knees.

"I don't even have a guess." He stood and smoothed the wrinkles on his shirt. "Something important."

She looked at him, his face suddenly grim and imposing.

"Just go along with it," he said, pulling firmly the bill of his fedora. "That is my advice to you, and it is sound."

With that, he stood and walked away, his figure square and smallish, and quickly lost in the hoard of passers.

She looked down at the tiny envelope in her gloved hand to make sure it was still there. She held it up to the light. She started to tear it open but stopped to make sure no one was watching. Someone was. It was a man on the other side of the path. Amid the grass, he stood alone, his hands in his pockets, dark sunglasses shielding his eyes. She lowered the envelope and watched him, her heart throbbing wildly within her chest. He kept watching, his face disappearing behind the people that passed and then reappearing exactly as before.

She pushed the envelope into her pocket and toyed with it nervously. She glanced to the left and the right, but there wasn't much to see. Her eyes drifted back toward the man, and she saw he was approaching. Her pulse raced as he closed the distance, her head growing faint, white flecks infesting her vision. Soon he reached the path and began sifting through the passing pedestrians, his face looking eager, mouth open and breathing.

After some difficulty, the man finally slipped through the human congestion and continued toward her. As he neared, Claire's body stiffened. She looked around. She started to call for help. But just as she opened her mouth, a young woman appeared from behind her and rushed into the man's arms. She buckled forward and breathed, her chest tight, hands trembling. She sat back and watched as the two entangled in what must have been a long-awaited embrace. At last, they separated and the man rubbed tears from beneath the girl's eyes. They smiled at one another and walked away, their hands interlaced as they disappeared from her sight and into their lives.

She sat a while longer until her heart settled and her hands stilled. Then she stood up, took the path a ways and caught a quiet cab ride home.

That night, she sat in her bed, the lights dim and considerate, her legs Indian-fashioned beneath the weight of her body and soul. The television ran live in one far corner of the room, but its offerings competed poorly for her attention.

She held the enveloped message in her hand, its secret at wait inside the cheap manila shell. Weightless and sharply rectangular, it was a part of something. Fractional to some greater purpose, but key to its actualization.

Inside this thing was the answer, and loath as she was, a terrible curiosity festered within. She was pursued by the influential and powerful. Forcible as it was, this entity considered her important, and a horrible, unfamiliar satisfaction with that seemed rightly fixed to support the countering weight of her natural anxiety.

In time, it would all make sense; and she would cope and evolve and grow from whatever came with it. This was her destiny and bound by it, she seemed definitively so.

But when she opened the envelope, she found it empty, and no action could make things any other way. And she cried to her core for a long time. For more time than she ever thought she could. And she did not, could not sleep the night, her crisp, brilliant mind growing wild and frayed and spoiled with dark thoughts.

Chapter 5

The spring dusted the city in gold, the warmth eroding all the browning snowdrifts and opening lush pastures for children to play. Almost at once, the parks turned lavish with flowers and green-smelling things, the sunlight opening rich veins of pleasure for those who knew how to take it.

For others, the season came without notice, their lives ensnared by schedules, deadlines and obligations. Like oddly-uniformed soldiers, they marched toward their zombie enterprises, some fixated on rings of brass, others driven by the patter of wolven feet.

Claire's spring was spent at her parents' home, supporting her mother's efforts to care for her father as they safely guided him toward his end. Intent on mindlessness, she cleaned dishes and dust and physical waste, pacified his delusions, and thoughtfully exterminated her mother's notions of perceived improvement. Bonded together, they forced food into his mouth, and his body into bed, restrained his panicked aggression with smoothed voices, and when that didn't work, combined to forcefully hold his arms and legs together to keep him from stumbling outright into the open, uncaring world.

At night, they drank together, the two embracing over old notes, photographs and stories, their thoughts cast back to sepia times, two minds remembering for three.

The summer brought fresh worry and a whole new kind of ache as they became strangers to the man they loved. Now, he cowered at the sight of their faces, balling up in corners and sobbing, like a shattered child at the unsettling approach of foreign smiles.

After a while, his mind became less a child's and more a void, dull and vacuous and uncomprehending. Most of the time, he stayed in his room, his eyes tracing minuscule fragments of dust that danced on beams of window light. All day he'd watch them move about, like wisps of evanescent magic left by fairy wings. Free and aloft and always refracting, until they passed through the sunlight entirely and vanished into the realm of imperception. Invisible and unconsidered, but there just the same.

One day, she handed her father a cup of juice and he immediately turned it over onto the carpet. While he sat on the bed watching, she scrubbed the floor. The heels of her hands grinded against the carpet as soap suds foamed atop the sucking fibers. After a while she stopped and looked up at him, his face vacant, drool gathering at the bottom of his lower lip. She got to her feet and approached him. She took his whiskered chin in her hand and lifted his head.

"Remember me," she told his face, her fingers firming around his jaw. "Remember me, Goddammit."

But he only stared through her, the drool pulling downward in a wobbly string and then falling free. She fell to her knees, dropped her head into his lap and wept. But he only stared vacantly at the space she no longer occupied, his eyes neither focused nor unfocused, mind uninhabited.

They subsisted by sparse consumption, eating when and what they could. Claire unable to tap her bank account, they devoured her mother's monthly pittance with painful care, like the last morsels of a cruel harvest, picked clean by hollow-looking things with dark, sunken sockets and manifest ribs.

Claire's problems remained her own, and rightly so. Her mother was too tired and too lost to consider anything else for even a single moment. Over the months, Claire had met with lawyer after lawyer with no real success. The script the same in every instance: they'd listen, fingers tapping chins, stroking beards, foreheads firmed by thoughtful thinking. With confident steady voices, they'd make big promises, each outlining his or her approach in clear, definitive language that would have been easy for anyone to understand.

Undeterred by her warnings, they'd pursue the case, some with very real success, at least for a while. But then things would change. One after another, they'd end the relationship abruptly and without explanation, their eyes advertising worry. Their voices trembling, asking her to please go away. Doors shut in her face and locked shortly after. Phones unanswered, calls unreturned.

By this point, Claire had applied to many jobs that were beneath her, the interviewers confused by her interest and skeptical of her intent. Ultimately, most passed for fear that she'd turn over the position too quickly in favor of opportunities that were inevitable for someone like her. Still, others jumped at the chance to have her, those offers rescinded days later for reasons that had become obvious to her, though mysterious and intangible, they remained.

One day in August, she made the last bowl of oats in a secondhand microwave she'd bought at a discount store. Her mother wouldn't touch the thing, older people having no use for those advances which serve to make their skills obsolete.

"It makes life easier," Claire had said to a sour face and shaking head. But this argument had died out among the sadness and fatigue, and now the thing sat upon the green kitchen countertop as if it had been there all along.

When the timer rang, she removed the bowl, added a spoon and toted the thing toward her father's room. Her mother met her in the hallway and snatched the bowl from her hands.

"Go out," she said.

"No. It's fine."

"No," her mother said. "Go out for a while."

She nodded and collected her purse, while the old woman carried the little bowl away.

Outside, it smelled of parched earth and dying grass, the sun's giving warmth now a nuisance to be wished away. She walked the neighborhood to the bus stop where all walks congregated for public transportation. After a while, the thing came, snorting and screeching, polluting the air with a foul, petroleum stench.

She ascended the steps and took one of the few empty seats. As the bus rumbled forward, her unblinking eyes pointed straight ahead, while the lewd gazes of strange-eyed, unwashed men itched against her skin.

After several blocks, the bus began emptying itself of all the wrong passengers, and soon she was left to ride with a pair of unwashed drifters who breathed through wet, open mouths. They watched her with covetous male eyes, their hands clasping the bus rails, gripping and relaxing, muculent prints of sweat left against the metallic chrome.

She noticed her stop approaching through the window and reached for the cord, only to take pause when she saw no other people outside. She glanced over her shoulder and reassessed the two men, her head conjuring images of torn clothing, screams and laughter, wide, gritting smiles. Without much thought, she released the cord and pushed back in her seat. Miles later, the bus entered a more cheerful area, and she finally tugged the cord and fled the vehicle to join a crowd of ordinary people dressed in sensible, coordinated attire.

She backtracked the way to her original stop, the sun intolerable, her blouse sticking against her sweating shoulders and back. After several miles, she crossed the street and entered a small café near a little grocery shop.

Inside, she found an immaterial line of customers that thinned quickly, and before she knew it, she held an iced coffee in one hand and a muffin in the other. Weak with hunger, she bit into the bread before the cashier could deliver the change. Errant crumbs fell against the coins in his outstretched hand, and she studied them with horror. The young man had a soft, handsome smile and he gave it freely, as she apologized through bulging cheeks.

"No worries," he said, as he poured the coins and crumbs into her hand.

She made a movement toward his plastic tip jar, but when his attention moved to another customer, she quickly placed the change inside her purse and turned to go.

Immediately, she saw Mr. Harris sitting in a far corner, his hat set upon the table, balding head tanned and glinting under the weak overhead light. He watched her like an impartial witness, his square face neither smiling nor frowning.

Without measure or hesitation, she crossed the room and bathed him in iced coffee, the foam settling on his face, the rest soaking the right portion of his sport coat.

Harris jumped to his feet, his stunned face studying the sleeve of his jacket as if a limb has been torn from underneath. An old woman gasped, a young couple gawked. The manager came out and asked her to leave.

"That's quite alright," Mr. Harris told him. "I had it coming."

The old black manager looked at one and then the other, his fists balled.

"Then I'm going to have to ask you both to leave, and immediately," he said, his jawbones at work beneath a layer of thin, coarse skin.

The two went outside, and Claire immediately turned and walked away down the sidewalk.

"Claire," Mr. Harris said. "Please don't go. I'm here to help you."

She kept walking.

"Claire," he said forcefully, his words cutting through the wind in a way that seemed beyond his capabilities.

She stopped and turned, eyes alive with fire, hate. She made the way back with fewer steps than before and struck him in the face. He staggered back and groaned, his palm against a swelling cheek.

"Who the hell are you? Once and for all, goddamit! Once and for all, who the hell are you?"

Mr. Harris steadied himself and removed his hand to reveal a gathering welt.

"I understand your frustration, but you have to believe that I didn't have a thing to do with that envelope." He spat blood. "I promise you, I did not know it was empty."

She moved toward him, and he flitted back like a much younger man.

"What the hell is going on?" she asked. "What do you have against me? Why the fuck are you destroying my life?"

He put his hands up.

"Not me," he said. "It's not me."

She balled her fists and screeched, passers flinching, birds fleeing trees.

"No more of that bullshit. I want to know what's going on."

He rubbed his face.

"I wouldn't even know how to lie," he said. "I promise you; I don't have the slightest clue."

She put both hands on top of her head, like a mother confounded by the ways of an errant child. Then she dropped them, staggered toward the exterior of the cafe and leaned against the brick.

"Why are you here?" she began to cry. "What now, for God's sake?"

He rubbed his face and spat again, his saliva looking pink against the pale sidewalk.

"I'm here to do what I've been told to do."

She shook her head.

"And what's that?"

He removed another tiny envelope from his pocket, and she moved toward him.

"Wait, wait, wait," he said, as he moved backward. "I checked this one."

She approached and snapped it up, tearing it open and lifting a white card from within. Her eyes burned forward as if to set it aflame.

"What is this?" she asked. "What is it?"

He put his hands inside his pockets.

"An address."

She looked at him.

"To what?"

He shrugged.

"I don't know."

She turned and tapped the card against the red brick.

"I'm sorry I struck you," she said. "That's not like me at all."

He took out his hands and dusted his shirt.

"I've been hit by people less angry than you."

She turned to face him and he flinched a little.

"Does the same hold true as before, Mr. Harris?"

He looked at her.

"I'm not sure what you mean."

"Before, you said I should come alone without telling anyone. Is the same true here?"

He nodded.

"Absolutely. Every bit of what you said is true and right."

She opened her purse and tucked the card inside.

"Then that's the end of this relationship. I don't want to see you anymore. Is that clear?"

He nodded.

"Perfectly, yes."

She turned and walked away without looking back. But once she achieved the edge of the building, she fled the walking path and retreated into a stairwell, where she wept for all that matters and all that doesn't, for her mother, for her father, but most of all, for herself.

How did you get so far in this life without any visible scars?

She pushed her back against a brick wall and sunk to the ground, crossed her legs and opened her purse. She removed the card and looked it over: it said 17 Copper Street and 2 A.M., and she took out a pair of old receipts and a pen and duplicated the address twice, placing one receipt in a pocket and one inside her shoe. Then she implanted the card back inside her purse, rose to her feet and shot back out into sun-drenched sidewalk that led the way home.

Chapter 6

    17 Copper Street was on the east side of town, and she would have to leave early to make the deadline. Invested wholly in the overpowering history of her daughter's seamless reasoning, her mother threw up few complaints. Instead, she said goodbye in the way that mothers say goodbye to daughters when their children are all they have left in this world. And they cried like children, each and the same, the right words spoken in case of an untimely or failed return.
    Her mother remained awake as long as she could before drifting away on the sofa, as television infomercials called softly in the dim pale light. Claire pulled a blanket over the old woman and placed a soft kiss on her wrinkled cheek. Then she shut the door noiselessly, leaving her mother alone to dream against unimaginable burdens and sorrow.
    The taxi had come late, and Claire let the driver have it for much longer than he deserved. Soon they were both apologizing to each other, and then it was quiet except for the engine and the intermittent crackling from the CB radio.
    At her request, the driver stopped a few blocks from her destination, and she entered the wind and night, where the street lights splashed weak hints of amber against the dark pavement. In that wind and night, indistinct shadows stretched outward, like ghoulish, spindly fingers across a vast and solitary urban terrain. But within that terrain, life moved all around her, and she knew it by the sound of clanking bottles and shuffling feet. As she walked, the downtrodden stirred in the shadows, pale-faced and curiously watching such a clean and foolish woman jog across their streets.
    By the time she reached Copper Street, the fear and anxiety had taken its toll. She stopped and bent forward, her hands on her knees, lungs sucking hungrily the air. She wanted to go home, but it was too late. She stood up and

rubbed the small of her back, her eyes darting about the shadows in search of dangerous men.

Then she saw them all scuffling about under a big pool of white light. She stumbled forward, her head turned slightly, the scene before her peculiar by context and setting:

At least a dozen men and women stood atop a dimly-lit basketball court that sat like a paved courtyard between three red-brick apartment buildings. Dressed professionally, they looked at their surroundings and one another through bewildered eyes, as if they'd suddenly appeared at this dusty, urban destination from thin air, or perhaps even another time. Claire crossed the street to join them, her heeled shoes applauding the pavement with thwacking noises audible to all. A good portion of the group unsettled, flooding toward her suddenly, like a shifting mass of migrating birds veering from the coordinated flock.

Claire stopped short of the curb, her feet tied to the dark, empty street.

"Are you one of us or one of them?" an approaching woman asked, her rotund figure laboring even at such an easy pace.

The small crowd filled in around the woman's shoulders, their faces eagerly awaiting a response.

"I'm definitely not one of them," Claire said, the words leaking through her knotted throat. "Whoever they are."

The backside of the crowd grumbled and turned away, leaving the woman alone to greet the newcomer.

"Oh," she said. "Well, come on then. We're all waiting over here."

Claire stayed fixed to the asphalt, a pair of small, brightening headlights bearing down on her position. The woman furrowed her brows.

"Are you coming, dear?" she asked. "You'd better get out of the street either way."

Claire turned toward the lights and jumped out of the road.

"I'm sorry," she said. "I'm just a bit flustered."

The woman gave her a tap on the back.

"Join the crowd," she said. "Figuratively and quite literally."

Claire followed the woman to the pack, many engaged in conversation and oblivious to her arrival, most of the men all together, one taking thoughtful drags from a polished wooden pipe. The fat woman joined two older, scholarly-looking women, and Claire trailed her and pushed into their group.

"What's your name, dear," the fat woman asked.

"Claire."

"And who are you with?" another woman asked, her jawline suggesting Scandinavian descent.

Claire's eyes washed over the group for a moment, their easy expressions offering no signs of fear or coercion.

"I worked under Paul Devaney at Clairmont University."

The asker's mouth firmed and her head nodded in approval.

"I'm Delores," said the fat woman, who then gave the other ladies' names and resumes in turn.

"Nice to meet you all," Claire said. "Do any of you know anything about this organization?"

The women traded looks.

"Not really," Delores said. "But we're all eager to learn more, everyone trading stories and such."

She raised an index finger and pushed her glasses back toward the bridge of her nose.

"Do you know what they're saying?" Claire asked.

The other women looked at Delores as if they themselves had asked the question.

"Oh, just a smattering," she said. "It's clear that no one knows anything substantial, but some have different attitudes than others. Some seem much more excited than others, than me."

Claire nodded.

"How did you come to be here?" she asked them all, but only Delores answered.

"They accepted an initial invitation. I resisted."

"So did I," said Claire.

Delores nodded and touched her elbow.

"I'm not sure everyone here understands them like we do," she said.

She opened her mouth to say more, but before she could, the faint sound of engines entered the quiet surround. At once, all the little social circles broke apart and each person lined up along the curb, some leaning forward and pinching their eyes to see deeper into the black yonder. The machine hum gathered in the distance until headlights finally broke over the horizon atop the paved hill. Through the bleary starbursts of shattered light emerged a train of five white airport shuttle vans, each spaced so evenly, they seemed tethered by samely-cut strands of invisible metallic cord.

As they approached, the vehicles slowed and turned their wheels, each pushing over the curb and onto the basketball court, shocks squealing, the drivers working carefully behind dark tinted glass that gave back the burnished street light, along with the faces of those who would attempt to look inside.

The watchers stepped back as the chain of vehicles looped around and steadied in an orderly line. Each man and woman stood waiting, their hair blowing in the wind, the engines idling softly, no signs of invitation or definitive reasons to run.

Finally, the door of the first shuttle opened, and a young well-dressed woman stepped out. She wore a broad, plastic smile across her beautiful, flawless face and she looked everyone over with high-voltage eyes.

"Hello!" She said as she stepped out to join them. "I'm so happy to see this great turnout."

She raised her hands and called them closer.

"Please, everyone, step forward, step forward."

They gathered around her.

"Now, if you'll just give me a few moments, I'd like to say some words."

Her impossible smile faltered for a brief moment, and then an even brighter one took its place.

"My name is Sherice, and I'd like to thank you for choosing this exciting opportunity to further your research and individual careers. Now, all of you are experts in your fields, and this has made you desirable to The Xactilias Project. What's The Xactilias Project, you may ask? Well, there will be time for broader explanations. In the meantime, I can say it is a mission dedicated to uncovering new discoveries aimed at advancing the human impact on the world."

She maintained her smile as she studied their faces.

"Now, I see a lot of different people from all walks of life, but one thing we all have in common is an insatiable desire to find answers to complex questions and, perhaps more importantly, the innate ability to construct the bridges that will take humanity from this plane to the next."

Her face suddenly grew somber, forming wrinkles and little bulges without affecting her beauty one bit.

"I understand you must all have numerous questions, but I'd like you to put a pin in those until we make our final destination."

A few of the attendees looked at each other. One man spat his gum onto the ground.

"Wait just a second," he said, all eyes turning toward him as he spoke. "What the hell is all this? You expect us to file into these vans and just go?"

He turned toward the rest of the party.

"I don't know about the rest of you, but I haven't been told very much about this organization, and I'd like to know more before I commit to anything."

The group turned its attention to Sherice, who appeared somewhat puzzled by the interjection, her eyes squinting toward the crowd, like a stage performer searching the darkness for drunken hecklers. After a moment, she turned and leaned back into the shuttle.

"Demetri?" she called. "Someone has a question."

The crowd waited for Demetri to appear, but he never did. Instead, the doors on the adjacent shuttle opened and three equally-built men exited, their thick, polygonal frames poorly concealed by dark suits, faces neither handsome nor ugly, expressionless.

As they approached, the free-willed man studied the increasing void between him and his colleagues.

"Please come with us, sir," one of the men said, the others bracketing him, sweeping him forward and into their vehicle, the whole thing swift and practiced, a thousand times refined.

"Now," said Sherice, her mouth regaining its familiar form, "while his individual concerns are addressed, let's talk about what happens next."

She stepped forward and the crowd gulfed. She turned her back to them and faced the shuttle train.

"All of you met with one of our representatives, and this is important because it will decide which shuttle you'll be taking."

She pointed to the left.

"If you met with Mr. Humphries, you'll be taking number five at the rear. If you met with Ms. Donovan, you will take number four. If you met with Mr. Grace, you'll take number three. And if you met Mr. Harris, you'll be riding with me in shuttle number one."

She turned to face the group.

"Obviously, no one will be riding in shuttle number two, except for existing passengers, of course."

She looked around as if she expected questions.

"Alright then. Let's all get into our shuttles and start this exciting adventure."

The groups within the group separated, some shaking hands, a few exchanging hugs, most content to keep their distance from anyone with features indistinct. They all lined up at their respective carriers and entered one by one, each vehicle equipped with white, leather seats and a steward to guide the incoming forth. At the front of the train, Claire fell in behind a line of tired, beaten-looking people with haggard faces aimed nowhere but down. Each went up the steps and took a seat, Sherice grinning madly as they passed, like an insane flight attendant, happily at work upon a conveyor of doomed souls.

When the passengers had taken their seats, an automated voice bled through a pair of overhead speakers: toneless, preserved words thanking them for coming, asking them to please fasten their safety belts and remain seated through the duration of the ride. When all was set, the shuttle train moved forward, circling the paved court and carefully descending the curb one by one, the passengers jostling within darkened windows, their existence imperceptible to the few passing motorists occupying the city's sleepy streets.

Outside, the night saw the city evolve from a place of efficient business to one of sour noises and hard tastes. The deodorized flock gone to slumber, the streets now played host to a homeless breed, which subsisted off indirect charities and the plights of its anothers. One after the next, they passed by the windows of the racing shuttles, each one staggering loopily along the filthy gutters: Some heavenly gazing after a fix; others looking downward, their faces knotted, broken minds sorting deviant languages murmured from within.

The shuttles traveled a familiar stretch of roads, and many of the passengers already knew their destination long before the airport lights bubbled atop the westward horizon. But instead of taking the usual route, the shuttles veered down unknown paths that twisted and turned before finally spilling onto the runway itself, each trailing vehicle impossibly close in its pursuit.

The train wheeled past all comers, baggage handlers slowing their work, reflective clothing vivid under the passing halogen beams. Some of the guests rose toward the windows, fingers fiddling with their seatbelts enough to realize they were locked.

Finally, the shuttles wheeled to a stop near a military cargo plane, its impossible volume enough for squadrons of men with plenty of room left over.

A voice rang from the overhead speakers, startling the passengers as they leaned over one another trying to see out. It was Sherice, and she seemed no less enthusiastic than she'd been before the drive.

"Passengers, may I have your attention?"

Throughout each vehicle, a hanging cloud of mutters dispersed into a hush, as everyone calmed to listen.

"Good," she said, invisible to all but those in the lead carrier. "I'm so glad to welcome you to our intermediate destination. Next, you will all be boarding a flight that will take you to a tertiary destination, and I must ask that you hold all your questions until journey's end."

As she cleared her throat over the microphone, the shuttles filled with an agony of trebled clatter, and some of the passengers clutched their ears.

"I'm sorry," she said, regaining her pitch. "Now, as each one of you exit, your steward will present you with an envelope meant only for you. Once we exit, you'll have an opportunity to lightly disperse. At this time, please read your card and then place it inside a pocket or handbag. Now this information is meant only for you, and we must insist that you refrain from sharing any part of it with your associates. If I am able to impress one thing upon you during our brief encounter, it is that the leaders of The Xactilias Project value cooperation above virtually all else; so please heed all warnings that pertain to the sharing of information."

They felt her smile among them, as she said to rise and exit, the seatbelts separating at the break of her voice as if she by will controlled each one using the few mental powers jangling around her empty head. One by one, they stood and walked and claimed their little envelopes before stepping out onto the tarmac, the summer breeze warm and kind even at this crooked hour. When they'd all exited, the doors to the shuttles snapped shut, while the crowd dispersed as instructed.

Claire watched the train get going, Sherice's shrill voice still rattling around in her head, like screws in a coffee can.

"That woman's been holding in the same fart for more than a few years," she heard from behind. She turned to see a glad-looking man with handsome features that might have seemed threatening on someone from the blue-collar world. He smiled through a set of polished teeth, his deep brown eyes devouring everything they saw.

"My name's Nathan," he said, offering his hand like it was a reward.

Claire took it briefly before leaving it in mid-air.

"I really don't think we should be talking. They said we should disperse and read our messages."

He smiled.

"Sure." He stood same-placed as she turned to walk away. "We'll just put a pin in this. Nice to meet you."

Most everyone had already secured territory, and she hurried past them as if working against a stopwatch, a frowning man with his thumb hovering over the button, tenths of seconds wasted with every misstep. She finally breached the outer circle and found a private place of her own where no one would see over her shoulder. Across the way, she saw distant runway personnel stopping to watch the scene playing oddly before their seasoned eyes. She turned to see their perspective, the envelope moist inside her pocketed hands. Indeed, they all looked foolish spread out that way: high-shouldered and slouched forward, heads alternating from left to right. They looked very much like children involved in some sort of curious schoolyard game, each one hoarding clues for a contest that might bring licorice or tiny adhesive gold stars.

When she was sure no one else could see, the envelope came out, and she tore it open to withdraw another card.

"Welcome, Ms. Foley," it said. "We are very pleased you have chosen to participate and are confident you will find great success with our organization. That said, we must insist that you discuss neither the details of your recruitment nor that of other guests. Failure to comply will result in immediate termination. - Demetri M."

She put the card back into its container and studied the others, their blank faces giving up little. Some clutched their memorandums tightly, while others crumbled the cards and tossed them onto the tarmac. One man laughed aloud when he read his card. A woman put a trembling hand to her mouth.

"Hello!" A man said from above.

They looked up and saw him standing high atop stairs that cut into the belly of the plane, his figure looking rigid in a tailored military uniform.

"Welcome, each and every one of you."

He had a thin mustache that was shaved into a pencil line across his lip. They all watched as he sailed down the stairs with ease, the toes of his polished boots tapping each one for only an instant, as if they moved only to give the appearance of walking, while he floated upon a descending draft of air.

"Please, all of you," he said, as he hit the level ground. He lifted his hands high above his head and summoned them all together across whatever fictitious borders kept them apart.

"Now," he said, as they fell in before him. "My name is Bernard, and I will be shepherding you to your tertiary destination."

He scanned them slowly, each brown iris looking small upon his bulging white eyes. He kicked his heels together and crossed his hands behind his back, his body growing even more wooden before their eyes.

"Now," he said. "You will all line up in any order and board the plane using the stairs. Inside, you will enjoy free seating unless you require special assistance, in which case you will notify one of the attendants who will see to your individual needs."

He looked them over once more before smiling enough to show most every tooth.

"I'm pleased to be in your company and hope you will find your journey without discomfort," he said. "However, I must ask that you hold any questions until journey's end, when all of your individual needs will be addressed to your particular satisfaction."

He turned his body in an automated sort of way, his left foot sliding backward like some giant invisible finger had pushed against his right shoulder. He raised his arm and turned his palm upward as if to introduce to their eyes the plane for the very first time.

"Please," he said.

They all shuffled together to form Bernard's line, and he watched as they ascended the motorized passenger staircase, everyone avoiding his stare, eyes fixed to the back of the one before them.

Claire fell in with the laggers at the back of the line, finally taking a spot behind the person who did not want to be last and the one who did. When she finally reached the top of the stairs, a thin young Latin woman greeted her with a fierce smile before pointing the way to the seating compartment, which held three to a row on either side. She walked the aisle looking for a seat, moving past the rows of strangers toward the first vacancy she saw.

"Hello," Nathan said, his arm casually resting atop the backside of the open seat middled between him and an old man. "I'm willing to offer the window seat if that's something you're interested in."

She smiled politely.

"That's very gracious of you. Nathan, is it?"

He rose up and shrunk backward, the old man following suit; each allowing her to pass by and take his offer, her rear end brushing hard against each of their fronts, with all parties pretending otherwise.

"That's right," Nathan said. "And what was your name?"

"Claire," she said, as she claimed her seat. "It's Claire."

"Nice to meet you."

The old man leaned forward and outstretched his hand over Nathan's lap.

"My name is Alfred, madam," he said, a hint of an accent bending each word, its origination left unidentifiable by decades of proficient suppression.

"Claire," she said, as she took his hand, soft in hers and courteously gripped. "Nice to meet you."

"Thank you," he said, smiling somewhat bashfully. He wore round, thickly framed eyeglasses and a free-willed bush of a mustache that had grown Einsteinian, by coincidence or intent, one could only guess. "Mr. Nathan and I were just discussing the odd tenor of this evening. Although I must say, he seems to be most comfortable despite the countless oddities we seem to have witnessed."

Nathan placed both hands on his knees.

"Well, Alfred, I just happen to enjoy the anti-norm wherever I find it." He grinned, and Claire could see he was chewing gum. "What about you?" He turned toward her. "What's your story?"

"I don't have one."

"Ah," he said, dashing the thought with a flip of a hand. "I hardly believe that else you'd be sitting on another plane headed to a seminar in Nebraska or Iowa."

She shrugged her shoulders.

"Oh, I get it," he said. "You're one of these lab rats who's spent a life hovering over microscopic worlds pressed between slides."

"Hardly," she lied.

"Are you sure?" he asked. "I think I can see a microscope imprint around your eye."

Alfred touched his arm.

"This is how you acquaint yourself with a beautiful woman?" he asked. "In my day, young men approached women with poetry on their lips."

Claire smiled politely.

"I take pride in your error, Alfred," Nathan said. "However, I'm neither young nor am I trying to woo our seatmate. I'm merely making conversation." He turned back toward Claire. "So what is it? Do you have a story or not?"

She looked at Alfred and then back to Nathan.

"Well, of course, I do, but I believe we've been instructed to protect our information from one another."

"Ah," he said. "The babbling woman with the painted face. As I recall, her guidelines pertained only to our little personalized memorandums. Am I incorrect?"

He looked at each of them, palms turned upward. Alfred frowned, his mouth disappearing beneath a forest of twisted gray.

"I suspect the ominous nature of the warning itself was meant as a chilling effect toward all communication; however, I cannot disagree with your assessment." The old man looked over both his shoulders before hunching toward them. "Perhaps we should whisper, nonetheless."

They both looked at Claire, each of them eager-faced, as if the three sat beneath a fortress of sheets, trading slumber party gossip above a low-watt flashlight bulb.

"I'm sorry," she said. "I don't feel comfortable."

Alfred looked disappointed, but Nathan only smiled.

"I'll do it for you then."

He cleared his throat and framed his hands like a director setting a scene.

"You're an idiot savant fresh from your laboratory cage, where your hyper-systemizing resulted in countless breakthroughs, which brought you countless edible treats and, ultimately, freedom itself, and, no less significant, an opportunity with the mysterious Xactilias Project."

Alfred's wrinkled face grew somber as if the words had been pointed toward him.

"Such talk," he said without a follow-up. Claire smiled.

"It's alright, Alfred," she said. "I've heard worse from better."

Nathan's face grew worried.

"Forgive me. I meant to be funny."

"Please," Claire said. "It's perfectly alright."

A single tone poured from the overhead speakers, causing everyone to perk up in their seats.

"Welcome passengers," a voice said with a German accent. "This is the pilot speaking. I'm quite pleased to have each of you with me this evening. Our flight will take between seven to 12 hours to complete, depending on weather and other circumstances. Should you need to use the facilities, please flag the closest attendant, and she will escort you. Otherwise, we must insist that you remain seated for the duration of the trip unless you have a medical condition, in which case, you should notify your nearest attendant immediately following this message."

They waited for more, but nothing came. Instead, the engines roared to life and the plane crawled forward, no catastrophe procedures or safety demonstrations, the passengers furiously fastening their seatbelts on their own accord.

The tone rang out again, sending pulse rates ever higher.

"This is your captain again," a voice said. "I'm sorry to say we have no choice but to deviate from usual procedures and take off immediately. Please fasten your safety belts and prepare for lift-off."

As the plane gathered speed, more than a few faces grew pallid, some digging fingernails into armrests, others deep in meditative breathing exercises.

Claire shut her eyes, but this only made the engines louder, so she raised her lids and looked about the aircraft if only to read faces of the flight attendants for signs of calm or concern. Instead, she saw panic throughout the cabin: the passengers hunkered backward into the plush of their seats, the attendants themselves looking rattled, hands on their hats, bodies jolting side-to-side.

And then she saw Nathan calmly looking over the rest, his head shaking slightly, an amused smile on his face. He turned suddenly as if her stare had burned a painful impression on the back of his neck.

"Isn't this fun?"

Claire shook her head.

"Not for anyone but you."

The plane jolted and the cabin filled with little yelps and deep groans.

"Embrace it," he said. "You feel your heart beating? That's how you know you're alive."

She bit her thumbnail as the lights dimmed and reset.

"Preexisting knowledge," she said.

He smiled and touched her arm, his hand weighty and impossibly dry.

"There's no point in worrying. We're in no position to control this outcome."

She moved her arm.

"This type of worry is involuntary."

He looked at her and unfastened his safety belt just as the plane lifted a moment and clumsily bounced back to earth.

"Really?"

"Stop that," she said. "You're making me more nervous."

"Why should my personal decisions make you more nervous?" he asked. "Are you afraid my loose body might lift from the seat and render you unconscious?"

She turned her head to the window.

"Let's just not talk until this is over."

He nodded once.

"Agreed. If we survive."

"Stop it," she said, and he grinned.

"I can tell we are going to be friends," he said.

"Shut up, shut up," Alfred said. "I'm trying to keep from having a heart attack."

Seconds later, the aircraft finally gathered enough speed to ride the air upward, a terrible thunder reverberating from its giant smoldering engines. The plane climbed and climbed, its long wings dipping and rising, some of the passengers driven to nausea, the smell of vomit wafting between shoulders and heads.

Once airborne, the plane finally steadied, and the passengers began to settle. The attendants unbuckled their belts and straightened their little hats. One by one, they turned to face the passengers, their stiff faces replaced by preset masks, friendly and calm and pretty as the world could offer.

Alfred put up a finger and motioned one over.

"I think I'll have a drink, miss," he said, as he ran his hand through his dry, coarse hair.

"Certainly, sir," she said. "Each passenger is entitled to two alcoholic beverages. What would you like?"

"A vodka tonic, please."

"I think I'll have one, too," Nathan said. He nudged Claire.

"How 'bout you?"

She looked at her wrinkled palms.

"Yes."

The attendant took out a note pad and made three checkmarks.

"Three vodka tonics."

While they waited for their drinks, Alfred toyed with a coin.

"What is that, Alfred?" Claire asked.

"A very powerful good luck charm, my dear."

Nathan looked at him.

"You carry a good luck charm, Alfred?"

"Indeed."

Nathan shook his head, as the old man leaned forward and handed it to Claire.

"Please be careful with that," he said. "It is very valuable."

Claire took the coin and looked it over. Nathan watched from the corner of his eye.

"It's just a penny," he said.

Claire turned it over in her hand.

"Does it hold some sort of sentimental value?"

"Yes," said Alfred. "But that's not what makes it valuable. It's a 1969-S Lincoln cent with a doubled die obverse."

He looked at each of them as if expecting expressions of appreciation.

"So," Nathan said.

"So," said Alfred. "This coin is exceedingly rare. If you look closely, you will see a clear doubling of the entire obverse except for the mint marking, which would suggest a case of strike doubling. In this case, the doubling of the obverse without the doubled mint mark indicates a doubled die, which is what makes this coin so exceptional."

Nathan and Claire looked it over.

"The 'Liberty' looks blurry," Claire said.

"That's it," said Alfred.

"So you think this penny's lucky because it's blurry?" Nathan asked.

Alfred looked disappointed.

"No, it is only valuable because of this. Monetary value has no bearing on its ability to provide luck."

"How valuable is it?" Claire asked as she turned it by the edges between her thumb and index finger.

Alfred smiled, proudly.

"That coin is worth between 70 to 80 thousand dollars."

Claire stopped turning the coin and immediately cupped it with two hands.

"Jesus," Nathan said. "What the hell are you carrying it around for?"

Alfred shrugged.

"Because it is lucky for me."

Claire offered it back.

"Please take it. I'm afraid I'll lose it."

Alfred smiled and took it from her palm.

"I'd be rid of that thing as quickly as possible," Nathan said. "Take it to auction and be finished. I couldn't stomach the thought of losing something like that, lying in bed at night thinking about it passing from one take-a-penny/leave-a-penny jar to the next."

Alfred opened his jacket and pushed it into a pocket.

"I thought you weren't given to worry."

Claire smiled.

"Touché," Nathan said. "Still, I can't believe anyone on this plane believes in luck."

The old man looked at Claire and winked.

"It's bad luck not to believe in luck."

It was quiet for a moment, except for the tapping of Nathan's foot.

"The Secret Service confiscated the early specimens until the U.S. Mint finally admitted they were genuine," Alfred said. "Imagine that. All that expense to avoid the simple admission of a minor mistake."

Nathan dusted his lap.

"Well, that's the government for you. Where the hell is the alcohol?"

As if summoned by his words, the attendant arrived with their drinks. They slowly took liquor from the glasses, the warmth sweeping their bodies like a strong emotion, rushing through their veins and over their skin. Alfred wiped the wetness from his mustache.

"Tell us about yourself, Claire," he said. "If you will."

Claire rubbed her forehead and drank some more.

"I'm sorry, Alfred. I want to, but I can't."

Nathan flipped his hand.

"Don't worry, Alfred; I can tell you anything you need to know." He took a deep breath. "Our friend here is one of us without being one of us." He took the old man's arm. "You see, she is one of the precious few on this flight who is blessed with the genetic ability to succeed without barter. Look around you, if you will." He raised his hands over his head and made swirling motions with his index fingers. "All these passengers are busy giving their resumes to one another, their accomplishments, proof of their viability." He reached over and took Claire's hand. "Claire here has no need for such gainless strategies, because she automatically knows she is better than anyone here."

Claire ripped her hand away.

"I'm guessing most people don't like you very much," she said.

Nathan nodded.

"Perhaps. But you shouldn't trust anyone who is well-liked."

It was quiet for a moment.

"People at my lab dislike me because I don't use the e-mail," Alfred said finally.

"That seems like a very thin reason to dislike someone," Claire said.

"I leave notes for them," he said before downing the remainder of his drink. "On their desks mostly. I despise computers, though I'm forced to use them frequently to record data and such. But when it comes to communication, I wholeheartedly believe when someone puts a pen to paper, their words are truer than those placed in movable type, or electronic type as it were. To write by hand, it requires steady attention, at least if one is to craft legible script considerate of the reader's understanding. These days, few maintain the muscle coordination to print or scribe legibly, at least for long periods of time."

He leaned forward, his eyes growing wide and serious.

"Did you know they have moved away from teaching cursive in traditional public schools? Can you believe such a thing? You'd better because it is true."

He leaned back and looked to the ceiling for answers.

"It's archaic, they say. But there's so much more to it than simple facts and expressions writ to paper or digital storage devices. Ever so much more."

Nathan looked at Claire and smiled.

"Oh, simple thing, where have you gone?" he asked. "Quick," he addressed Claire. "Take this pen and scribe some coiling sentences to soothe our friend."

Alfred crossed his legs and raised a finger.

"Laugh all you want, but refinement for ease is not refinement at all."

He dusted his legs and looked from one to the other.

"You consider e-mail refinement for ease?" Claire asked.

"No, not at all," he said. "I'm a scientist, after all, not some old fool commit to useless relics that remind him of better days that never were."

He raised the finger again, as he seemed to do at the conclusion of every point.

"But when I want to send someone a message, I will have the consideration to raise a pen to the occasion."

Nathan tapped his elbow against Claire's arm.

"Wouldn't it be funny if his penmanship was indecipherable?"

Alfred shook his head.

"Oh, to be young and brilliant."

Nathan looked at him crossly.

"I'm 40, thank you very much."

The old man's face grew impressed.

"Oh, 40, my goodness."

Nathan raised his eyebrows.

"And what of smoke signals, Alfred? Will you be taking up their cause, as well?"

The old man leaned forward and took Claire's hand.

"Let me ask you this, my dear. Would you rather receive a love letter written by the very hand of your lover or one printed in New Times Roman?"

She smiled.

"I very much see your point."

His mouth grinned as he released her hand.

"And you," he turned to address Nathan. "Don't judge the old until you have gotten over the hill to see. And if your sweetheart ever writes you a letter by hand, you'd do well to regard the content with keen, attentive eyes."

Nathan put his hand atop the old man's shoulder.

"It's between the lines what counts, my old friend. True today as it was yesterday, machine text and handicraft alike."

The airplane bellied a thick pocket of air, loping suddenly and then falling just as fast. Some of the passengers groaned over the passing weightlessness, but Claire only felt Nathan's stare upon her while she gazed through the window glass.

"Tell me about yourself, Precious Few," he demanded.

"I have flat feet," she said without looking at him. "Is that the kind of thing you're asking?"

He bent over to take a closer look.

"At least they're only flat on the bottom."

She shook her head slightly, elbow on the armrest, chin nestled within her hand. Her eyes watched the moonlight pour over the tops of clouds, like an ethereal sun above a land of gossamer makings.

"I mean, what's your story?" he said.

She turned.

"It's not very interesting," she said. "Maybe you should just read that magazine."

He reached into the pocket on the backside of the chair before him and withdrew a Turkish publication called "Skylife."

"That's old news," he said. "It's been on the back of my toilet for weeks."

He rolled it up and began tapping it against his knee, as Alfred leaned back in his chair and shut his eyes.

"How'd you come about this little journey," he asked?

She looked at him crossly.

"Haven't you read your card?"

He reached into the interior pocket of his sport coat.

"What, this?"

He pushed the magazine back into the pouch and pulled his card from the little yellow envelope.

"What of it?" he said as he passed it over.

She pushed his hand away and looked around.

"I don't want that. For God's sake, put it back in your pocket."

A puzzled look spread over his face as he looked around.

"Jesus," he said. "It's just a little card."

She turned back toward the window.

"Let's not talk anymore. I don't think it's a good idea."

He took another look around the plane: most of the passengers trying to sleep, a few reading beneath pale little lights. He sat back down.

"Why?" he asked as he leaned toward her. "What does yours say?"

She did not respond.

"What does yours say?" he said loudly, another passenger clearing his throat at the disturbance.

"Shh," she whispered, placing her hand over his bare arm. "It says not to discuss myself with other passengers."

His jaw fell a little as her fingernails dug in.

"Alright, alright," he said rubbing the skin she'd just released.

His eyes grew suspicious of the woman before him, as if she'd just exposed herself as delusional. Just in case, he opened his envelope and withdrew his card to be sure he hadn't overlooked anything. When he was satisfied, he tossed it onto her lap, text up.

"Here," he said.

She flinched from it, her body turning wooden, as if he'd thrown a writhing serpent onto her legs.

"I don't want that," she said. "Please, stop this and take it back."

He shook his head and collected it in his fingers.

"Fine," he said, pointing it at her, his face stern. "You need to relax, Precious Few. This is going to be a long flight."

With that, he killed the overhead light and pushed his seat back, eyes closed, forearms wholly consuming both his armrest and hers.

She watched him for a moment, his mouth open and breathing. Dark morning stubble grew along his jaw and neck, but he was still a handsome man, with or without a shower, civility or refinement.

After a while, she turned her eyes back to the window, but her thoughts remained on his card, its message odd and troubling, the tone innocuous and soft.

"Welcome, Mr. Walker," it said. "We are very pleased you have chosen to participate and are confident you will find great success with our organization. Please let one of our agents know if you need anything during your trip, and thank you again for your commitment to The Xactilias Project. - Demetri M."

Chapter 7

  The plane landed three times on its way to wherever it was going. Each time, its passengers remained seated without the slightest idea of where they were or how long they'd be there. As the hours passed, they muttered to one another and fidgeted in their seats. Outside the idle plane, they saw only paved tarmacs, the skylines empty of mountains or buildings, everything barren and lifeless and even as the blade of a knife. After countless hours in transit, the gravity of their choices had taken on size, whatever lives they had left behind growing both smaller and greater with every mile put between them and whatever was left behind.
  Soon, little freedoms seemed to go away, attendants hard to flag, beverages and bathroom trips difficult to secure. Before long, a soft mutiny began its slow birth beneath the sustained quiet and order, but this was quelled by an unexpected announcement that they'd be landing soon and for the final time.
  Within minutes, the plane began its descent, its passengers looking over one another out the windows, stiff-legged and aching and ready to get to their feet. Outside, they saw a forest land beneath them, tropical and lush, tiny toy motorboats zipping over the ocean along a flawless coast. They looked at each other with raised eyebrows and pleased expressions, some showing outright excitement, others the ease of relief.
  The airplane rode the air downward and landed, the tires gripping seamlessly the runway as if caught up by an invisible corresponding track. The pilot brought the aircraft to a slow and wheeled it off the runway, settling on the tarmac and coming to a halt.
  "I'm pleased to announce we've arrived at our tertiary destination," the pilot said through the intercom speakers. "Please unbuckle your safety belts and exit the plane in order, allowing those nearest the exits first opportunity. Once you've left the aircraft, Bernard will provide you with further

instructions. I'm grateful to have had the opportunity to transport you and wish you much success with your new opportunities."

They exited the plane as instructed, the sun bright and centered above them, like a piercing white hole in the bold blue sky. There was an unfamiliar sweetness in the air, and it mingled with the scent of ocean salt, and as they descended the steps, a comforting wind cooled their sweating skin.

"Gather around me, please," said Bernard, his strict demeanor unaffected by the length of the flight. "You will all board shuttles, which will transport you to your temporary residences. In these, you will stay for three weeks."

He looked over them and smiled politely.

"It has been my privilege to oversee your journey; however, I must now leave you in the hands of Romero, who will be your guide over the next several weeks."

He put his hand out and a svelte-looking man stepped forward, his tanned arms and legs looking muscular and healthy against his white shorts and polo t-shirt.

"Welcome, guests," Romero said. "I'll be your host while you're here." He gave a crooked smile that made his perfectly symmetrical face seem more human. "I'm sure you are all very tired from your trip, so if you will all board a shuttle of your choosing, we'll be on our way."

Everyone looked at Bernard to see if Romero had erred in his orders, but the former had already begun walking the stairs back to the plane.

"Let's go," Romero said, and the passengers formed lines before various shuttles, many sticking with their seatmates from the plane. Claire took a place behind Alfred, and Nathan followed suit, his fingers furiously scratching the dark whiskers flourishing along his jawline.

"I need a shower and a shave," he said, as he ran his fingers through his hair.

"That sounds like heaven," Alfred said, as he took a seat inside the shuttle.

Claire selected the seat next to Alfred, while Nathan claimed the two in front of them, his leg draped across the other empty seat. Other passengers passed without seeming to notice and selected one of the many other seats available on the spacious shuttle bus.

When all the passengers had boarded, the doors clamped shut and the vehicles departed, the train's pacing far less precise than the one that had brought them all to the airport so many countless miles ago. The shuttles traveled along a sharp network of sculpted roads that ultimately devolved into dirt paths which could barely be called roads at all. The passengers held tightly, as the vehicles plunged over large water-filled holes, driving up great curtains of brown sludge that spread high and outward before spattering apart against oddly barked exotic trees.

Soon, the wildwood closed in around them, blotting away the sky before finally swallowing it whole. The headlights on the vehicles came to life; while unfamiliar bestial noises popped and shrieked in the not-so-far-away distance. As they burrowed deeper into the forest's heart, branches lashed out at the vehicles, breaking off at the windshield and stealing away some of the body paint. The passengers flinched at the sound of each metallic bong, the vehicles skidding left to right against the muddy earth.

"Where in the hell are we going?" Nathan whispered.

"Into a tropical forest of some sort, it appears," said Alfred, his hands clutching the cushion of his chair.

A crack of thunder shot across the unseen sky and rumbled into the distance. Droplets of rain followed almost immediately, slapping against huge leaves and pattering the roof overhead. Nathan showed gritting teeth as the vehicle jerked violently against a sudden void in the road.

"Any idea where we are?"

"Somewhere south of the equator," Claire said.

"How do you know?" Nathan asked.

"I noted the sun's position in the sky when we landed."

Suddenly the vehicle before them stopped in the middle of the road, its taillights burning red through droplets of dark mud. Alfred looked out the window.

"Something's going on."

"What is it?" Claire asked, but no one answered. "What is it?" she whispered.

"It's men," Alfred said. "Men with guns."

Nathan put his head out the window and quickly jerked it back inside.

"He's right. There are at least six on this side, all with machine guns."

Outside, the men fanned out around the vehicles, some barking orders to others in an unfamiliar tongue.

"What are they speaking?" Alfred asked.

"Portuguese," said Claire.

She passed a glance at one of the men through the window, his face heavily whiskered and bleeding sweat. Another man approached and stood next to him, each dressed in matching green fatigues, automatic machine guns in their hands. The two exchanged words as they peered into the forest, their eyes wide and seemingly concerned.

"What are they looking at?" Alfred asked, but none of the other passengers had an answer.

The driver of the shuttle turned and stood.

"Please, you must go now," he said in broken English.

Everyone looked at each other but no one stood. The driver pulled the lever and the door swung open.

"Please," he said. "Go now."

No one moved despite his request, most every seatbelt still securely fastened. The driver looked at them all through uncertain eyes, as Nathan stood and raised his finger.

"Shut that door," he said.

The driver looked at the door and then back to the American.

"Shut it."

The man shook his head and turned the lever, the door pressing shut, the other passengers closing their windows until the noise from outside reduced to a mutter.

"What do we do?" Claire asked, but she already knew the answer.

"I don't know that we have much choice but to sit still and hope our Mr. Romero can talk these people away," Alfred said.

They all waited in silence, the beat of the rain steady, like countless fingertips softly drumming atop the roof. While they sat, their heated breath fogged the windows until the outside world disappeared, its affairs seemingly distant and unreal.

Outside, the gunmen traded words, their conversations deliberate and slow. The passengers huddled silently, hearts throbbing violently within their chests. After a few moments, Nathan lifted from his seat.

"What are you doing?" another passenger asked, but Nathan didn't answer. Instead, he moved toward a window and used his finger to trace an eyelet in the condensation.

"What do you see?" Alfred asked. Nathan held up a finger and pushed his eye to the window. Outside, the gunmen busily emptied the other shuttles and lined the passengers alongside their vehicles, the rain picking up, mud hungrily sucking the soles of their dress shoes.

"They're taking the others from the shuttles, lining them up outside," he said.

A woman gasped and the other passengers quickly subdued her. Almost immediately, there came a hard banging against the shuttle door.

Without looking at the passengers, the driver turned the lever and the door swung open. The passengers stiffened as Romero stepped inside.

"I'm sorry for the surprise, my friends, but you must all exit the vehicle and join your colleagues outside." He took a step down before turning back. "Come on, now. Everything is perfectly alright. You have no reason to fear."

After hesitating for a moment longer, they detached their safety belts and shuffled toward the door. Outside, the raindrops seemed to fall in slow motion, before fracturing at last into countless water beads which melted against soil and clothing alike. Romero handed out green vinyl ponchos to each person as he or she exited the vehicle.

"Please, join the others," he said, as they slipped the rain gear on and pulled the hoods over their heads. When they'd all fallen in together, Romero stood before them and cleared his throat.

"Everyone, please, may I have your attention," he said. "I'm truly sorry for the inconvenience, but we must abandon these vehicles and travel afoot a short distance."

He pointed toward the gunmen, who were busy peering into the woods, rifle barrels pointing through gaps between trees.

"These men will be our protection as we make our journey," he said. "Without arising unnecessary fear, I can say they are an important defense against the potential dangers associated with the geography we currently occupy." He looked at their shoes. "I understand most of you are ill-equipped for this type of journey; however, we don't have the time to remedy this problem, so you will have to make do with what you have."

He turned and motioned one of the gunmen over. They spoke for a moment and then the man began walking up the road.

"Please follow me," Romero said. "You will all be well-served to trace the footsteps of the person before you. And please be kind enough to offer a helping hand to those who have difficulty staying up with the rest."

With that, he turned to go, adjusting his stride so his feet placed neatly in the lead gunman's water-filled tracks. Without speaking, the others followed suit, the rain popping against their ponchos and making a racket in their ears.

Overhead, the tall trees seemed to grow together to form a tunnel that choked out the light while disrupting the rainfall not at all. Beneath their waving branches, the men and women walked in a line with their heads down, eyes focused only on the path, minds calculating each and every step. As they plunged their feet into the existing steps, the foot holes grew deeper and deeper, until the mud tore the women's footwear from their feet, its suction greedily clutching the soles as they stopped to wrestle them free. Soon, most walked on bare feet, the road peppered with pricey pumps and loafers that jutted from the soppy ground like little hollow relics, as if the wearers had vanished without explanation, leaving only their shoes to declare they'd existed at all.

An elderly man buckled, his knees coming down hard against the ground. He struggled to his feet and moved on, only to go down again a few steps later. Nathan rushed forward and helped him to his feet.

"I'm afraid I can't manage this," the old man said, his fear concealed behind a thick pair of fogged eyeglass lenses. Nathan looked back at Claire and Alfred.

"Go ahead," he said. "I'll catch up."

They approached, their faces painted with concern.

"How can we help?" Alfred asked.

Nathan reached into his coat and removed a small pocketknife.

"Just keep up with the rest," he said. "I'll catch up." He looked at the old man. "Wait here a moment."

He slogged through the mud and stumbled onto the thicket's grassy edge. Claire and Alfred gave the old man a nod before moving forward, all the others growing distant in the murky curtain of drizzle before them.

They trod through the sucking muck, their figures swallowed up by the fog that lifted from the road. Through the rain, they heard nothing, not the birds, the strange noises from before, not the gunmen or even the sound of their own panting. The mud grew loose and deep, and they forced their quivering legs along, each one leaning against the other's body, pulling and pushing as necessary, not a sign of anyone before them, nor anyone behind.

Finally, Alfred stopped.

"I'm sorry, my dear; you will have to go on ahead."

"I won't hear of it, Alfred. Now, let's go."

He sat in the mud.

"I can't. These old bones just won't let me."

Claire sat on the ground beside him.

"I'm not going to leave you."

They waited.

"Will they be coming back?" Alfred asked.

She put her arm over his shoulder, and they leaned in together.

"Surely," she said.

Claire looked through the rain at all the lavish growth flowing in the wind, the tremendous leaves innumerable, tiny rivers flowing brown in the alleys alongside the road. As the water puddled around them, thunder rolled overhead, as if God impatiently thrummed the heavens at wait for their next move.

At last, they sat in the road, feet aching, skin made fragile by soggy shoes, peeling away in spots, stinging. Someone approached from behind and Claire turned to see the old man, his arm around Nathan's waist, a crude walking stick in the other.

"No time for a break," Nathan said.

Claire stood while Alfred regarded the old man's cane.

"Cut me one of those, and I'll see what I can do," he said.

An hour later, they crossed out of the fog to see Romero crouched over the ground, a small stick in his hand, linear patterns carved into the soil. To his right sat a pair of large armored military buses, their engines idling,

"I'm relieved to see you," he said, unconvincingly. He nodded toward the woods, and a pair of gunmen exited the thicket. "These men have kept a watchful eye on you; however, they are only being paid to protect and not to aid. Forgive me for your plight, but as I told the other passengers, we are taking special measures to ensure that we do not fall victim to opportunistic parties."

He walked over to one of the bus's giant tires and used the edge to cleave mud from his boot.

"Please," he said. "Join your colleagues. You will find towels and water inside."

As they entered the bus, each received a towel and a large bottle of water, which they nearly emptied on sight. As they moved through the aisle, they passed numerous weary faces, gaunt and timid and streaked with crusted mud that had given away its earthy tones and settled to an ashy gray. They found plenty of open seats near the middle of the bus and settled together, Claire and Alfred on one side of the aisle, Nathan and the old man the other. Nathan turned backward and addressed a pair of stupefied women.

"What did we miss?"

One of the women looked up and scratched a flake of mud from below her ear.

"He didn't really say anything. Just told us to get on the bus, take a towel."

Nathan nodded and turned around.

"May I ask your name, good sir?

The old man smiled.

"My name is Arnold."

He lifted his water and drank, his hand trembling. Nathan waited while the old man lowered the bottle and used his sleeve to dry his mouth.

"Thank you so much for your kindness," Arnold said. "I was once a formidable athlete, I'm ashamed to say. But in life, you lose things."

Alfred leaned over.

"I can relate, my friend," he said. "I once ran track and field, but I can hardly imagine moving that quickly anymore."

Arnold nodded. "Time has a quick hand, so it seems."

The bus began moving, its giant tires churning the soil and spitting up mud.

"I'm sorry. I haven't learned your names," Arnold said.

They introduced themselves and traded handshakes.

"Are you feeling alright," Claire asked. "Would you like some of my water?"

Arnold smiled and held up his hand.

"No, dear, thank you. I'll be fine. I just need to rest. Perhaps we can pick up our conversation when we arrive at wherever it is, we are going."

She nodded, and they left him to rest against the wall of the bus, his towel wadded into a makeshift pillow.

Nathan leaned toward the aisle.

"This whole thing is getting out of hand," he whispered.

Alfred nodded.

"Agreed. But I don't know what means we have to alter our course."

Claire scratched the mud from her calves.

"I agree with Alfred. It's only practical to wait and see what happens."

Nathan lifted his head and rubbed the stubble beneath his chin.

"I'll feel better when I can cut this down, have a shower."

They rode in silence the rest of the way, the old man asleep, whistling through his nose. Alfred slept, as well, while Claire and Nathan watched the scenery blow past through pink, wired eyes.

Two hours later, the buses breached the forest's perimeter and spilled out onto a long road that divided rambling fields of sugar cane. Almost immediately the rain ceased, the sun boring forth as if to welcome them from their journey through a dark and ancient land. The light evoked a stirring amongst the passengers, who climbed to their feet and gazed out the windows. Outside, they saw rows of plants flowing under the sunlight, the leafy blades bright green and whipping all around in the wind.

They continued through the fields, the ground turning hard and choppy, the chugging tires jolting the passengers for several miles. Finally, the buses climbed out of the fields and onto a stretch of flat, combed land. Soon, structures began to appear: silos, water towers and large storage buildings surrounded by tall electrified fences. Several miles later, they saw the coast appear in the distance, the water glinting brightly under the sun as it roiled against long away sands.

An hour later, they reached their destination, the buses slowing and then stopping before a gate, which gave access through a chain-linked fence that spanned the outer edges of what appeared to be a massive concrete dome. Security personnel guarded the entry, automatic weapons firm in their hands. Romero exited his bus and gave one of the guards a glossy little card. The man looked it over, his face broad, square and expressionless. He raised his hand and swung it forward and the gates drew open so the buses could pass through.

The dome sat at least 500 yards inside the gate, and as they approached, its mass seemed to both rise and expand, the passengers pressing their faces against their windows to get a better look at its size.

"This just keeps getting stranger," Alfred said.

"I agree," said Claire.

As they approached the dome, more armed men appeared, and the buses settled to a stop. Once again, Romero exited and showed his card, the guards nodding and then returning to their posts. Romero signaled the drivers, who opened the bus doors.

"Please exit carefully," Romero shouted.

The passengers flowed from the buses and gathered outside.

"We'll now be entering the enclosure," Romero said. "Please form a line."

One of the soldiers approached a keypad mounted on the sidewall next to a metal door. He typed something and the door popped open to reveal a steel grid walkway that led inside through a narrow hall toward a large elevator door. One by one, everyone entered and walked toward the elevator, their shoes and bare feet slapping hollowly against the cold metal below.

"Excuse me," Romero said, as he squeezed between them and approached another keypad positioned just to the right of the elevator. He typed something and the doors separated to reveal a large platform. "Please enter."

When all had done so, Romero typed against yet another keypad and the doors closed. The elevator dropped rapidly and without sound, a tickling in their stomachs upon its descent. Seconds later, they came to a stop and the doors opened to reveal an elaborately decorated lobby stocked with plush-looking couches, which were buttressed by end tables supporting stacks of varying genres of magazines. Directly in front of them, about 80 feet away, a very tall, beautiful woman sat behind a large curved receptionist desk, her attention fixed downward, hand furiously writing.

"Please exit," Romero said, and when they all had, the woman raised her head and smiled.

"Welcome," she said, as she pushed a stack of documents aside and moved to join them.

Romero held his hand out.

"This is Gretchen, and she will attend to all your needs during your stay at the spa."

The guests exchanged looks, as the lofty woman approached.

"For the next two weeks, you will reside here at our spa," Romero said. "During this time, you will be allowed access to a variety of relaxation services and recreational activities. The purpose of this time is to acquaint you with your new responsibilities, while providing you the opportunity to acclimate to your new surroundings and familiarize with your co-workers."

He turned to Gretchen and nodded.

"I'm very pleased to have you all here," she said, eyes gleaming and impossibly blue. "Here at our spa, we provide the best of everything. Should you need anything of any sort, you are to visit me or one of our other recreational therapists, understood?"

She turned to Romero and smiled.

"I know you all have plenty of questions," Romero said. "However, these are best kept for another time. For now, I'll be leaving you with Gretchen. In two weeks, I will return to move you to your permanent quarters in the lower levels of the facility and introduce you to the work area, where you will conduct your individual research based on The Xactilias Project's specific needs at that time."

Romero turned to Gretchen and nodded. Then he checked his watch and reentered the elevator. The guests turned to watch him disappear behind the doors. Gretchen returned to her post, her broad upper body towering above the desk.

"Please form a line and I'll get you each checked in one-by-one."

As they registered, she offered each a keycard labeled with a large number.

"This is the key to your quarters," she said. "Please do not lose it, or you'll be forced to move to a new room, as we do not issue new keys."

When they'd all registered, she instructed them to visit their quarters and clean themselves.

"You'll find suitable articles of clothing inside your closets," she said. "Each will be tailored to your individual needs if necessary. Just let us know."

The guests looked around but saw no staff lurking about.

"You'll find a button mounted to the wall of your quarters, adjacent to the door," she said. "Should you need assistance, press this button and a recreational therapist will arrive shortly."

She left the desk again and stood before them.

"Tomorrow, we will meet at 9 a.m. for orientation, when you'll be introduced to the spa area, cafeteria and recreational facilities, which include a weight room and racquetball court."

She folded her arms and smiled, her lips pressed firmly, eyebrows raised, as if she expected applause or some other form of giddy feedback. The others traded looks and then dispersed to search for their rooms, muddy feet staggering wearily down a bright, expansive hallway.

Claire and Nathan followed Alfred to his room and waited. He opened the door and tipped the light switch up.

"Not 5-star, but it will do," he said.

Inside, there was a bed, a nightstand, a dresser and not much else.

"All I care about right now is a shower," Nathan said.

They entered and Alfred walked to the bathroom.

"Standing shower," he said.

"Don't tell me you're a bath guy, Alfred," Nathan said.

Alfred shook his head and sat on the bed.

"I may just go to sleep without bathing."

Claire took Nathan's arm.

"Let us leave you, Alfred," she said. "Sleep well. We'll see you tomorrow."

Outside, the hallway sat empty, the red carpet fouled by wild trails of dried mud, as if it had been unevenly dusted with bucket-throws of cinnamon. Nathan followed Claire to her room and waited while she slipped her key card into the slot.

"I look a lot better once I've cleaned up," he said, as he gouged a hunk of mud from his boot.

"Too bad you can't wash your personality."

As she opened the door, he smiled and put his hand out.

"Thanks for the laughs."

She looked at his dirty fingers and gave them a brief shake.

"I'll see you tomorrow, Nathan."

He gave a trademark smile and walked away, sport coat thrown over one shoulder, lips whistling bright notes, as if he walked through his own home on the most ordinary of days.

She watched him the whole way, head poking further out into the hallway with each step, before he finally stopped and turned back to see only her hair flitting by, and then the shut of the door.

Chapter 8

Glenn Foley cannot read, but that is alright. For what he wants, it truly is. A truck driver and proud of it, he scrapes what leavings the world allows him into a life that makes him feel rich, valuable and whole. Others agree with his appraisal. Those others, not peers, but members of his family. For them, he gives everything. For them, he paves paths he never knew.
    Before that, he is of the sorry and blaming, of the can't and never will. Born into the world strapped with bad genes, clueless parents and no mind of his own, Glenn middles along intentionless for a long while with no real reason to keep going, save the automatics working within his brain.
    Out of school at 14, he spends the first part of his adult life working ditches, mowing lawns and laboring over endless conveyor belts for long hours and laughable pay. With no goals or angles, he is an odds-on favorite for nothing special, until he meets Dawn McWilliams, a local grocery cashier with a similar background and a future that seems parallel.
    But Dawn McWilliams can read, and read more than the printed gossip in the magazines that seduce customers within her aisle. She can read people. And when she meets Glenn Foley, she reads his face and his soul and her future in the depths of his sad brown eyes.
    Twice a week, he chooses her aisle over all others, giving no credence to the length of the line or his wavering will. See their flirtation, but don't judge its tranquility. Within it, there is stirring and bold desire, and the world is shut out by it, and the clocks keep ticking, though there is no time at all.
    Their marriage brings a child and a reason, and Glenn works with Dawn on a lie that paints his abilities in false lights. He becomes a truck driver and stable provider, and his little family prospers, the world oblivious to their makings and throwing up few complaints.

In the beginning, he speaks of serendipity, of the nation and all its sites. He talks of the mountains, with their coiling roads, the bold ascensions and the terrifying drops, his boot against the brake, the pads against the rig's weight, the smells of burning rubber, of sore arms and foreign hotel beds.

He is gone almost all the time; but at home, on certain days and nights, the child sits at the feet of this hero stranger, while he speaks of faith and persistence, love and duty, the world's largest ball of twine and the St. Louis Gateway Arch.

Over a span of decades, he dips in and out of his family's life, not for want but necessity. If he could, he would be there always; but he can't, and they know it and understand. He goes on this way for as long as he must; his back constricting to a permanent arch; his soul grayed by all the missing, body ruined by years of bad food. By the end, he is broken down and used thin. But his victory extends outward; for his daughter is educated and pulled forth by the gravity of her promise, with abilities that are confusing to him, but wondrous just the same.

Claire hears this story enough until its weight falls against her every choice. A torch pushed into her diminutive hand at an early age, she carries a slim flicker of reason for her parents' woe and quickly becomes the embodiment of their hope. They know neither the inner workings of the world's secrets nor the strings that others use to make it spin. But they know enough to recognize that she wields the power to someday see each and both at the same time, and they recognize this gift while she is at a very young age.

At 13 months, she is talking in complete sentences. At 18 months, she has memorized the alphabet and knows the colors in English and Spanish: red and yellow, aureolin and fawn. At two, she can count to 20 in three different languages and do simple arithmetic using only her fingers. At four, her parents enroll her in a Montessori school, and she learns Spanish in just over a month.

Every day, she rises early with a constant, compulsive drive to learn, her mind receiving an almost sensual ecstasy from it, her brain like a heart in love. To her, learning is not of mastering; it is of experiencing. Vivid and absorbing, it penetrates and arouses, its absence causing pain, its presence, relief.

To her parents, it is a troubling addiction, and no amount of ordinary play will coax her from it. When knowledge is withheld, her mood turns gray and she becomes anxious and withdrawn. She must know everything about everything: lizards, grasses and planets, organic sediments, minerals and rock.

Sometimes she wants traditional cartoon stories at night. Mostly, she wants books on natural history. These, her parents use to train her in toilet habits, a sizable stack fixed strategically to keep her in place.

The schools are no good for Claire, a feeble curriculum, the lessons but pointless tasks. They ask her to solve 6+8; she makes 36-piece origami forms on her dining room table. They give her Frog and Toad Are Friends; she reads Les Miserable at home. How long can you anesthetize a child before you finally put them to sleep? This is the question her parents ask themselves every day.

The playground expounds on the classroom's folly, the other children distrusting of this odd figure before them, venomous in their response. She tries hard to be like everyone else, failing miserably in almost every way. At home, she becomes sleepless and depressed until her abilities turn from gifts into something to wish away.

At last, she is moved ahead several grades against the resistance of the school heads, their brows pressed with worry, mouths uttering warnings regarding social inadequacies. But in the end, her parents agree: what could be worse than this? For it is just as difficult to kneel or stoop as it is to stand upon toes.

At first, the move offers improvement, but soon, she is stretching the teachers past their abilities. The older students will spend a year on their textbooks; she sucks them dry within the first several days. Ultimately, they craft personalized curriculums and teach her on the side. But the more they feed this mind, the greater its cravings, until their cupboards are empty, and the deprivation returns.

They visit a private school for the gifted, and her test scores astound. There, they craft improvised parallel curriculums that soar above the heads of the gifted others. She ranges far beyond her classmates, mostly fixated on a newfound world of subatomic particles. At the conclusion of the program's fourth grade, the school heads agree she can go no further in such an institution.

Through personal connections, the headmaster secures a meeting with an influential representative from a prominent research university devoted to engineering and applied science. He is a doubtful man with big gray unkempt brows that have begun to hang over his eyes.

He meets with her parents and the headmaster for only a short time, and then she is placed alone in a cold sterile room before a tall varnished table that comes to her chin. There, the stern figure slaps a stack of papers under her nose, its questions requiring answers that will measure her IQ.

As he paces the width of the table, she populates each field, her hands appearing infant-like as she scribbles against the paper. When she stops writing, he snatches the test away, his eyes darting about the pages, his tired face made bright and pale by unbelieving. The exam's IQ distribution chart ends at 145; somewhere beyond, lies Claire.

Chapter 9

For nearly a week, the guests wandered the facilities without responsibilities, dipping in and out of hot tubs, taking massages, and drinking at the bar. In the mornings, the room lights would ignite automatically, a gentle combination of pinks and yellows that flared gently and considerately, until the senses enlivened, and the rooms took on a warm, comforting glow. For meals, they met together in a large but comfortable cafeteria, the food like something from a dream, with flavorful meats, brightly colored fruits and rich, flaky pastries that were always fresh, delicious and warm.

In the early afternoons, most gathered in the little round courtyard, where they sat among the sweet scent of flowers, chatting over coffee beneath willowy trees that shaded courteously the soft, green grass. Most kept tightly within the circles established during their journey; Claire, Nathan and Alfred no different, the three of them together the majority of the time, trading stories and theories, growing closer and happier for it.

At night, Alfred would usually retire early leaving Claire and Nathan at the bar, where they pried at each other's layers with subtle tactics both cunning and kind.

"Tell me about your research," he said one night, as he sipped a small glass of bourbon under an amber light.

"It mostly revolves around experimental research on human aging," she said. "Strategies to replenish DNA telomeres to make cells immortal and thereby prevent aging."

He pursed his lips and nodded.

"Have you made any strides?"

She sipped from a glass of red wine and nodded.

"Major strides; however, any sort of telomere-based anti-aging treatment is apt to increase cancerous growths and therefore increase mortality."

He nodded and lowered his head, his finger tracing the wet circle on the bar top where his glass had been.

"What's the nature of your research?"

He looked up at her and smiled.

"Experimental methods for cancer prevention."

They sat quietly after that, their minds pondering the meaning of these things and others. The mystery of The Xactilias Project. The mystery of each other.

The next morning, everyone congregated as usual in the cafeteria, where they filled their trays with thickly cut bacon, sausages, fresh berries, warm strudels, croissants and tarts. Like every other day, Alfred blended into the line and filled his tray with a wealth of rations, his face bashful and apologetic, as if he had taken each morsel from the plate of a starving child.

Once he'd acquired his share, he surveyed the tables and found Claire and Nathan sitting across each other, their trays samely glutted with far too much food. He hurried across the room and took a seat next to Claire.

"Every day I come into this room, my mind recalls the story of Hansel and Gretel," he said, as he raised a fork.

Nathan nodded.

"I've gained at least five pounds," he said, his words distorted by a mouthful of half-chewed food.

Claire watched him and scowled.

"Close your mouth. That's disgusting."

He smiled broadly, his cheeks pregnant with food.

Alfred took a sample from his tray and gently placed it inside his mouth. He lifted from his chair and took a long look around the cafeteria.

"Why do you suppose all the rooms in this place are round?"

Nathan glanced about and shrugged.

"Tell us about your research, Alfred," Claire said, as if she hadn't heard his comment.

The old man swallowed a mouthful of food and brushed a few stray crumbs from his mustache.

"I'm afraid it's not as fascinating as yours," he said. "It's mostly centered on practical solutions for utilizing water to produce hydrogen fuel." He stabbed his fork into a chunk of ham and held it for a moment. "Long before that, I was quite fascinated with neurological research. However, it didn't suit my abilities."

He raised the ham to his lips and then pulled it away.

"Sometimes, you have to choose to either pursue a passion in a limited capacity or apply your abilities to more practical endeavors that will allow you to acquire the lifestyle you desire."

Claire started to say something, but he cut her off.

"I did always enjoy neurological research, though. It was all I could think about as a boy."

Nathan passed a look to Claire, who gave a small apologetic smile for getting the old man started.

"When I was 12, I entered a school science fair with a project in which I manipulated rats into doing quite remarkable things."

Claire winked at Nathan, who grimaced a little.

"What sort of things?" she asked.

"Well, let's see," he said. "I taught one to stack blocks, and another learned to use a small key to open a door within a maze."

Nathan stopped eating.

"How?"

"Oh, it was really very simple. I got them addicted to amphetamines. They'd do anything for it. Plus, the drug itself made them quite adept at picking up new skills."

They all ate quietly for several minutes, others finishing up their meals and filing out the room.

"Well, did you win?" Nathan finally asked.

Alfred looked up, his face contorted a bit as if he'd forgotten the nature of the conversation.

"Oh, no," he said. "Another student invented a sock with a pocket on it." He shook his head and smiled. "The judges were captivated."

A man approached the table.

"Mind if I join you?"

Nathan turned to look at him.

"Howard! Good to see you. Of course, take a load off."

He sat next to Nathan and placed his tray on the table.

"Claire," Nathan said. "This is Howard."

Howard shook her hand. Alfred looked over Howard's plate, which held two hardboiled egg whites and some boiled asparagus.

"A meager appetite amidst such gluttony. Are you dieting?"

Howard looked at his plate.

"Oh, I'm afraid my stomach wouldn't tolerate much more than this. It's been a problem of mine for years."

They all frowned for Howard.

"It's not such a tragedy," he said. "I've grown used to it."

Nathan nodded, as he shoved a forkful of food into his mouth.

"Yeah, he's fine," he mumbled. "Don't worry about Howard."

They all returned to eating, a slightly uncomfortable silence between them.

"I know," said Howard. "Let's play useless facts."

"Fire it up," said Nathan, as he scooped another heap of food into his mouth.

Claire looked at Alfred.

"What's this?"

Alfred shook his head.

"Apparently, one attempts to impress the other with factual oddities which have no discernible use."

Nathan pointed his fork at Alfred and spoke through a full mouth.

"It has to be interesting, though. Otherwise, you lose."

Howard nodded.

"I'll start." He cleared his throat. "Flamingos get their color from the carotenoid pigments in the algae and crustaceans they eat."

Claire jabbed her fork into a pile of green beans.

"I can think of discernible uses for that information."

Nathan swallowed his food.

"Ignore her, Howard. She doesn't get it."

He thought for a moment.

"People have been chewing gum for more than 5,000 years."

"A blue whale's tongue is as heavy as a full-grown elephant," Howard said.

"A cheetah can run from zero to 60 in three seconds," said Nathan.

"Seahorse reproduction requires the male to birth the young."

"Anteaters eat 35,000 ants a day."

"An ostrich can move 16 feet in one stride."

"An ostrich can kill a lion with a single kick."

"Elephants can smell water from miles away."

Claire looked at Alfred.

"Why so National Geographic?"

Nathan glanced at her.

"It's more interesting," he said.

He thought for a moment. "Alright. This one's for Claire." He cleared his throat. "NASA's vehicle assembly building is so large, actual rain clouds form below the ceiling."

He looked at Claire and smiled.

"It has its own weather."

She shook her head and ate.

"Each person has two to nine pounds of bacteria in his body," said Howard.

He looked at Claire, who'd stopped chewing.

"Sorry."

Nathan grinned.

"When a male bee climaxes, his testicles explode, and he dies."

He laughed.

"You're ridiculous," she said.

"You go ahead, then," he said. "Illuminate us."

She set her fork down and used a napkin to wipe her mouth.

"There are more atoms in one cup of water than there are cups of water in all the oceans of the world."

They sat in silence for a moment.

"Boring," Nathan said.

She thought for a moment.

"Half of all humans who have ever lived on Earth died of malaria."

Nathan shook his head.

"Now, that's just depressing."

"Charlie Chaplin once entered a Charlie Chaplin look-alike contest and came in third," Alfred said.

"There you go," said Nathan. "Is that true, by the way?"

Alfred nodded.

"Owning a cat can reduce your risk of stroke by 33 percent," said Claire.

Nathan and Howard looked at each other.

"It's not uninteresting, but try something a little less scientific," Howard said. "Perhaps a shocking oddity of some sort."

She thought for a moment and pushed her tray aside. She leaned forward and all else followed suit until they were huddled in a circle across the table, like accomplices conspiring over some plot.

She cleared her throat.

"The Mexican General Santa Anna had an elaborate state funeral for his amputated leg," she said.

They traded looks.

"With speeches, poems, a 21-gun salute, a flag over the coffin," she continued.

Nathan shook his head.

"For a leg," she said.

They traded smiles and looked at Claire, but her eyes were fixed on what was coming up behind them.

"Ms. Foley," Gretchen said, as her towering body swallowed the space behind both men. "Mr. Romero requests your presence in the conference room."

Nathan and Alfred looked back at her and then to their friend, who pushed her tray away and stood.

"Of course," she said. "Would you be kind enough to empty my tray?"

Both men nodded as she followed Gretchen out of the cafeteria.

They made their way down the hallway, which curved sharply around a bare cement wall. When they reached the conference room, Gretchen opened the door and then walked away without speaking. Claire watched the mountainous woman retreat the way she'd come, then she entered the room to find Romero seated alone at the opposite side of a long conference table.

"Please, take a seat," he said, his hand pointing to the chair across from him.

She sat.

"Ms. Foley, I've called you here to prep you for your meeting with the head of our organization. Do you understand?"

"Yes."

"Good." He scribbled something on a clipboard and set it aside. "Most of your associates will take their instruction from the heads of the departments that govern their particular fields of study. A select few have attained special status for one reason or another. You are one of these select few."

He straightened in his chair and folded his hands neatly.

"Tomorrow morning, I'll greet you in the lobby at six. From there, we'll take the elevator into the mid-level division of the building, where you'll meet the leader of our project."

He waited for a response, but she gave none.

"Do you have any questions?"

She rubbed the back of her neck.

"No."

"Alright, then. Let's proceed."

He reached for his clipboard and read.

"You are to dress professionally with no jewelry of any sort. This means no bracelets, necklaces, earrings, pendants, hair clips. Do you understand?"

She gave a nod, but he never looked up to see it.

"Leave your purse behind. Carry no metallic objects whatsoever. Not even coins."

He looked at her.

"In fact, don't bring any money. That's very important."

She swallowed.

"May I ask why?"

He shrugged.

"You can, but I won't be able to answer."

She frowned.

"Alright."

He read from his clipboard.

"Don't bring anything edible, and this includes chewing gum. Wear flat-soled shoes and double-check to make sure they don't have any metallic clips or attachments."

He turned to the next page.

"You may wear lipstick, foundation and concealer, but no eyeliner or eye shadow. Do not wear perfume. Do not use hairspray. Pantyhose are fine, but they must be flesh tone. You can bring photographs if you have them, but you must not take photographs under any circumstances."

He stopped talking and passed the clipboard over, along with a pen.

"Now, please sign at the bottom if you agree to everything I've just told you."

She took the pen and signed her name.

"Do you have any questions?"

She shook her head.

"Good." He smiled politely. "I'll meet you in the lobby tomorrow morning at six. Please be on time."

They both stood and exchanged cordial nods. Then she left the room to look for Nathan and Alfred.

After checking the usual places, she finally found them drinking coffee in the courtyard, and when Nathan saw her coming, he stood.

"Everything alright?" he asked.

She approached with her head down, eyes darting softly at the handful of others that sat on benches or in the easy, delicate grass.

"I have no idea," she said as she joined them. "Things are no less strange, that's for sure."

"How do you mean?" Alfred asked.

She told them everything and they lingered quietly for a moment, Alfred smoking his pipe, the rich smell driving some of the others inside. Nathan looked up at the retractable concrete ceiling and then down to the neatly cut grass.

"This place is bat-shit crazy."

"When are you supposed to meet this person?" Alfred asked.

"Early tomorrow morning."

"I'd assume this is our Mr. Demetri."

Alfred pinched his bushy brows together.

"Demetri?"

Claire and Nathan exchanged looks.

"From the card," Nathan said.

Alfred reached inside his pocket and withdrew his welcome card. He turned it over.

"Mine's signed Dominic Betancur."

Claire took the card from his hand as if the old man could lie.

"I guess we don't know who's in charge after all," Nathan said.

They stood a while longer in that bright little place, talking about each other, about their past, about the lives they'd put on hold. But no one was really present. And no one seemed to notice when the conversation waned.

That night, Claire retired early, leaving Alfred and Nathan alone at the bar, long handshakes and good lucks, some reassuring smiles.

"It will be fine," Alfred said, as she walked away.

"I know," she said, with a nod. "Don't worry about me."

But later, alone in her room, she was different, an unforgiving anxiety in her stomach, like some breakaway sickness that could not be stalled. And it persisted while she showered, while she lay in bed, and into the late hours when a gentle knock brought her back from a close brush with sleep.

She sat up in bed and gathered the covers against her chest, her eyes on the door, ears straining for any hint of noise. Three more soft taps at the door. Then nothing. Then a whisper, "Claire." She escaped the covers and put on a robe. She approached the door and put her hand against it, as if she might learn the visitor's identity by a hint of warmth or lack thereof.

"Yes?" She said with a graveled voice not her own.

"It's Nathan."

She relaxed and took a breath.

"Just a second."

She moved to the mirror and tried to coerce her hair without accomplishing much of anything.

"What are you doing here?" she asked through the door.

"I wanted to see you," he said. "Can you just let me in?"

She quit the fight and moved to the door. She opened it and he came inside.

"It's late, Nathan," she began, but before she could finish, he kissed her.

She turned her head and pulled back.

"I'm sorry," he said, but his arm was still around her waist.

She looked down for a moment, and then her eyes drifted upward, and whatever he saw in them strengthened his resolve. He gathered her up in his arms and brought the tips of their noses together. This time, she lifted her chin to oblige, her body awash with chills and warmth all at once. Their mouths came together flush, his soft lips skilled and practiced, his touch so overwhelming, her head felt light.

For several minutes they went on this way, and then they were on the bed and she was atop him, her legs spread over his lap, nightgown pushed back over her knees. He took her lower lip between his and sucked it, while she clawed her fingers through his thick, black hair.

While she worked his mouth, his hands explored her body, his fingertips traveling slowly from her bare shoulders down to the small of her back. As he kissed her, the smell of his unfamiliar cologne made its way into her mind, like some invisible narcotic that would not be turned down.

She looked up into his dark eyes, an animal looking out from the other side. Then it was all seamless, their bodies together in an easy, relentless harmony, as if they weren't new friends at all, but familiar lovers after a long separation. When it was over, they laid together without speaking, their breathing heavy, bodies exhausted, and each one gathering up energy for a long night ahead.

Chapter 10

The next morning, she found Romero waiting patiently in the lobby, his usual attire replaced with a military uniform complete with polished black boots and a hat which he held at his side. When he saw her, his eyes traveled the length of her body.

"Very nice," he said, with a smile that seemed unfitting to her eyes.

She glanced down at her skirt and cleared her throat.

"Are you ready?" he asked, as he placed his hat on his head and pulled the bill low over his dark eyes.

"Yes."

He turned and tapped codes into the keypad and the elevator doors yawned open. They both entered in turn and he repeated the process in reverse.

"It will be a bit of a walk," he said, as they made the brief descent to the lower floor.

When the doors opened again, everything looked different. Before her eyes, a network of narrow metallic platforms seemed to sprawl in all directions. The floors weren't really floors at all, but stainless-steel grids lined to make a walkway over what? Who could say? The darkness below stretched down hundreds of feet or more.

"This way," he said.

He hurried forward without looking back, Claire following closely, like a child on the heels of her father in some dark, uncertain place. Every several feet, the platforms shot off to the left or to the right toward destinations that might be surprising to all but the knowing. To eyes like hers, the layout seemed ill-conceived to be anything else but intentionally confusing.

With every step, she held firmly the safety rails on both sides. As her hands slid atop them, a curious chalky dust bloomed up into the air and then quickly dissipated under the bold halogen lights, which effectively illuminated the steel walking platforms and not much else. Romero achieved impressive gains with each step, and she hurried along to keep up, her flat-soled shoes shooting off little metallic pings that echoed in all directions.

They walked for some time, taking lefts and rights through a seemingly endless maze of platform walkways that featured no markers, signs or numbers, nothing to tell you where you were going or how to get back. Finally, they arrived at yet another elevator and Romero accessed it by tapping more numbers into a keypad.

"Please," he said, holding his hand toward the open elevator.

She entered, but he did not follow.

"You'll take this elevator down to the third level of the facility, where you will meet with the head of our organization. Do you understand?"

She nodded, and with that, he typed against the keypad and the elevator doors pressed shut.

She barely felt the elevator move before the doors opened again, this time revealing a very dark, very long room. At the end of the room, an old woman sat at a small desk, and when Claire exited the elevator, the woman looked up and smiled.

"Come forward, dear," she said. "It's alright."

Claire approached the woman, her aged features poorly lit by a small work lamp, the only lighting in the vast room.

"I'm sorry for the darkness," she said. "Mr. Betancur is very particular about a great many things."

Claire stood before her desk. She looked for a chair, but there were none. The old woman finished writing something and then stood. She moved to the other side of the desk and made a complete circle around Claire, an old crooked finger to her lips, tongue making ticking noises against the roof of her mouth.

"Your makeup and attire look right," she said. "Did you wear any jewelry?"

"No."

"Good. Very good." She circled her again, this time stooping low to get a look at her legs. "Flesh-toned pantyhose, good."

She straightened with some obvious discomfort, a hand on her lower back, another on her knee.

"Did you bring any money or photographs?"

"No money," Claire said. "I have a photograph of my mother."

"Let me see it," the old woman said.

Claire withdrew the picture and handed it to her. The old woman held it by the edges and returned to her desk. She sat down with great care, as if her whole body were made of glass, then she held the photograph to the light and examined it.

"This looks alright."

She reached inside a drawer and removed a rubber stamp. She turned the photograph upside down and made a wet red impression of an inverted triangle.

"Ok," she said, as she fanned the picture in the air and passed it back to Claire. "You can go inside now."

She pointed to three equally sized steel doors.

"His is the one in the middle."

Claire approached the door and stopped. She looked over her shoulder at the old woman.

"Go ahead, dear," the woman said with a tender smile.

Claire nodded and turned. She grasped the handle and gave it a twist.

Inside, everything was dark, except for a very large desk that appeared to glow beneath the light of a small work lamp. Behind it sat a man, his hands folded neatly, a firm expression upon his face, like that of someone lost in meditation or a ticklish set of thoughts.

She crossed the threshold and closed the door behind her. She tried to speak, but he silenced her with a finger. He sat there a moment longer, his eyes fixed on nothing in particular. Then he picked up a very expensive-looking pen and wrote something on a small yellow notepad. When he finished, he opened a drawer, slipped the pad inside, and closed it without making any sound. He looked at her and smiled.

"Hello," he said, as he pushed his chair back and stood. "My name is Dominic Betancur."

He approached and stood before her, his height imposing, a Spanish accent dripping from his tongue.

"I am very pleased to finally meet you," he said.

He offered a handshake and she accepted it, her fingers disappearing inside his large, enveloping hand.

"Please," he said, "sit down."

He pointed to a chair that sat immediately across his desk and watched as she seated herself. Then he returned to his side of the desk and folded his hands.

"I'm sure you have various questions knocking around your head. I invite you to ask them now."

Claire squirmed in her seat.

"Anything?"

A smile leaked from the corner of his mouth.

"Well, let's move slowly and see how things go."

She looked him over in the low light, his dark features very rugged, eyes bold and brown.

"What is this place?"

He leaned back in his chair.

"A research facility, of course."

She crossed her legs.

"What sort of research?"

"All kinds, really. Certain varieties receive more funding than others. More attention."

"What sorts?"

He smiled.

"Nothing that could be weaponized."

She uncrossed her legs.

"Then what?"

"Well, we're interested in the same things you are. We want to cure diseases, extend lives, things like that."

She began to say something, but he interrupted.

"I'm sorry. It's very early and I didn't offer you any coffee. Let's have some coffee."

He tapped a button on his telephone.

"Carol, can you please bring coffee."

"Of course, Mr. Betancur."

They sat in silence while Carol brought coffee.

"Do you take cream or sugar?"

"Just a little cream," Claire said.

She poured them each a cup and then retreated from the room without saying another word.

"I'm sorry," said Dominic Betancur. "You were saying?"

"Why all the secrecy? Why the compound? The armed security?"

He sipped his coffee and thought for a moment.

"We have our reasons and they are sound, I can assure you."

She sampled the coffee, its flavor quite ordinary in relation to everything else at the facility.

"What is it you want from me?"

He sat up in his chair and placed his forearms on the desk.

"I want you to do what you do. I want you to continue your research. Or, I guess I should say I want you to pick things up where others have left off."

"You mean continue existing research?"

"That's correct," he said. "We've already made significant strides in your particular field of research. You're in store for some surprises when you get down to the third level of this facility. Suffice it to say, we've far exceeded what you've accomplished so far at your university. I say this with respect of course."

She drank her coffee.

"Whose work am I taking over?"

"I'm afraid we don't divulge this information. Just as we won't divulge your identity to your successor."

"I don't understand," she said.

"Well, I'm afraid our operation won't bestow you with any fame or glory. We work in a piecemeal fashion, with numerous researchers all contributing anonymously to one project for a certain amount of time and then surrendering their work to a successor. You will not receive any credit for your contributions. Not a page in the newspaper. Not even a letter of recommendation. You'll be required to sign a confidentiality agreement, and we will enforce it through any means necessary."

He sipped his coffee and waited for a response, but she gave none.

"What you will get," he continued, "is substantial monetary compensation, depending on how far you extend the research, of course."

She looked into her coffee cup for a moment.

"What do you mean by substantial?"

"Between one and ten million dollars based on how far you push the research ahead."

She looked up suddenly, and he gave a slight smile.

"We only want the best you have to offer. If you don't add a single thing, if you aren't able to advance the research one iota, you'll still receive a minimum of one million U.S. dollars. This will come at the end of a maximum 12-month commitment. That said, we may choose to relieve you from your responsibilities after only a few months or even a few weeks. But never more than twelve months. That will be the maximum duration of your involvement with our enterprise."

He shrugged.

"That doesn't sound so bad, does it?"

She sipped her coffee and thought for a moment.

"I can't say that it does."

"Good," he said. "Now I hate to cut things short, but I have others to see."

He stood and put a hand out.

"It was a pleasure to meet you, finally."

She stood and placed her coffee on the desk.

"Likewise," she said, as she offered her hand.

They shook and he followed her to the door.

"Carol will escort you to the elevator. You'll be moving to the third level of the facility in the coming days. You'll receive plenty of guidance when the time comes. Anything you need, you'll receive."

He opened the door to reveal the old woman, who stood straight and attentive, a kind smile decorating her weathered face.

"Come, dear," she said, as Dominic Betancur closed the door behind her.

They walked the length of the waiting room, and Carol opened the elevator doors with a few taps of the bright green keypad on the wall.

Claire entered and turned, her body finally relaxing, mind nearly exhausted from the stress of the engagement.

"Best of luck to you," the old woman said, as the elevator doors slid shut.

When they did, Claire leaned her back against the elevator wall and exhaled. She held her hands out before her eyes and watched the shaking cease. She breathed deeply and waited for the doors to open once more to reveal Romero, who would lead her through the maze of metallic grid scaffolding that led back to the facility's top level.

But when the doors opened, she did not see Romero. Instead, another man stood before her, his face like a hammer, eyes black as sucking holes.

She tried to look into them, but it was like looking into the sun.

"Hello," he said. "My name is Demetri Mendoza."

-

This has been a ten chapter preview of Girl in a Rabbit Hole. Get the full book to continue Claire's story.

The story continues in
GIRL IN A RABBIT HOLE,
Get the FULL FIRST BOOK and FOUR Thrilling Sequels at AMAZON!

Available NOW at AMAZON!
https://www.amazon.com/dp/B094DY44FQ/

Purchase Claire Foley Book 1, available NOW at Amazon, and take a ride you will never forget!

This is a work of fiction. Any names or characters, businesses or places, events or incidents, are fictitious. Any resemblance to actual persons, living or dead, or actual events is purely coincidental. No part of this eBook may be reproduced or transmitted in any form or by any means, electronic or mechanical, including photocopying, recording or by any information storage and retrieval system, without written permission from the author.

Copyright 2017 RJ Law All rights reserved.

Printed in Dunstable, United Kingdom